WORDSLINGERS:

An Epitaph for the Western

WORDSLINGERS

AN EPITAPH FOR THE WESTERN

☞ WILL MURRAY ☜

ALTUS PRESS
2013

EDITED AND DESIGNED BY
Matthew Moring

PUBLISHING HISTORY
"Wordslingers: An Epitaph for the Western" appears here for the first time. Copyright © 2013 Will Murray. All Rights Reserved.

Cover and interior images from *Dime Western, Star Western, New Western* and *Rangeland Romances* courtesy of Argosy Communications, Inc.: Copyright © 2013 Argosy Communications, Inc. All Rights Reserved.

Robert E. Howard quotes reprinted with the permission of Robert E. Howard Properties.

THANKS TO
Author Services, Nicholas Cain, Jack Cullers, John DeWalt, John A. Dinan, Doug Ellis, Michael Feldman, Joel Frieman, Galaxy Press, John Godwin, Kenneth R. Johnson, Richard Kyle, John Locke, Dave McDonnell, Gerald W. Page, Mary Power, Laurie Powers, James Reasoner, Tom Roberts, Milton Shaw, Anthony Tollin, Albert Tonik & Joakim Zetterberg.

For Ryerson Johnson, the best damned Hudson River Cowboy I ever met.

CONTENTS

INTRODUCTION

BOOKS ON the Western have largely been confined to the genre's literary or cinematic history. Yet commencing with the Great Depression and continuing into the post-war period, the fictional cowboy story was largely a creature of the pulp magazine.

A definitive study of Western pulps has never been undertaken. Nor could it ever be. During the first fifty years of the 20th Century, over 200 pulp-fiction magazines specializing in frontier and cowboy yarns were printed, most every month, and several published as frequently as weekly. That's not counting the general-fiction pulps which also offered Western stories.

All told, uncountable quantities of words of pulp Western yarns were published during this era, all different, yet all the same. No mortal could hope to live long enough to absorb them all, much less synthesize that reading into a coherent survey of what was once as American a form of entertainment as baseball, but is now verging upon extinction. Would even five million words of commentary suffice to skim the surface of such a prodigious body of work?

Nor do I attempt such a Herculean undertaking here. What follows is a species of oral history, employing found quotes, developed so that the author recedes into the role of omniscient organizer, sometimes disappearing altogether, in order to allow the participants of the past to spin the saga of their literary labors.

The origins of this book reside in my decades of research into the pulp magazine period. I freely admit that, although a lifelong fan of the Western genre in films and TV, the Western pulp magazines never drew my strong interest. But one day while paging through the bound volumes of *Writer's Digest* at the Boston Public Library, I ran across two articles which destroyed my casual impression of the Western as an indestructible perennial genre: Walker A. Tompkins' "Just Another Western—" and Rogers Terrill's "The Evolution of the Western." Together, they painted a portrait of a powerhouse pulp genre in crisis at the tail end of the Great Depression. I photocopied both essays, intending to quote liberally from them for a modest article, "The Gun-Dummy and the Swivel-Chair Westerner."

My initial stab at penning the piece led me to look for further insight into this forgotten turning point in the Western. Further research suggested a larger canvas, a massive untold story. The Western genre, its techniques and its problems, proved to be one of the most thoroughly documented of all. The draft article soon swelled to the size of an illustrated coffee-table book.

One day, like an amoeba reproducing, it divided into a part 1 and 2. These sections in turn divided and subdivided again, until a book of eighteen chapters resulted. Two years into the process, I was suddenly inspired to pen a prologue. I had only to reach into a box of photocopied articles, and quotes seemed to assemble themselves into a coherent whole. It was an organic, yet spooky process. Almost any new article discovery shed light, offered insight, and gave up commentary that almost invariably filled gaps in the manuscript, many of which I had failed to perceive. Often, I felt as if I were piecing together an intricate jigsaw puzzle—which in some strange sense preexisted this project.

My quest took me from the libraries and universities of greater Boston to the New York Public Library and finally, the Library of Congress. Principally, but not exclusively, *Wordslingers* is culled from the pages of *Writer's Digest, The Author & Journalist, Writer's Review, Writer's Journal, The Writer's Monthly,*

The Writer, Writer's Markets and Methods, and *Report to Writers.* Early issues of the Western Writers of America's official organ, *The Roundup,* also proved invaluable.

To include a bibliography of all of the articles and essays consulted would swell this substantial volume by another fifty pages. Since this is a study of a literary genre intended for a popular audience, I have elected to spare readers that mind-boggling burden.

I am indebted to my fellow researchers, John A. Dinan, John Locke, Richard Kyle, Kenneth R. Johnson, Gerald W. Page, Jonathan G. Jensen, Anthony Tollin, Albert Tonik, Elizabeth Carter Bissette and Laurie Powers, for their help amassing this account. From Archie Joscelyn comes the quaint coining "word-slingers."

With that, I am stepping back from the customary role of author, shifting instead to active raconteur, the better to permit the colorful and distinctive voices you are about to read return to life and tell their own shared saga....

WORDSLINGERS:

An Epitaph for the Western

"I have often wondered why we don't have greater Western stories than we do. Great stories are there waiting to be dug out. There are hundreds of people far more worthy than the notorious Billy the Kid (upon whom the spotlight has fallen for years), unknown outside of their home neighborhood, robust people living in a raw and virile land, a land that is huge and beautiful and rich in material wealth. There's the challenge and perhaps that is the difficulty. The West was too big to be written about and bound between two hard covers."

—Wayne D. Overholser, author

"When men began to write of the West, it was to exploit its more lurid aspects for sensational purposes. Hence, rose the 'cowboy' tradition, the 'Wild West' trash—an absolutely criminal distortion of the literary growth and traditions that made a vulgar jest out of what should have been one of the most vital and inspiring pageants of American History."

—Robert E. Howard, Texan

"The reader of Westerns don't want no part of 'history' that isn't history—he never was crazy about history in the first place. All he's hunting is a good absorbing story of he-man adventure, the horse-and-gun kind of story he used to get from the pulps… He don't want to be preached to, harangued at, nagged at, taught, or anything that adds up to discomfort. He wants to be entertained, period."

—Nelson C. Nye, first President,
Western Writers of America

PROLOGUE

"**O**NE GUSTY spring day in 1903," recalled Western novelist Syl MacDowell, "in the small raw cowtown of Rifle in western Colorado, our school let out for noon recess. As the kids whooped out-of-doors, there appeared at the crest of a hill where the road dipped down into town, a weird rubber-tired vehicle without any visible means of locomotion.

"It came with a series of clattering explosions until it reached a slushy stretch in front of the schoolhouse and there it wheezed to a tired stop.

"We crowded around it with great curiosity. Some of the kids guessed that it ran on kerosene, plain old lamp kerosene. Others said steam. The older ones spoke of a little-heard-of fuel called gasoline.

"That was the first automobile any of us had seen. We did not know then that we were witnessing the end of an era, an era that had begun exactly one hundred years before with the Louisiana Purchase.

"The appearance of the first automobile signaled the end of the American Frontier."

The dawn of the 20th Century also marked the beginning of a turning point in Western popular fiction. Where before magazine stories, dime novels and nickel weekly pamphlets had served up what amounted to fanciful contemporary tales of a still-untamed West, that period was slowly shading into legendry. *The Virginian,* Owen Wister's classic distillation of the

U.S. cowboy, was published in 1902 to widespread acclaim, elevating to near-mythic status a figure formerly mere fodder for dime novel derring-do.

In 1903, Andy Adams' fictionalized memoir, *The Log of a Cowboy* appeared, as did B.M. Bower's classic *Chip of the Flying U.* Edwin S. Porter shot the first movie to tell a narrative story. *The Great Train Robbery* also inaugurated the first cycle of Hollywood Western movies. It was, however, filmed in New Jersey. Los Angeles still qualified as a frontier town.

That same year the mighty Street & Smith publishing company issued their first all-fiction periodical, *The Popular Magazine,* heralding another significant shift, this one away from juvenile dime-novel fare to more manly accounts designed to compete directly with the serious hardcover novels and yellowback paperbound books. Cowboy yarns abounded in *The Popular*'s pages, as they would in every general-interest pulp from Frank A. Munsey's pioneering *Argosy* to the greatest of them all, *Adventure.* Within these thick magazines many of the seminal Western romances of Emerson Hough, William MacLeod Raine and Zane Grey first saw light of day.

Unquestionably, the Western story never enjoyed as great a vogue prior to the advent of the pulp magazine. Named for the rough grade of newsprint on which they were printed, pulps proliferated when dime-novel publishers realized they could side-staple a slab of their folio-sized periodicals into book signatures and slap a four-color cover around the oat-colored makings. As a cost-saving measure, they declined to trim the works, giving the open edge a rough yet feathery texture. Thus did a common grade of unbleached paper become a colorful label for a type of cheap, affordable popular fiction.

The sheer popularity of the Western tale led inevitably to magazines completely devoted to the young genre. At their peak, Western pulps bought and published some three million words of fiction a month, a staggering 35 million words per year, year after year, between the Golden '20s and the Grim 1950s. The more successful titles were issued weekly, each offering a market for over 500 manuscripts a year. Discounting the so-called "slick" magazines like *The Saturday Evening Post* and lending library books, an estimated one *billion* words of Western adventure were published during the pulp era. A vast, voracious market, it virtually hijacked the nostalgic myth of the cowboy and took him to exuberant extremes, never witnessed before nor since.

William Savage noted in his book, *Cowboy Life: Reconstructing an American Myth*, "Most real-life cowboys were just that—boys between 18 and 25. Unwilling to stay at home with pasture and plow, they became hired hands on horseback. Most did not even own their own horses and few rose above their humble station."

That may have been the unvarnished truth behind the legend, but it was the legend which thrived, thanks to Owen Wister, who set the tone for this new literary genre in his nostalgic preface to *The Virginian:*

"What is become of the horseman, the cowpuncher, the last romantic figure upon our soil? For he was a romantic. Whatever he did, he did with his might. The bread that he earned was earned hard, the wages that he squandered were squandered hard,—half a year's pay sometimes gone in a night,—'blown in,' as he expressed it, or 'blowed in,' to be perfectly accurate. Well, he will be here among us always, invisible, waiting his chance to live and play as he would like. His wild kind has been among us always, since the beginning: a young man with his temptations, a hero without wings."

While not confined to its shores, the appeal of the Western is distinctly American. As pulp magazine editor Leo Margulies explained in his 1945 *Writer's Digest* article, "The Pulp West:"

"Western stories are translated into all languages of the world. The Chinese mandarin chuckled at the mishaps of the luckless cowboy who was 'tied hard and fast' to something he would like to let go of. The Russian sees a counterpart of his own great land of unexploited opportunities in the achievements of the men who made the West. The Englishman thrills to the adventures and conquests of those descendants of the grand old Mother Country who went to seek fortune in a strange land under new stars. The Frenchman sees La Salle's followers wander forth from Saint Louis Bay in the Texas coast to meet Indians who tell of 'rivers where silver mines are found'. The Norseman sees Eric the Red land again on the shores of Vinland, with a continent before him of towering mountains, mighty rivers, fantastic deserts and limitless plains. The Spaniard walks with Alva Nunez Cabeza de Vaca, Black Stephen and Hernan Cortez and dreams of the days when the Lion Flag of Spain flew over this land of promise and adventure."

The above is pure purple pulp prose—mightily exaggerated, melodramatic to the point of burlesque, but sincerely offered. Above all, the Pulp West strove to be sincere.

It had to. For it wasn't real.

More properly, it was what William MacLeod Raine called, "a hope, a state of mind, a dream, a utopia…."

"But it is not the West the cattlemen knew," observed writer Lee Floren. "The greatest foes of the cattlemen were not rustlers or bandits. His greatest enemies were drought and hard winters. Therefore, the Western story is set in the 'never-never' land."

One Western magazine editor discovered this when, on his first day on the job, he paged through a sample magazine issued by his new employer. Confronted by myriad alien words and phrases, he asked, "What does 'bushwhack' mean?"

"You hide behind a bush and you whack your enemy with a bullet," a senior editor told him.

"People don't talk like that back home."

"Where's home?"

"The West. Los Angeles."

"No, no," the exasperated senior editor insisted. "That's not *the* West. That's west of *true* West."

The true story of the Pulp West has never before been fully told. Here it is, culled from contemporary sources, and narrated by the authentic voices of those who made it the never-never land that it never was.

"It all started one rainy Sunday in 1928 when, foraging around the house for something to read, I happened upon a copy of **Western Story Magazine** *that my older brother had discarded. It had a story in it by Max Brand, and by the time I'd finished the first paragraph, I was hooked. I had always wanted to be a writer. Now I knew it was* Westerns *I must write.*"

—*D.B. Newton*

"*It began on the XIH Ranch in northern Colorado lo, these many years ago when, to my horror, I found a stack of Street & Smith's* Western *magazine—the old-time pulps—that were so riddled with errors that I decided try my own hand.*"

—*Lauran Paine*

THE PULP FRONTIER

ROGERS TERRILL is a forgotten man today. But in his day, he oversaw the biggest string of Western pulp-fiction magazines ever published, the Popular Publications chain. Reminiscing about his early career, he wrote, "One of my earliest recollections of the publishing business is a lunch-time conference at which we discussed the sad probability that the Western story, as a pulp medium, was about washed up.

"One young editor was thoroughly convinced that the then current slump in Western sales marked the beginning of the end. 'I can't figure,' said he, 'why the Western story, with its stereotyped plot and limitations as to time and place, has re-mained popular as long as it has.'

"Another young editor pointed out that the cowboy and Indian movie, recently popular, had been relegated to Grade C pictures for corn-fed counties.

"Said he, 'If even a movie fan gets tired, eventually, of chase scenes and gun fights, do you wonder that the Western story fan is beginning to get fed up?'"

The year was 1927. The Western genre was still in its glory. Western fiction magazines had a long way to go before they finally bit the dust—some 30 more years as a matter of record.

Next to the romance fiction pulps—whose prodigious cir-culations dwarfed all others—Westerns were the top pulp-era genre. One of the true perennials, more sagebrush titles were published than in any other category. They never seemed to go out of fashion. That they were considered washed up as early as 1927 flies in the face of their apparently-indestructible popularity. More surprising still, over the years the Western pulp field had many times found itself on the verge of being dry-gulched and left for dead.

Here follows the dramatic story of how the Western pulp-fiction magazine was saved from the hangman's noose over and over again. Until, finally, nothing was left to string up.

Fortunately, much of the tale has been preserved in the dusty pages of the writers' magazines of the day—principally *Writer's Digest* and *The Author & Journalist*—told in the words of those who were an integral part of it all—Western pulp authors and their agents and editors.

Terrill's anecdote comes from "The Evolution of the Western," (*Writer's Digest,* May 1941) written at the point where the pulp oater was in the throes of yet another crisis of transformation. In it, Terrill laid out the entire development of the genre between 1927 and 1941. But in order to understand how the Western got that way, we must go back to its very beginning.

As literature, the Western traces its roots back to the *Leatherstocking Tales* of James Fenimore Cooper, who borrowed from the life of Tennessee frontier scout Daniel Boone to create his semi-fictional protagonist, Natty Bumppo, better known as Hawkeye, the *nom de guerre* he used in *The Last of the Mohicans.* Cooper's *The Pioneers* first saw print in 1823, thus establishing the genre's literary beginnings. Writers such as Francis Parkman, Washington Irving, Bret Harte and Mark Twain took the genre from the early eastern frontier to the far West. Their books became classics.

"The Western story started back in the days when it was a part of everyday life in America," observed 20th Century Western writer Lee E. Wells. "The Apache was still on the warpath, Buffalo Bill was in his heyday, Tombstone still had faint echoes of recent gunplay. It was a part of then modern

America, though a very exciting and romantic one."

"After the Civil War, the Western came into its own," related fellow pulp writer Tom Curry. "Mass printing and distribution were applied. The West opened to settlement, and with practically free homesteads, appealed to the American spirit. The fathers of such people must have been courageous to leave civilization and seek a new deal in a savage setting....

"Impoverished Confederates, to gain a little Yankee cash, rounded up longhorns and drove them to railheads in Kansas or to Gulf ports. The cowboy quickly became a fascinating figure. Runaway lads appeared on the ranches, eager to lead such an apparently glamorous life."

But there was another side to the West. The pulp paper side.

"With this wealth of material," continued Curry, "the background of mountains and canyons, rivers and lakes, deserts and the plains, ranches and mines, peopled by colorful adventurers of every stripe, the writer could not lose. Authors such as Ned Buntline and Alfred Henry Lewis were with the Frontiersmen. They elaborated on what they saw and often believed everything they were told."

In his 1945 *Writer's Digest* memoir, "Tabu Buster Or, Growing Up With the Western Story," longtime pulp writer John A. Saxon—then one of the oldest hands in the game—offered up his investigations of how the Western pulp story became a genre unto itself.

According to Saxon, the earliest proto-Western tales first appeared in the *Police Gazette* as far back at the late 1850s. These were tales of Western outlaws, he said, "...supposedly based upon fact and using real names, but dressed up by New York writers who believed there were still Indians roaming the streets of Chicago, scalping the citizens." The forerunners of Billy the Kid, Jesse James and their ilk were its subjects.

The next turn on the trail came when New York writer Edward Zane Carroll Judson persuaded plainsman William F. Cody to lend his name and reputation to a fictionalized account of his life, *Buffalo Bill, King of the Bordermen*, for publisher Street & Smith and written under the pen name, Ned Buntline. The year was 1869.

"Thus was born the *Buffalo Bill Weekly*, which enjoyed almost as phenomenal a circulation as our present-day *Superman*," noted Saxon. This was the true beginning of what Saxon called "the fictionalized form of the Western story… based partly on fact, but mostly on imagination."

Judson was a notorious example of the so-called White Plains Plainsman—an Easterner who went West and reported as fact every tall tale a poker-faced Western card told him.

"Of boundless imagination and unlimited confidence in the credulity of Americans," wrote Charles B. Roth, "he sat down one day and wrote a novel about a subject of which he was entirely ignorant… A Buntline hero could do anything with a gun that Buntline wanted him to. He shot from the hip, fanned, slew Indians from the back of a galloping mustang, and cut playing cards in half from the thin side.

"Lying blissfully content in some hay-mow, your eyes bulged as you followed a Buntline hero. You believed what you read. And millions of other Americans read. And believed. And thus, right under our eyes, we had a mythology created—a mythology as lusty and persistent as that of ancient Greece—the mythology of frontier marksmanship."

After Judson moved on, Street & Smith simply hired others to continue Buffalo Bill's exploits. One, Colonel Prentiss Ingraham, may have been the archetypal Western action writer. To him goes the credit for first popularizing the cowboy as fiction hero.

Buck Taylor, the King of the Cowboys, was a star performer with Buffalo Bill's Wild West Show whom Ingraham ran through a series of cheap novels circa 1887. But the heroic frontiersman and Indian-fighter, rather than the workaday cowpoke, held the public's imagination for a long time.

Ingraham was fond of telling camp followers, "Never plot.

Just find a hot opening. For example, here's one: 'Crack! Crack! Crack! Three more redskins bit the dust!' There's your opening situation. Now go on and write the story!"

"Ned Buntline and the later lurid paperbacks were filled with blood, thunder, gunplay—and that was about all," wrote Lee E. Wells. "It was not good writing, with very, very few exceptions. It was labeled 'trash,' and perhaps it was for the greater part. It was read secretly behind the corncrib or hidden from irate parents under the mattress.

"So the Western started with accent on adventure, upon action for action's sake, on blood, chase, and roaring Colts as often as possible," continued Wells. "The story was a mere minor detail to give some semblance of order to the rest."

Buffalo Bill was soon followed by *Diamond Dick, The James Boys,* and other nickel weeklies devoted to frontier tomfoolery. The dime novel also worked this particular vein of lucrative fool's gold, beginning with *Malaeska, The Indian Wife of the White Hunter,* an 1839 magazine story reprinted in soft cover as *Beadle's Dime Novel Number One* in 1860. Beadle also launched the illustrious career of Edward L. Wheeler's long-running dime novel Western series, *Deadwood Dick,* in 1877. Called "The Black Rider of the Black Hills," Deadwood pushed the genre away from the plainsman as folk hero. But he was no cowboy. Rather, Dick was the outlaw leader of a band of rough-riding road agents. Curiously, John A. Saxon overlooked him, as he did the fact that Buffalo Bill ran in several general periodicals before *Buffalo Bill Stories* was launched in 1901.

But the era of the buckskin plainsman was already drawing to a close. It concluded with the publication of Owen Wister's *The Virginian* in 1902. An instant bestseller, it became a popular stage play and fodder for future films. Most importantly, it transmuted the common cowhand into a 20th Century Solar Myth.

"Wister rode in on the era of the cowboy," observed Texas pulp writer William L. Hopson. "Towards the end of the 19th

Century cattle had come to stay in Texas and the cowboy was king, in real life, and in the Western. All Wister's plots revolved around cowboy heroes…. When the Virginian and Trampas hammered it out with six-shooters, in the final chapter, in the town's main drag, Ned Buntline, who ruled the Western in the 1870s and '80s, and his dime-novel contemporaries were dead ducks."

Wister's impact was thunderous. In surviving nickel weeklies, characters like Diamond Dick and Diamond Dick Jr. hastily doffed their diamond-studded duds for the rough flannel garb of the working cowboy. A milestone in the ascendancy of the cowboy hero was Street & Smith's offering of an all-Western issue of *The Popular Magazine* in August 1906.

When the nickel weekly reluctantly gave way to the pulp magazine after World War I, Western stories began popping up in *Argosy, Adventure, All-Story, Short Stories, Blue Book,* and similar general fiction magazines. As often as not, they were simple homespun tales of ranch and range life, or chuck wagon yarns—essentially Western tall tales. The genre had not yet solidified into the White Hat versus Black Hat morality plays which overwhelmed the Western story, nor had the familiar aura of the contemporary completely faded.

Owen Wister had set out to pen the last word on a dying era in *The Virginian.* Instead, he unwittingly birthed a cottage industry in the book trade. Literary writers like Stephen Crane, Jack London, O. Henry, and Stewart Edward White and others continued to produce seminal Western works. Perhaps because it was both contemporary and historical, the genre became respectable.

"When these trail blazers were in full swing the Western story was the literary vogue and no popular magazine was complete without several of them, no publishing list dared go without a book or two," noted Western editor Harry E. Maule. "New writers came onto the scene: Zane Grey, William MacLeod Raine, Eugene Manlove Rhodes, Clarence E. Mulford. Wyoming's Johnson County war, under other names, and against different settings, was fought a thousand times. Billy the Kid, under countless aliases, served as the classic model for the bad man.

"It was inevitable," Maule added, "that the popularity of the subject matter would attract the lesser writers and the formula story would emerge, getting more threadbare with each repetition. Consequently, the 'Western' fell into some literary disrepute."

The Western's appeal was unabashedly American and almost entirely masculine. "The Old West was a man's country," wrote critic Harold Waldo. "There he contrived a Gargantuan society celebrated by Mark Twain and Bret Harte, a cosmos of laughable, outrageous figures, a preposterous epos that astonished and delighted... a faraway land."

"The cowboy story was established as a romantic saga of The Hero at the very beginning, with *The Virginian*," critic Bernard DeVoto observed. "But Wister abundantly sprinkled his work with humor and for a long time the form was regarded as primarily humorous; it was turned into the path that has led to its present solemnity by its one novelist, Rhodes, and by the fabulists Harold Bell Wright and Zane Grey...."

After a decade or so, interest waned, shifting to the naturalistic Western novels of Frank Norris and Willa Cather. Critics thought the masculine Western had run its course.

"Thus the dark horseman of the Golden West is fading," asserted Waldo in 1920. "The Stetson school of fiction and the Stetson school of 'statesmanship' show equally deflated, and their puncturing may well be charged along with other items to the new woman and the rising city—with its vast insignia of urban taste—built for her. [...] "Man is pulling in his horns, in short. And so is the West. The Old West is gone. Romance is dead.... The red-blooded brand is obsolete."

Waldo was wrong.

The Western story had always adapted well to all previous disposable print forms. But the pulp magazine proved to be a perfect vehicle. In the cities, newsdealers sold them to urban readers curious about life in the wide-open spaces. Shipped by rail, they were widely available in railroad depots or by subscription, and read by rural readers to whom the Western milieu was comfortable and familiar. Pulp magazines were passed from consumer to consumer until, exhausted, they were consigned to the outhouse for a final perusal, and in those days before toilet paper, eventually dismembered for sanitary purposes.

"Authorities seem to agree that whatever else may happen to the 'fiction market', the demand for frontier stories remains almost constant, year in and year out," wrote H.W. Boynton in *The Bookman*. "Largely, no doubt, it is a fiction for the sedentary and the city-bound, a magic casement, some four inches by seven, opening on perilous peaks and icy trails forlorn…. For it is frankly meant to give people a glimpse of a sort of robust fairy-land, full of red blood and ozone, in which youth, courage, and huskiness have things pretty much their own way, within limits. Beauty is there too, but mostly as a property. Things doing in the open are what we must have here, and if they are the same old things, that doesn't seem to worry us, so long as the author contrives for them the slightly fresh twist, the necessary bluff of novelty, which we willingly take at face value, to save our own faces."

The genre was already coming under criticism for its extravagance. In 1921, *The Bookman* contracted a Western gambler with a taste for Wild West fiction to assess its veracity.

Writing anonymously, this worthy reported, "There are, in general, a number of slips in the Western life stories, but I want to state at the outset that most of the stories are pretty true to things as they are. I have, of course, read many other brands of fiction besides that devoted to the West, but of all the various kinds, I believe, from my own knowledge, that the fiction dealing with Western life is possessed of a greater *resemblance* and veined with a closer appreciation and knowledge of the subject under treatment than any of one of the other classes of fiction stories. Western fiction, in short, is fact. And the answer,

I hold, is not far to seek. Your average writer on the West has lived in the West, knows it from top to bottom, and loves it."

All that was about to change.

The first dedicated Western pulp periodical emerged from Street & Smith's presses. *Western Story Magazine* debuted in 1919. William MacLeod Raine, Emerson Hough, Franklin Richardson Pierce, B.M. Bower, Bertrand W. Sinclair, Clarence E. Mulford, Will James, W.C. Tuttle, Jackson Gregory, Charles Alden Seltzer, Robert Ormond Case, Robert J. Horton, Johnston McCulley and newcomer Ernest Haycox were among its star writers.

Touted as chock full of "Big, Clean Stories of Outdoor Life," *Western Story* was aimed at a middle-class family audience and prided itself on the fact that no matter how violent the fiction, it never printed the word "damn" in its pages. At its peak, *Western Story* was issued relentlessly every week and sold a half-million copies per issue. Not for nothing did *The Literary Digest* once call Street & Smith "the uncontested Ford of the magazine field." They were a literal fiction factory, with editorial offices, presses and bindery housed in one forbidding red brick building.

The architect of *Western Story Magazine* was business manager Henry W. Ralston, who conceived the idea. But the man who built it into an institution was editor Frank Engs Blackwell. A former *New York Sun* reporter, in 1915 he had successfully transformed the faltering *Nick Carter Stories* into the first mystery pulp, *Detective Story Magazine*. *Western Story* was an outgrowth of the last incarnation of the *Buffalo Bill Weekly*, then dying a slow death after the passing of William F. Cody. A Long Island native with a love of horses, Blackwell used to commute to work in a horse-drawn sleigh during his first winter at S&S, which he joined in 1912. He also preferred to work in an old-fashioned wicker rocking chair, thus earning him the grim sobriquet "Rocking Death" among his associates.

Described by a contemporary as "…a wiry, tough-minded

veteran who would have gone insane long ago if he were not a humorist who could take the daily beating with a wise-cracking jape at life and literature, which he affects to despise," Blackwell was a man of fixed ideas. He believed in only two plots, which he called "pursuit and capture" and "delayed revelation." And he could be a hard editor to deal with.

"...*Western Story Magazine* paid well, as competition grew apace," recalled star writer Robert Ormond Case, "though each 1 cent per word raise came almost directly out of dour old Scotchman [sic] Blackwell's blood stream. He would start a writer at 2 cents per word... then, with anguished cries, he would raise to 3 cents. To achieve 4 cents per word was to reach a high plateau resounding to Blackwell's wails of grief and predictions of bankruptcy for Street & Smith.... Nevertheless, three of Blackwell's writers were finally paid 5 cents per word, to Blackwell's incredulous horror."

Fledgling writer Ernest Haycox found him impossible, as Case recalled in *The Roundup*:

"Blackwell was a thin little man, bald as an egg, with a sense of humor buried dark and deep. He always played it dead-pan. Instead of raising his voice at a climax he would hitch his chair closer to his listener, hunch over portentously and whisper.

"'Haycox,' he said, 'I've bought three of your short stories, and I think we're running into plot trouble.' (Hitching his chair closer) 'In your first story, Haycox, you had two men and one woman. In your second there were two women and one man. In your third you had one man and one woman. My God, Haycox—' (whispering) '—*where do we go from here?*'"

In his less puckish moments, Blackwell set the tone for all the fiction that comprised the Great American Mirage that was the Pulp West, whether published by Street & Smith or not:

"We want stories that are clean and wholesome, and that will urge people to live the open life of the West—to make them dream of doing so some day. We do not care for 'stories within stories.' Unless the story is straight historical, *Western Story* likes to have it one that could happen in the present. While it is true that some of these stories could not happen in the present, because of a change in the old order of things, we wish them to be written as though they could. For instance, do not begin your story by saying, 'It was in the good old days of 1877,' but write it so that those who know will say, 'Of course, the author means that this happened in 1877,' while those who do not know whether it could happen today or not, will assume that it could. While it is true that a great deal of the West has been built up, fenced in, and plowed under, there is still a whole lot of it lying around loose out there where people of an adventurous frame of mind can find plenty of attraction."

The magazine's lifeblood was the immortal Frederick Schiller Faust, AKA Max Brand, who often had two or more serials running concurrently under a herd of pen names. Despite his staggering popularity, Faust was no authentic Westerner, but a Californian who was inspired to enter the genre when legendary *All-Story* editor Robert H. Davis suggested he try a novel along the lines of Zane Grey's best-selling *Riders of the Purple Sage.* The result was a mythic extravaganza of the Old West, *The Untamed.* Its protagonist, the preternatural cowboy "Whistlin' Dan" Barry, was part Pan and half Tarzan of the Apes on horseback. He ran through two wonderfully improbable sequels and made "Max Brand" a name to conjure with.

Faust began generating Western serials for the major pulps, concentrating on *Western Story* in 1920, for which he disgorged an estimated 300 novels and novelettes under 11 pen names.

Street & Smith acquired the services of "Max Brand" through a fluke. Rival publisher Frank A. Munsey had sunk considerable capital into acquiring a string of newspapers, forcing a buying moratorium on poor Davis.

"Bob Davis was over-bought," Blackwell later boasted. "Munsey found it out, told Bob he'd have to shut off buying for as long as six months, and use up some of the stuff in the safe. Faust, always in need of money, no matter how much he made, came to me with a story. I bought it. He was mine, and mine only from there on."

Blackwell credited Faust's inhumanly reliable output with inspiring the decision to go weekly in 1920. Within two years, *Western Story* circulation zoomed to over one million copies a month. To meet the seemingly insatiable demand, Street & Smith resorted to running multiple Faust stories under different pen names.

Like most of his tribe, Faust was a formula man. "Action, action, action, is the thing," he averred. "So long as you keep your hero jumping through fiery hoops on every page you're all right. The basic formula I use is simple: good man turns bad, bad man turns good. Naturally, there is considerable variation on this theme… There has to be a woman, but not much of a one. A good horse is much more important."

He was also an unabashed fabulist, writing a species of Western-based fantasy, rather than true-to-life tales of a time gone by.

"As the years went by," wrote Samuel A. Peeples, "Faust began to develop his own Never-Never Land to provide a locale for his stories. It lay somewhere in a 'West' that never was. It was described as the 'Hole-in-The-Wall Country' but bore absolutely no relationship to that very real outlaw territory. He created from whole cloth a mountain-desert, edged by his fictional 'Blue Water Mountains' and when he wasn't laying a tale in an equally mythic Far North, or just as unreal Mexican Border, he placed his characters in this imaginary region, where they brawled and adventured their way through millions of words."

One of the reasons Blackwell owned Faust's output was that other pulp editors simply did not want it. Charles Agnew MacLean, editor of Street & Smith's upscale *Popular Magazine*, was unquestionably speaking of Faust when he said: "I cannot publish the work of a certain writer of Western stories, because he writes of a country that is non-existent and of a people that do not now exist and in all probability never did exist."

Yet the Herculean Faust set the standard for much of what became the 20th Century pulp Western. He was so disinterested in historical or geographical facts that when one of his editors paid his way West to soak up some first-hand local color, Faust simply holed himself up in his hotel room and banged out a novel or two, then trained home without investigating further.

Equally important to the early Pulp West was Faust's polar opposite, Walter John Coburn. A rancher's son, Coburn had knocked around the range until a pile-up between a mounted Coburn and a wild bull effectively ended his cowboy days.

Coburn described himself as the genuine article:

"About myself there ain't much to say. I punched cows from the old Circle Diamond Range in Canada to the Mexican border. Have worked in a center-fire country and a double-rigged country. Have dallied my rope and have tied hard and fast which, in the language of the cowboy, means that I forked a pony in just about every man's country between the Rio Grande and Alberta. Having busted up a couple of legs I quit the cow business and from then on follered different rackets. Worked on survey gangs, fired a boiler, ran a garage, was life guard, put in some months with the Rebel Army in Mexico, bummed my way on freight trains, lived in the Jungle Camps with hobos and fought in a prize ring as a preliminary fighter. Have been a deputy sheriff and have ridden with boys that carried a price on their heads. Outside of that I have lived a very conservative life."

During his surveying phase, Coburn happened to read a Western yarn in *Adventure*. "There were enough mistakes to convince me the writer did not savvy anything about cow punching," recalled Coburn in his autobiography, *Western Word Wrangler*. "It was only after I finished the yarn… that I looked to find the name of the author. The story was written by Robert J. Horton, and this surely rang a bell."

Horton had been an old drinking buddy of Coburn's. The busted-up wrangler also recognized the plot as a yarn Coburn once spun for the veteran sportswriter-turned-fictioneer.

"According to my boneheaded cowhand way of thinking," Coburn later wrote, "if an Eastern tenderfoot like my old friend Horton could bat out a fiction story about my own cow country, I certainly could do the same. I spent the rest of that afternoon writing a lengthy letter to Bob in care of *Adventure,* asking his advice regarding my tackling writing a Western fiction yarn, informing him that my own cow punching days were over."

Coburn sold his first effort, "The Peace Treaty of the Seven Up," to Munsey's *Argosy All-Story Weekly* in 1922. He later claimed to have been so broke he had to borrow the money to buy that issue off the news stands. Coburn soon became a familiar byline in *Western Story Magazine.*

A critical turning point in the careers of all concerned came in 1924 when Fiction House owner Jack Kelly bearded Coburn in his Montana lair for the express purpose of luring him away from Blackwell. Kelly had started a magazine of general adventure fiction called *Action Stories,* which increasingly emphasized Western yarns. In Coburn, Kelly saw a "Westerneer" as rough and realistic as rawhide.

Offering him the feature spot in *Action Stories* every month, Kelly promised, "I'll build you up, cowboy, until you're the highest paid Western writer in the game. Max Brand will never catch up with you. While he's a good writer, he knows nothing about the West."

True to his word, Kelly christened Coburn "the Cowboy Author." To sharpen the nickname, he prevailed on the young writer to trim back his byline from Walter J. to the more laconic Walt Coburn. And a legend was manufactured.

When Fiction House launched their first all-Western title, *Lariat Story Magazine,* (Headlined "Real Cowboy Stories by Real Cowboys") Coburn had the cover and lead story in virtually every issue of that one, too.

Without mentioning names, Kelly went out of his way to publicize his top hand in terms calculated to put the Frederick Fausts of the pulp writing world to shame:

"Of Western story writers there is no end. They are as common as democrats in Texas. Many of them learned their locale from a Pullman window; some of them just sat down to a typewriter and got it all from a package of cigarettes. You will not have to read many paragraphs of this magazine to appreciate that Walt Coburn is the real McCoy. Montana is his home state and old-timers still talk of the Coburn Circle C spread where Walt, man and boy, wrangled horses and punched cows before the days of barb wire. Perhaps you have read Walt Coburn before, but, man, if this is your introduction to this high ridin' cowboy's stories, how we envy the thrill of your discovery. Walt Coburn's story people are the hard-living, hard-dying breed who built an empire—who wrote pages of high courage in American history. Walt Coburn is of them and one of them."

Other publishers were slow to realize reader tastes were shifting away from the all-fiction magazine to genre-specific periodicals. When the Clayton chain issued a more focused version of the old multi-genre fiction cornucopia, *Ace-High Magazine* sales lagged so badly publisher William Clayton wondered aloud, "They must be printing them out West somewhere and shipping them in to fool us, for we seem to get twice as many returns as there were copies originally printed."

He should have looked to his editor, Harold Hersey, out of Greenwich Village by way of Bozeman, Montana.

"We started *Ace-High Magazine* as a general adventure sheet," Hersey recounted, "and were forced to make it a Western, due to the title and the fact that Frontier stories with cowboy heroes were what our readers wanted. Clayton used to say that *Ace-High* succeeded in spite of my articles, not because of them. Having been born of pioneering parents, I was raised on stories of the Last Frontier. Its heroes were my heroes. The trouble was when I began editing *Ace-High* that I had not yet learned to

concentrate on the entertainment features in a popular magazine. The moment I caught on to this the magazine became a
national success."

History records William Clayton himself as the man who
turned *Ace-High* around. Looking over his product, Clayton
decided to take the comma out of the masthead blurb, "Western,
Adventure and Sport Stories", and focus on the Wild West
with a smattering of prizefight yarns. Sales took off.

Doubleday, publisher of the all-fiction title *Short Stories*,
foundered briefly with *The Frontier*. Originally dedicated to
frontiers all over the globe, it soon discovered pulp readers
preferred the frontier period of the Old West.

"Most Western stories," explained editor Edmund Collier,
"deal with the working cowboy and his work. They are laid
(roughly speaking) between the Rio Grande and the Yellow-
stone, between Abilene, Kansas, and the Rocky Mountains. In
time they range (also roughly speaking) between the Civil War
and the... Johnson County War... They are based on what
William MacLeod Raine describes as 'the greatest pastoral
movement of the world'—the trailing of millions of cattle from
Texas north, first to the booming Colorado mining towns, next
to the Westward-building railroads, and finally to the fertile
Northern ranges. This tremendous stream of cattle, driven by
Texas cowmen and cowboys, met the stream of Easterners
heading West—prospectors, merchants, gamblers, dry farmers,
trappers, settlers of all kinds, and of course Indians and soldiers.
This meeting and mingling—in a practically lawless land—of
Southerners, Yankees, and Indians forms an unsurpassed
breeding-ground for drama; and this great movement, more
than anything, is responsible for the tremendous and continued
popularity of Western fiction."

The Roaring Twenties were in full cry. It was a crazy time.
The Pulp West emerged as a wild, untamed place, with characters drifting in and out and back again as fortunes and reader
preferences shifted.

The experience of Frederick Robert Buckley, even if exaggerated, is that of a lost pilgrim wandering through an unknown, incomprehensible land.

A former Vitagraph film editor and actor, Buckley wanted to write literature, but his work failed to support him. In the throes of a nervous breakdown, he stumbled into the offices of a pulp he called *The Cowboy.* In reality, it was Street & Smith's *Western Story Magazine.*

"What kind of stories do you want for your magazine?" Buckley asked innocently.

"What we require," Frank Blackwell told him, "is stories of clean, rapid action with a wholesome love interest, as, for instance, bandits rob a train, sheriff goes after them, *bing-bing-bing,* ride ride ride, bandit shoots back, *bing-bing-bing,* terrible fight, marries the girl."

"What girl?"

"Any girl," said Blackwell.

"Well, who marries her? The sheriff or the bandit?"

"Either," rejoined Blackwell. "Good afternoon."

According to Buckley, "I went home and wrote that identical story."

Several days after submitting it, Buckley dropped in to see Blackwell. Instead of being met in the formal reception room, he was invited into a dark-paneled editorial sanctum.

Blackwell began, "Aren't you the chap who came in last week and asked what kind of story we wanted, and I said bandit robs a train, sheriff chases him, *bing-bing-bing,* ride ride ride—?"

Buckley admitted that he was.

"W-e-e-ell," drawled old Rocking Death, "you went and wrote just that, didn't you?"

"Yes."

"We-e-e-ell, you know, I was only joking. I thought you— well everybody asks that fool question; so I just gave you a fool reply; said anything that came into my head—gave you a kind of parody, you know."

"Then you're not buying it?" Buckley asked.

Blackwell smiled. "Oh, yes, I am." Pitching the manuscript into the safe, he added, "And—say; go home and write some more stories like it."

"Just like it?"

"Exactly like it," returned Blackwell.

Buckley did as instructed. After selling a variation a week for three consecutive weeks, his conscience started bothering him.

"I remember," he wrote, "how on the third Saturday following my interview with the editor, I returned to him worried. I had received two hundred dollars for the first story, two hundred and fifty for the same yarn with different names for the characters, and two hundred for yet another telling of it, with Wyoming for the locale instead of Nevada. This seemed too easy to be moral and I said so. The editor smiled. He also pointed to a *Webster's Unabridged Dictionary* on a stand...."

"You're getting a cent a word," he remarked. "You can have a cent and a half after this, if you're a good boy; but even at a cent—you see that book? It contains a quarter of a million words—worth a penny apiece. All you've got to do is rearrange them a bit. Not very much. See?"

Buckley knuckled down to the task. He became one of *Western Story*'s rising stars. His only challenge was bending his imagination to the narrow formula.

"I actually wrote a Western novelette in which the heroine did not marry the most unspeakable ruffian in sight," he admitted, "and when this was rejected, hurled her into his arms in five lines and a manner which was designed to be a blood-insult to the editor's intelligence. I got six hundred dollars for the revised version; it then sold into the movies for a thousand dollars; and since then it has brought me about four hundred in second-serial and similar minor rights."

By this time, Buckley was so entrenched that Blackwell put

him to work pushing the steadily-petrifying cowboy formula in a daring new direction.

"Delighted, the editor chose me as the standard-bearer in a daring new departure. He felt like trying something kind of imaginative, and he insisted that I should write a fantasia on the original theme... I went home, perched on my wooden box, and raved twenty-five thousand words about a hollow mountain, near Dallas, Tex., in whose interior lived the Lost Tribes of Israel, drinking out of golden mugs."

As his reputation grew, he started hitting other markets, and playing editors off one another. Once while intoxicated, Buckley wrote a letter proclaiming that his word rate was now double.

One editor called in abject agreement, begging for stories.

"Your *old* stuff," he insisted. "None of this damn highbrow business. Just have a nice cowboy on a nice cayuse or whatever they call the damn things, and have him ride along, and have things happen to him, and then have him stop riding and get married, and let it go at that."

"What else have I ever done?" Buckley demanded.

"Why, you've been working this damn trick of having him ride out of one place, going to another, and then meeting him when he gets there, in the next chapter. Our people don't get that, I tell you. They say, 'Who the hell's this guy, anyway, and where's he come from, and what's it all about, anyhow?' And then they write in and say I don't know the Great West."

Buckley took that as the gross exaggeration of a proof-addled pulp editor—until the bright day in March 1923 when he pulled his Ford into a filling station.

"I hear," said the proprietor, "that you're a writer... What book do you write for?"

Buckley began ticking off a list. The man stopped him at the first title.

"The Cowboy? Why, I read that every month."

Buckley brightened. "And I'm in it almost every month, so we must have met."

The filling station proprietor looked uncertain.

"I don't pay much attention to the names of the authors," he admitted.

"Perhaps you know the character I use," Buckley suggested helpfully. "He's been running for nearly three years. Scarecrow Wilson, his name is."

"I don't pay much attention to the names of the characters. Lessee—that's five gal—"

"Well," Buckley pressed, "surely you remember the big fight with the sticks of dynamite in last month's complete novel. Yes? Did you read the complete novel?"

"I guess I did. I always read the book through from cover to cover."

"Well, the fight with the dynamite, now—where Scarecrow is in the cave, and all the Mexicans and Indians attacking him, and one stick of dynamite blows the trousers off Snorting Horse showing he's a white man and the heroine's missing father?"

Clearly embarrassed, the man muttered, "I don't—"

Buckley burst out, "In the name of the Captain General of the Society of Jesus, what do you mean?"

"Well," the proprietor said slowly, "I don't take much notice of the stories. I—just read 'em."

A stunned Buckley confessed, "I went straight home and conceived a plot containing less than nothing; during the next three days, I wrote it, in a style as devoid of even elementary tempo as is a hen's pup of dun-drearies; and from then onward unto this last, I have never looked back."

Came a time in 1924, when F.R. Buckley could hack them out no longer. Ten thousand words a week at two cents per had made him prosperous, but the call of literature grew too strong to ignore.

It was time to quit. Visiting Blackwell's office, he expected to be met by gnashing teeth and the rending of editorial garments. After all, he was a popular *Western Story Magazine* writer.

Instead, Blackwell cut him off.

"All right—all right! I know the rest. You chaps don't meet each other, tucked away in dog-holes the way you all are, but I meet you all, you know. Jenkins got through three months ago—he's in England, translating Horace, of all the birds that fly in the air! Yes—the Bloody Jack Blair man. Wilkins was in yesterday, talking about essays just the same as you are. He finished up his pile by selling us that Roberts character of his— and his own name—and he's going to do his essays under a pseudonym. Ah, well—you boys were the first generation of this method. Due to the war or something, I suppose. There's a second growth coming up to take your places, though. By the way, do you want to sell us this Scarecrow Wilson character, and your name? Give you a thousand cash. It's your own name you've been using, isn't it? Second generation's got you beaten there. They're putting pen-names on this stuff, so they'll have their own for the real etcetera. One of 'em did sixty thousand words last week. You'll have to get a nom-de-plume, like Wilkins."

Buckley took the cash. Under his new byline, John Pentifer, he penned an *American Mercury* essay on his experiences.

The first cycle of the pulp Western magazine was drawing to a close. But the gold rush was just beginning.

"Critics of the 'Western' are legion. Because of its swift action and original diction, they concede it to be nothing better than the progeny of the Diamond Dick and Nick Carter yarns. Tainted, then, as the 'Western' is, by the Diamond Dick thrillers, critics years ago predicted its summary demise. Yet the 'Western' today is riding 'high, wide, an' handsome,' and new magazines are appearing almost monthly in its name."

—Francis W. Hilton

2

KING COWBOY!

PROSPERITY PUSHED the pulp magazine to new heights. During the early '20s, with the nation struggling through a brief recession, a handful of publishers were content with issuing general fiction magazines. Only one all-Western title prospered. For a while, it seemed as if the weekly *Western Story Magazine* was all the market would bear. No one took William Clayton's new *Ranch Romances* very seriously.

Emerging as the chief rival to Street & Smith's supremacy was Fiction House, formed in 1921. It came about through a chance meeting between two gents named Jack. When magazine circulation manager Jack Kelly told Jack Glenister about his plans for the new pulp enterprise, Kelly suggested they team up, with Kelly editing and Glenister handling the business side. Glenister was also in circulation. *Action Stories* was their inaugural effort. It showcased detective and adventure stories at the start, with a smattering of cowboy yarns. It wouldn't be long before the cowboys ran most other horseless heroes off.

In 1925, a third Jack, a former newspaperman from Corning, New York, tired of his day job as a bank teller, approached Kelly about an editorial job. No sooner had John F. Byrne introduced himself, than John Byrne Kelly jumped out of his chair and exclaimed, "You're hired!" They were not related, but Fiction House quickly expanded through the hard work of the three Irishmen with the coincidentally common names.

Byrne was an editor of strong opinions, as writer Richard

Wormser learned when he submitted a Western entitled "The Five Irish Villains."

"I received it back by mail with a curt note; anybody who was damn fool enough to send a story like that to an editor named Byrne deserved to be banished to the outer darknesses."

Jack Byrne represented a new breed of pulp magazine editor.

"But with the mounting prosperity after the war," recalled writer Tom Curry, then following in the footsteps of his brother-in-law, F.R. Buckley, "new magazines came into being. Strings of them. There had always been Street & Smith, of course, and they controlled the field for years, except for *Argosy* and *Munsey's* perhaps. Now William Clayton brought out *Ace-High Western*; he expanded… Fiction House put out several titles, and there were others coming into the field. All these sheets had to have material on the line—and editors to run them.

"They could not wait for beards to grow and the mellowed knowledge of middle age; they installed editors who were young, eager. Even if they couldn't grow a beard because it hadn't yet sprouted."

Fiction House had released *Action Stories* in the Autumn of 1921, simultaneously with Clayton's inaugural issue of *Ace-High Magazine*. Undoubtedly the trigger for this double-barreled discharge was Street & Smith's decision the previous year to publish *Western Story* every week. For three years, this trio of magazines—all chockfull of Western yarns—were sufficient to satisfy the American appetite for Frontier fiction.

Calvin Coolidge's 1924 election to the Presidency kicked off a new prosperity that took less than a year to reinvigorate the economy—and the magazine publishing business.

In the Autumn of 1925, only weeks apart, Fiction House offered up *The Lariat*, Street & Smith brought out *True Western Adventures*, and William Clayton issued *Cowboy Stories*, which had been test-marketed the previous Spring by rebinding old issues of *Ace-High Magazine* with the tentative new title. It sold briskly.

Clayton, too, was fast becoming a major player. Started by a British-born speculator with a penchant for playing the horses, the Clayton chain expanded rapidly and paid authors generously.

"When I first became an editor," recalled Clayton's Henry A. McComas, "in the Winter of 1925-26, we had the mostest fun. There was plenty of room for the magazines then being published. As a matter of fact, there was so much room that each company decided to double, then treble, the number of its titles. The radio was just beginning to be called radio instead of wireless. We had movies, but 'talkie' was merely Chinese dialect. And for several years, we lived and worked in the dawn of a new era, and the sky was the limit only because we didn't feel like boasting too much. This was the time when the editorial problem was that of getting enough new writers to fill the maw that emptied into the roaring gluttons called presses. Slowly but constantly increasing word rates turned the trick. That, and the fact that many an author learned how to double or treble his output. William Wallace Cook was not the only one by far who wrote 30,000 words a week—and sold them! Our friend H. Bedford-Jones once admitted, I think, earning $70,000. This was no fluke. It was simply a new big business."

Just as city boys once migrated to cattle ranches to escape their sorry lot in life, real men of the West swiftly succumbed to the gold-fever lure of the pulp-paper trail.

Allan Vaughan Elston was one. A doughboy during World War I, he wrote a letter home that was published in *Munsey's* magazine. "I took it in stride," Elston recollected, "never supposing I'd write anything else. And I didn't—until 1924. By then I was operating the family ranch in south Colorado and due to a flood, a fire and a blackleg epidemic, plus soaring land taxes and bank interest, I'd come upon hard times.

"That's when I remembered the Munsey article and thought maybe I could do it again. Failing to think of anything to write about, I tried fiction. And because of the pulp magazine boom of the 1920s, I got away with it."

In this booming young field, the cowboy was king, and the saddlehorse was his throne.

"Nothing can blind us to the fact that the cowboy-sheriff yarn is by all odds the most popular form of fiction that is being published today," observed *The Author & Journalist*. "Readers apparently are insatiable for it. Numerous writers are pulling down thousands of dollars yearly with mediocre stuff, writing for this demand, and the editors howl for more. To those naive young writers who frequently write asking us what type of fiction is in demand—their practical minds set on turning out just that type, and thereby taking a short cut to fame and fortune—we are wont to reply, sorrowfully but truthfully, 'The Western yarn.' It is the nearest thing to a 'sure-fire' seller that exists in the fictional field. In spite of which, how anybody can write 'em, or how anybody can read 'em, remains a mystery to us."

Conventional wisdom said the all-Western pulp was an historical aberration. They couldn't last. "Readers would soon tire of magazines devoted solely to tales of cowboys, sheriffs, and cattle ranches," predicted Willard Hawkins of what seemed but a passing fad.

"The cowboy has had the limelight too much to himself," insisted *Western Story* novelist Arthur P. Hankins. "There is plenty of adventure and romance in the Western mountains, in the Western railroad construction camp, in the lumber camps, in California mines. The cowboy West is not only a thing of the past—it has been 'done to death.'"

Yet the cowboy magazines kept on coming. At the beginning of 1927, Doubleday issued *West*. Unlike the more literary *Frontier*, *West* was aimed at the same young readers who devoured *Action Stories*.

"The main fare of this magazine will be the Western story of plot and action, cowboys, roundups, stage coaches, prospectors, gold rushes, etc," announced editor Harry E. Maule. "But what we are trying to do especially is to get into the magazine that sense of the rollicking, devil-may-care, hip, hip, hurrah which characterized the cowboy in his best days."

After five years of offering up general fiction, *Action Stories* became a de-facto vehicle for Westerns. Although South Seas and other high-adventure fiction continued to be offered, post 1927 it was a rare cover story that was *not* a Western.

Later in the year, Street & Smith converted a lingering dime novel series into the unabashedly juvenile *Wild West Weekly* under the direction of Ronald Oliphant. It showcased rambunctious series buckaroos like dime-novel holdover Young Wild West (tamed down to just plain Billy West), as well as Kid Wolf, the Whistlin' Kid, Sonny Tabor, Silver Jack Steele, Flame Burns, Bud Jones of Texas, and a noisy posse of like-minded others.

Suddenly, there were seven all-Western pulps on the market, not counting those others which ran Western yarns as part of their magazine mix.

No two were exactly alike, insisted agent Agnes M. Reeve:

"Some take only stories that have little or no romance; others favor tales in which the gentler sex has a part; some want stories with setting and atmosphere—real pictures of the different phases of Western life, be it Northwest, Southwest, or the Western plains. One or two put no emphasis at all on the setting—merely the name of a ranch will do. But all unite in the cry for action—action at the beginning, action at the end, and action all the way between."

The very nature of the genre called for it, claimed wrangler-turned-writer Francis W. Hilton:

"'Westerns' must, of necessity, be fast-moving, for the life of the West was that way," he noted in "Writing the Western Story." (*The Writer,* June 1930) "The cowboy was a man of few words but great action. He lived in the saddle; was always on the move. The problem he faced was weather—terrible, death-dealing winters and blistering, rainless summers. The things he fought for were the two essentials of life—food and water. The men he was pitted against were, in many cases, fugitive desperadoes who bowed to no law save that which the cowboy 'toted' on his hip. Small wonder then that the tales of the 'puncher,' who was up with the break of dawn and away, never to stop moving until long after dark, are filled to the brim with action!"

Jack Kelly's Fiction House was the company responsible for taking pulp-style action to its highest expression. He codified the house brand of pulp thusly:

"Our formula for *Action Stories* briefly is this: Action, stripped to the bone, denuded of all superfluous trimmings spelt with a capital A… no lengthy descriptions, no long-winded digressions, no weather reports… Just the stripped action meat of a dramatic, swift-moving plot—laid in any adventurous land under the sun, with a Yank for a hero."

The reasons for this approach were purely economic. "The consensus of opinion of all editors with whom I have come in contact with is that the intelligence of the public we are aiming at ranges from 14 to 18 years," admitted Fiction House managing editor Richard A. Martinsen. "The conclusion is obvious and inexorable: simplicity of style and plot, and an absorbing, swift-moving story. Fourteen to eighteen is the age of hero worship."

More than any other publisher, Fiction House set the tone for the cowboys of the boomtime '20s. "Picture your story as a succession of action scenes that will unfold a situation and solve it in the climax," added Martinsen's successor, Jack Byrne. "Don't start out with Joe Smith arriving in Gila, saving the girl from a bully's attacks; taking a position as foreman of her father's ranch and solving the mystery of the disappearing herds. That sort of plot attack brands your story right off as 'one of those things.'"

Hollywood, not the rules of good fiction writing, set the tone for Fiction House's style of high-pressure action. "It may help you if you think of your plot as a movie director would visualize it if he were making a six-reeler," explained Byrne. "Ask yourself what scene he would use as an opening to get immediate attention and interest—what continuity would he follow—from what angle would he shoot various scenes to get his best effects?"

Byrne directed writers, "We must have a good, fast opening. Smack us within the first paragraph. Get our interest aroused. Don't tell us about the general geographic situation or the atmospheric conditions. Don't describe the hero's physique, or the kind of pants he wears. *Start something!*"

Jack Kelly himself placed great emphasis on muscular writing. A declarative line like "He picked up the gun from the table and shot his victim," was considered hopelessly dull. "Seizing the gun from the table, he pressed the trigger and his victim crumpled to the floor with the explosion." was the preferred shade of purple.

He was also a ruthless editor. Kelly often lectured his Western writers, "If you want to describe a sunset, O.K. Describe it. But we'll shove it at the end of a story as a footnote, and just put a star in the yarn so the reader can refer to it later after the story's been read."

A monotony of melodrama lead to considerable editorial hair-splitting over what constituted acceptable action writing.

Rogers Terrill, then cutting his editorial teeth at Fiction House, dwelt on this distinction-without-a-difference in *Writer's Digest*. "Much has been said of the 'typical' Fiction House opening," he wrote in "Why Manuscripts Come Home." "All of it worthless—for there is no such thing. For any successful magazine—or group of magazines—there can be no such thing. There are a good many ways of writing a good Fiction House opening as there are ways of writing the story itself. No way is typical. But—and here is the difference—there *are* certain very definite qualities which are to be found in a large majority of

Fiction House openings."

After citing a straight-action opening, Terrill then dipped into the work of Walt Coburn for what he called the "action-type" opening:

"There were six fresh bullet holes in the wooden slab that marked the grave of Bob Hutton… Which meant that Pablo Costello had returned from the Chihauhau country. It meant that Pablo had ridden along that trail, and had halted long enough to pay sinister tribute to the dead man buried there. For whenever Pablo rode by Bob Hutton's grave, he always emptied his six-shooter at the wooden slab—even as he had, some five years ago, emptied his gun at the living Hutton." [1]

"There is no direct action here," Terrill commented. "There is in reality—and this is rather remarkable—no character actually before the eyes of the reader. There is only a grave and a wooden slab with 'six fresh bullet holes.' But that this opening packs real dramatic punch no one will deny. Its atmosphere, its setting, its tersely worded explanation of those six bullet holes—all give a definite, intriguing promise of action swiftly to follow."

The success of the Fiction House action formula goaded pulp editors into lashing their stable of writers to perform superhuman feats of wordslinging.

"Start with action—not with atmosphere, description or whatever sounds pleasing, even if it belongs there *logically*," instructed Arch Joscelyn. "Get your hero into a situation, as quickly as possible, where it seems that he can't get out, then proceed to get him out of—or shall we say past?—that situation, by getting him into a worse one. Repeat the formula two or three times, add a bang-up ending, and you're approaching the idea."

Editors called this frenzied formulation the "super-action plot."

"Everything in the Western story, from the title to the last period, must be a mass of action," counseled writer Walter Des

---

1 *"Gun Hands" by Walt Coburn.* Action Stories, *February 1931.*

Marais. "The title should give you a flying start. The first paragraph must show the hero in some position from which he will have a difficult time to extricate himself.... The main idea of an action-adventure story is conflict. Get your hero in trouble and keep him there. Let him fight his way out. What he does while he is fighting his way out makes your story."

Under this kind of pressure, opening situations inevitably descended into straight-faced parody. "Joe Star's first concrete evidence of the awful danger threatening the Slash Diamond came while he was being hanged," began one pulp oater.

A backlash was inevitable.

"The editors have gone hog-wild on action!" complained Albert William Stone of *Western Story Magazine*, and Denver. "I've crammed action into a story until it hung over the side, like an old-fashioned loaf of bread with too much yeast in it, only to have the editor write, 'I'd like this better if it had more sheer action in it.' Or: 'If you'll rewrite the first five pages, and get a bigger dose of action into them, I think I can use the yarn.' And I have done the requested re-writing, only to have the editor comment sourly, 'I'm sending you a check, but next time see if you can get a little more *action* into your yarns.'"

"What is action?" asked rancher and writer S. Omar Barker. "A cowboy lopes into town, anchors his horse at the hitch rail and strolls into a drugstore to buy a stick of gum. That (probably) is mere movement. A cowboy lopes into town, steps off without bothering to hitch his horse, hurries into the courthouse to look for the sheriff, only to find that the ol' booger has been murdered sometime last night. That (probably) is action."

Jack Byrne simplified the formula when he proclaimed, "A good sock in the jaw is action."

Not all editors saw action in the same terms. *The Frontier*'s first editor warned his writers away from action for action's sake:

"Action is not melodrama," insisted A.H. Bittner. "To some writers the more revolver-shots and the more murders the faster the story is moving." […] "Action is not a string of useless stunts dragged in to make a story snappy. If the action of a story cannot come out of the plot itself there is something wrong with the plot; anything which is imported to make a story move is bound to ruin it."

Among pulp editors, this was a minority opinion. They were not looking for quality writing, but the literary equivalent of standardized horseshoes. It was more important that stories fit a formula than break new ground.

"In some quarters this adherence to formula was—as should be the case—flexible," admitted writer Stephen Payne. "In other quarters it was carried to the point of ridiculousness, as witness an editor speaking: 'Our staff had agreed that this story was a "must" for our book before they passed it on to me. I liked it, too, and was about to okay it when I suddenly discovered it didn't fit our formula. So of *course* I had to reject it.'"

In Bittner's case, he moved on from *The Frontier* to editing the prestigious *Argosy*. Under Harry E. Maule, the former magazine was retitled *Frontier Stories*. Under constant reader pressure, it gradually went all-Western. It really took off after Maule dropped pioneer-era stories, exiling all Indian characters in favor of Cattle Kingdom days and cowboy ways.

Resisting the action trend, *Western Story*'s Robert Ormond Case struggled with the problem of "clicking" with his capricious editor, Frank Blackwell. "I sold a million words to *WSM without once killing a man*," he recounted. "What made the stories saleable in a magazine where six-guns thundered and corpses littered the landscape on practically every page? I hadn't the slightest idea.

"When I began to wonder vaguely if there was something about technique, or the ingredients of a story, that made it saleable as opposed to one that rated only a printed rejection slip. I naively mentioned to Blackwell, in one of our innumerable exchanges of letters, that he had never complimented me on any one of my stories. He had never said that one *was* better than another. I wasn't asking for praise: what I wanted to know was why, from a seasoned editor's viewpoint, one story was better than another.

"Blackwell was no help at all. What he replied was a pearl of wisdom no doubt, but no help to my search for a good yardstick. 'Young man,' he wrote back severely, 'the highest compliment I can pay to you, or to any writer, is to buy your goddam stories.'"

Elsewhere, Blackwell confessed in print, "Often I read yarns in which I can find no flaw, yet reject them. They lack that intangible, indescribable quality I call the 'story.'"

The plain fact was that beyond the safe boots-and-saddle formula, pulp editors didn't know what they wanted. It showed in their broad market notices, which ran to rude clichés and cruder generalities.

"Over on the *Triple-X* range there is a continual howl for short and long Western stories—authentic cow-country yarns with bullet holes for punctuation marks," quoth editor Jack Smalley. According to his successor, Douglas E. Lurton, "We want the regulation Western story… that smacks of the sage brush and tumble weed."

Calls for manuscripts loaded with "range feel" or "sage tang" or "packed with snappy action" were as precise as editors were willing to go.

Boldness was not part of the pulp editorial vision. Agent Lurton Blassingame once told the tale of an editor who refused to be pinned down on the type of plots he favored, finally exploding, "Hell, man, I don't know, and I don't care as long as it won't offend too many readers and is convincing. What I want is a story about interesting persons. I want a yarn which will make the reader say to himself, when he's finished it, "*There* was a man!'"

Montana writer Arch Joscelyn dissected the type down to the meat and bone of a solitary sentence. "Editors cry loudly for the new, the unusual, but they are mortally afraid of it when they see it," he observed.

Yet in the hardcover book field, things were starting to change. As Lee E. Wells later observed, "In the '20s Emerson Hough's *The Covered Wagon* appeared, a powerful and important book that was made into a motion picture classic, as was also Edna Ferber's *Cimarron*. These two books were historical novels, the time definitely placed, every detail correct to the period and year. I believe these two books mark a very definite change in the approach to Western writing. They stood head and shoulders above their contemporaries. Why? It was not solely because of strong character motivation and powerful stories, though they definitely had these. It was because here was the first recognition that the West, heretofore a romantic dreamland, was a definite part in the building of America, a development of the westward course of empire, and of far-reaching effect to the America that was to come. The West had meaning, its people could now be seen in their proper perspective as forefathers of ours who pioneered, who built an extension of American civilization in a wilderness."

This development away from blood-and-thunder superheroics was not embraced by the fledgling pulp-paper magazines. It would be another generation before pulp editors got around to rejecting the "romantic dreamland." They were too busy strip-mining the myth to trouble their readers with mere history.

"From the first, the field of Western fiction has been a paradise for the beginning writer. Story plots were there for the taking: rustling, land and water squabbles, the legendary feats of cowboy and outlaw, of peace officer and gambler and stage robber. Using these properties alone meant only placer work, surface mining. Missing the one essential element of all, it led to the 'bang-bang' era, and monthly audiences of more than twenty million readers absorbed the too often fantastic tales that ignored credibility and the true principles of the craft."

—*Joseph T. Shaw*

3

CARDBOARD COWPOKES
AND WOODEN INDIANS

THE PULP Range was a thing to be worked in sections, just like the genuine article. Writers learned to navigate its different cow-trails to selling, but it was not always easy to find the shortest path the first time out.

During the 1920s, Californian Ludwig Stanley Landmichl segued from being a roaming Fox newsreel cameraman to productive pulpster, "slowly working into the field of 'Westerns,' which type of story is one of the hardest forms to put over, because the field was, still is, and probably always shall be over-crowded, and the stuff so much exaggerated.

"It was a tough grind," he acknowledged. "Competition was keen—the boys that had been doing Westerns for years knew their horses and oats, they had learned how to handle their material, and they had a good idea of what the editors and the reading public wanted in their Western yarns.

"But I had done considerable traveling throughout the so-called West. I had made long drags out into the sageland and desert country, and far in along the backbone of the Rockies with pack-horse outfits. I knew the West as it was. And being out with old-timers, I learned from them how it used to be before I saw it.

"In this way I picked up some good material for a number of stories that went into *Two-Gun Magazine.*"

That was the Western approach to research. One Eastern-based freelancer devised a scattershot strategy for selling his

Western wares, which he shared with other writers:

"I've evolved a two-way target that's been working pretty well for some time," Richard E. Martinsen told *The Author & Journalist*. "If a yarn is tossed back by *West* as too melodramatic, *Triple-X* usually corrals it, while if *Triple-X's* reaction to a yarn is violently jaundiced, *West* not infrequently picks it up. If both these books jump on a yarn, however, I toss it in the lowest drawer forthwith. There's something radically wrong.

"Generally speaking, a yarn that *Triple-X* and *Lariat* will clutch avidly won't sell to *Western Stories* or *West,* and vice versa." […] "For each of these mags has a number of its own peculiar wants and don'ts—*West* a particular lot of 'em. And *Western Stories,* f'instance, is a deal more addicted to the sentimental side of range life and character than *West.* And *Lariat* wants elementary simplicity. A yarn with the least trace of the supernatural, bogus or real, used as a frame-up by the villains or as a fact, is out for *West.* And *West* isn't keen on railroads in the cow country, and doesn't like Indians…."

One of the weirdest wrinkles in the early Pulp West was not the seemingly bullet-resistant cowboy, but the banishment of entire tribes of Native Americans from the imaginary landscape.

Although welcomed in cinematic Horse Operas, the Red Man was virtually *persona non grata* in the pulps. He appears to have fallen out of favor in the mid '20s as a result of the sympathetic portrayal of the Navajo Indian protagonist of Zane Grey's *The Vanishing American.* Romance between a white woman and a noble savage was too much for audiences of the time—no matter how noble the savage. The backlash was so intense that for decades after, *The Ladies Home Companion*— which first printed the novel—and companion magazines like *The Saturday Evening Post* refused any Western submission containing a Native American character in anything greater than a supporting role.

When he was editing *The Frontier,* Harry E. Maule admitted,

"…our readers do not show any preference for the all-Indian story which does not have a white man as a hero. Indians must necessarily appear in certain Western stories, but it is more popular with the reader if they appear rather as subordinate characters than leading ones."

Possibly this was a reaction to the dated old dime-novel formulas where the Red Man was a convenient object of slaughter. When instructing his writers on how to pad out longer sagas, one turn-of-the-century editor curtly directed: "Kill more Indians."

Writer J. Edward Leithead fought this restriction the length and breadth of his pulp career, which encompassed the birth of *Western Story Magazine* to the death of the pulps three decades later. "I constantly argued with editors to publish Indian stuff," he recalled, "as I always liked Indians from the time I read Cooper's *Leatherstocking Tales* and Edward E. Ellis' Indian stories. I argued that they couldn't present a true picture of the West and leave out Indians. They replied that the Indian was 'dead' as a fiction character for readers of those times."

Another Indian aficionado, complaining in *Writer's Digest* about the dearth of Native American stories and markets, pointed to one explosive trigger for the boom in pulp Westerns after 1924. Wrote Del Radway:

"The years 1914 and 1915 saw Thomas Ince, that hardy pioneer of the motion picture industry, turning out Indian and Western films by the carload. And these films were devoured by a thrilled public. These pictures were the forerunners of the present day action photoplays and short stories. The fickle public liked them at that time. Have the last few hectic years changed the people's minds in regard to Indian pictures and stories? I think not.

"For example," continued Radway, "single out the motion picture that was shown in all theaters of the country five years ago: '*The Covered Wagon*.' Wasn't that cinema a huge box office success? Why? Because it came at a time when the majority were fed up on society dramas and secretly longed for a change. In *'The Covered Wagon'* they found that change. And if my memory has not failed me, I do believe that was a saga of the Old West with *painted Indians....*"

Adapted from Emerson Hough's 1923 novel, James Cruze's *The Covered Wagon* was a turning point in Western cinema. The first epic pioneer film, it triggered a fresh cycle of silent Westerns, including *The Pony Express, The Iron Horse* and *North of 36,* a 1924 film based on Hough's final book. A big-budget treatment of cattle trailing days, *North of 36* did for that era what *The Covered Wagon* had done for the Oregon Trail time period. Westerns films were not new, of course. Horse Operas starring William S. Hart, Hoot Gibson and Tom Mix—who starred in many based on Max Brand novels—regularly rose and fell in popularity. But from mere melodrama, the genre had been elevated to serious cinema.

More than any other event, *The Covered Wagon*'s roaring success triggered the launching of *The Frontier,* setting the stage for the avalanche of Western magazines still to come.

But as much as it grew, there was no place in the Pulp West for the Indian, except in minor roles. Del Radway concluded his complaint with this:

"I earnestly wish that I could persuade a publisher to launch a new magazine, tentatively called "Indian Stories," and then have said publisher sit back and watch the profits pour in. What say, editors and publishers?"

Twenty-one years later, a pulp house would issue an *Indian Stories.* By then it would be too late for the pulp cowboy, never mind his eternal nemesis.

Writer Albert William Stone was not alone in resenting the increasing editorial cattleprodding toward action. He was one of the early pulp Westerneers, who took as their models the more literary books of Eugene Manlove Rhodes and Emerson Hough. This first generation happened along while memories of the Old West were still vivid. They numbered among the most popular contributors.

A mere sprout growing up in ranch country, Texan Eugene Cunningham recalled reading B.M. Bower's 1903 classic, *Chip of the Flying U.* It was a revelation.

"This is the first Western I ever read," Cunningham later wrote, "and I recall how bewildered a young fellow was, to find the come day-go day life of a ranch put into a book. I looked out of the barn to where a bronc' peeler was topping some Indian Territory rough ones for my father, and I thought amazedly: "'Imagine him—in a book! Like Captain Cook, Midshipman Easy, and Natty Bumppo!'"

It was a common cow-country epiphany.

"My background was exclusively Western," reported Frank C. Robertson. "My father was a Texas trail driver in his youth, my mother a Dakota prairie schoolteacher. My two brothers were cowboys and ranchers. I spent a lot of time on the range, myself, with cattle as well as sheep. I followed construction work throughout the West for a time. The normal chores around a Western ranch, such as breaking broncos, were as ordinary to me as wrapping packages would be to a store clerk....

"Not until I read the Western stories of the late B.M. Bower did it dawn on me that the West might be a field for fiction. Having no idea of ever being a writer, I marvelled and forgot."

For many of them, those clear recollections plumb got in the way. Arthur Hawthorne Carhart got to jawing with an old cowhand when the following exchange occurred:

"I wish I could write that stuff," mused the aging Westerner. "But I know the West as she was, and when I start to writing of some wild adventure I clog all up in my thoughts 'cause I know it didn't happen."

"But it could have happened," Carhart protested.

"Yes," the other allowed. "I suppose it could have happened."

"All right," said Carhart, "kick that inhibition of yours out of mind. You saw the West, in its high-flowering days, and you didn't see just this sort of thing. But you admit it could have occurred. Frankly, I had this same sort of complex and I licked it. Now, here's what I do. I take true-to-life characters—people that are flesh and blood of the period I am writing, whether it is the explorer's period of Pike and Long, the fur-trading time of Carson and Bridger, the gold period of Russell, Jackson and Gregory, or the trail-herd period of Goodnight and Iliff. All right; I have my people. Next, what sort of hot jam could they get into? Something typical, something based on fact, something that rings true *as to its essentials.* Run 'em into it, now, and let things begin to happen. Just sit down and figure what grief, ruction, turmoil and strife they could have gotten into over the basically sound contention. If your characters live, and you get them to fighting severely enough over a situation, if what follows is true to human nature and basically sound as to period factors—then it could have happened."

Carhart was typical of that first generation. A former Recreation Engineer with the U.S. Forest Service in Denver, he penned articles for various outdoor magazines while working as a landscape architect. Then the Western pulps boomed. Drawing on his Colorado background, Carhart plunged in. As his literary career drifted West, his publicity photo did too. He exchanged his outdoorsy Tyrolean hat for the ten-gallon variety.

Yet Carhart took his fictioneering seriously, at one point solemnly informing fellow pulp writer Edward Hunt Hoover, "You know, Hoover, you can't dodge the U.S. Forest Service in any Western tale you write, if you write of any time after 1905."

They got their background where they could, as did Colorado journalist Ray Humphries, who specialized in the now-obscure art of rodeo reporting, turning observation into fiction.

"I could not sit down and write story after story on rodeos—on bucking broncos and swaggering cowboys and lightning lariats and dodging steers—if I had not 'covered' a dozen of such celebrations for my paper. I know rodeos. I know cowboys. I know the West, and still I am not a puncher. I am a newspaperman."

Honest-to-God out-of-work cowboys constituted the chief elements of this far-flung legion. If you could write and plot, and hailed from the True West, you were worth your weight in gold dust. Motivations were as varied as backgrounds.

"I cooked and wrangled on a round-up when I was twelve years old," claimed Francis W. Hilton. "I rode the range from childhood. Most of my life has been spent in Wyoming, Colorado, and Montana.... Many of us writing 'Westerns' are writing from first-hand knowledge, of a people we know and love, and writing of days so long past that they would be forgotten but for us."

Arch Joscelyn reminisced, "I chased cayuses from the backs of others, smelt burning hair from the branding iron and rode all day behind half-tamed dogies with the barbed wire steadily encroaching. And then I tried to put some of it down on paper—to catch something of that lingering whisper out of the past, a bit of the remaining glory of a golden age."

Others were not so romantic. Recalled *Wild West Weekly's* Samuel H. Nickels, "...if I hadn't been flat broke and in bed I'd probably never have started writing for publication. But I'd had a smash-up while roping a big steer on the side of Tucson Mountain, from the back of a half-broken horse. My chest and one side were bunged up and I was in bed for nearly a year. I had a wife and three small children looking to Dad for support, so Dad had to think of something besides cowpunching for a living."

Wrangler Glenn Vernam of Kansas took the opposite path.

"I never 'broke' into print. I just kind of sneaked in, when somebody left the gate open. I still don't understand it. All I know is that when old *Triple-X Western* sent me a $25 check, that fine April morning of 1928, they sure ruined a tolerably good cowhand. Things were never the same after that though I still had to chase cowtails for a considerable spell."

One of the best of the Western pulpeteers was Wilbur Coleman Tuttle, a Montana newspaperman who came into the world above the jail of his sheriff father. Back in 1915, he started writing on a dare. "One day, on a newsstand, I saw a copy of *Adventure* magazine, on the cover of which was an editor's note—'this is the funniest Western we ever published.' I bought it, but tale didn't give me any chuckles. You see, I was a product of the Montana range country, and usually managed to keep a straight face."

Tuttle dashed off his own idea of a cowboy comedy yarn, and one of the Pulp West's few geniuses, W.C. Tuttle, was born. He single-handedly invented the range mystery Western sub-genre in his long-running tales of Hashknife Hartley and his saddle pard, Sleepy Stevens.

Tuttle wrote from his gut. "I have never mapped out a story in my life," he claimed. "I do not bother about plots nor situations. A typewriter and some paper seem to be all I require, and I let the story tell itself. When my lead character gets bothersome enough to worry me I know he is ready to tell me the story."

Another giant was Harry F. Olmsted. Groomed to follow in the footsteps of his civil engineer father who had been hired to conduct topographical surveys of China, Olmsted turned maverick and began grinding out Westerns for Fiction House instead, soon rivaling Walt Coburn in both popularity and prolificacy.

"When I was starting," he recalled, "that fabulous editor, Jack Kelly, told me to read, read, read, not to imitate, but to fill myself with the lore, the mannerisms, the ways of speaking, so that the flavor and the spirit of the old West became part of my tools, leaving me free to plot and turn out just so much more copy."

Texan Dick Halliday took to roaming the range with his typewriter lashed to his saddle. Insinuating himself into working ranches, he stayed for weeks, soaking up local color and character types. At night, he pounded out stories based on his encounters, then rode on to a fresh setting tricked out, contemporaries recalled, like a cross between a dashing Silent Screen buckaroo and an Eagle Scout.

Halliday once showed up at a New Mexico bunkhouse, explaining, "I'm here to get atmosphere."

One cowboy roared, "God-damn! If you're looking for *atmosphere,* you've come to the right place You cain't beat the Diamond A for *atmosphere!* Mister, cain't you smell it?"

Novelist Alan LeMay, who used the byline Alan M. Emley when slumming in the pulps, was a practicing astrologer. His novel, *The Searchers,* later became a classic Western film.

Montana ranch hand Chis'm MacDel Rayburn submitted a sample of his handwriting to a mail-order graphologist and after being told he'd make a better writer than a rancher, carved out a fair career for himself under the alias of Del Rayburn.

Harry Sinclair Drago, who rose from Western books to scripting oaters for Tom Mix and other Hollywood cowboys, came to the cowboy hero via another legendary horseman. "I wrote several books about the mounted police in Canada because that's where my people are from," he said. "But once I got an interest in the old West, I couldn't help writing about it." He finally settled in White Plains, New York, to be close to his markets.

Perhaps the most unusual of them all was California miner Charles Snow, who turned to fictional cowboying after a babbitt explosion robbed him of his sight at the age of 37.

"I was at loose ends," he confessed, "until my brother suggested that since I was a great liar and as we had seen a great deal in our travels to make interesting lies, I might make a living by putting some of them on paper."

Teaching himself to type on an Oliver machine whose keys were dabbed with mucilage shaped for easy touch identification, Snow took to writing Westerns, ultimately churning out some 500 novels under five pen names with the assistance of four secretaries.

This human fiction factory once quipped, "Sometimes I don't

know my real name until about 10 o'clock in the forenoon." Collectors remember Snow today for his 1936 *Wild West Stories* yarn, "One Hopped Up Cowboy," featuring the Marijuana Kid.

On occasion a valuable writer simply rode in over the transom. "...a year after I had started *Ace-High Magazine,*" recalled editor Harold Hersey, "a little dog-eared manuscript came into the office dealing with the adventures of the Hooker Brothers. The story was told by Johnny, the older of the two, and it related their adventures in Canyon Lobo, a ranch they were holding somewhere beyond the Mississippi. I began to chuckle, and so an unknown writer walked into the pages of *Ace-High* and a Hooker Brothers story appeared in every issue for four years. Ray Nafziger, the author, in addition to these short stories, wrote for me under various pseudonyms, contributing many thousands of words during each year and in all the time that I was editing this magazine he did not have a single rejection, nor apparently has he missed since, for his yarns continue to pour out with clockwork regularity."

Many of these emerging Western wordslingers were dedicated to high-speed production, and damn all history.

"Write swiftly," instructed Texan George C. Henderson. "Be sure of yourself—even if you are wrong. Do not peck out a few thousand words and then decide what it lacks. Keep it moving. Prod that cowboy hero into the thick of it. Get him into a bad mess and then have him use his head to get out.... In the action Western, when all else fails, you set .45 calibre revolvers to spilling lead and make it logical, provided you remember that a six-shooter can be fired only six times without reloading, and some but five, and that the other fellow's bullets cannot all go wrong."

The author of "The Gunslick from Hellangone" offered fellow pulpsters a sure-fire way of tackling their pulp. "To break the force of inertia that tends to keep the thoughts revolving in a groove," Henderson claimed, "the professional shunts his cowboy through the swinging doors of Bad Town's worst saloon, plumb into the center of a fracas. He may throw away the first pages after the story unfolds, but more likely the rollicking cowpunch, hopping into trouble with six-shooters flaming, will give him all he wants to handle for a good many thousand words. In the meantime he has hazed the hell-bustin' range waddie into another ruckus even worse than the first and before he knows it his 35,000-word novelette or even 60,000-word serial is done. It has literally written itself. Immediate action changes the characters from dumb clay into real people, who take things into their hands thereafter. The best Western stories are inevitably after the first chapter."

Production rather than personal expression became the watchword of the still-developing Pulp West.

Henderson again: "One question I am asked is: 'How does the professional manage to sell such a large percentage of his product?' I may say that many Western writers sell 100 per cent. The answer is that they standardized their product. They know that action is wanted in action stories; that it must be logical and that it must lead to the hero's triumph. Love interest, sex, politics, preachment, the weird, horrible, and repulsive—all are taboo. The hero must be kept in constant peril, and truth and justice must triumph at the curtain."

As Margaret MacMullen observed in *Harper's*, "The 'Westerns' have their own code. The heroine, though capable of extraordinary physical feats, is a much less sophisticated creature than her Eastern counterpart. In the old-fashioned way, she expects to be sought instead of being the aggressor. The hero, though a rough, tough man among men, dewily awaits the dawn of love, but is as a rule too much engaged in foiling bandits, leaping from precipices, swimming rapids, and discovering gold-mines to have his attention more than briefly distracted by the softer emotions. It is all in the good adventure-story tradition, less well written of course than the doings of Richard Hannay and Allan Quatermain, but hardly less credible. There is sometimes a rather nice feeling for nature—an element never allowed to intrude on the action of the other types of cheap magazines, all of which are sternly urban in tone.

If one does not object to the merciless pace at which shooting follows shooting, and can understand the lingo talked by the actors, these Westerns are pretty good stuff."

Editors dictated this standardization in no uncertain terms. *Triple-X* framed its formula this way, "The setting preferred is on a ranch, the time of the story neither modern nor ancient, but roughly half way between the present and Indian days, presumably when the cattle business was in its prime, fences were few and far between, and Judge Colt was actively in command."

This is what led critics to decry the cut-to-pattern pulp formula.

"The mass production of day-dreams by the Pulps has been accompanied by a phenomenon unique in literature: the standardization of fiction," commented *Vanity Fair's* Marcus Duffield. "Even as Fords and hairpins are standardized, so are stories. These magazines represent the incursion of the Machine Age into the art of publishing."

Duffield was in error. Contemporary pulp magazines were no more standardized than their dime-novel forebears. If anything, they were less so. Duffield continued:

"The reason for the standardization is not to help speed the mass production—although it does enable the Pulp writers to turn out the reams of stories they do—but rather to make the yarns conform with the pattern of their readers' natural day-dreams. The Pulp customers never allow social problems to intrude into their own flights of fancy: hence the magazines rigorously bar any touch of contemporary realism."

The term that best described the pulp product was plain "hokum."

"In my opinion there's much to be said in favor of the good old hokum," admitted Fiction House editor Richard E. Martinsen. "Certain plots, employing combinations of circumstance and a certain atmosphere, play on correlated passions and emotions in human beings. The yarns that were 'knockouts' in

Homer's age are knockouts today and will be equally sure-fire knockouts a thousand years from now. It's merely necessary to throw the characters into contemporary garb."

"But hokum is grievously misunderstood," declared agent Laurence D'Orsay. "It is nothing to despise, nothing to shudder over. It is simply *what people want,* what people like. For example, there are those favorites of silver screen and printed page, the honest-to-goodness superman hero who wouldn't dream of doing anything wrong, the honest-to-goodness super-woman heroine who wouldn't dream of letting him… and the villain who slinks away at the happy fade-out, baffled by the hero's might and the heroine's constancy. These well-known characters, and all the thrilling things they do and suffer, are hokum—and *good* hokum, one hundred per cent palatable to editors, if properly cooked and daintily served."

"The average 'action' editor today demands that the hero shall be a super-man," cautioned Arch Joscelyn, "but don't carry that trait so far as to be ridiculous. If you are going to have him kill a dozen men with his six-guns, at least have him re-load it once! Remember too that there can be plenty of 'bloody' action with very little killing; that men who are wounded cannot do half as many things as are often attributed to them; it becomes physically impossible. Convincing situations and explanations must be given if your super-man is to deserve the title."

This wild exaggeration of the cowboy hero into superhuman proportions caused Nebraska rancher and novelist Eugene Manlove Rhodes to scoff at "the dreariness of invincible and tireless super-heroes" then running rampant in Western popular fiction.

Coming from a more serious literary tradition, Rhodes met the phenomenon of the Pulp Western with a plea, "You who write today the stories of our yesterdays—can't you give our grandchildren something to remember of the cowboy, besides gunplay? …There was gunplay amongst the cowboys; but what cowboys did best and most was to work the cattle. It was not unnatural to write up the fighting days of the cowlands; but the skill, the daring, the fine faithfulness and the splendid fun of the working days has been neglected."

Rhodes was bucking, not a literary movement, but a stampede. Given a choice between the realists offering the historical West, and the fabulists who depicted a mythic Wild West, readers invariably chose the latter. The complaint had started with *The Virginian,* where nary a cow troubled the cowboy life. The public ate it up. The bigger the buckaroo, the better he went over.

"This was the size of the problem facing the average Western hero," observed Tom Curry. "Alone, he must settle at least a war."

Pulp editors were a cynical bunch. Their opinion of their audience could be summed up in a single pithy epithet.

"Wood-pulp literature caters exclusively to the adolescent mind," observed Alvin Barclay in *The New Republic.* "The first editor I worked under told me on the first day of my editorial career: 'Always remember that we are getting out a magazine for The Great American Moron!'"

Barclay toiled for Street & Smith and Frank A. Munsey, who is said to have uttered that famous line which poisoned pulp editorial thinking for a generation.

"Since the stories are edited for mental children and persons suffering from arrested development," Barclay continued, "they are kept strictly moral in tone. However invidious they may be in suggestion, however harmful the influence of the unreal world they depict and the phantasies they foster, their surface is almost repulsively virtuous.

"The stories themselves—I am speaking now of Westerns— usually consist of frantic chases and violent fights, and they end, in the good old Sunday-school manner, with virtue triumphant. The woman interest in the Westerns is almost non-existent and without sex coloring. The heroine is simply the prize awarded the hero, along with the ranch of his dreams, at the end of the story."

In part, pulp publishers were trying to avoid the stigmas of their popular predecessors. "The woodpulp magazine was a natural development of the dime novel," explained Erle Stanley Gardner. "But the woodpulps were trying desperately to be respectable so that they could ease out from under the parental ban imposed on dime novels, and their purity defied description. This was particularly true in the Western magazines, where every young heroine was a symbol of purity, a glacial statue of virgin ice."

And no respectable pulp-paper puncher could ever stand accused of what S. Omar Barker so quaintly termed "urgin' a virgin." Not if he wanted to retain his White Hat status.

The producers of pulp fiction were also tarred with the same black brush of immaturity. "Few mature intelligences want to write for the wood-pulp magazines," claimed Henry Morton Robinson in "The Wood-Pulp Racket." (*The Bookman*, August 1928) "Few can. The physical battle of hurling six thousand words a day onto paper, the brain-pulverizing business of devising enough hair-trigger action to stretch over the plotted area of your tale, and the ghoulish necessity (when invention fails) of coming back again to feed off the dead flesh of last year's yarns—these are some of the reasons that make wood-pulp literature the last miry trench of men who write against despair."

The pulp writers themselves would have laughed at that judgment. During a time of growing national prosperity, they were literally turning blank stationary into currency. Their penny paid per word possessed the buying power of a modern quarter. At that rate, a 5,000 word short story netted over a thousand 21st Century dollars. And Street & Smith's three Western titles alone represented an annual market of nine million words.

"Commercially speaking, you can stick to five plots and make a fortune," advised Richard E. Martinsen. "The Lord knows how many yarns have been printed about the Texas Rangers and the Royal Mounted. Old stuff, you bet. Just the same I'd use two Ranger and two Mounted stories in each issue of *North*

West if I could pick up good ones. Why? Well, the Rangers and the Mounted are no longer organizations, so far as the American public is concerned. They are far more. They are symbols of *courage*, which is immortal."

"There was gold in them there thrills," writer Allan Bosworth later recalled. A *San Diego Sun* reporter, Bosworth bet a fellow staff member that he could sell his first story before he turned 25.

"The first story was a 4000-word Western," he recounted, "and I wrote it from start to finish in three hours. I called it 'When Bar S Went Bolshevik' and it dealt with a ranch that had to complete a fencing job in a certain time in order to retain its lease, and a crew of cowboys who hated fence building. I was drawing partly on experience. The crew left in a body for the oil fields; the ranch-man fell heir to a bunch of hoboes rounded up in the railroad yards and given their choice of going to work or landing in jail. In 1926, the country as a whole was not as sympathetic toward labor problems as it is today, and it remembered unpleasant incidents involving the I.W.W. I had my crew of cowboys return just in time to fire a few shots, break a few heads, and save the ranch and its owner."

Bosworth sold it first time out to *Triple-X*, winning the bet. He was not the first reporter to swap a copydesk for the free-lance life—and he would not be the last. These were the days that gave rise to the million-word-a-year man, a species of high-production human fiction factory who, legend claimed, sold six figures worth of copy per anum.

Frederick Faust was the king of them all. Not far behind was the Grand Old Man of the pulps, H. Bedford-Jones, whose prodigious career began circa 1908, then expanded beyond all reason. A master at virtually every pulp genre, Jones specialized in pioneer-era Westerns and produced a memorable series of novelettes focusing on lost Indian tribes for *Western Story Magazine*. It was alleged that in order to maintain his prodigious production, Jones kept stories going in three different electric typewriters at once, shifting from one to another when one yarn hit a snag.

"The writer who could turn out 2740 words, ten pages of finished narrative every day of his life (Sundays included), an average short story every two days, or eleven book-length novels a year was a product of special conditions," explained Fletcher Pratt in *The American Mercury*. "He was born in the booming era of Harding normalcy, when the dime novel was turning into the dime magazine, conjured forth by a new reading public consisting of two groups: first, the thousands of second-generation immigrants just leaving high schools where they had been taught to read but not to think; and, second, other thousands of men just emerging from the army, where violent death had been a matter of imminent expectation, and who now found ordinary literature flat."

Pure career strategy drove these demon wordsmiths.

"Volume of output is essential to the building up of a following for any author," insisted *West's* Harry Maule. "An occasional story in any one magazine by a writer will not accomplish this end. The writer's value to the magazine is determined by the size and character of his following—the number of readers who like his work, buy the magazine because of it, and let us know how they feel about it."

No one valued such iron-fingered typewriter burners better than Street & Smith's Frank Blackwell. For each issue of *Western Story,* he needed a novelette, three ongoing serials and six short stories. At the height of his reign, Blackwell was in the market for a staggering 750,000 words of fiction every month, most of it Western.

"Stories, stories, stories!" he once told a visiting author in near despair. "It's almost a nightmare, sometimes, to get them. Every now and then I draw a long breath and say: 'Well, this number is taken care of, at last. Now I can breathe!' And then will come notice from some department, to the effect that four or five thousand words more are needed to fill a hole. We've got to start digging hard, to fill that hole." [....] "And every time we find a yarn that will fit we give a whoop of joy. This job is a perpetual search. It is endless. A prolific author, who can turn out the kind of fiction we want, is worth his weight in gold to us."

"Wood-pulp literature is bought by the bale and sold by the long ton," observed Henry Morton Robinson. "They're nine parts action and seventeen parts romantic improbability, done to a sizzling turn by writers whose credo runs 'Action is the true God, and plausibility is His only prophet.'"

In that, Robinson hit the nail on the head, according to *Triple-X* editor Jack Smalley:

"I knew one editor who would be transformed into a calliope of steaming-hot 'blues' at the spectacle of an otherwise-impeccable hero who comes to get his revenge on the villains girded for the fray—with an empty six-shooter! At this stage the hero whispers a husky farewell to his horse—and us—that he forgot to bring along bullets. Or else he brings his gun ruthlessly to bear on the cattle rustler, and a *click* is all that comes of it. He ranks with the fool who didn't know it was loaded, yet the author picks out this man for his hero!

"With shaking fingers, the editor would lay down the manuscript, clip out an advertisement for a memory course which always ran in his magazine, and send it to the author, with his regrets—and the manuscript.

"Yet it was this same editor who would acclaim the passage where the hero—with the same innocuous hardware, apparently—slays five of the rustlers and wounds three more, without reloading. He didn't mind a little thing like that because it was merely impossible. But the other sin was unforgivable because it was improbable."

Prolificacy was the rule rather than the exception. One author remarked, "There's nothing remarkable about a pulp writer turning out 16 stories in six weeks. That was a fairly normal output and some did much better, but the point is, there was a market out there that could take that sort of output...."

Fifteen or 20 stories floating around New York at all the times assured you of a fairly steady income."

It was no business for a shiftless former cowpoke, assured William MacLeod Raine:

"It's physical labor as tiresome as digging ditches in the streets," he declared. "People don't realize what it means to put a piece of paper in the typewriter and begin without having a single idea. The typewriter stares you coldly in the face. You shamefully look at it, and then you walk around the room. You smoke several cigarettes. You look at your watch. It's getting late. You sit down at the typewriter. You begin. Once the first paragraph is started, the rest is easy."

The pressure to produce sometimes wrought havoc on writers and editors alike. Top pulp wage earner Eugene Cunningham told this tale in 1929:

"Not very long ago an editor in one of the cowboy magazines read a manuscript, and when he finished it, he turned to another editor in the room and said, 'This guy Jones is getting rougher every day. In this story he has a bad man bursting out of a saloon, leaping into his saddle, and lashing his horse madly with his sweetheart!' The author, cursed by a little knowledge of the Spanish language, and properly feeling that a nice two-bit Spanish word would sound impressive, had his bad man lash the horse with a *querida* instead of a *quirta!*"

Alvin Barclay recalled, "I once heard an associate editor remonstrating with an author about the lack of plot in a yarn he had concocted. 'But Mr. F—,' she said, 'you simply have your hero ride up the hill. Tagallop! Tagallop! Tagallop! Fire off his pistol—bang! And ride down the hill. Tagallop! Tagallop! Tagallop!'"

Quipped Barclay, "That nicely describes nine out of ten Westerns."

That author was surely Frederick Faust, and the assistant one of Frank Blackwell's Vassar girls. These assistants were sometimes guilty of murdering the manuscripts they copy-edited, innocently changing "dogies" to "doggies" and committing even more grievous extra-literary crimes.

"Occasionally," Barclay recalled, "the stories become too genteel for the tastes of their writers. I remember one yarn, laid in a Western saloon which the virile author had decorated with cuspidors. These seemed improper to the lady who edited the copy, and pretty wire baskets were substituted for the dirty spittoons. The letter in which the author expressed his opinion of the change could never have been printed in the magazine. Somewhat similar was the reaction of the writer whose hero was made to rise from the floor after a knock-down blow, wipe his brow, and exclaim, "Goodness gracious!""

"Despite the fact that a Western story is usually a man's story," explained Walter Des Marais, "there is very little, if any, swearing.... Your hero may swear a blue streak in one magazine, but Street & Smith will cut out his tongue if he but mutters 'damn.'"

"Man, we were moral then," added *Western Story* contributor W. Ryerson Johnson. "We couldn't use words like 'damn' or 'hell' in a telegram. Or even in a magazine story! It got to be a game. You kept trying. Once, in a story I wrote: '"Great God!" he cursed.' I won half of that one. An editor changed it to '"Great Scott," he cursed.'"

One title, whose editor required that it be "packed with cow-country action," received a perfectly good yarn marred by the unfortunate development that in the climax, the cowboy hero was rescued by a trio of hombres flying biplanes.

"Now, airplanes were strictly taboo in the magazine," reported *Vanity Fair,* "so a sub-editor was instructed to eliminate them. He did; he changed 'whirring' to 'thudding,' and 'gleaming wings' to 'foam-flecked haunches.' The three airplanes became six horses and the story went to the printer."

The consequences of not being editorially vigilant were serious. One sub-editor absent-mindedly allowed the crimson vulgarity "brothel" to pass into print, and was summarily fired.

"The magazines were so squeaky clean," another recalled, "they shimmered almost with divine light. Censorship came from within the organization. The pulps in New York were always afraid of an Armageddon of censorship if obscenities proliferated."

But the greater burden of filling the double-columned pulp pages fell to the authors, who began proliferating as a species. A sub-culture of pulp writers started forming in the late 1920s. Scattered throughout the nation—if not the globe—they gathered in social pockets and writers' colonies—and speakeasies. Evolving into a company of comrades, they took to calling themselves "pulpeteers" or "fictioneers" if they were high-minded, and "pulpsters" or "wordslingers" if they looked askance at their profession.

Many of them spun their melodrama with tongue secretly in cheek. "For the most part," admitted Allan R. Bosworth, "I always chose names for my villains that began with a sibilant sound. I imagined most of my readers moved their lips when they read, and this enabled them to hiss the villain satisfactorily. But once, having run out of Sneeds, Schriers, Spradlins, Zapatas, and the like, I killed a man named MacDowell. The story was no sooner on the news stands than I received a letter from a well-known pulp writer I had never met—Syl Mac-Dowell—informing me that I had over-stepped the line. He said that his next victim, doomed to die like the dog he would be, was going to be named Bosworth."

They fell into the roles of the fantasy heroes they created:

"Often," confessed Bosworth, "when I had just ventilated the villain with a .45 slug, I would get up from the typewriter chair that gave me saddlesores and practice a quick draw of an imaginary gun before the mirror, so that I might be able to describe the shoot-out better, next time. I could see that my eyes were becoming narrowed to mere lidded slits from the glare of sun on alkali, and my legs looked as if a horse had just run out from between them."

Or they assumed outrageous personas and told wildly improbable stories on themselves, as did Tom Curry, who claimed to have sold an unfriendly editor his first effort through the friendly persuasion of a Peacemaker borrowed from F.R. Buckley.

"I wrote a short Western, hid the Colt under my jacket, and called on an editor. I laid the story on his desk and as he began shaking his head because he didn't even like the first paragraph, I pulled the hogleg and stuck it against the back of his skull. 'I don't want to kill you sir,' I said coolly. 'But so help me, if you don't buy this, I'll do it. No use to call the sheriff. I'll be in hiding till I receive your payment.'

"He swallowed his adam's apple and with shaking hand reached for his phone. I rammed the Colt into his neck. 'What d'you think you're doing?' I snarled. 'Just... just calling our financial department to issue you a check,' he quavered. 'I think this is the best story I'm ever going to read.'"

Even their more plausible anecdotes possessed a folksy tall-tale odor. "I will admit that my education forced me to write everything in the first-party," confessed W.C. Tuttle. "It did for at least five years. One winter I was on a pleasure trip to Southern California, and when my feet thawed out, I had to stay in my hotel room; so I rented a typewriter and wrote my first third-person tale. In fact, it was the first of a mighty long series, 'The Hashknife Tales.' I doubted the sale. Then I got a fat check from *Adventure,* and a note from Art Hoffman, in which he said, 'Queer incident, Tut. Yesterday we held a meeting, and it was the general opinion that you should write a third-party tale, very seriously. This morning the tale came in the mail. Here's our opinion—in cash. You're a mind reader."

Paid by the word, pulpsters were trained to think by the word. And they counted every penny. A pre-Perry Mason Erle Stanley Gardner told this revealing story on himself:

"Without my realizing it, my heroes developed a habit of missing the first five shots, only to connect with the last bullet in the gun. At one time an editor took me to task for this. How did it happen that my characters, who were chain lightning with a gun, were so inaccurate with the first five shots?

"I told this editor frankly, 'At 3 cents a word, every time I'd say *'bang'* in the story I get three cents. If you think I'm going to have the gun battle over while my hero has got fifteen cents worth of unexploded ammunition in the cylinder of his gun, you're nuts.'"

Gardner made pounding pulp sound frivolous and insincere. Some approached it that way. But for most Western pulpsmiths, it was hard, hard work.

"Few readers realize the rigid demands imposed upon a writer of Western fiction," said fictioneer Francis W. Hilton. "To produce a salable script, the writer of 'Westerns' must incorporate the requisites of other short stories and stretch his imagination back forty years for a setting, for editors will not admit that the West of the old trail-herd days is dead." […] "But the trail herds have vanished. What few cowboys are left wear mail-order clothes. The 'bronc-peelers' long since have quit the 'home ranch' for the rodeo game, leaving the writer stranded high and dry for a background for his fast-moving 'Westerns', which, undeniably, have created a new field of fiction—a type of story that, above all else, is typically American, and which in its typical American way defies all precedent, smashes all the rules of good writing, and utterly ignores the example set by the masters of another age!"

One reason was that many Western pulpeteers took their cues from Hollywood Horse Operas. Lud Landmichl was one writer who pounded out pulp alternately with scripting silent Westerns. He rode the boom on two mounts.

Landmichl wrote, "Dick Carter, that husky young 'Western' star who played 'lead' in 'The Golden Trail' and other Western pictures; Pete Morrison, also starring in 'Westerns' for Lariat Productions; and stars and executives of the Chadwick Pictures Corporation, all have informed me that 1926-1927 are being looked forward to in great anticipation as probably being big 'Western' years. Some of the folks on the Fox lot have told me the same thing, so I am beginning to take some stock in the prophesy."

Early in 1927, Fiction House's Richard E. Martinsen forecast the roaring Pulp Western boom then in full cry was just a mouse squeak in comparison to its future potential. "My prediction that 1927 is going to be a humdinger of a year for popular fiction writers is by no means pure hearsay," he stated in *The Author & Journalist*. "Two important magazine houses have for some time now been engaged in a competitive scalping-bee which has already rebounded bee-utifully to the benefit of copy producers, and the going has just begun to be interesting. An editor of a well-known magazine gave it to me today as his firm conviction that wood-pulp periodicals now paying a top rate of two cents for material will within two years at most be driven to three, and possibly higher."

Martinsen—who in that very year quit Fiction House to cash in as a freelancer—had every reason to be optimistic. As far as the editorial eye could discern, fictitious Western skies were a clear and cloudless blue. No one had any idea what was coming over the golden horizon.

"*Once upon a time the demand for Western stories far exceeded the supply… Now 'way back in 1925 and on into the '30s, plot and action, coupled with plausibility, of course, were the main essential factors. One string of magazines even went so far as to adopt for its slogan, 'Action stripped to the bone.' It is an interesting sidelight to note that they soon began to cry: 'We want a human being, not just a gun dummy!'* "

—Stephen Payne

4

DAY OF THE GUN-DUMMY

DURING THE latter 1920s, the Western fiction magazine achieved unprecedented popularity. Emerging pulp publishers staked their claims with *The Golden West, Two-Gun Stories* and a strange shotgun marriage of a magazine aimed at female fans that was much copied and ultimately outsold them all, *Ranch Romances*.

Showcasing sentimental stories of the early 20th Century West, *Ranch Romances* gave birth to a new subgenre, the dude ranch yarn, wherein East met West and found Heaven on Earth under Western skies.

"Love must dominate the situations," insisted first editor Bina Flynn. "The characters must be sincerely portrayed, the men being either cowboys, miners or adventurers in outdoor range life, the women of the human, warm-blooded, sentimental type. Action will be subordinated to the love element always, but the Western idea as portrayed by the popular novel and the motion picture will be essential. Sex stories are not to be used."

This turned the regulation Western on its head.

"Away back then," recalled pulpster Stephen Payne, "writers and editors of man-interest magazines were openly scornful of love-interest Westerns, and looked askance at *Ranch Romances*. The West was a man's dish, and thousands of stories in the short lengths during that time held no woman interest whatever."

Fiction House found an unusual formulation with a half-breed title called *North-West Stories,* in which Westerns and "Northwesterns" shared the same bunk.

A close cousin of the Western, the Northwestern was a popular sub-genre of the early 20th Century. It focused on the exploits of loggers and trappers in the Great North Woods, with the Royal Canadian Mounted Police substituting for sheriffs.

"Nor are cowboys the only fit material for fictional treatment," observed commentator Malcolm Ross. "There are miners, rangers, lumbermen, and many breeds of workers whose essential appeal to the imagination lies in the fact that they lead hard, dangerous lives in picturesque surroundings. The same fictional types which writers like Willa Cather have described in the Middle West exist in the Far West; and, in addition, the latter section offers the dying, but still extent, color of pioneer life."

Practitioner Al P. Nelson contrasted the difference between the cowboy Western and the so-called "timber" Western this way:

"The true lumberjack is probably the most inspiring of all outdoor men," he asserted. "While the two-gun cowboy depends largely on his flaming guns to cow his enemies into submission, the lumberjack wades into battle with only his two sturdy fists as weapons. Many are the tales of heroism that come out of the big woods where the best man wins, not the man who is quickest on the draw."

Many pulps included Mountie yarns for variety, and perhaps to entice Canadian readers, but American audiences preferred the two-gun fantasy. Within a decade, the RCMP field would be all but extinct, while the "galloping" love story as codified by *Ranch Romances* became a genre—if not a force—unto itself.

Western yarns even rubbed shoulders with the early efforts of Dashiell Hammett, Erle Stanley Gardner and Carroll John Daly—all of whom dabbled in the genre—in the pages of *Black Mask.* Daly is credited with inventing the hard-boiled detective genre in the early 1920s via his two-fisted urban hired guns. Some of his first crime stories were virtually indistinguishable from Westerns of the day, making the trailblazing hard-boiled crime story a bastard offshoot of the woodpulp Western.

But Western fiction magazines remained stubbornly rooted in the dime novel. Many writers had cut their teeth on the gaudy little pamphlets, and some, like former Buffalo Bill ghostwriters W. Bert Foster and William Wallace Cook, were survivors of its latter days. They simply retold the same brand of gunpowder-packed stories for the new pulp magazines.

"Practically all of the Western magazines demand the hard-riding, fast-shooting, action type of story with a single predominant character—a very noble, he-heroic, gallant, sympathetic sort of a chap—overcoming great odds," explained Stephen Payne. "The old stereotyped Western given just a little bit of freshness and of novelty is plumb good."

This was encouraged from the start. When Frank Blackwell assembled the first issue of *Western Story Magazine,* he did so from scraps of Street & Smith's *Buffalo Bill Weekly,* which he had been editing for a solid decade. Early issues ran Buffalo Bill stories until a stable of authors were groomed to support the new venture.

Another pulpster, New Jerseyite Hamilton Craigie, declared that the first thing "the successful carpenter of Westerns" should do to master background and form was read old dime novels. Craigie claimed to be a former Confederate soldier born in 1837 and an acquaintance of Buffalo Bill Cody and Annie Oakley. Maybe he was, maybe he wasn't. Soon, the winds of change would sweep him from the forefront of the field.

The carpentry approach to fiction-making was fostered by the editors themselves. Frank Blackwell liked to tell aspiring pulpsmiths, "The dictionary is your lumber yard. It is for you, the writer, to study the words and so put them together that they make sense and interesting reading." Even by the standards of his day, Blackwell was old school.

Editors were single-minded in their preference in protagonists. "The main character must be a cowboy," proclaimed *Lariat's* John Byrne. "Make him a real personality, capable of arousing reader sympathy. Keep your yarn on the range with some good subordinate atmosphere and range-tang."

"Naturally, a Western story must take place out West," asserted Walter Des Marais. "But, it must take place in the 'out of doors' West. If you are going to write a Western, keep your characters out of doors as much as possible. If they act out the story in a house, they may as well be in Harlem or Yonkers for all the good the West will do them."

"Let us get it straight that the reader wants first of all to be entertained," elaborated Arch Joscelyn, "and that he reads a Western almost solely because he wants to get into those Wide Open Spaces of the old frontier, be they prairie, mountain, mine or saloon. That, after all, is what makes a Western a Western. For nine out of ten Western plots can with some ingenuity be transplanted to the sea, the East Indies, Down East, or almost anywhere else. It isn't the plot here, it's the setting."

Over time, the humble cowboy was elevated to near-mythic status, becoming what one critic dryly dubbed "a sun god", akin to a 20th Century solar myth—the super-cowboy.

"The usual formula is to describe him as something over six feet tall and broad in proportion," Joscelyn outlined, "give him chaps and two guns, a silver hoss and a dash of dialect."

This was the era of stalwart drovers like Pecos Peters and the Cactus Kid tangling with malevolent arch-desperados cursed with names like Hack Gore and Scorp Drago.

As Arthur Hawthorne Carhart sized up the situation, "A hero named 'Tex' could hardly be anything but tall, handsome, generous—well, you know heroes. A villain named Wolf Barbour ain't no gent, and he has teeth and a long nose. You believe that, don't you?"

Most readers did. The cast of characters consisted of stock players, torn from the pages of recent history—and silent films.

"There are heroes in every aspect of Western pioneering and development," editor Edmund Collier instructed, "prototypes that satisfy with perfect efficiency the reader's natural inclination toward hero-worship—Kit Carson as a scout, General Miles as an Indian fighter, Captain McNelly as a Texas Ranger, Dick Steele as a Mounted Policeman, Colonel Goodnight as a cowman, John Wesley Hardin as a lovable outlaw."

"The panorama of the West offers a writer a rich lode from which to draw color, characters, and ideas," explained Tom Curry. "Giants cross the stage, adventurers of every type. There are gunfighters, law officers, and bandits, cattle kings and cowboys, Indian chiefs, gamblers, miners, scouts, and hunters. Army personnel, ornery egotists, sheepmen and settlers, females naughty or nice."

In time, this varied cast would be worked to exhaustion.

"As a byproduct," added Curry, "there is feminine interest, but aficionados prefer to see the hero kiss his horse rather than waste lineage seducing a girl."

Under relentless recycling, this paper stereotype soon degenerated into a soulless symbol. This seemed only to make him even more popular with Western fans.

"A well-written cowboy yarn is about the easiest kind of a Western story to sell," claimed Reginald C. Barker, who sold over five hundred of them. "In fact, it is probable that the cowboy will never lose his place of honor as being the most popular character ever produced by a new country."

Eugene Cunningham distilled the era's formula plot when he described planning his 1929 *Lariat Story Magazine* serial, *Buckaroo*. "Naturally, one begins with the hero," he related. "The exigencies of the plot demand of him certain characteristics with which I endow him. Then, out of all the real men I have known over the cow country I select a type which 'physiognomically' suits the inner man—the sort who would make action; the daredevil type that readers of 'Westerns' like. And a type likeable—with punch. Somehow, into this *hombre prin-*

cipal, as I consider him, there comes the quiver of life....

"Next the lady.... I know if a woman can be permitted on the premises, and how long she can stay and how she must comport herself! It seems to me that she would naturally furnish most effective contrast for a Ranger sent to settle lawlessness in this country if she is the daughter of a big cowman mixed up in the lawless habits of the land. I hardly know how she takes shape, but there she is, a vivid, black-eyed, black-haired girl, domineering of habit—her father is 'king' of that range, you see—and as untamed as any colt on the plains.

"But the initial situation I am plotting is too big a job for one man—even one Ranger. So, in come a couple more Rangers, cut from the same bolt as the 'lead' character—at least from the same general material. But each is an individual. Here is an important mechanical point—these men have each of them their marked mannerisms and they can be identified by speech in the darkness. There is never confusion in the reader's mind as to whether Shorty or Buck is the speaker.

"My villain? Well, he is obviously the mainspring of the villainous activities of the land. A dashing puncher-type, tiger-skin chaps, pearl-handled, silver-plated Colts, fifty-peso Stetson and handmade boots. Surrounded by the lawless element—its idol. Hand in glove with the girl's father, who is half-intimidated, half profit-seeking in this relationship. He is the girl's ideal also, and natural foil for the Ranger.

"This is enough to show that in my initial situation I have laid the groundwork for that sort of breathless contest between deadly-efficient villain and super-efficient hero to the very last minute of my story."

Pulp villains required sound motivation, but in the Western, choices were limited. "Every action must have a logical explanation," cautioned Tom Curry. "A villain who steps up and pops John in the jaw or takes a shot at him just for the sport of it is not in his right mind. He will start the conflict for a very good reason, and the best reason is that he is after some form of wealth. It may be gold, or another metal; it may be land, or water that's valuable. There are only a few proper motivations for fiction.

"The conflict in the straight action story will be chiefly physical," Curry added. "We grade up from this to very light fiction, where it's entirely mental. But it's there, just the same, that conflict, that problem the hero or heroine must solve for his or her salvation."

Emotions were not barred from these elemental proceedings, but they too were proscribed.

"In this kind of fiction," noted Agnes M. Reeve, "brute strength, courage, hatred, loyalty, jealousy, and—where the woman figures—chivalry are the emotions that are stressed. The central character must triumph through some one of the finer emotions coming into ascendancy."

It was an easy time for Western yarn-spinners. Rates were high. Markets proliferated. Rejects could always be sold down-river to less picky periodicals desperate for copy.

"The natural assumption is that the West is a sterile fiction field," suggested Malcolm Ross, "and that the Nick Carter tradition must go on being dressed up for cheap tastes until the last cowboy moron wins the gal and the fortune and moves to Paris."

Editors could not afford to be too fussy. They accepted the roughest of first-draft copy from writers who might boast of having learned their letters from branding irons. These editors joked not of editing, but "slashing" a Western manuscript into shape. One cardinal rule hung over their heads: "When you cut, never cut a fight scene."

Fledgling Westerneers were encouraged by overworked editors to read the latest issues in order to understand a particular magazine's requirements. This often backfired on both parties.

"Authors have a miraculous capacity for reading a magazine and then selecting for a model the worst story in it," observed editor Edmund Collier. "The author must always keep in mind that an editor buys the best things he can lay his hands on at the time he has to schedule an issue, and more often than not what he gets is woefully short of his ideal."

A vicious cycle of mediocrity was thus initiated.

Popular magazines available by subscription had to pass muster with the Puritanical U.S. Postal Service. While Frank Blackwell recoiled at what he deemed to be "unpleasant sex situations" in submissions, by which he meant the natural hormonal attraction between the sexes, others were more lenient.

"You can let your heroine be chased all over Montana, Idaho and Nevada," allowed Clem Yore of Colorado, "but at the end of your story she still must be chaste."

Violence against the sacred equine was another paramount sin to be shied away from. "I came near to doing it once, with a mule in a story," writer Kenneth Perkins confessed. "But at the last moment I lost my nerve and the plot was changed to fit the exigency."

"What do we consider taboo in a Western yarn?" asked one *Triple-X* editor. "Well, we count the shots a man fires, and that's about all."

Nor were they particular about technical matters, as writer-turned-editor Allan K. Echols discovered when he went to work for William Clayton. "I was born on a ranch in Texas," he admitted. "When I started in this business, I had to learn the differences between the cattle industry as practiced by cattlemen and as practiced by editors in New York...."

Competition for readers turned into a drive for writers in 1927, the year the market was at its pre-Depression height.

"We're howling for new blood," said one Fiction House editor. He was not the only one.

Street & Smith attempted to rustle some of the rival Clayton chain's top hands away from them by offering 25 dollars merely for a first look at any new Western manuscript. When S&S raised its base rate from a penny to two cents a word that year, the rest of the field followed suit.

Word rates reached for the stars. "Clayton's minimum was 2 cents a word and they did better for their regulars," Tom Curry recounted. "Two cents was the accepted minimum at the better pulp companies, and some would go three, four or five without a quiver. The *creme de la creme*, a few pulp writers at the very top, receive as high as eight cents a word."

Desperate for top stories, Clayton's *Cowboy Stories* offered a $2,500 bounty for the best Western story to cross their desks, with a thousand dollars to the runner-up. Submitting anonymously, Colorado cowboy Stephen Payne snagged both first and second places. Born John Stephens Payne, he was so prolific friends called him "Story-a-Week" Steve. Former wrangler Francis W. Hilton came in a distant third.

"Never before in American literary history was there such an opportunity to get the attention of people on authentic pictures of the American scene," lamented Hilton. "It should not be allowed that the West remain the only section given over entirely to writers who keep one eye lifted ecstatically to the far purple mesas and the other bent down to the royalty check."

"All a man had to do to earn a fast fifty or hundred bucks," recalled Texan Allan R. Bosworth, "was to roll a sheet of virginal dime-store foolscap into his typewriter and begin with what the masters of the craft called a 'narrative hook.' It went something like this:

"Slouching in his saddle as sundown painted the rimrocks and dusk rolled down like a purple tide into the canyons, Concho Collins looked down into the Bar 7 pasture at the bunch of longhorn steers he was going to rustle that night."

After the writer got his yarn rolling, it was a carefree canter to The End. "Every short story is built around a problem and its solution—usually against increasing odds," observed Bosworth. "No story is stronger than its villain, who is one and the same with the problem. Put the problem on paper and use it for a springboard of thought; put it down and let your subconscious work on it for a few days. Some kind of solution will come, and if it is logical, and if you can make it tie with your hero's character, you've nothing left to do but write the story."

They made it sound easy, because it *was* easy. "Time was when about all the Western pulpeteer had to do to create a salable hero was to gig him into a gunfight, or a series of them, and let the blaze of burning powder serve for drama," said another early yarn-spinner, S. Omar Barker, who sold *Top-Notch* his first rodeo story while he and the century were still in their early '20s. *"Why* he fought often seemed a matter of minor concern, just so he slung hot lead—and didn't get hit anywhere except in a few shoulders and legs."

Gunplay in the pulps was raised to a level of rude art. The hero had to take his manful share of lead, dish it out, yet survive to fan his irons another day. One editor, upon going through a novel he would reject for the capital offense of excessive clichéd perforation, remarked, "…no less than four Stetsons were shot away from the heads of heroes; and the rest of the indomitable band bore nonmortal wounds galore. It really became odd how infallibly the desperadoes punctured the peripheries."

By no means were the pulps gun-shy about violence. Villains existed as much for target practice as for dramatic purposes, according to Bosworth. "We used to kill off a bad man every thousand words—always, of course, in fair fight and against heavy odds," he said. "There was a flair to their dying, those mangy rustlers, horse thieves, bobwire cutters, and sheep-herders, and any writer worth his lick of salt could expand the final death scene into three or more paragraphs and increase his check by ten dollars. They always lurched sideways, as if struck down by a giant, unseen hand. Or they clutched their bellies and pitched forward in a limp, grotesque heap, smearing their evil faces (suddenly drained of all color) in the hot alkali dust. Their guns slipped from suddenly nerveless hands, and they mouthed incoherent curses through a froth of crimson that bubbled from their twisted, ashen lips." […] "Sometimes a thin trickle of scarlet crept down their stubbled cheeks, but this was seldom called blood. Few of the pulp magazines would print the word, even though blood was all over the homestead."

This style of writing caused critic Robert T. Pound to joke, "The easiest thing to do in a story laid in the West is to commit human murder, and the next easiest thing to do is commit literary murder."

"After the shoot-out," concluded Bosworth, "the hero—a Galahad in chaps—holstered his smoking hog-leg and rode away, leaving the bad men to lie where they fell. The unburied dead of the old pulp West must have run into the tens of thousands, and their bones are still bleaching somewhere under the suns of high or low noon."

It was as simple as that. Editors called this formula "bang-bang" after the preferred onomatopoeic symbol for gunshots as typed on paper.

"Any story that would stick together was a sure sale," boasted Tom Curry.

The field evolved swiftly from tales of the working cowboy on ranch and range to the free-riding Western Robin Hood, who, reflecting shifting attitudes toward law and order fostered by Prohibition, was often at odds with local authority. This plot got so overused one *Lariat Story* editor started decrying what he called "the old sheriff-cowboy-bandit triangle," saying, "We want the real thing in cowboy stories. Go easy on the sheriff stories. Cowboys have other adventures besides mixups with sheriffs."

Wringing a new wrinkle out of the Old West became a game of inches. Clem Yore, who pounded out his pulp when not practicing law, recalled being taken to task for writing what editor Harry Maule perceived as the same story over and over and was firmly told to concoct a new plot.

"I wrote back that I certainly would," Yore later recounted. "Then I changed my setting a little and introduced a new character. Harry read the yarn, wrote, 'That's fine, Clem. Now you've got away from that old plot, give us another new story.'"

One desperate editor, *The Golden West's* Tom Chadburn, began salting his magazine with "modernized" yarns, "…using some other means of offense and defense than the six-gun, such as the attack on a fortified cabin by an armored car, gas-bombs, or what-not, rather than besieging or blazing arrows." Readers voted with their dimes, and *The Golden West* went back to basics.

When the symbolic super-cowboy could be reduced to his commercial fundamentals no further, he collapsed into an irredeemable cliché.

"The Western pulp has one central character: a roving cowhand, usually with a buddy who serves as his foil," outlined Harold Hersey. "They drift from ranch to ranch, ride into town like Comanche Indians, shoot up the place, engage in violent battles with fists and guns, and ride on to fresh adventures. They are superb horsemen, needless to say, swingin' in and out of their saddles with familiar ease, capable of forkin' a cayuse from daylight until dusk. Undaunted by death, disease or disaster, they are eternally cheerful, courageous and gallant to wimmenfolk."

But not realistic, according to Francis W. Hilton, who knew. "All cowboys were not hard-shooting, hard-drinking renegades, as many 'Westerns' picture them," he wrote. "That is admittedly true. But on the other hand, he was no angel. He was a victim of environment. Working as he did on the silent trails, miles from the crude civilization of the plains, his only companions dumb brutes, when finally he did get among men, he did what the sailor does, what the soldier does, what any red-blooded human does—he unleashed his pent-up passions and 'cut loose.'"

Hilton also claimed that, "Many of the heroes of 'Westerns' today would have been hanged forthwith, had they ever dared to show up in a real cow-camp."

The entire field could be accurately boiled down to a clichéd cast of victors versus villains, salted with virgins, vipers and varmints.

Readers were not oblivious to the regulation plot. One complained to *The Frontier:*

"Western stories… are not popular but tiresome. There is always the old cattleman in financial difficulties, with the beautiful daughter just home from college who can ride anything on four legs. He has a foreman who intends to marry the girl and is invariably in league with the rustlers. Likewise there are the Chinese cook and the sheriff—no need to describe them; you know them by the book. Out of nowhere comes riding a stern-jawed young puncher, mounted upon a steed of supernatural intelligence whom he addresses as Little Hawss and holds in familiar converse. And he licks the foreman, busts the rustlers, marries the girl, and, I hope, lives unhappily ever after, damn him! When a magazine writer wants a Western plot he goes to the movies and lifts one off the screen. When a scenario-writer wants a plot he buys a magazine and lifts one off the pages. And so it goes in a dreary, soul-wearying circle."

"By this time the fiction formula had been fixed and it remained so until about 1925-1930," claimed John A. Saxon. "There was always the 100 per cent hero, a villain at whom the readers could hiss, a heroine with soul of purest white. Plots were stereotyped. The protagonists were always what later day editors called 'gun-dummies.' Action!! Action!! Action!! was the constant cry."

It's problematic to say for certain who coined the pulp pejorative, gun-dummy. An anonymous *Lariat Story Magazine* editor first invoked it early in 1927, the year the Western fiction magazine stumbled into its first crisis, when he wrote, "We want the cowboy on the range, a human being—not a gun dummy, with a real story behind him that rides along rapidly and smoothly with a fresh twist."

Jack Kelly or Jack Byrne were the likeliest originators. The term soon spread like wildfire.

After skimming a pile of manuscripts being rejected by an unnamed Western pulp editor, author's agent Lurton Blassingame defined the notion this way in his *Writer's Digest* essay, "Dummies with Names."

"In all the stories," he discovered, "the heroes could have been inter-changed without anyone, even the author, being able to tell the difference. Because each hero was like every other hero—a gun, a name and a pure purpose, and each villain only a name, a gun, some profanity and a bad purpose."

Yet writers who deviated from this narrow norm often met with rejection, explained pulpster Everett H. Tipton: "Most of the stories which have brought ready checks have had the same character for a hero and had him doing conventional things. In one yarn he may be Smith playing a harmonica, in another Jones, Jew's-harpist, limping slightly; in another he packs two guns, in another he is not even a good shot but has other virtues, in a fifth he's a rodeo champ. Sometimes he's small, sometimes he's tall. But he has essentially the same characteristics and does not stray far from the conventional cowboy trail. If the reader wants Smith-Brown-Jones, you can't pan off Murchison or Worthington on him as 'just as good.'"

As one would-be Westerneer protested, "I have read *Wildest Western* from cover to cover. The writers merely tell their story. They don't use this characterization stuff."

For a long time, violent action was all that mattered. "Any story that didn't have a killing in the second page—it didn't matter who it was or why he was killed—was doomed to instant rejection," observed Saxon. "No wonder that old-time Western writer 'Chuck' Martin has his own 'boot-hill' on his ranch, where each of the many characters killed off in his stories has its head-stone. The pattern having been set, the Western story rolled its merry way for many years without changes."

Even the editors recognized and accepted this grim reality.

"While he was editing *Wild West Weekly*," wrote contributor Arch Joscelyn, "Ronald Oliphant pointed out to me that the Western, by its very nature, had a sameness which was hard to get away from. To insure freshness in a story, it was essential that the characters should be personalities."

"Because the Western story was the most dependable nag in any publisher's stable, year in and year out," opined Walker A. Tompkins, veteran of *Wild West Weekly* under his own name and innumerable other aliases, "it was inevitably constricting formula that became the editor's nightmare."

Tompkins went on:

"Characters became standardized into an ever-varying cast of (a) cowboy, (b) outlaw, (c) sheriff. Western story locale was set against backgrounds consisting of (1) cattle range, (2) cowtown saloon, (3) mining camp, until they became as crinkly and pin-holed as the backdrops of a small-town theater.

"Every conceivable method of killing off a villain had been figured out in the heyday of the Jesse James dime thrillers: quicksand, hangrope, dynamite, cattle stampede, six-gun duel. The bullets fired from cowboy .45s, if piled into one heap, would make the ammunition dumps of the warring powers of Europe seem a mere molehill.

"But the reading public gobbled up Jack Q. Author's Western formula for three generations with undiminished gusto. Redskins bit the dust, rustlers blotted brands, cowboys twisted cigarettes with one hand and triggered a Peacemaker with the other, stagecoaches were robbed, and the U.S. Cavalry brought Old Glory to the aid of beleaguered prairie schooners so regularly that it was lucky the automobile replaced the hoss before the equine breed dropped dead from sheer exhaustion."

"It seemed that anything and everything went into the great yawning maw of the press," admitted Lud Landmichl. "And it was the ruination of practically all of us. We were not accustomed to revising and cutting. Most of us were disposing of our entire output to one publisher...."

A former *New York World* reporter who started writing fiction way back in 1909, Saxon saw the first glimmerings of change prior to the Great Depression. "Up until that time, with minor exceptions, we had pretty much the same old 'bang-bang' with lots of 'action,'" he observed. "However, there were some editors who were beginning to realize that their readers were tiring of the tripe about the wandering cowman, the crooked foreman, the hero on the wrong side of the law, the banker who held the mortgage, the rustler, and above all (although to some extent still persisting) the returning cowboy who comes back from afar to avenge the death of his father, brother, or friend, or who returns because his father, brother, or friend, is in a jam. That one dies hard. You can find it in nearly every book you pick up today. It's a classic 'situation.'"

Pioneer pulp publisher Street & Smith seems to have been the earliest house to shake the trail dust from the old tried-and-true super-cowboy formula. This transmutation occurred in the work of one of its rising stars.

Portland Oregonian reporter Ernest Haycox sold his first pulp yarn to Street & Smith's *Sea Stories,* and a second to *Western Story.* Flush with imagined success, he moved to New York to work the S&S word mines. He found it tough going.

Facing starvation, Haycox received a short lecture from Frank Blackwell: "Young man, I have just one piece of advice for you. Learn to write Westerns. Once you have mastered that, the rest is up to you."

Haycox didn't simply master the pulp Western tale. After his apprenticeship, he took it to the next level. "…Ernest Haycox blazed a bend trail away from the moron myth…" noted novelist Leslie Ernenwein. "He made popular a type of Western hero who possessed the ability to think as an enlightened man."

"From his earliest pulp appearances," wrote D.B. Newton, "the real strength of Ernest Haycox, in my opinion, lay in his willingness to take the Romantic Adventure, and its readers, seriously…. First, he had to get rid of the stereotyped characters of the pulps. He invented for his purposes a new kind of hero—older, haunted by a troubling past, possessed of depths of great feeling."

Observed William L. Hopson, "He seemed to be imbued

with the idea that what a character thought and felt in moments of crisis was about as important as how fast he could thumb a six-shooter; that if a man had to kill he could do so with a sense of deep regret rather than swaggering off to the nearest bar, blowing smoke out of his gun barrel on the way."

"When Haycox describes a gun battle you can believe in it," praised Frank Gruber. "The villain and hero don't go for their guns the moment a fighting word is said. The set-up may not be just right. When they do finally fight usually the hero doesn't shoot the dirty villain right between the eyes with his first shot. It doesn't happen that way in real life, as history records."

"The robust vitality of the man's writing," added Stephen Payne, "and life and punch of his style, wrought a significant and tremendous change in the *presentation* of Western fiction."

But writers of the caliber of Haycox were rare, and fresh twists on the standard Western protagonist rarer still. Thus the two-gun super-cowboy *cum* gun-dummy continued to ride the pulpwood range virtually unchallenged for a time.

For example, the most popular Western pulp writer of the 1920s, Frederick Faust, whose serials lifted *Western Story Magazine* to incredible circulation highs, suffered only three rejections during that era. His crime? Excessive characterization. Faust's feverishly-written tales appealed to the imagination, not to the true Westerner.

"In Westerns as in any other story," noted Utah pulpster Frank C. Robertson, "characterization is far more important than plot or background. ...Max Brand was able to people his stories with glamorous but completely improbable characters. He was enough the master craftsman to get away with it. Unfortunately, Brand had many imitators who have succeeded only in creating unreal and often grotesque characters. To fit them into the background and atmosphere of the real West would be impossible, and so the synthetic West was invented."

"...Max Brand outwrote and outsold us all," wrote Harry F. Olmsted, "despite the facts that his West was a weird and terrible place of fens and moors and gorse and other British idioms, and his characters fanciful supermen who outraged the intelligence of serious readers. Yet with such genius did he bait his plot trap that even the disgusted reader went on to the bitter end, and bought the next magazine to see what fool calisthenics Max's imagination performed there."

The blame fell on either side of the fence, depending on who was doing the finger-pointing:

"There was a time when it seemed that the field of Western writing was being worked out," claimed the peppery "Little Giant of the Pulps," the Thrilling chain's leonine Editorial Director, Leo Margulies. "That was the fault of the writer, not the subject. Too many writers were deceiving themselves in the belief that all a Western story needed was plenty of gun slinging; plenty of people killed; plenty of fights, but never mind a good reason; lovely girls with mortgaged ranches who would be saved from destitution by the hero, garbed as no cowboy was ever costumed, riding up just in time to pay off the mortgage and send the villainous banker into the darkness off-stage with gnashing teeth, black mustache raising in a leer and 'curse you—foiled again,' on his lips."

As an author, John A. Saxon naturally saw it through different eyes. "The greatest single influence in retarding the development of the Western story were the hide-bound traditions of the editors and publishers who bought them. Most of them knew little about the West and cared less. They were governed by one creed—Circulation. If the editor had an idea for improving the type of stories, he was usually met by the objection of the publisher: 'Why? We have printed the same story for years. Our circulation is building up. Why change? It's what the public wants, we can't afford to experiment.'

"So, they didn't experiment—at least not for years."

Which brings us back around to Terrill's account of his 1927 lunch, also attended by Fiction House managing editor, Jack Byrne, and his editorial associate, T.W. Ford—soon to become one of the most prolific of pulp Western scribes. Rog Terrill—later affectionately known in pulp circles as the Rajah—accepted full blame for what was ultimately a failure of editorial judgment.

"The answer," Terrill recollected, "is, of course, that all of us at that luncheon had accepted the Western story in the form in which it had been passed on to us by our editorial predecessors. To us, the word 'Western story' meant gun-dummy action. We didn't know then that the cowboy and Indian movie would someday produce *The Covered Wagon* and *The Plainsman!* We were blind to the vivid historic color and bonafide human drama inherent in the then 'gun-dummy' Western."

These editors were also blind to a daring new breed of he-man. A bushwhacker would soon swoop down on the wood-pulp wrangler from an unexpected direction.

"You know how Jack Kelly over at old Fiction House used to drum it into us about action. I thought I knew just what he meant. Now I don't believe I had the idea at all. In those days, if a story opened with a gunfight, I thought it surely had the stuff. It might, or might not."

—John F. Byrne

5

BOOMTOWN BUST

THE RISE of the pulp cow-hero was swift, and his fall from grace precipitous.

In January 1927, literary agent Laurence D'Orsay crowed in *Writer's Digest,* "The cowboy, with his two smoking guns, is the heir of the ages. If Homer were alive, he undoubtedly would be writing Westerns."

In the world of book publishing, two of the most popular writers going were Hopalong Cassidy creator Clarence E. Mulford and the Max Brand of the hardcover Western, Zane Grey.

"Zane Grey makes a hundred thousand dollars a year translating the man-myths of Greece into the terms of cowboys and cactus," observed writer Homer Croy. "If he had lived in Greece he would have written epic poems about somebody wrestling with thunder and lightning. There's more money now in cowboys."

On the pulp side of the fence rail, business was also booming.

"Many Western tales," wrote Street & Smith editor Arthur E. Scott, "I know, are ground out by Greenwich Village cowboys who have never been farther West than Hoboken, or at the most, Indiana, their birthplace. The boys sell regularly and get good rates. But they won't keep it up as long as a man like Zane Grey, who loves the roll of a saddle and the smell of the sagebrush."

So popular were these paper super-cowboys that *Black Mask's* new editor, Joseph T. Shaw, began playing them up big. Despite the fact that his magazine was the primary exponent of the new hard-boiled school of detective fiction, more Western covers decorated *Black Mask* in 1927 than in any other year, before or after. Circulation shot up fifty percent.

Over at Fawcett, *Triple-X* editors were retiring their detective authors and putting out the call for range mystery yarns, a cow-country sub-genre where wild chases and gunplay replaced clues and detection. In the back rooms, sub-editors mercilessly Westernized paid-for Eastern detective manuscripts with their lightning blue pencils.

At the same time, they followed *Lariat's* shift away from gun-dummy hokum, announcing:

"*Triple-X* is actively getting away from the melodramatic style of Western fiction which seems to be quite popular at the present time and, consequently, we are reaching in all directions for genuine cowboy stories of the old range. We don't feel that the cow-poke is quite as bloody as some writers are wont to picture him, and we know the old-time cowboy had plenty of action and speed without resorting to a six-gun to punctuate the drama of his colorful life."

In his *Author & Journalist* piece, "A Year in the Saddle," Fiction House Associate Editor Richard A. Martinsen painted the future of the Pulp West as unlimited:

"The demand for popular Western fiction which already seemed stretched to the breaking point, has continued to soar to incredible heights. It has never been so great as it is today, and the end is not yet in sight. Even the quality smooth-paper magazines, in many of which up to a year ago a gun-totin' waddy would have been sacrilege, are now catering to the demand."

Martinsen pointed to the influence of Hollywood as a contributing factor. "Never have two powerful influences like the movies and magazines worked so effectively hand in hand to boom a field of literature. So long as Tom Mix remains a greater box-office attraction than John Barrymore, and Buck Jones, Hoot Gibson, and half a dozen others retain their places in the very top rank of celluloid money-earners, the demand for Western stories in all likelihood will not abate—and vice versa. It's an example of gorgeous team-work."

Editors continued to cite the success of the 1923 silent film, *The Covered Wagon,* as having helped to ignite the pulp Western boom in the first place. But change was blowing through Hollywood, and its consequences would touch the Pulp West with a shriveling finger. The first sound picture was released in 1927. By the following year, the film industry was rapidly converting to sound.

"When the talkies came in like an Oklahoma gusher," explained Fawcett's Jack Smalley, "Westerns went out. It was difficult to produce outdoor pictures with the talking equipment available. Indoor pictures confined the new 'Art' to stage plays, crook dramas, chorus pictures of 'the show must go on' type—and the he-man on the horse languished. Movie cowboys tightened their belts and went to work for a living."

Literary agent August Lenniger noted the adverse impact Hollywood was having on pulp writers:

"The Western 'movie,' which except in rare instances has degenerated almost to the point of slapstick comedy, is also in a large measure responsible for the mediocrity of the average story of this type offered to the magazines. The obvious insincerity overlooked in the rapid action of a motion picture becomes incongruous implausibility in fiction."

Hollywood's negative impact on the Pulp West is difficult to measure. The field was already oversaturated. Harold Hersey left Clayton in 1928, and promptly issued *Western Trails.* Another publisher came out with *Wild West Stories.* Street & Smith converted the faltering and ill-conceived *True Western Adventures* to *Far West Illustrated Magazine,* which continued to falter.

Editors were struggling to keep the genre fresh, according

to August Lenniger, who was rapidly emerging as the leading author's agent in what he straight-facedly called "the industry of manufacturing the horse opera."

"It is time that the writers of 'Westerns' realize that the days of the 'lightnin' draw' artist, bullet-proof hero, and the stereotyped blood-and-thunder plot are about over," he stated. "As the editor of one of our most successful Western story magazines puts it, 'The Western story has shed its swaddling clothes. There is no reason why we cannot have good stories—even in Westerns!'"

But this drive to rise above hokum came too late. In his market forecast for the coming year of 1929, Lenniger warned:

"In the Western-adventure field a severe shaking up seems to be in progress, doing much toward stabilization of the market, and the general improvement of the Western story. The synthetic blood-and-thunder, rustler, bandit, box-canyon yarn is being looked upon very much askance in editorial circles. The Western magazines are demanding more convincingness and originality in plot construction every day, and they are insisting upon real stories."

Dark storm clouds were gathering over the Pulp West, insisted Lenniger. "I have heard rumors, well substantiated by analysis of magazine newsstand sales, to effect that the air story is causing heavy sales losses to the Western action magazines, that readers who used to worship the two-gun cow poke are turning their eyes to the sky. That there is much food for thought in this rumor for Western-story writers is proved by the large number of air yarns which are appearing in magazines formerly devoted almost exclusively to Westerns. It is another manifestation of modernism in fiction."

The buckskin hero was rapidly passing out of favor, a victim of changing times. A fresh frontier beckoned.

Aviation pioneer Charles Lindbergh was the culprit. His successful May 1927 transatlantic flight inspired Fiction House to issue an experimental pulp called *Air Stories* that summer.

Figuratively speaking, it took off. Other houses launched flights of imitators. *Flying Stories. Airplane Stories. Air Trails. Zoom.* To an air-minded American reading public, the dusty horseman was suddenly passé. By year's end the Western boom had gone dead bust.

This was the juncture where Rogers Terrill took over as managing editor of *Lariat* and discovered the gold mine he'd fallen heir to had been thoroughly worked out.

"The hero worship of the American reader is being transferred from the two-gun buckaroo to the leather-clad man who flies," explained Lenniger. "We now have air pirates in battle planes waylaying the air mail instead of the Western masked stick-up man holding up the stage-coach or pony express."

Literary agent Thomas H. Uzzell reported that pulps like *Short Stories, Top-Notch, Triple-X* and *Three Star Magazine* had evicted the Western from its pages. West took the novel step of putting its cowboys in airplanes. Citing "the growing use of airplanes for all purposes in western North America," editor Harry E. Maule remarked, "Air stories are not only appropriate, but they also offer a welcome change from the straight Western story which has shown a dangerous tendency to become stereotyped." Harold Hersey's new *Western Trails* soon followed suit.

A *Triple-X* editor, trying to have it all ways, pushed for more air fiction, but added, "If the air story was a war story, with a cowboy hero, the combination is the acme of perfection."

This new sub-genre, called "cowboy-air", spread to other magazines, including aviation pulps like Street & Smith's *Air Trails,* where Robert J. Hogan's "Smoke" Wade of Arizona chased the new breed of airborne owlhoot in his pinto-hued Spad.

The only new entry in the field, *Two-Gun Stories,* was being swamped with the rejected refuse of bewildered authors. It was a sorry time for the Western pulpeteer ignorant of aviation.

"This does not mean, however," Uzzell admitted, "that the

story of cowboys and pintos is dead. Most of the straight Western magazines still hold on and will continue to; the glamour of the West exists, though it is slightly tarnished."

Yet by 1929, some were penning the pulp-paper cowboy's epitaph. "The Western began to lose popularity over a year ago when the War and Air stories came into vogue," said Uzzell. "Some old writers in this field had to shift over. Newcomers were frequently greeted with the editorial comment, 'We're bought up on Westerns for a time. The aviators have dry-gulched the cowboys.'"

The genre appeared doomed. No less than top fictioneer H. Bedford-Jones himself had pronounced the Western fiction magazine dead in his 1929 book, *This Fiction Business*. But two years later, with the Depression in its early stages, he was forced to recant:

"…Western stories were on the wane, doomed to pass out of existence. Certain editors had banned them entirely, others were buying very few. And what happened? There was an abrupt about-face, largely induced by the Western movies of Warner Baxter and others in his train. Western stories leaped back into favor. Western magazines held up where others crashed in circulation, and there you are."

Baxter played O. Henry's Cisco Kid in the extremely successful 1929 sound film, *In Old Arizona*. It was the first "all-talking" Western, for which Baxter garnered an Academy Award. Sequels followed. The Western genre was thus revived. It would not be the last time Hollywood prodded the Western fiction field into finding surer footing.

The impact on the Pulp West was immediate. *Fiction House Flashes*—a bulletin mailed to writers—reported in late Summer, "A lot of you writing gents who have doffed the Western sombrero to climb into the cockpit will do well to shift back again. Those friends who told you that the Westerns were dying—well, go out and give them the horse laugh."

The Author & Journalist noted the abrupt reversal of fortune in an August 1929 editorial:

"After a flurry in the manuscript market, caused by the apprehension on the part of various editors a few months ago that the Western story had run its course, the action magazines using this type of material seem to have settled down to steady buying again. The rise in popularity of the air story did not, after all, supplant the hunger which seems to exist for gunfanning stories of cowboys, rustlers, and the range.

"Even the prediction that the quick-action, gun-play type of Western yarn would give way to quieter stories dealing with character and modern conditions does not seem to be borne out. The present trend, if anything, is more than ever toward 'blood and thunder.'"

That was not entirely true. In the less gunsmoky action pulps, a firefly flicker of maturity could be gleaned.

"Being a Westerner, born and raised in the West," revealed Arch Joscelyn, "I used to feel rather a contempt for most Western fiction. That was true in part, I imagine, because 'Westerns' had not yet shed their swaddling clothes. Any old-timer at the type-punching game knows that there has been a radical change in fiction in the last decade. Stories nowadays are swifter in action, meatier in plot, more convincing, better told in general." […] "Consequently, the efforts that would once 'get by' for Westerns, would not go today in the magazines, though they still do go in the movies.

"You will notice that the better type of Western story today is not so bloody as it once was," Joscelyn elaborated. "The hero is no superman. He seldom kills fourteen men in a story. In fact, many of the best stories today have no killings in them. The hero is courageous and resourceful, but human, and therefore more true to life, more convincing, more likable. To have a good action story of the new type, a better, more original plot is demanded."

One of the most prolific of up-and-coming pulsters was the so-called "Speed-King of the Pulps," Arthur J. Burks. A former Marine, he penned few Westerns but much aviation fiction. He may have put his finger on the true secret of the paper cowboy's longevity when he wrote, "The reason for the continued popularity of Westerns is the fact that the cowboys and punchers always have a gun strapped on them which they use at many and various times throughout the story. Take the gun away from the cowboy and Westerns would lose their present popularity overnight... If... perchance you are now trying to write Westerns with gunless cowboys, switch over on the other tack and put a couple of dozen six-guns in your hero's hands."

Struggling against the rising tide of gun-dummy melodrama, *West's* Harry Maule was soon forced to surrender. "We've got to hew pretty close to the line with regard to action," he warned writers. "Every time we let our personal tastes for character work and atmosphere get going a bit strong, we hear it from our readers in a most unmistakable way. I refer to newsstand sales as well as letters from readers."

Once again, Fawcett's Jack Smalley credited the latest vogue in cinematic horse operas for the status quo. "Now the talkies have hurdled mechanical obstacles and outdoor films are coming into popularity," he wrote in 1930. "*'The Virginian'* is a tremendous success; so is *'Romance of the Rio Grande,'* both good old melodramas, given color and life through sound. And already their influence is being felt in magazine circles, for Westerns are definitely in again, and—is it coincidence?—such stories must be of *'The Virginian'* type, the reliable melodrama of other days."

Harkening back to a half-forgotten boom-and-bust, *A&J* editor Willard E. Hawkins cast his gaze into the future of the Pulp West and prophesied only endless fertile prairie:

"The Western story, with its swashbuckling, adventurous disregard for human life, probably will be leading the field many years hence. Some eighteen years ago—after a brief rise to popularity—writers were told that the Western story had run its course and was dead. As a matter of fact, its reign had not even begun. A great new magazine-reading public—actuated by the search for thrills rather than for literary excitement—has been discovered, developed, and exploited. The West is dead—long live the West!"

But change had come. Before 1930, a writer could peddle a reject manuscript for months—even years—until inevitably some greenhorn editor snapped it up. Now most of these duds were sent back lame.

Writer Reginald C. Barker insisted that the cowboy story was the easiest kind of Western to sell, but he also claimed it was the most difficult to write. "A few years ago a well known eastern writer wrote a cowboy story in which his hero roped and held a buffalo bull with a 'horsehair rope' (a *mecate*)," Barker related. "No sooner had the yarn been published than the author received letters from irate cattlemen all over the West, who told him the thing simply couldn't be done."

The bar had been raised to a more realistic level. "Remember," he cautioned, "when writing a cattle story, you are competing with such authors as W.C. Tuttle, Walt Coburn, Stephen Payne, and others; all of whom were cowboys before they became writers. If you don't know the difference between a claybank and a pinto, between bat-wing chaparejoes and angoras, between a snubbing post and a corral fence, between a hondo and a dally, between a maverick and a bronc, don't try to write a cowboy story."

True sons of the West had it no easier. "The author must continually watch his step," lamented *Wild West Weekly*'s Paul S. Powers, "and an error or even the semblance of an error will be immediately spotted by the clientele. The readers of pseudo-science and of sports are particularly keen witted, and the writer of a Western story who makes a mistake in the caliber, rotation motion, or trajectory of a Winchester rifle bullet will, before the storm of disapproval has subsided, feel like using one of the bullets on himself. One Western fan wrote me a scalding letter regarding the color of the smoke of a black-powder cartridge charge when seen against a twilight background of snow.

Another writer for the same magazine received a protest from a native of Mozambique, East Africa, when he caused his stage-driver hero to leave his team standing in the street unattended."

Not every editor adhered to the new vogue. Early in 1930, *Argosy*'s Arch Bittner reeled off the many types of stories he favored. After adventure, sea, war, sports, mystery, circus and even Northern stories, Bittner added, "…and even Westerns when we can find one which is *different.*"

The top all-fiction magazine that once helped popularize Max Brand now relegated the frontier genre to the bottom of the slush pile.

"While Western action stories retain their popularity," explained August Lenniger, "there seems to be a great deal of material of this type floating about which comes under the category of 'just another Western.' But it is the really worthwhile story with some novelty of plot and treatment that makes a place for itself. While the Western action magazines offer excellent opportunity of a steady and well-paying market to those who can do them well, there are a great many mediocre Westerns going begging. Several of the Western magazines have broadened their policies to permit a secondary woman interest: *Ace-High, Triple-X Western, Western Trails* and *Western Rangers.*"

If formula ranch-and-range Westerns were getting harder to concoct, new hope arose from little-grazed pastureland. A fresh flock of *Ranch Romances*-style titles began springing up.

"The Western romance is a type which has gained considerable popularity and offers a field that is not quite so overcrowded and perhaps less demanding because it is comparatively new and all the old gags have not yet been exhausted," Lenniger pointed out. "These magazines require a simple love story in a Western setting, and a bit of gunplay and physical action, but frequently these stories are from the heroine's point of view and the danger and action are implied rather than emphasized in action."

Even that narrow slant was expanding. With the launch of Dell's *Western Romances,* publishers were going after the woman reader with a vengeance. "In the past the demand, for the most part, was for Westerns with a slight thread of romance," noted *The Editor.* "The romance was usually dragged in by the heels for the sole purpose of giving the hero (and the reader) a chance to catch his breath before he again went forth to battle at least six desperadoes who were intent, it seems, upon doing wrong by Nell and our William, too."

This expansion was measured in yards, not rods. "Stories of a conflict between your hero and one or more outlaws are always welcomed by editors, if all else is equal," wrote Reginald C. Barker. "If you can have your hero fall in love with a rancher's daughter, or any nice open-air girl, so much the better. But keep the girl in the background in the average Western. Above all else, don't let eroticism creep into a Western story."

Barker also reported a slight shift away from the cowboys and cattle. "But not all the West is given over to the cattle range; in fact there are very few great ranches left, and with the passing of the unfenced ranches, a demand has grown for other types of Western stories. One can write stories of trapping wild animals, stories of mining or stories of love and adventure among the mountains or deserts."

At Dell, *Western Romances* editor Carson W. Mowre suddenly decided that geography equaled variety, announcing, "Any story of the old West, be it cattle-country, mining, timber, or border, is welcome… Empire builders and the period yarn are also welcome." He also warned, "Writers must understand Western color."

Publishers began gearing up with new titles. Harold Hersey trademarked a *Sage and Saddle Magazine,* while William Clayton filed for *The Westerner.* Neither magazine was ever issued. Publishers were proceeding cautiously while they watched for signs the economy would soon shake off the stock exchange blues.

A year later, the revival was in full cry.

"A trend toward Westerns has been noticed for some time," declared Fawcett editor Jack Smalley early in '31. "The present magazine readers are being influenced by motion pictures depicting the Western scene of pioneer days, rather than modern stuff, and the good old ranch and wagon-trail melodrama is reviving."

Western writer J.R. Johnston explored it in "The Western Story Lives" (*The Author & Journalist,* July 1931). Forgotten today, Johnston contributed to a wide array of cowboy pulps. Polling the major Western editors on the future, he heard only sunny optimism. Fawcett's Jack Smalley, whose *Triple-X* had reversed its anti-Western policy and adopted the *Triple-X Western* brand, stated, "We have no doubt that *Triple-X* will continue to function as a Western magazine for some years to come. The popularity of Westerns seems to rise and fall in a cycle of five or six years, and were it not for the general depression, Westerns would be in the lead right now.

"For a while there was an attempt made to give variety to this type of story by injecting the modern note, employing airplanes and even gangsters in an effort to pep them up. But I believe that the good old standard cowboy yarn with a ranch setting is the type of story most likely to find favor...."

Quoting *Triple-X* editor Douglas E. Lurton as calling for "less hectic action and more character delineation," Johnston noted, "If that doesn't strike you as a decided change, consider the fact that little more than a year ago, it was just the other way around. That was the old order. What professional Western writer isn't familiar with the cry of editors for action, action, and more action? Nothing else used to matter, so long as there were swift-moving situations tumbling over one another to get out of the way of a rootin', tootin', hootin', shootin' climax. A writer couldn't stop to do a thorough job of character building without risking the ire of the editor. It slowed up the action!"

John F. Byrne of Fiction House declared:

"Right now we are just beginning to dig into the depths of the glamour and romance that has been written into the history of the West; and as our writers continue to familiarize themselves with the history of the great Western era, their stories gain increasingly in appeal value."

Clayton's Henry A. McComas, in charge of *Ace-High* and *Cowboy Stories,* stated, "I still believe that it is one of the greatest of popular fiction themes and that it will be enjoyed by a vast public just so long as that public is red-bloodedly American and so long as the stories given them are really good ones."

Johnston turned to "Coteau" Gene Stebbings, an old-timer who ramrodded numerous readers' columns in assorted pulps, for the writer's view:

"Do I think the Western story is dead? Hell, no, not if you mean stories of the real West. If you mean the synthetic, flash-dash hooey, I say yes, decidedly. It never was Western. It is a sort of fairy story said to be written in a style some jugheads imagine to be Western.

"But reasonably true-to-life stories of the West, Lord! There are untold millions of potential readers hungry for them. The field is practically virgin. Even our 'best' publications demand that Westerns be jazzed up. But one of these days some publisher will wake up, and then there'll be an awful scramble to get on the band-wagon.

"No! Real Western stories are not dead, nor will they ever die. The West, old or new, has been and is the greatest producer of honest, real human interest stories ever known to man!"

Stebbings made a claim that, if true, makes one wonder what the pulp editors were thinking when they bought cow-country fiction:

"In all my experience as a conductor of departments for readers, I have never received a single letter praising the blood-and-thunder hooey everyone is familiar with. Kicks? Plenty of them. But the rare, reasonably true-to-life Westerns, the readers deluge me with letters of praise for them."

Naturally, Frank Blackwell weighed in. Seeming to miss the point, he expounded:

"As editor of the old 'Buffalo Bill' weekly, and as editor of *Western Story Magazine* for the past twenty years, I have never used development stories of the West. That is, for instance, I have never used stories showing what the gasoline engine or the automobile has done for ranch life. I have tried to keep as much romance and color in the story as possible. The minute you have the cowboy scooting to town on a motorcycle, you have lost appeal. It is like putting a sailor on a horse."

Clearly, Blackwell misread the word "development." Probably the very notion that the formula boots-and-saddle Western tale *could* evolve was foreign to his old-fangled editorial sensibilities.

Betraying his dime novel origins, Blackwell added, "The average person doesn't want realism anyway. We all need some romance: romance is the relief from stark reality. The writing ability being equal, the romantic story outsells the realistic story ten to one. Romance is life, realism is death; romance is Heaven, realism is Hell!"

Blackwell would soon regret those words.

"There you have it," Johnston concluded. "Old Man Western Story isn't dead. His ghost, a very live one, is riding ranges once more."

He would not ride very far before encountering unexpected trouble. It started later that same year.

"…the Western story has alternately thrived and languished," recounted Rogers Terrill. "Better writing and better plotting gave it a new lease on life from '27 to '30—for the early days of the Great Depression left the pulp field untouched. Then, in '31, came the deluge. Over night, the bottom dropped out of pulp sales—and none hit the toboggan harder or faster than the Western. By the Spring of the '32 there wasn't a Western magazine on the news stands that wasn't in difficulties."

Major pulp publishers dropped titles, skipped issues or

reduced frequency. Some, like Dell and Fawcett, shifted their focus away from fiction magazines. Clayton and a few lesser outfits collapsed into insolvency.

"All the old-timers remember the toppling crashes of bankruptcy," Chuck Martin remembered. "Most of them have Clearing-house reports from Receivers, stating that after the Printers, Pressmen, and all the office boys had been paid, and after the Paper manufacturers had been satisfied, there was nothing left for the Creditors, said Creditors being the Authors and Artists who had made the Magazine possible."

The prolific suffered most. Fifty years later, L.P. Holmes reported, "I still have in my possession as a reminder of this jolt a promissory note of $1,595 from Clayton Magazine that never did get paid, dated July 12, 1933. But what the hell, Clayton, while he had it and was making it, sure paid off big to me."

Ray Nafziger alone was said to be owed four thousand 1932 dollars.

The giant Fiction House chain, rocked by the death of co-founder Jack "Candy" Kelly in April, killed off several titles, struggled uncertainly into the Fall, finally suspending publication at the end of 1932.

Lariat Story contributor Tom J. Hopkins recalled, "…Jack Glenister, then president of Fiction House, told me 'the Western story is dead. We're folding up all our Western books.' Jack Byrne, his editor since the untimely death of Jack Kelly, nodded agreement." […] "Times were bad—very. The depression was hitting everyone and every business, it seemed. 'And,' Glenister added, 'when times are better and we open up again, we'll use mostly general adventure stuff, and air stories. You'd better switch, Tom, get away from the Westerns.'"

A major problem with the Western story was simple fatigue. Virtually every premise and plot had been used and abused. Since the writers were attempting to mine a narrow field constrained by limited historical horizons, all concerned were prisoners of its hidebound conventions.

And a thorny thicket of taboos had grown up around the simple cowboy yarn.

Author & Journalist's Willard E. Hawkins—himself a dabbler in Westerns—enumerated the problems the earnest pulpwood Westerneer faced when trying to break the mold:

"Consider the Western writer when he sits down to weave a plot. An idea presents itself—but it won't do because it involves Indians. Another idea—but Mexican revolutions are barred. Another tack involves too much woman interest. The unsympathetic hero is out; so is the tragic ending. The hero who is not an American may be picturesque—but he won't sell the story. A foreigner can't be cast in the role of a villain—because his countrymen might consider it an insult. An 'Old West' or period story—better not take the chance. Humor must be handled as if it were dynamite—for what may bring a laugh from one editor may cause the next one to groan. There must be no hospitals in the story. The slightest taint of unethical methods about the hero—and out he goes.

"Most of the above taboos exist in one or more editorial offices—and the list is not half complete. What wonder that the Western writer clings to old plots and situations, and to conventional characters who have proved satisfactory in previous yarns—and what wonder that Western stories show a dangerous tendency to become stereotyped."

These observations notwithstanding, in his 1931 *Writer's Digest* essay, "Craftsmanship in Westerns," agent August Lenniger noted ferocious editorial resistance to the regulation Western that had formerly been a certain sale.

"Too many writers have the impression from their superficial reading of Western magazines and from the motion pictures they have seen that one simply takes rustlers and a cowboy, drops in a girl for luck, shakes them like dice in a leather cup, and rolls out an acceptable Western. It is this tongue-in-cheek attitude that is responsible for the many synthetic Westerns that are going begging. If you consider the Western story 'hokum' that is exactly what you are going to turn out."

Yet the formula had been perfectly acceptable to editors and readers only months before. The true reason for all this sales resistance was economic, not cultural. People weren't buying Westerns because dimes were tight.

H. Bedford-Jones chronicled the root causes in his March 1931 *Author & Journalist* article, "The Changing Market."

"For the first time," he wrote, "every prior experience of fictioneers has been reversed, with a dismal and horrifying thud. Formerly, in every time of panic and crisis, even during the World War, magazines prospered mightily; people turned to magazines to get their minds off their troubles, to get out of themselves and the world they knew. The magazines were immune from financial disaster.

"This time it was different—the stock market crash was too universal. Also, magazine prices had gone up. The ten-center of the old days now cost two-bits, much less easily spared for an evening or two of diversion. Depression had struck deeply into all lines. Everybody was in the stock market, and everybody suffered. Further, the magazine market was—and is—flooded with publications that had far passed the saturation point; anyone with a little backing was putting out new magazines. They were either using the cheapest sort of material by unknown writers, or they were filled with stories first published years ago and now reprinted at a very cheap rate."

Most of these low-rent pulps were Westerns. They had not only proliferated beyond reason, but the specialization that Street & Smith had kicked off with *Western Story Magazine* had gotten out of hand, with new magazines devoted to cowboy sub-genres crowding one another on the newsstands.

"During the flush days of 1929," Jones continued, "the editors had bought largely and at high prices; at least two fiction magazines were paying up to ten cents per word. The new year dawned with a crash. The safes were full of MSS.; everybody had lost money, circulation was dropping to the danger-point, advertising was thin. Money was being rapidly lost, not made.

Extinction threatened."

By the Summer of 1932, magazine circulation was off a reported 25 percent. Editorial salaries were reduced by 10 to 20 percent.

At Clayton, *Cowboy Stories* editor Henry A. McComas had discovered a bullseye painted on his chest. "Publishers asked editors what was the matter with their magazines. Editors asked authors why they had fallen down on the last dozen yarns." […] "The editorial problem was simple. Their readers were being thrown out of work each week by the thousands. Where once 20 cents was the price of a few nights of reading, it was now two loaves of bread. Soon, one after another, the magazines slowly but surely reduced their price per copy, and 10 cents became the usual selling price."

"The result was quite logical," Bedford-Jones continues. "Editorial policies were abruptly changed, and so were editors, in some cases. Budgets were cut down, the rates of authors were lopped on all sides, and in many instances no more manuscripts were bought from high-rate writers; nobody could sell except the struggling beginner who was content to take a small price for his wares. The magazines could exist for months upon what was actually bought and laid away in the safe, and that is exactly what they did."

It wasn't until late 1932 that manuscript inventories began to disappear, and publishers ordered editors to resume buying, while they considered how to meet the challenge of an industry-wide retooling. Some, like *Black Mask,* banished the Western story entirely. Industry leader *Western Story Magazine* slashed its rates—and overnight alienated their ace-in-the-hole, Frederick Faust.

Panicky pulp magazine publishers and editors, unwilling to cede that the situation was spiraling out of their control, started blaming the reading public. Their tastes had changed, some insisted. Nothing could be done until this mutiny was understood and catered to.

"Can it be that the depression has stimulated the brain of

the pulp paper reader?" an aghast Frederick Faust wrote one friend. "I hope not, but the editors tell me that it is a fact."

Writer's Digest's Aron M. Matheiu quickly put that lie to rest. In his August 1932 editorial, "Praised be Cinderella!" he observed:

"The more capable and honest critics of the rise and fall of the publishing business place almost the entire blame for the downfall on one little sentence that stole mouselike into this journal a month ago. That sentence reads: '"The old hokum is not going so well."' Upon that one sentence rests the main and prime criticism of magazines and books today.

"And in our opinion that criticism is just so much utter nonsense."

Mathieu continued: "…any man that says a change in the public's reading tastes caused the publishing business to retch itself into red ink is simply and earnestly a fool. The publishing business as a quick money big profit venture was cooked, fried, and finished when the market crashed, and to say that a change in reading tastes caused the market to crash is absurd."

In that same issue, Dell Executive Editor Carson W. Mowre weighed in:

"The pulps are in the doldrums. Circulation has fallen and many are the dire predictions concerning their future. Remedies are suggested. Expensive experiments are being indulged in by publishers. Students of publishing make searching analysis and tell us that the pulps are breaking their old cocoon and merging into another form of butterfly. They sourly tell us that the pulp as we now know it is doomed. That present publishers will fail and a new group with a new idea will usurp the field long held by the pulps.

"Hooey!

"The fact is that the buyers of pulps have been hardest hit by the depression. They look longingly at the money they formerly spent for a magazine. Many of them don't have it. Had they the money they would buy the same magazines they always did. Their tastes have changed only slightly; the readers of pulps represent a distinct section of our population. Morons, if you like. They will always be with us.

"Thank God!

"Give them the money of good times, or even fair times, and the pulps will again flourish with their action type of thrilling adventures and honest story value. Human nature is basically the same. The panic has not changed it. There have been other panics."

Yet in the face of all this, most editors were unwilling to tinker with the fundamentals of the regulation Western.

"'We will use the same sort of thing as always,' several Western story editors unanimously replied when I recently queried about the immediate future," reported August Lenniger. "They added that they wanted writers to give them novelty, to avoid the overworked old plots—but that's what all editors say!"

"The readers want something new," warned Reginald C. Barker, "but not something so blamed new that they don't believe a line of it! There is a limit to human credulity, even in the matter of fiction. Make your situations possible, probable, and as nearly within the range of understanding of the readers you expect your story to reach, as lies within your power."

The limits of realism were in the pulps elastic. As *Writer's Review* put it, "For instance, in a Western story don't make your hero capture a dozen bandits single-handed. The reader knows that this can't be done. Make him a super-he-man, but within the realm of possibility."

The period of the impossible Western was drawing to a reluctant close. Simply put, it was spent.

Bedford-Jones concluded his piece with this prediction, "So I may be pardoned pessimism anent the future. The outcome will be a perennial flood of ultra-cheap magazines of distinctly higher type, upbuilt by some editorial genius—who has not yet appeared."

But he was about to.

"Western editors and Western readers are just as weary as Western writers of the Western story that is written over and over on the same formula without the contribution of a single new twist or turn or slant or development to freshen up the old stuff of twenty years ago. Why do editors continue to buy them, then?"

— *Douglas Lurton*

6

MUSICAL SADDLES

IN 1932, industry-watchers were forecasting the imminent doom of the lower-end pulp genre magazine. Only the top-shelf all-fiction titles like *Argosy, Adventure* and *Blue Book* would survive, some predicted.

Western writer Clee Woods offered the contrarian view in the August *Author & Journalist*. "Look at the magazines which thus far have survived the depression," he wrote. *"Wild West Weekly* is still going strong. It's about as far removed from *Blue Book* as Job's hide was from the skin you love to touch. *Ace-High* continues to splash blood and burn powder, though with no little skill in the artistry of the deeds. It is very much alive, while *Far West Illustrated* staggered through two or three titles and then died a natural death. When the latter magazine changed its content and title to a mild type of Western love story, its end was in sight, while the virile, hard-riding heroes and gun-packing little cowgirls still gallop across the pages of *Ranch Romances."*

[…] "There has always been room for *Western Story Magazine's* quieter type of story right alongside the swift-trigger pages of other magazines. Doubleday, Doran's *West* stands about midway between the two types, perhaps, and it too survives."

The industry in 1932 could be divided into three distinct types of publishers. There were the venerable old houses like Street & Smith and Munsey, which had weathered financial panics before and would weather this one. The boomtown houses with no corporate memory of hard times, like Dell, Hersey, Clayton and Fiction House, were struggling to stay upright in their saddles.

The third category were the new lean outfits, principally Popular Publications, started by former Dell editor Harry Steeger with Harold Goldsmith in 1930, and Standard Magazines—generically known as the Thrilling Group—owned by timber millionaire Ned Pines and edited by former agent and Munsey man, Leo J. Margulies, which rode onto the scene in 1931. Paying a flat penny a word (or less) and charging a thin dime per copy, they were poised to make a go of hard times.

Late that year, Rogers Terrill abandoned the collapsing Fiction House chain for Steeger's upstart company. Popular's first twenty-cent titles—*Western Rangers* among them—had foundered amid distribution problems. At the suggestion of their distributor, Popular issued *Dime Detective Magazine* in 1931, and discovered a silver buzzword that eager buyers transmuted into pure gold: Dime. Now Steeger aimed to try again.

"At Popular," Terrill recalled, "we talked things over and decided that the Western, by the very nature of its historic coverage, stood as good a chance as any of survival. In December of that year we launched a new magazine, *Dime Western*—and we sent a bulletin to our Western authors. In it we told them that 'gun-dummy,' fast-action yarns were a thing of the past in the Western field. 'We are dealing,' we said, 'with a place and a period which, combined, produced the most dramatically colorful chapter in American history—the winning and securing of our Western frontiers.

"'Such fiction should have glamour and movement; human drama, and the occasional passages of swift, suspenseful action and bleak tragedy which are to be found upon all frontiers. It should stress the pioneer virtues of dogged determination and high courage; intense loyalty and cordial neighborliness. It should have the emotionalism of primitive peoples, and the glamorous adventure feel of the far-flung, untamed wilderness.'

"The Western story was becoming humanized!

"From a thing of mere bravado and fast action, it was now demanding not only good, well rounded story telling, but a flavor, characterization, and content which was characteristic of pioneer life.

"It was no longer sufficient to have a wandering waddy ride casually into a cow-town (any cow-town), shoot it out with the wicked town boss, and thereby save the weakling, gun-shy brother of the girl with whom our heroic, but otherwise uncharacterized, hero promptly fell in love. If that plot was used at all after 1932, it was given a little better motivation and at least a twist or two in the nature of added complications."

Maybe it was plummeting sales. Perhaps it was the pulp writers choking on their own imaginary gunsmoke, but 1932 seems to have been the year the tide turned against the "gun-totin' dummy" (to use writer Clyde A. Warden's personal coinage) in most of his tumbleweed manifestations.

Frederick Faust finally gagged on the mythic landscape he had summoned up from equal parts sheer imagination and Old World mythology. Having contributed to some 700 separate issues of *Western Story Magazine*, Faust had ridden the genre into the ground much the way his larger-than-life protagonists routinely spurred their super-stallion mounts beyond the limits of equine endurance.

Even the cowboy fans were fed up. One took Faust to task under two of his pseudonyms when he complained in an issue of *Western Story*, "I have been a reader of Street and Smith *Western Story Magazine* for a number of years, so I think I am entitled to register a complaint. I am getting tired of seeing Max Brand and George Owen Baxter take up so much room. Why don't you give them two a vacation for about ten years? If you want them to write a story, why don't you change the name of your magazine to Street and Smith fairy tales?"

Pressed by steadily sinking circulation, Frank Blackwell began rejecting Faust's work, complaining of one unsatisfactory novel, "…the entire story is clothed, in its manner of telling, in a very old world atmosphere. There is no American Cowboy 'relief' in it…."

Faust described one 1932 meeting with Blackwell to his wife in tones verging on despair:

"Blackwell to-day refused the first novelette that I handed him. This time, he said the plot was all right but the writing was 'dated.' He picked out a page that he thought was bad and read it aloud to me. He said it was old-fashioned. It wasn't a good page, but on the other hand I didn't think it was a bad page. He simply has come to a point where he cannot find anything good about my work."

Paradoxically, Blackwell was candid in telling Faust that he didn't believe *Western Story* could continue being published without him. The magazine was in desperate trouble. Both men struggled to find a solution. But Faust was at the end of his creative rope. "When I come to the writing of Western stories," he lamented, "I have so thoroughly exhausted most of my possibilities that I don't find new stones to describe, or new emotion, or a new lingo for new ideas."

In 1933, Blackwell was again forced to roll back the Olympian wordrates of the Roaring Twenties. Rather than take the new cut, Faust moved over to *Argosy*. Several of Blackwell's rejects found welcome in new rival magazines. But Faust would pen few Westerns after that terrible year of 1932.

Two other writers were getting five cents a word from Blackwell. Robert Ormond Case was one. The other was Walt Coburn's old mentor, Robert J. Horton. All became victims of their own success. Blackwell was instructed by Street & Smith management to eliminate these expensive Westerneers. With regrets, he did so.

Somehow, despite their absence, *Western Story Magazine* soldiered on, although Blackwell soon dropped serials in favor of self-contained novels.

In the higher world of hardcover books and slick magazine

serialization, genre tophand Zane Grey came to a similar cross-roads. He had commanded fabulous rates for his magazine serials before they hit hardcover. But in 1932-33, the advertising-dependent slicks could no longer meet his price.

Writing to his father, Grey's son Romer outlined the terrible state of affairs as of January 1933:

"We can't sell any stories to magazines—they all find some excuse to send them back—and I will say that I believe if we could I doubt if we could get $10,000 for a serial now. We can't sell any motion picture rights because the studios are using up their old material, and not spending any money on new story material. 'Westerns' came back and then 'went out' again because they are so rottenly made the public can't stomach them. I seriously doubt if we could get $10,000 for a picture just at this point.

"This isn't due to conditions being any worse, but to uncertainty, and to the result of all the studios, magazines, etc. finding out how much money they lost last year. I think things will get better; but I can't be sure and neither can you. Nor can we be sure how soon they will get better."

It was the beginning of the end of Grey's career. The Frederick Fausts and Robert Ormond Cases were taking his place, willing to work for fractions of his rate and seeing it as a step up in life.

Sales of hardcover Western books dropped alarmingly. Zane Grey lost a reported sixty percent of his audience. For the next twenty years, the serious hardcover Western virtually vanished. The ten-cent pulp magazine helped kill it.

Authorial fatigue accounted for other losses, according to *Triple-X Western*'s Douglas Lurton:

"Many of the prolific old-timers have gone by the boards in recent years," he wrote in 1932. "If you don't believe it scan the contents pages of Western magazine files of five years ago and those of today. There are others who are slipping, some who have already slipped; and neither they nor the editors have recognized it as yet, although the readers are suspicious."

Some, like Robert J. Horton and Arthur P. Hankins, died unexpectedly. There were suicides by discarded writers who failed to grasp that the fault lay in the editorial offices, not in their work. One pulpster was discovered sitting on a park bench, a bullet in his brain, a smoking pistol by his side, his pockets stuffed with rejection slips.

Others slunk back into the ordinary working world.

Erle Stanley Gardner simply gave up on Westerns around this time. Living out in California, he took to working round-ups on one of the last big cattle ranches still in traditional operation. A few seasons of this did the trick.

"Once I began to participate in these cowboy activities," he confessed, "I quit writing Westerns. I could no longer see anything dramatic about the life of a cowboy."

Two writers temporarily driven out of the game were John A. Saxon and Charles M. "Chuck" Martin.

Saxon went plain bust. "I lost my grip," he confessed. "I couldn't sell. Lenniger told me what the trouble was and as soon as I believed it... he began to sell about all I could write."

As for Martin, a California deputy sheriff who claimed acquaintance with Wyatt Earp and Emmett Dalton, sole survivor of the Dalton Gang, and who moonlighted writing easy gangster stuff as Carlos Martinez, he found himself drygulched on both counts. The gangster pulps also died with the repeal of Prohibition.

"Personally, I was caught with my Plots down," he admitted. "I had eight tomato vines growing in my back yard, and I fished on the pier every day for a year. If you want to see a cowboy run amok, just mention 'Fish and tomatoes' to me. That's all there was to eat. There just wasn't any money or market for my stories."

Lenniger saved his hide, too.

Douglas Lurton explained why the Saxons and the Martins were rebuffed as old-hat. "Western editors, in using up old stocks, have been forced to print many yarns purchased in a weak moment by themselves or predecessors down through the years. In replenishing their stocks, these editors have a tendency to be more exacting. They *must* have strong stories to hold their own. Believe it or not, the readers of Western fiction are more exacting today than they were several years ago."

New thinking caused August Lenniger to ask in print, "What's wrong with our typewriter cowboys? They seem to need a new bag of tricks, for editors are complaining of the scarcity of Westerns they can buy with enthusiasm. Yet thousands of ordinary messes of Western plotage go begging."

As one nameless pulpster lamented in *The Author & Journalist,* "Oh! for the good old days when you could write a 40,000-word range-war Western beginning with that infallible formula, 'When the smoke cleared, every rustler lay dead on the barroom floor' and get away with it! But them days are gone forever. Stories are short and getting shorter."

With the Depression at its bottom, younger, hungrier writers, not insulted by a penny a word, rushed in to fill the gap.

Walker A. Tompkins' experience was emblematic of the new blood entering the field:

"In my late teens I was a reporter in a small California daily, for $22.50 a week. Chancing to read a Western pulp magazine some hobo had tossed out of a box car, I said to myself, 'Hell, I can do that good!' So I batted out an 11,500-word cowboy story in four afternoons and sent it to *Action Stories,* proof right there of my ignorance of markets. It bounced, naturally, so I decided to try it one more time, and mailed it to Street & Smith's *Wild West Weekly,* a decision that was to change my entire life. 'Gold-plated Handcuffs' starring a cowboy detective, Tommy Rockford, struck *WWW* editor Ronald Oliphant's fancy and back came a check for the astronomical sum of $115. I quit my newspaper job pronto, wrote another Tommy Rockford novelette, and sold it. And so on, novelette after novelette, for years...."

"In 1931," continued Tompkins, "when I broke into the pulps, rates had been slashed from a dime to a penny a word. Some of the long-established authors thought they could go on strike and boycott the publishers, but it was too late for that; the depression had changed things forever. I, however, was only too glad to make a cent a word. I could type a hundred words a minute, far too slow to keep up with my imagination, and I was adept at thinking up plots, working from a formula which never failed me."

Established writers found it tough going, but it could be done. "The depression made quitters out of a lot of people," recalled Californian L.P. Holmes, "particularly the spoiled boys who thought they were extra special, but weren't. Rates fell way down, but there was always a market somewhere if you had guts enough to stick it out and keep on plugging. Those tough years were the best training in the world—a man found out what his real capacity was."

Then there were the returning pilgrims. H. Bedford-Jones was one. Commanding from six to ten cents a word at the top of his game, he had tapered off his relationship with Frank Blackwell and *Western Story* during booming '20s. His better markets in collapse, and accustomed to living high, he buckled down to spin fewer, better yarns for reduced word rates. Blackwell was glad to have him back.

Allan R. Bosworth was another. A former Navy man, he had deserted the Pulp West for the air-war field during the high-flying days of 1927-29. When magazines like *War Birds* and *Navy Stories* went belly-up, he slunk back to the range.

Concocting a yarn about a muleskinner named Shorty Masters, Bosworth found *Triple-X Western* was bought up. So he sent it to *Wild West Weekly*. Ronald Oliphant took it.

Bosworth said later, "I delightedly proposed that we make it a series, and he cautiously admitted it might go for a very short series; he didn't think the character was strong enough to stand up in a long one."

Eight years later, Bosworth had produced nearly 200 Shorty Masters yarns, as well as buckets full of other work under sundry house names, in a few cases "collaborating" with himself when two of his characters joined up in a single tale.

But the series really didn't take off, Bosworth revealed, until he introduced a regulation sidekick. "Five stories later, I teamed Shorty with a mystery cowboy, a gun-slinging waddy who was sought for bank robbery. We built up suspense—it was thirty-two stories later before the Sonora Kid cleared his name. In twenty-six of those, the partners were engaged in the pursuit of a border bandit who held the secret of the bank holdup."

The cowpoke still ruled the range, but in his versatile mule-skinner Bosworth caught a glimmer of the Pulp West's future.

The Great Depression was proving to be the ultimate equalizer. As older writers were flushed out of the game, new blood poured in, spurred by the shifting economy. Publishers re-dressed their magazines, throwing out the pastoral Western canvases of yore and insisting on lurid action-soaked "bang-bang" covers. Strangely, the more blazing the cover illustration, the fewer gunfights appeared inside. It was a reversal of the old packaging, which had amounted to masking the violence of what had come to be derisively called "the Bloody Pulps."

A new era was dawning.

"It wasn't so long ago that magazine editors and writers were bewailing the passing of a grand old citizen, a revered specimen who had almost become an institution. The sages had gone into a huddle and emerged with sad faces and the solemn pronouncement that *Old Man Western Story* was a goner, dead on his feet. All he lacked, they said, was to be laid on his back with a lily in his hand, and have somebody shovel dirt into his face."

—J.R. Johnston

7

OFF-TRAIL BLAZERS

DELL'S NEW venture, *All-Western Magazine* was probably the first to strike out into the unexplored territory of the "true" West. Editor Carson W. Mowre put out the call early in 1932:

"Our magazine is making no effort to appeal to Easterners who get a vicarious thrill out of much lead-slinging, rustling, etc. It is making its appeal direct to the Westerner, and people who have lived in the West. So many of the so-called Western books have nauseated real Westerners that we are trying to give them something different to read. Anything savoring of the old Western story that has been published in countless variations will receive instant rejection. We want to portray a true picture of the West and all its color and glamour, not a ribbon clerk's version of an hombre with a Colt in each hand, killing 47 sheriffs, not to mention 16 U.S. marshals and countless rangers."

A former Naval aviator and horseman, Mowre was another Fiction House fugitive.

Struggling to explain the new magazine's concept of "different" *The Writer's Year Book* offered, "See if you can't find a new Western plot to appeal to old Western fans (Not too different, you understand, but different enough)."

At virtually the same time, ex-Wyoming cowpuncher turned New York publisher Aaron A. Wyn was telling potential contributors to *Western Trails*, "The hero doesn't have to be a gun-wizard; he can be a man who has certain clearly-defined character traits, and through these oddities he is able to overcome the obstacles in his path. The trouble with the majority of the Western stories that fail is that the characters are not sufficiently emphasized to become real; they are mere gun-dummies."

As August Lenniger explained, "The mediocrity that is so evident in the majority of Western stories is due to their failing to get under the reader's skin. They are mere vague cowboy names moving through a blur of gunsmoke. The reader doesn't know what they were all about five minutes after he's finished them. They are too obviously machine-made; they lack sincerity."

Douglas Lurton noted this new trend in "Selling Western Stories" (*Writer's Digest,* March 1932). "There seems to be an increasing demand for Westerns in which the heroes are more than a mere name; a demand for characters who can be identified any place in the story through their dialogue, their appearance, their actions and reactions. The hero who is simply a zero with a name and two spitting Colts and a Stetson is on the way out."

As Rogers Terrill saw it, "The Western story was not entirely 'gun-dummy' any more. Its characters were beginning to suffer other viscissitudes [*sic*] than lead poisoning. Its plots were beginning to develop complications which, if not entirely unexpected, were at least a change from the old straight-line action formula. Of more significance, perhaps, was the first awkward emphasis on human and emotional values."

So began *Dime Western.* Terrill enlisted a small band of seasoned writers to produce the kind of Western tales he envisioned. Among them were *Western Story Magazine* deserter Walt Coburn, Fiction House fugitive Harry F. Olmsted, Clayton orphan Ray Nafziger, as well as Eugene Cunningham, Arthur H. Carhart, Edward Beverly Mann, Cliff Farrell, John Colohan, Gunnison Steele and one tophand who had never before written in the genre, but had been a star contributor to Popular's *Dime Detective,* T.T. Flynn, of Santa Fe, New Mexico.

In market notices appearing in all the writer's magazines later in 1932, Terrill outlined his plan of attack on the jaded cowboy fan: "Popular Publications is in the market for Westerns of all lengths up to twenty-five thousand words. Story and character values are being emphasized rather than the forced action of the gun-dummy type, but all stories to make the grade in this market must pack dramatic punch. Unusual story situations and unexpected plot twists are particularly wanted, as a real attempt is to be made to get away from the trite and the hackneyed in Western plotting. Gunmen and gun-fights are of course not barred, but they must have real motivation behind them.

"In other words, don't manufacture a gun battle just to give your story the proper high-powered send-off. If you can give your characters human, valid reasons for dragging their hardware, let 'em go at at. We like action, in its proper place and value. But we don't want the old brand of hectic, unmotivated bullet-throwing that gets the story nowhere and calluses the reader to the real thing when it comes along. All stories must have bona fide Western color and atmosphere, but the story material may be dug from the entire history of the White Man's West, since there are no definite period limits implied in our story policy."

In a follow-up bulletin, Terrill added:

"We are particularly in the market for off-trail stories. I am emphasizing human character values and plot twist... These stories must be dramatic and must have the quality of stirring the reader emotionally. I will use period stories definitely dated and dealing with any one glamorous era in the history of the White Man's West. This means the U.S.A. and Mexico. I do not want Canadian settings; this always suggests the men in scarlet on horseback. Scenes may be laid, however, right up on the northern border in the cow country.... Woman interest? Yes. And it can be fairly strong. The story must always be from the man's angle, though."

This paragraph alone broke three separate taboos in pulp

Western fiction—no actual dates, no token women, and no straying outside the formula. The old-style regulation Western was definitely not welcome on Terrill's range.

The first issue, its cover showing a Western wench in *dishabille* shielding her wounded cowman from an unseen opponent, promised George C. Henderson's "Lead in Their Teeth."

Rogers Terrill opened the proceedings in his trademark style:

"It is the hope of *Dime Western* to bring you each month a large cross section of the most glamorous adventure-land the world has ever seen.... Human, man-stuff yarns that will put a new tingle into your blood and pull your heart strings. Stark, real-life drama ripped raw from the lives of those sturdy men who lived out their lives on horseback. You'll know the tang of hot saddle leather under the blazing sun of Texas cattle trails—feel the zero-pinch of sweeping Montana blizzards—listen to the blatant blare of honky-tonks main streets in a score of Colorado mining towns!

"And last but not least, you'll share adventure and hardship, trail-side battle thrill and heady romance with the finest type of two-fisted, hard-riding adventurer this country has ever produced—our Western cowboy!

"The editors of *Dime Western* realize that they've tackled a he-man job in attempting to crowd all this into any one magazine. But we're willing and game to die trying.

"Come hell or high-water, we'll never sell our saddle!"

Popular's timing was perfect. Harold Hersey and Fiction House were no longer publishing. Debt-ridden William Clayton was reeling in his saddle. Fawcett unceremoniously cancelled the renamed *Triple-X Western* at the close of 1932. Of the 16 Western pulps being issued before the stock market collapse, only seven remained.

"Magazines fluttered into bankruptcy like the falling leaves of autumn," recalled Alfonso Cliff Farrell. "I wrote fifty-seven short stories in that year and, somehow, sold fifty-two of them. A life preserver had been cast to foundering writers. A magazine that sold for a dime and therefore was named *Dime Western*... had appeared. I believe I appeared in about its second issue."

Another maverick newspaperman, Farrell was born in the same Ohio town as Pearl Zane Grey. *Cowboy Stories* introduced him to readers in 1925, and it was a sweet ride during the easy years. Applying himself, the Zanesville native rode the new market with desperate industry.

"I became a fiction factory," he recounted, "turning out up to 400,000 words a year, most of which appeared in Mr. Steeger's string." Like Coburn and Grey, Farrell cut his byline down to size in order to sound more Western, becoming Cliff Farrell.

One of Terrill's other finds was named Robert E. Mahaffay. After suffering 25 years of rejects, this veteran of the Washington and Oregon cattle country sold Popular his first Western, and quickly adapted to *Dime Western's* slant:

"The yarn in which the hero shows up somewhere by accident, lands a job, is shot at, endures a welter of physical tribulations, and eventually tracks down the rustlers, winning the cowman's daughter, is pretty difficult to sell these days," Mahaffay wrote. "Not impossible, you understand, because some markets demand a story that is basically action, but difficult.

"The new Western is in a way reminiscent of Greek tragedy, with the bitter ending sheered off. The hero has his share of physical difficulties, of course, but coupled with them is a good deal of mental turmoil. He is no longer simply a brawny, panther-like figure with a gun. The fact that he is quick on the trigger, able in a brawl, capable of saving a captured young lady and riding hard to intercept the rascals who have robbed the stage, is no longer enough.

"He must be a man who reacts like a human being—as you or I might, for example—and he must be honestly torn by the circumstances in which he finds himself. You, the writer, must provide the circumstances that put him over the hurdles of indecision, hurt, anger, perhaps hopelessness, perhaps despair."

Likening the newfangled pulp cowboy to Oedipus Rex, Mahaffay said, "Put a saddle on him and change the circumstances a little and he might have been a Western hero." It's possible Mahaffay was overstating this comparison. He had been a university dramatics teacher when he first crashed the pulps. Terrill convinced him to go freelance during the Depression.

"I don't contend that these Westerns I'm discussing are developing into literature comparable to Shakespeare or the Greeks," Mahaffay admitted. "But I do maintain that they are expanding along lines that those lads proved are sound."

He proved it by selling Terrill a novelette entitled, "Friends, Romans—Gunmen!"

Between the cowboys and the dramatists, Rogers Terrill managed to fill his daring new magazine with exactly what he wanted. Readers perked up. *Dime Western* became Popular's top title. One of its subscribers was said to be Al Capone.

"'This,' we thought, 'is the cat's!'" Terrill recalled. "We had 'emotional values' 'n' everything! *Dime Western,* using the new type story, was prospering. *Star Western,* newly launched, was prospering, too."

"Rogers Terrill... injected something new and vital into Westerns," asserted Stephen Payne. "When he called for something different, he really meant it and wasn't afraid to publish it when he got it."

Terrill seemed an unlikely candidate to remake the Western genre. Born in Irvington, New Jersey, he enrolled in Columbia with the firm intention of becoming an actuary. Midway through, he switched to studying literature, concentrating on the short story. After graduation, Terrill briefly sold hosiery and did actuarial work before landing at Fiction House in 1927. He sold considerable pulp fiction in genres ranging from sea stories to Westerns, some of which appeared in *Western Story Magazine* and *Lariat.*

Terrill was not alone in this push. His primary Western

associate editor, Francis "Mike" Tilden, was at least a co-conspirator. Tilden had previously toiled at Fiction House and been fired from Street & Smith during an austerity move earlier in the year.

"Western pulp fiction began to swing toward what some have called the 'realistic' story," recalled John A. Saxon. "Walt Coburn topped the field in this division for years. His characters are real. His backgrounds are real. While some of his stories still feature a lot of 'bang-bang' they differ from the old type in that there is always a reason for the shooting.

"Rogers Terrill and Mike Tilden began querying their writers for what they called 'The Emotional Western,' something that appealed to the emotions of the reader rather than having only the thrill of action and gunsmoke.

"I believe Cliff Farrell and myself—and there were probably others—began writing this type of story about the same time.

"Harry Olmsted was infiltering this idea into his Indian and Overland trail stories."

"The growth of Westerns has been slow and sure as tomorrow's sun," wrote Olmsted, one of the genre's top proponents, in "After Selling Ten Million Words (*Writer's Digest*, September 1945)." "Not steady necessarily, for there have been times when the acceleration has exceeded average. It was my pleasure and agony to write through one such period (1932-1940) and it is my humble opinion that Rogers Terrill was the prime mover in that speed-up. An editor who knew what he wanted and set out to get it. A calm man and a forthright man, with the patience of Job.

"'Look now,' he'd say, in letters that frequently went four pages. 'Forget deep complication of plot. I don't care if your characters draw a gun, fork a horse or notice a girl. You fellows who touched the old West and knew its old-timers can take care of the color. Give me honestly motivated conflict spiced with the human values that take the reader by the throat and hang on until the last wisp of smoke from the last gunshot blows away to reveal a startling and unwanted THE END. And give me repression.'

"That's what Rogers wanted," wrote Olmsted. "The day of the jostled arm and the spilled beer, as a motivation for wholesale slaughter, is done. The old idea of recounting the ghastly details of a killing, from boot toes beating a grisly tattoo to blood like rubies dropping from his lips, must give way to a delightful 'John killed him.' And thus, when we came again to measure our brain child, lo, he had grown up… a little."

Characterization replaced the Colt as the new key to the Golden West. Real writers with fake-sounding handles like Tom Roan, William Colt MacDonald, Harry Sinclair Drago, Claude U. Rister, L.L. Foreman, William F. Bragg, and others new to the scene, like Tom W. Blackburn, Wayne D. Overholser, and F.D. Glidden—who appropriated gunslinger Luke Short's name as his *nom de plume*—did their dead-level best to adapt.

Two of the most important were relative old-timers, Ernest Haycox and Walt Coburn—the latter remaining the top Western pulpster in the new era. After his apprenticeship in the pulps, Haycox broke into the slicks in 1931 and never came back. There, he took the regulation Western tale to the next level.

"Ernest Haycox did as much as any one writer to liberate the Western novel," wrote Wayne D. Overholser. "He influenced all of us who were writing Westerns at that time. Some writers frankly copied him. Haycox was the best when it came to creating strong, multi-dimensional characters, male and female, and he was able to create stories that pulled the reader into scenes that were vivid and situations that were moving."

"Haycox very nearly succeeded, single-handed, in doing for the standard Western what Hammett and Chandler did for the private eye detective story—made it respectable," averred D.B. Newton.

According to critic Bernard DeVoto, Haycox was single-handedly responsible for the "solemnification" of the Western.

"It was he who added the Hamlet strain to the sun god that is now standard," wrote DeVoto. "The Hero is always a shadowed man and a regretful fatalist. He is born to ride dim and lonely trails to an end known to be lonely and meaningless… It turns out, of course, that the end he rides toward is a multiple murder, from which he takes three steps into the arms of a rounded girl whose sleeping fire his six-gun has awakened, all the more so if he himself has been wounded in the shoulder or upper chest."

Critics credit Haycox with injecting a species of sex into his Western word weavings, specifically coalescing a formula that became as regulation as the stirrup. DeVoto described it like so:

"Two loves are in competition, the pure girl who is prim but can be awakened, and the loyal, generous, obviously passionate girl whose appeal to The Hero must lose out because her past is shadowed."

Haycox himself analyzed his new Western hero this way: "Make him a good man, but give him *possibilities* of badness."

"Haycox, with a genius for word facility, may not be measured by characterization," opined Harry F. Olmsted. "He keeps those tools very sharp, but the things he writes about convey a sense of 'bigness,' of vast moving forces which slowly but surely enmesh his principal in an unbreakable web. Coburn has much the same genius, limited perhaps by a more restricted horizon. Walt has led the pulp field for two full decades. Walt sweated and bled and wept his way through the years of change. It speaks volumes for his bigness and Terrill's patience that Walt's yarns grow tighter, more logical, and altogether more readable as he matches the growth of the Westerns from the *whimsical prospector and loyal, lop-eared burro* stage of juvenility to a grown-up delineation of primitive struggle, where weaklings perish and the strong are conditioned to fight peculiar and specialized odds."

Dime Western fed off the Haycox formula like calves at their mother's udder. But Rogers Terrill can't alone be credited with reviving the pulp Western magazine. However, if 1932 was the year of disaster, 1933 witnessed a revival.

It started off badly, as witnessed by Stephen Payne. "In February of 1933," he recalled, "determined to see if there was any way by which I might be able to 'stick and hang and rattle,' I went to New York. The contrast between what I had seen in editorial offices in June of 1929 and saw in 1933 was like a visit to a real booming mining camp and then a return to the same camp which had become a ghost town!"

At Clayton, they were shutting down everything but *Ranch Romances* and *Five-Novels Monthly*. The unpublished story inventory to *Cowboy Stories* and others was unceremoniously dumped on the market at bargain prices via authors' agents, flooding the market and putting writers in competition with their own wares.

Stephen Payne also discovered that among the desperate survivors, the specialization trend had reached the ultimate extreme.

As Willard E. Hawkins related in the March 1933 issue of *The Author & Journalist*, "In former times, a story would be 'slanted' toward a *group* of magazines. A Western story, for example, could be so written that it might be submitted to one after another of the Western magazines, with a fair chance of landing somewhere down the line. These times have passed.

"Every pulp-paper editor now has his formula, so distinct from others that if the story is not written directly for his magazine it is a waste of time to submit it.... The essence of the formula is something intangible—something which neither the editor nor his writers can express, although they have come to 'feel' it instinctively."

Hawkins painted a bleak landscape for would-be contributors. "For example, he writes a yarn for Miss Fanny Ellsworth, who conducts the Clayton magazines, *Ranch Romances* and

Rangeland Love Stories. If the story fails to land in this one market, it is 'through.' Miss Ellsworth demands an out-and-out love story, in the Western setting, preferably told from the girl's viewpoint. No other pulp magazine uses this type of story. The nearest approach to it is *Western Trails,* edited by A.A. Wyn. Mr. Wyn desires a strongly plotted Western story, with woman interest and a touch of mystery. It must not, however, have anywhere near the same love-theme predominance as a *Ranch Romances* story; and it must be told from the male viewpoint. Further, the Clayton magazines do not care for the mystery element desired by Mr. Wyn. If a story written for him fails to land, there are no other markets for it. Most of the other Westerns will admit an occasional minor woman element, but they differ from each other in respects equally marked."

"*North-West Stories,* for instance, prefers a young man, and likes a touch of real romance," Arch Joscelyn elucidated. "*Lariat* is strong for the devil-may-care swashbuckler type; but he must be youthful also. *Wild West* is strong for youth. Here there is one broad recipe—youth—which varies somewhat with the magazine…. One editor will admit a present-day atmosphere to some of the old–time Western stories. This is poison to editor number two. And so it goes."

Hitting the editorial bull's-eye had become a job for a dead shot—if not a mind reader. "Nearly all of the pulp-paper editors, especially those in the Western field, emphasize the requirement for 'something different,'" Hawkins noted. "The well-worn 'rustler' theme, for example, is sure of rejection. Pressed to explain what they mean by 'something different,' these editors become rather vague. The best bet is to study their magazines."

The phrase "something different" would torment Western pulpsters for the next twenty years. For no one could or would define it.

A anonymous writer of comical Westerns who skulked like a bushwhacker behind the assumed byline of Thomas Thursday, cynically observed:

"The editorial ladies and gentlemen will moan and yelp for the story that is new and novel, but they are scared stiff when it enters their sectors. What they mean by something different, I take it, is that if your hero wore hair-pants in your previous yarns, dress him in a tuxedo in your next and, instead of having him fall off his horse onto his head, as you did in your last opus, have the gentleman fall off a hay-stack onto his ear. Thus we have the editorial idea of something distinctive."

The sad state of things was summarized by Walker Tompkins this way:

"What had once been the 'dime novel' industry of the nineties, mushroomed to sixteen Westerns by the start of the thirties, to be whittled down to seven books during the depression Winter of 1932-33."

By the close of the year, most fallen titles found new publishers. Street & Smith bought Clayton's *Cowboy Stories* at a bankruptcy auction, while Dell restarted another Clayton castoff, *Ace-High Magazine*. Fawcett reactivated *Triple-X Western* as an annual. A fierce bidding war erupted over *Ranch Romances*. *Field & Stream* publisher Eltige Warner handily outbid all rivals, paying a reported $35,000 for the biggest cash cow in the pulp field. That summer, the magazine changed publishers without skipping an issue.

Simultaneously, Fiction House reversed itself and revived five suspended titles. Three, *Lariat Story Magazine, Frontier Stories* (which it had acquired from Doubleday in 1929) and *Action Stories,* showcased Western action yarns. Jack Byrne returned to the editorial saddle, repeating the old refrain of "no gun dummies."

Walt Coburn returned, too. Burned by bankruptcy, he was no longer exclusively with Fiction House. He kept a stake in *Dime Western,* which had gotten him through the tough times.

"In that noon-hour long ago," recollected Rogers Terrill in "The Evolution of the Western," "Jack Byrne said that the Western story was too limited in plot, character, time and place.

He knows better now—was, in fact, one of the first to realize the fallacy of that statement."

One man had predicted the comeback of the Pulp West. When told by Jack Glenister that the Western story was a dead issue, Tom Hopkins bluntly retorted, "Westerns are not dead and will never die." Hopkins came back to the Fiction House outfit, too.

The change wrought by *Dime Western Magazine* was profound. Wild new grass was growing out on the Pulp Prairie. Even editors who chose not to copy Terrill's formula—which he came to call "emotional urgency"—were forced to elevate the fiction they offered the public. Where before writers were instructed to write down to the level of the imagined teenage semi-literate reader, now editors encouraged better writing and richer character delineation.

This revival encouraged Standard publisher Ned Pines and his editor, Leo Margulies, to issue their first Western titles. *Thrilling Ranch Stories* was released late in 1933, with the more traditional *Thrilling Western* hard on its heels.

Writer's Year Book described its slant as "…thrilling tales of the gallant West where danger lurks and cowboys are supermen."

In other words, the same old stuff. Thrilling became what was called a "dump" market—one that would happily print stories rejected by the better pulp houses.

Early in 1934, August Lenniger told *The Author & Journalist,* "After a period of eclipse, the Western and the Western romance are today stronger that ever. Although many of them cling to the old formulas of somewhat exaggerated action, there is generally a greater demand for verisimilitude, more convincing characterization, and at least a superficial suggestion of significance. Several of the Western pulps definitely demand the better-class Western similar to those we find frequently in the smooth-papers like *Cosmopolitan, McCall's, Collier's, Saturday Evening Post*—but nevertheless with enough virility and fast action to give them appeal to the pulp reader. There are three times as many markets for the Western romance as a year ago, and about twice as many substantial markets for the straight masculine Western action yarn."

In "The Changing Western" (*Writer's Monthly*, November 1934), Arch Joscelyn painted a clear picture of the new reality:

"A few sturdy souls have pioneered and shown that stories of any particular type, though placed between the covers of a pulp magazine, will meet with a kindly reception, though written for people of adult mind." […] "Accordingly, the old-type Western is coming back. By that I mean the Western which made the story-type famous and well-liked before the pulp magazines ever were heard of—the Westerns that sold in book form, the same sort that now appear as serials in the big, smooth-paper magazines.

"There will never be, of course, the old-time leisureliness in Western stories, or any other type. People want movement, without digression into side-paths, however diverting those paths may be of themselves. But beauty of description is not barred out now merely because it is scenery...."

Both writers and editors began paying closer attention to their audience. Writer Norman A. Fox loitered around news-racks just to see who was snapping up Western pulps.

"Any newsstand dealer will tell you that the man who reads Westerns, for example, wants nothing but Westerns and buys them by the bushels, scorning other types of fiction," Fox revealed. "Who are they? College boys who look like ranch hands… ranch hands who look like college boys… professional men and wide-eyed schoolboys… butchers and bakers and candlestick makers and women, too—a cross section of humanity in fact.

"Yet, roughly," Fox said, "the readers of Western pulp can be divided into two classes—the more astute or adult type of reader who is looking for 'escape literature' but who hopes to find better fare in the pulps than was to be had in the old-time dime novel—and the juvenile reader, be he eighteen or eighty, who wants his fiction fast and furious and is not one to ponder over subtle writing or anything else that doesn't directly meet the eye."

Out of these observations, Fox evolved a fresh approach to the science of pulp "triggernometry."

"The trick, then, is to produce a story to satisfy both types of readers—a double-barreled yarn. Fortunately the juvenile reader is easily satisfied. He may be a little sated with the old opening that has the hero riding peacefully along until a gun bangs from the rimrock and the hero's sombrero goes sailing but if you can recast the old situations with plenty of lead-slinging, thundering hoofs and thudding fists, your juvenile fan will be happy and may even forgive Max Brand for deserting him by turning to Dr. Kildare.

"But to have an ample amount of the old bang-bang to satisfy the juvenile *and* to inject something else into the story— something to make the adult reader feel that the magazine was worth the ten or fifteen cent investment—is a trick in literary technique.... The gunsmoke, suspense and action which are injected for the juvenile's sake will keep the yarn 'in the groove' while the use of off-trail characterization, conflicts, backgrounds or style treatments will give it that extra something that brings long white envelopes instead of bulky brown ones."

Fresh to the field, N. Coral Nye (later to rebrand himself as Nelson C. Nye), warned against the pulpster's natural tendency toward violence. "Never permit your dead men to wallow in a smear of gore. Be genteel in your homicides; don't have a single killing which is unnecessary. If possible, write your yarn *without* a killing. It is harder, yes—but the days of the 'blood-and-thunder' yarn have passed. They went with the buffalo and the Indians."

This was a gigantic reassessment for all concerned.

"In those stories of action written yesterday, the plot and its movement carried the hero; today the hero has to carry the plot," explained Arthur Hawthorne Carhart, one writer who struggled to shift away from Fiction House-style of yarning to the new Popular Publications approach. "The cardboard hero is in the ash can."

"The key to the checkbooks of these magazines is complete sincerity," insisted August Lenniger, "the creation of real red-blooded Western characters who conquer the vicissitudes of their hard, dangerous, but glorious frontier West. You have to write these stories so that the reader will feel the blistering sun of the Mojave, so he'll choke with the dust of the trailherd of whitefaces being hazed over the prairie, so he'll smell the purple sage of the rolling [plains], so that his eyes will blink at the glare of the great Salt Lake desert."

Once again, the pulp Western had been ransomed from the rope.

"Will it last?" asked Robert E. Mahaffay. "Or is it a fad that will sooner or later be stampeded from? I think not. It may be modified when the freshness is gone. Perhaps some of the melodrama will mellow into drama, though not all of it. The strain that has been added is too basic to be thrown overboard altogether."

Mahaffay seemed to be peering into the future, and not very far, either.

As the Depression wore on, Rogers Terrill learned to his chagrin that all this reconsideration was merely a stay of execution, not a full pardon:

"We began to ask boldly for more emotionalism," he recounted in "The Evolution of the Western," "and though we warned that 'Emotionalism, handled skillfully and with repression, makes strong reading; weakly handled, it degenerates into sentimentality and cheap melodrama.' We failed to realize that we were letting ourselves in for something almost as bad as the straight-line, unadorned 'gun-dummy' action yarn which we had so confidently cast aside.

"There are, perhaps, half a dozen situations and general plot types which lend themselves most obviously to an emotional handling. The sacrifice theme was promptly done to death. There came a flood of stories about bold, bad killers who, in the last tenth of the story, suddenly turned good and saved the ranchers who had been hunting them.

"A lot of pulp Western heroes escaped from prison with the express purpose of reeking [*sic*] vengeance on the gents who had sent them there, only to discover in the last few pages of the story that the supposed villain was really a loyal and lovable chap, himself about to be victimized by the undercover scoundrel who had really been responsible for the hero's incarceration. Back to back, they then proceeded to fight it out victoriously against overwhelming odds, each warmed and mellowed by their re-established partnership.

"The Western was undergoing a new and deadly type of formularization."

"*Westerns? I've written—and sold—over a thousand of them, and that makes me an expert. Nothing to it. Take a brawny, gun-belted hero, a cold-eyed villain, maybe a sun-kissed range girl. Mix well. Season with large amounts of gunsmoke, fist fights, a stampede or two. And there you have a sure-fire Western.*

"*Hogwash!*"

— "*Gunnison Steele*"

8

DODGING HEMP

HAVING INSTIGATED a revolution, Rogers Terrill saw it as his responsibility to rein in the wild mob he had unleashed before it ransacked his burgeoning line of Western magazines, which eventually included *Ace-High Western, Big-Book Western,* and *New Western*—all purchased from failed pulp houses.

"We wrote to the authors and begged them for fresh plots and new situations," he recalled. "We outlined story ideas and suggested as yet unused historic material. But, alas, we had told them—not once, but many times—that we wanted human values and emotionalized situations. The authors obediently gave us new settings, new characters, new themes, but after a while we began to realize that no matter what fresh settings or characters they gave us, they were, unconsciously, re-writing the same general story type time after time.

"They were giving us, they thought, exactly what we had asked for—emotion! We realized then for the first time the terrific, destructive dynamite in that word, and we proceeded to drop it from our vocabulary. We couldn't, however, afford to throw overboard all of the progress the Westerns had made toward a more human, more believable, more moving story form.

"We sent out another series of letters, in which we told our authors to forget any conscious striving for emotional effect. We told them that consciously or otherwise, they had gotten into the habit of writing just one particular sort of over-senti-mentalized story for our market; and we added that we hoped they'd drown in their own tears if they ever sent us any more. We listed six or seven plot situations of which we had seen enough for a long time to come, and we told them that we thought each and every one of them was a good enough crafts-man to give us the sort of solidly dramatic, suspenseful, vigor-ous stories we wanted without recourse to the old too-often-tried and not-too-true situations.

"Progress was slow this time. There was not the immedi-ately noticeable change in story form and tempo which had greeted our earlier request for emotional values. Slowly, however, there was evolved in the late '30s the well balanced, human, believable, not-too-sweet and not-too-salty Western story, which is to be found in all of the better pulp Westerns today.

"It isn't necessary," Terrill summarized, "to enumerate in detail the various pitfalls which have marked the course of pulp Western fiction. Clearly melodramatic writing, lack of charac-terization and the monotonously straight-line action plot first imposed grave audience limitations on the Western. After a few years of this, its readers, quite naturally, walked out on the entire field.

"With better plotting," he concluded, "and with the addition of human and emotional values, it won a new following in the early and middle thirties—a following which it almost lost a few years later through our failure to supply the amount of variety and freshness in plot, theme, character, location and time which any all-fiction magazine must have in order to long survive."

One of the problems was the Western pulp had rebounded *too* well. Over 1933-34, established pulp publishers and a few mavericks attempted to unleash a posse of new Western titles.

In 1933, publisher Martin Goodman, along with fellow cir-culation man Louis H. Silberkleit, started a shoestring chain called Newsstand Magazines with a reprint title, *Western Su-*

pernovel. It soon became *Complete Western Novel Magazine,* specializing in what was called the "rapid-fire type" of Western tale.

A year later, Silberkleit struck off on his own, forming Columbia Publications. His first title was *Double Action Western Stories.* Like Goodman, he started off as a low-rent reprinter, but soon became a "dump" market, where rejects could be sold off at rock-bottom word rates. Both publishers quickly expanded their Western titles.

The following year another Goodman affiliate, A. Lincoln Hoffman, started yet another chain with *The Masked Rider Western* and *Greater Western Magazine.* Hoffman's Ranger Publications soon sold out to the Thrilling Group, but Goodman's Red Circle line and Silberkleit's Blue Ribbon Magazines competed for the bottom-end of the marketplace to the bitter end of the pulp era.

"It is almost impossible to keep track of the new magazines starting up to feature Westerns," reported *Writer's Markets and Methods* late in 1934. *"Real Western, Great Western, Greater Western, Western This* and *Western That,* spring up overnight and fold up in the morning."

Most folded immediately. Two, *Super-Western Stories* and a revived *Golden West Magazine,* never got out of the corral. One publisher released a mixed-genre title called *Conflict.* When sales sagged, it went all-Western. Readers, mistaking it for a war title, passed it up.

"Three months ago everyone and his uncle was shouting, 'Detectives are down, the Western story is the thing,'" explained *Writer's Review* that December. "For a while Westerns outsold detective pulps, with a half dozen new Western magazines started overnight. But suddenly the taste has reverted to its old love—and Westerns are second."

Of these, only the publishers brave enough to follow in *Dime Western*'s wagon tracks produced winners. A.A. Wyn released *Western Aces* late in 1934, but kept *Western Trails* going along the old familiar gunsmoke trail. Fiction House moved *Lariat Story* away from straight action cowboy fare, but *Action Stories* continued to live up to its pulpy title.

Jack Byrne modified Fiction House's fare with reluctance.

"The pulp world is going sissy," he told *Family Circle* in 1935. "Even now I have to admit that during the past five years the love interest in stories has become an integral part of our formula. It's a terrible change. Nevertheless, the chief appeal of our magazines is still to he-men, who like their drama strong, fast, and straight from the shoulder; their heroes brawny and bold; and their heroines winsome, worried, and weak."

Such was the impact of *Ranch Romances* on the field.

There were holdouts, of course. *The Writer's Year Book* for 1934 reported, "Just forget all about the women in the world when you're writing the good atmospheric Western for Dell."

The most conservative house of all was the Thrilling Group, where editor Leo Margulies told writers that for his watered-down *Ranch Romances* knockoff, *Thrilling Ranch Stories,* he wanted "…straight cowboy stories, with a girl helping in the motivation, and no love scenes until the end. As far as the single plot is concerned, one might read a boy into the girl's role without changing the main action."

Popular Western was soon added to this string, which in-cluded *Thrilling Western.* Women were not welcome in the latter, but in the former, it was a different story. "The stories must have a definite plot," Margulies advised writers, "and by that I don't mean the cattle rustling and the old 'avenge-my-buddy' themes. The women interest is permissible—the author can give us a love story—but it must not be dragged in by the hair."

Like Terrill, Margulies found that he had to continually ride herd on his writers. Relentless formula submissions forced him to issue the following dictum virtually every year for over a decade: "Unless there is a some new slant the following is at present taboo: The man-hunt yarn in which a cowhand gets a letter to come and help an old friend, arriving in time to see the buzzards whirling and starts out after the murderer."

By dishing up fast-action yarns, the Thrilling Group of Western pulps carved out a comfortable niche of their own. But they lingered at the back of the herd, where it was safe.

Edmund Collier, associate editor of the upscale *West,* spoke for a new editorial generation when he said, "We feel on *West* that the Western epic in spirit and in detail, as it actually occurred, is more interesting to the largest potential audience than faked-up, purely melodramatic, over-fictionalized, over-actionized stuff."

One of the casualties of this period was an unnamed title announced by A.A. Wyn's Magazine Publishers that was to star a cowboy star in a monthly novel of his own. Lawrence A. Keating was hired to write it under the house name of Clint Douglas. John A. Saxon was originally tapped to tell the exploits of demi-owlhoot Kid Calvert, but as *Writer's Review* reported, "He said he would write as Saxon or not at all."

Wyn dumped Kid Calvert into the first issue of *Western Aces,* but soon abandoned him in favor of L.L. Foreman's distinctly off-trail Preacher Devlin, who went on to a phenomenally long career. Yet the Western pulp magazine built around a solitary lead hero was an idea whose time was coming.

By 1936, a year in which the Depression seemed to be lifting, pulp magazine publishers again unwisely expanded. An unprecedented 37 Western periodicals of different types crowded the newsstands. A year later, the number had leapt to 42.

Terrill himself contributed to the boom when he launched two titles, *Pioneer Western,* devoted to the 1820-1850 era, and *.44 Western,* which covered 1868-1892, the period between the opening of the Texas cattle trail and the Johnson County cow wars. The novelty of *Pioneer Western* was lost on readers. It expired after three issues, while the more mainstream *.44 Western* flourished for two decades.

Reader unrest continued to simmer. "The novelty of the cowboy's or the gunman's routine exploits has worn thin," explained Robert E. Mahaffay. "The demand—and it must be from the public or the magazines wouldn't sell—is for stories of real men and women who experience the emotional upheavals common to all of us."

Early in 1936, August Lenniger observed, "Perhaps the most significant trend which popular fiction as a whole seems to have taken within the last year, is a much heavier emphasis on characterization and real human-interest emotional values. We find this particularly manifesting itself in the 'pulp' Western, Western romance and detective fields. Action and plot are no longer enough for most of them; they want 'real stories that get under the reader's skin,' as one editor puts it.... The merchant of 'blood and thunder' is doing less business. But while this holds true in general, there are notable exceptions."

Over at the Munsey corral, a reformed Jack Byrne took over over the faltering *Argosy* that Spring. "I agree with you about the regular Western fiction which fills so many of our magazines," he confided to one writer. "These yarns are as a whole pretty dull stuff, it seems to me. I like to think of our *Argosy* Westerns now as historical yarns. I believe too that the majority of adult readers in the field are also chiefly interested in historical aspects. Wherefore we can kill two birds by giving them the real thing as far as background goes and still develop the colorful fiction story in the bargain."

In the more progressive pulps, fences kept falling. "The scope, in time, of the Western story extends from the days of the Spanish explorers to the present—or conceivably the future," noted *West's* Edmund Collier. "Geographically it includes everything from Mexico to the North Pole, from the Alleghenies to the Pacific Coast. While most Western stories take place somewhere between northern Mexico and Alaska, the boundaries have more to do with types of occupation than with space. If a story were sufficiently outstanding, an editor of a Western magazine might even go so far as to admit South American gauchos, Arkansas mountaineers, Minnesota lumberjacks, or Kentucky pioneers of the Daniel Boone type.

"While the cowboy and his work and the problems of the cattle industry form the backbone of all straight-Western magazines," Collier continued, "stories of the Texas Rangers, the Canadian Mounted Police, the golden days of Nevada, California, Dakota, and Alaska, both the Southern and Northern oil booms, the salmon fisheries, the United States Forest Service, trapping, trading, Indian fighting, buffalo hunting, the building of the railroads, the lusty life of the lumber and construction camps, and other subjects too numerous to mention go to give the Western story its endless variety and glamour."

Even hidebound old Rocking Death was forced to rethink *Western Story Magazine,* according to John A. Saxon:

"Editor Blackwell of Street and Smith was one of the first to ask: 'Why must the hero always be a cowboy?'

"He got an answer to that from H. Bedford-Jones who began sending him the 'Medicine Dan' stories which ran for a long time.

"'Medicine Dan' was a wandering, self-constituted protector of the rights of the oppressed, with an eye always cocked toward his own gain so long as it came from the undoing of a villain. He would come into town with his 'medicine wagon' from which he peddled all sorts of nostrums for man and beast. Before long he managed to get embroiled in some sort of local fracas, straighten everything out, punish the guilty and be gone before sun-up, to appear again in the following month's issue."

Saxon's memory fails him slightly. The character he remembers as Medicine Dan was actually called Pawnee Joe. He first appeared in 1934. After only two years, his creator was thoroughly sick of him.

"I remember when 'BJ' decided to kill [Joe] off," Saxon wrote. "I was living on the opposite side of the Indian reservation from Jones, up at Palm Springs.... One day he told me that he had written Street and Smith there would be no more [Pawnee Joe] stories; that he was tired of doing them.

"Editor Blackwell wrote: 'Hell, BJ, you can't do this to me.

[Joe] is a fixture. He will go on forever.'

"Jones, in his laconic way advised Blackwell: 'Not under my name he will not. I'm weary of these fakeroo Westerns about things that never happened and never *could* happen.'"

H. Bedford-Jones described the desperation the field had reached during that critical juncture in "Something Different!" (*Writer's Digest*, August 1936.) Jones was in the editorial office of what he called "a magazine of alleged Westerns" when the unnamed editor launched into a frantic request.

"I want something different," he stated. "And that's not baloney. You can write the bunk, sure; I want the real quill. You say nothing different can be written in Westerns? It's got to be. Listen! I keep smelling salts on my desk so I don't pass out when I read my own proofs. That's how things are. Same way in the whole field."

Jones asked the editor (who could only be *Western Story's* perpetually-harried Frank Blackwell) exactly what was wanted. The reply was feverish:

"Something that will smash. A serial. Put any damned thing in it you want, but make it smash. None of this six-gun blah. No guns blazing from the saddle of a galloping horse. Make it gallop just the same. None of the old words and sentences, get it? New all around."

"And then you'll be scared to use it because it isn't the same old rot," Jones shot back.

Sure enough, when Jones outlined a modern Western set in a lost Aztec city, the editor complained, "It creaks like my chair."

Jones shot back: "Sure; oil it. Your readers have supposedly never known that people have reproductive organs or desires to use 'em, or that situations are compromising, or that there is anything to love and courtship and marriage except chaste kisses. There's a trend in all the pulps to reality. Not to dirt, mind you. Some of 'em will run to that, sure, being already filled with the rottenest writing extant. Reality, sophistication, actual life; that's the oil for creaking joints. It can be kept clean, too.

It must be kept clean, but it can hold the thrill it holds in real life."

"Maybe. You've got to show me," he said. "What next?"

"Just what you said yesterday; words. Old stuff deliberately done new style. Character stuff; not the old pulp formula type characters, *but real character conflict* and impulse and motivation, as in real life."

"That isn't what my readers expect," the editor grumbled.

"Right," snapped Jones. "Give 'em what they don't expect, for a change. Your rag is going downhill because you give 'em what they expect; it's the old system of pulp editors. Do you take a chance or do you eat crow?"

"Go ahead and show me," he said with resignation, but no hope.

As Jones had predicted, that editor balked at the finished product. Jones put *The Hour of the Eclipse* in his trunk, years later finding a home for it in *Short Stories*. Having failed to start a new cycle in Westerns, he simply abandoned the tired genre.

As Saxon recalled, "'B.J.' told me at the time he would never write another Western." And he never did.

But Bedford-Jones' notion was in the wind. Late in 1936, August Lenniger commented, "You'll find quite a few stories in the better class, mature-appeal Western magazines these days which feature situations that would have been 'taboo' several years ago. We sold one swell Western yarn recently wherein the author tactfully but definitely made clear that both the heroine and the hero had been anything but pure and virtuous in their past. And stories wherein the hero rides with a sad heart into the sunset, having renounced the girl to the man she loves, even though the reader knows she should have chosen the hero, are not uncommon."

The ultimate stretching of the Western pulp formula came as a result of Trojan Publications' attempt to replicate the stunning success of their *Spicy Detective Stories* and companion titles, all of which were curious hybrids of straight genre fiction mated with hot girlie-magazine "spice."

"Sex, in these palpitant pulps," remarked contributor Allan R. Bosworth, "was limited to the verbal fondling of the feminine bosom, and it had to be done every second paragraph or the story would not sell. Every story became a game, a contest between writer and editor, a search for a simile, a ludicrous striving for action, such as the jolting of a buckboard across the rough prairie, or Laura Belle's horse in a trot."

Spicy Western Stories debuted in December 1936. *Writer's Digest* marked its arrival with a equal parts market notice and vague horror:

"The cover of Volume 1, Number 1, of *Spicy Western Stories,* shows a mostly nude blonde young woman roped to a madly dashing horse while the villain pursues with a horse whip (intended for the girl, not the horse). The magazine contains 10 stories, all of same caliber as the cover indicates. Best other example is the girl getting branded by the villain, instead of the bad man or the steer." […] "The stories are all frankly sexed up. If the new *Spicy* sells, the contamination will spread into the hitherto untouched Western field."

Spicy Western Stories did sell well, but its peculiar "Horse-and-Hotcha" slant remained unique to itself. Its contributors were mainly *Spicy* pulp hacks not otherwise known in the Western field. Exceptions included John A. Saxon, who employed the transparent pseudonyms King Saxon and Rex Norman to protect his reputation, Texan Edwin Truett "Bud" Long, disguised under multiple aliases, and T.W. Ford. Its star writer, E. Hoffmann Price, frankly denigrated pulp Western stories as "pure crap and gunfire of the most stupid sort" riddled with "the weird jargon of nowhere on earth, which was invented by Manhattan Cowboys." Ironically, Price later became a significant serious Westerneer during *Western Story Magazine's* twilight years.

In his 1936 article, "Western Pulps," *West's* Associate Editor Edmund Collier took stock of the ever-changing field.

"Now there have been four separate tendencies in the last four years," he observed in *The Writer*. "Western love has increased. Serials have almost disappeared. Reprint magazines have multiplied, and the melodramatic action stuff that flooded the field from 1921 to 1929 has had a revival."

Of these, Collier found that latter development the most baffling. "…I thought that the day of melodrama was past," he admitted, "and that there would be more insistence on story value, character, atmosphere, and emotional effects based more broadly than on pure action. While these things have been in demand by certain editors, the return to the production of the gun-fighting story with incessant violent action and 'a murder on every page' has been much more marked, and we must sadly add, with considerable financial profit to the producers thereof."

Later that same year, August Lenniger divided the Western magazine field into five distinct categories: The Fast Action Western; The Masculine Character Conflict Western; The Masculine Action Romance Western; The Western Love Story; and The Realistic Emotional Masculine Western, to which *Dime Western* and its imitators belonged. Lenniger outlined what he perceived as the essential approach writers needed to take with the fast action category:

"These magazines cater to a large proportion of adolescent readers and also to the older Western fan who demands fast, dramatic action without too much sentiment. Usually a youthful hero is faced with a situation where danger and death lurk at every turn; he knows that to accomplish his purpose there isn't a chance in a hundred that he'll come out alive, but never for an instant does he hesitate. His reckless courage, his native intelligence, his 'do or die' spirit enable him to win against overwhelming odds. We may find him as a deputy sheriff single-handedly mopping up an outlaw stronghold; as a stagecoach guard preventing the theft of the gold; in the role of the small rancher fighting the encroachment of the big unscrupulous cattle combine; as the cowpoke on the vengeance trail who realizes that the murderer of his 'buddy' will undoubtedly beat him to the draw; as the U.S. Marshal or Cattle Association 'detective' in double jeopardy from the local law and the rustlers because he can't reveal his identity; or even in the guise of the prisoner who has been 'framed' and must escape to bring the real criminals to justice."

In others words, Lenniger is describing the regulation Western circa 1926. The gun-dummy was out of his coffin, and the public was snapping up blazing tales of fast-draw wonder workers as never before. The success of the series character, whether Max Brand's Montana Kid or *Wild West Weekly's* Flash Moran, compelled publishers to try building entire magazines around the exploits of a single cow-hero every month.

Street & Smith initiated this sub-genre when they launched *Pete Rice Magazine* late in 1933. Written by Ben Conlon under the house name Austin Gridley, the Pete Rice novels failed to hold readers, perhaps because they were set in the modern West, with motorcycles side-by-side with the mustangs. Pistol Pete Rice was a quasi-Victorian lawman who never smoked, drank or swore and, despite being the Sheriff of Buzzard Gap, Arizona, still lived with his mother. After his magazine was cancelled in 1936, Pete was exiled to *Wild West Weekly*.

Teck Publications tried to steal some of *Wild West Weekly's* thunder with Larry A. Keating's special ranger, Flash Steele, in a series of novelettes for *Wild West Stories and Complete Novels Magazine*. Ranger Publications offered up *The Masked Rider Western*. It struggled for years, but its similarity to radio's Lone Ranger along with the magazine's purchase by the Thrilling Group gave it a new lease on life. Popular experimented with misunderstood heroes who rode the owlhoot trail in *Mavericks* and *The Western Raider* with no success. Tom Mount ghosted both series under different names. Few of these gun-dummy heroes endured long.

It was Leo Margulies who struck gold when he asked writer Alexander Leslie Scott to create a series character, Jim Hatfield. Scott had been a specialist in railroad yarns when the Depression forced him to rethink his trade. Margulies suggested that the floundering pulpster specialize in frontier fiction, and another foundering career was saved.

Scott was soon backed up by Tom Curry, who reported the identical inspiration: "Leo Margulies has the wonderful faculty of putting life into those with whom he comes in contact," Curry wrote in 1945. "His enthusiasm is boundless, and it is contagious. He encouraged me to write straight Westerns, and I grew extremely interested in this kind of story, especially historical fiction of the Golden Era of our frontier, the period from the Civil War to 1880."

Launched in 1936 to commemorate the centennial of their founding, *Texas Rangers* ran over 20 years, with Scott and Curry alternating under the house name of Jackson Cole. Perhaps success was as simple as offering an historically valid Western hero.

"The general theme must be that the hero, being young, handsome, strong, personable and endowed with great moral courage and character, as well as being an expert shot, fist-fighter, cowpuncher and rider, must, in willingly facing the most hazardous missions, track down, confront and defeat the villain in violent physical combat," explained Curry. "And, like all romantic adventures stories, these yarns musty have a happy ending, as far as the hero is concerned, that is."

Many writers avoided these books, seeing them as throwbacks to the extinct dime novel, or at best commercial repackagings of the old super-cowboy/gun-dummy hero. But the readers made no such distinctions.

Ned Collier closed out his survey of the field with a look to the far future. "Westerns come and Westerns go, but it is our prediction that if any now on the stands will be there twenty years from now, they will be those which follow a policy different from any that heretofore has been pursued consistently by any straight Western. They will be those which study the great epic growth of the West and express its reality. And this reality is much more exciting and dramatic than anything ever created in the mind of a professional fictioneer."

But to have a future in 1956, the Western pulp periodical had to survive the Great Depression—which was far from over. Quiet consolidation continued to narrow the field that year. Doubleday promoted Harry Maule to vice president of Doubleday, which relinquished *West* and *Short Stories*. *West* bounced to shoestring Ranger Publications, then became a Margulies magazine. Ned Collier followed it to both outfits. Popular Publications ransomed Clayton's *Ace-High Western* from the temporary custody of Dell, and absorbed *New Western* and *Big-Book Western*. Street & Smith folded *Western Winners* after a brief spell. Finally, Fawcett published its last *Triple-X Western* annual. The old-line houses were slipping out of Dodge.

After an optimistic period in which the Depression showed clear signs of easing, the stock market imploded once more. More severe than the '29 crash, the Wall Street collapse of October 1937 kicked off what came to be called the Roosevelt Recession.

Pulp publishers didn't wait for the inevitable sales downturn. They cancelled borderline magazines while the ink was still drying on newspaper scareheads. Recession soon set in, turning the brief boom into a bust, clearing the field of the weaker titles, and forcing others to drop frequency. Publishers circled their wagons. John Burr—formerly with Clayton and Dell—replaced Dorothy Hubbard as associate editor of *Western Story Magazine*. Her superior, Frank Blackwell, was kicked upstairs, and ultimately out to pasture. The survivors limped on uncertainly. The gun-dummy still ran wild and free. The pulp Western yarn seemed beyond rehabilitation.

This was the condition of the range into which rode newspaperman Fred Glidden, soon to be rechristened Luke Short. He was not much impressed by what he surveyed: "…newly married and lacking any kind of a job, let alone the newspaper job I wanted, I decided to write for the Western pulp magazines. Their contents seemed simple-minded to the point of idiocy; their stories appeared easy to write if you could complete a sentence. I studied them with a secret contempt since I'd graduated from Zane Grey at the age of twelve. Then I hacked out Western pulp stories that sold."

Glidden neglected to mention that his earliest works were a short stack of adventure tales set in the Far North. When these timber Westerns failed to sell, Glidden's agent suggested he rework them into straight Westerns. Every revised reject was snapped up by copy-hungry editors.

Another new arrival's early struggles were emblematic of this latest turning point. Tom W. Blackburn got started the way many Westerneers had—ghostwriting stories for a one-man fiction factory named Ed Earl Repp. Tiring of the relentless grind of plotting and typing, Repp began hiring greenhorn writers to churn out first-draft Western fiction. After a fast polish, they would duly appear in print under Repp's byline. Repp also kept the foreman's share of the loot.

In 1937, Blackburn, who was born on a New Mexico ranch, was learning his craft via this apprentice route. Soon, he decided to break away on his own. Blackburn showed his first solo effort to Harry Olmsted, who asked a blunt question: "Tom, do you like writing about cowboys?"

Blackburn sheepishly admitted he did not.

"Then don't do it!" Olmsted barked.

"But—the Western field is all I've studied."

"Never write about anything you don't like to write about," Olmsted lectured. "Writing is an honest business. You have to believe in your yarns. You can't make them real any other way. Look at the West. There were more than cowboys in it. See if that doesn't help you."

Offering to write a letter of recommendation to Rogers Terrill once Blackburn produced a story he had faith in, Olmsted left the dejected writer to his thoughts.

Blackburn's wife asked him, "Now that Mr. Olmsted was here, what are you going to do?"

Blackburn shrugged. "Write another novelet."

"About what—?"

"Well, there's an old boy has a ranch and a daughter. The villain has a neighboring ranch and he wants the girl and the old boy's place. The old boy's foreman gets killed by assassins unknown and he hires a drifter—"

"Who is the hero," Juanita Blackburn interrupted. "A slab-muscled son of the Texas salt-grass. A face like a saint and a draw like a diamondback. He hates women but the girl witches him and he falls in love like a land-slide coming down the side of Pike's Peak. With no other profit in sight than forty dollars a month and maybe a kiss on the last page, he single-handedly wipes out a vast land combine operated by the villain and saves the girl, the ranch and her father!"

"That sounds kind of familiar," Blackburn admitted.

"You've been writing it for ten solid months! Ed's name sold the ones you wrote for him—and the first ones were good, anyway. But they're getting monotonous, now. Maybe Mr. Olmsted's letter would sell one more. I don't know. But he told you to get a story you believed in—then he'd write the letter."

"It's no use!" Blackburn moaned. "I'm no Western story writer. What the hell do I know about cowboys?"

"What do you know about, then? You've talked about writing ever since I've known you. What kind of writing?"

"Historical adventure stories!" Blackburn shot back. "History is something that happened in the past, isn't it?"

Juanita pointed out. "Isn't the West history now?"

Blackburn later recalled reflecting on this simple but neglected truism:

"Western stories currently on the stands—and I had read a lot of them—had never appealed to me as documents. Yet, in the light of my wife's comments, I saw that they could be. Their purpose was to conjure up for a new generation a past era. This realization immediately opened up a new vista for me. What I had told Juanita was true. I had always been an avaricious student of history. It was no effort to swing the enthusiasm of this study to the Western field. Sitting in the shop that night, I realized I already possessed considerable historical knowledge of the West which I had not attempted to use in my yarns."

Fired up by this realization, Tom Blackburn sat down to write a tale based on a factual account set in Wyoming's Green River Valley, "When the Killers Crossed Green River." Rogers Terrill took it for *.44 Western.*

Thus, one of the most important pulp Western writing careers began in earnest. Terrill bought seventeen Tom W. Blackburn Western yarns in the months that followed. The year was 1938. Something new was blowing in the Western wind, and Blackburn was the first writer to sniff it. For a little while, he was the only one.

Out in the real world of the 20th Century other, more bitter, forces began gusting. Sales dropped off alarmingly all through calendar 1938. The so-called Roosevelt Recession was deepening. Nervous pulp magazine publishers began cutting back even further that summer.

Writer's Digest columnist Harriet Bradfield reported, "There used to be a 'summer depression' about this time of year, when nobody expected to sell much and editors used the manuscripts for fans. This year it started earlier, and got a head start before anyone realized it."

One agent told *The Author & Journalist,* "Many publishers are waiting to see what happens in July and August before deciding which way to move on projected magazines.... I have never seen the market so mixed up before. This is because editors anticipate changes in policy and formula by September and are buying little in advance. Everything now is on deadline."

In July, Owen Wister passed away. The impact of his death— if any—was no doubt purely psychological. Wister's romantic interpretation of the cowboy had ridden unchallenged for 36 years, but now it was tired.

That year, a greenhorn editor named Robert O. Erisman took over Martin Goodman's chain of nine Western pulps. He proclaimed that he wanted pulp Westerns with "literary quality," but also confessed, "'Literary quality' refers only to the writing, not to the plotting."

Attempting to describe his editorial needs, Erisman echoed Rogers Terrill circa 1935—as if to suggest that there existed but one type of Western story: "Characterization must be emphasized, and endings can be tragic if some big cause, or some fine person, benefits; and the guy who has the tragic end should be an outlaw who reforms in the climax. Otherwise standard Western action plots; best to have a hero with his own problem to solve which, particularly in the longer lengths, he takes care of simultaneously with the bigger range war he gets mixed into."

Soon his stable of Westerns would shrink—as did most others. Dell dropped both *All Western* and *Western Romances* in the Fall. Both would eventually return, but as anemic bimonthlies.

Anxious to hold his readers, Street & Smith's Jack Burr lured Walt Coburn over to his outfit with the promise of five and a quarter cents a word. Burr rustled L.L. Foreman and his long-running Preacher Devlin series from *Western Aces*. T.T. Flynn was hired away from *Dime Western*. Even Frederick Faust was induced to pen a fresh Western. A new panic was on.

Interviewed at this time, Coburn was asked if he noticed any change in the Western formula. "I don't know of any change," he replied. "I get letters from my editors wanting this or that type of story. But it's usually put something like this: 'Remember, Walt, that border yarn you wrote about such and such a character? How about another yarn along that line?' Because I don't ever read my own or any other Western writer's stuff I can't recall the yarn he mentioned and I'm not looking it up in my files. But he wants a yarn about the Mexican border. I give him one. The editors are mighty tolerant about riding me with a hackamore instead of a spade bit. And it works out better all around. No new treatment. No new slant."

This studied unwillingness to push the frontiers farther out was endemic to the field.

It led to disaster.

Walker A. Tompkins picks up the tale:

"Then—in 1939—the public gagged. Plots are few in number in any field of writing, Lord knows. When a market is as wide open and insatiable as the Western field has always been, these plots finally began to whip into a vicious circle of repetition. The same old yarns began to mill around through editorial sanctums like the familiar rotation of faces in a column of men marching past the camera of a small-budget movie outfit filming a mob scene for a quickie.

"The pulp Western market started experiencing digestive pains as early as 1935. Finally, to quote a letter which came to my desk from a Western story publisher last year: 'The cowboy market is suffering from a plethora of that genus of fiction known as "just another Western." From now on, they're out.'"

The editor who issued that decree was *Western Story's* John Burr, but the cutting phrase had been in common use since the previous cow-fiction crash.

"Stories that in 1938 or 1928 would have assured a check," Tompkins continued, "began making round trips. 'What's wrong?' went up the chorus of anguished authorial voices. 'My plots are as good as ever. My scenes are the tried-and-true Western locale that have gone over big for years. My characters are as colorful as ever—'

"'Yeah!' came back the editerrible echo. "'Just as colorful as ever! But that's the trouble, scribes. Our Western mags are slumping. We've got to cooperate with each other and find out why this toboggan slide is gaining momentum. We know the American public is clamoring for Westerns. We've got to isolate the germ that is destroying our market.'

"Editors, authors and public *did* isolate the germ. 'Just another Western' summed up the whole disease. Plots were trite. Characters were stereotyped. Locales were going sterile."

Robert Erisman was forced to rethink his stable of nearly

30 Western magazines, which were divided into adult and juvenile types. Outlawing the juvenile yarn, he told his writers, "No ancient gun-shooting super-action stories."

Luckily, Erisman discovered a new writer in the slush pile, Oregonian Victor H. White. After taming White's overwild style via Pony Express, Erisman began publishing this exciting new discovery under bylines such as Ralph Berard, Ken Jason and Vincent A. Twice when he had more than one story in an issue. White went on to pen some three million words of pulp—never once signing his actual name to his product—allowing Erisman's magazines to stagger on.

Before long, *Thrilling Ranch Stories* became a *Ranch Romances*-style love title. It was that, or die.

Other, more distant smoke signals were also presaging change.

Norman A. Fox was just getting a toehold in the field. A protégé of Arch Joscelyn, Fox sold his first Western to F. Orlin Tremaine's *Cowboy Stories* in 1934. Reluctantly heeding Joscelyn's advice to specialize in the West, Fox started selling regularly to Rogers Terrill. *Western Story* soon added him to its stable. Fired from a solid bookkeeping job, he elected to freelance. By the Summer of 1938, Fox was easily exceeding his old income.

"Happy days!" he recalled. "But the fly in the ointment, a heel named Hitler, tramped into Poland, and John Bull gave up reading about gunfights to try the real McCoy. Up went the price of paper. Down came English sales. Western magazines that had been coming out every month started appearing bimonthly or vanished. The Winter of '39-'40 was mighty poor pickings after the way the cartwheels rolled the summer before."

The new retrenchment was so severe that in 1939, Street & Smith replaced long-time *Wild West Weekly* editor Ronald Oliphant with his former assistant, Francis L. Stebbins. A six-month circulation slide was the reason given.

A year later, "Steb" Stebbins was in turn thrown over in favor of *Western Story*'s John Burr, who in swift order proceeded to clean up that corner of the Pulp West by de-emphasizing the series buckaroos in favor of quality lead novels and serials. The most popular of the juvenile Western magazines was forced to mature.

"Well, these are evil days for pulp writers and editors, both," Stebbins confided to star contributor Paul S. Powers before his departure for the downriver Thrilling spread.

"What worried me," admitted Powers, "was my suspicion that the new editors were trying to turn *Wild West Weekly* into something like the run-of-the-mill Westerns that were crowding all the news stands. I hoped that the magazine would be kept 'wild' and that I wouldn't have to send my characters around on motorcycles."

The gun-dummy was again off on the dodge.

"*1940… One year before Pearl Harbor. The days when, to sell a Western story, the main character had to be a watch-maker, house-painter, or anything but a cowpuncher. 1940, when a Western magazine editor would not buy a story starring a cowboy.*"

—Lee Floren

9

NO COWBOYS NEED APPLY

"IN THE Fall of last year," reported star *Wild West Weekly* writer Walker A. Tompkins in "'Just Another Western—'" (*Writer's Digest,* April 1940) "Western markets began to take on new vitality. Readers commenced mailing in fan letters instead of pan letters. Without fanfare, a new trend in Western stories was ushered in; another cycle, a different vogue.

"Old, experienced pen-pushers hopped on the band-wagon with alacrity. *Tyros, not reading the writing on the wall, continued to garner rejection slips for the work they had patterned after the Old Masters during that apprenticeship.*

"The secret? The panacea? It was a golden nugget that had long been gleaming, neglected and tarnished from disuse, in the barren soil of Western fiction material. And here, sans cellophane, was the answer:

"Historical fiction! Western yarns based on fact.

"The movie industry was the first to catch the popular fancy. In rapid succession during 1939, audiences saw such factual films as *Dodge City, Stagecoach, Wells-Fargo, Union Pacific, Frontier Marshal* and *Geronimo.*

"The movie industry suddenly came alive to the fact that our own American back yard is teeming with episodes which make the old-run cowboy plots anemic by comparison. The annals of our American frontier are jammed with characters who really lived, breathed, fought, loved, and died."

The trend's origins can be traced back to Paramount's 1936

celebration of the Texas Rangers centennial, *Texas Rangers*. Cecil B. De Mille's *The Plainsman* soon followed, and what one contemporary film critic called "the old, hard-boot Western" was back on the screen.

"Today studio interest in rangeland stuff is concerned with 'epics,'" explained MIT dropout and self-professed "Manufacturer of blood and thunder," Nelson C. Nye, "stories whose production costs will run around a million dollars. While horse operas are still being spawned by the smaller companies, such 'quickies' are vile anathema to producers who are backing their approval with cold hard cash in figures that amount to something. These men are looking for stories with important or historical backgrounds."

Once more, Hollywood had redeemed the genre—and the pulp editors hastily joined in the new stampede. It was that, or be trampled flat.

Tompkins went on: "A prominent New York agent, whose business it is to keep his stethoscope on the chest of the public fancy, told me over the phone only yesterday:

"'March and April will find editors crying for historical novels. I get calls for yarns dealing with the old Oregon Trail; for the Pony Express epoch. Here on my desk now are urgent orders for novelettes dealing with the Virginia City gold rush in Montana, a field which authors seem to overlook despite the fact that it is more fertile than the El Dorado phase in California. Here is an order for a serial featuring Custer's last fight on the Little Big Horn. The more unorthodox the period, the better the public likes it.'"

The agent in question was August Lenniger.

"Regarding characterization," continued Tompkins, "the above-mentioned agent was particularly eloquent:

"'Do authors think that the old West was populated solely by cowboys, rustlers and gamblers? Why don't they try writing a story in which not one of those stereotyped hombres appears? I just got a story laid in a woman's dress shop in a cowtown, and it's a dilly!'

"That doesn't mean the market is taking a trend toward the puerile or wants gigolos or sissies," Tompkins asserted. "The old West was peopled by all types, and they clamor for attention. Remember when the Clanton dynasty was shattered by the guns of Wyatt Earp? Of all things, a *milliner's* shop figured in that brawl, as much as did the O.K. Corral!"

The Western revival inspired Street & Smith to throw the dice on its first new Western pulp in years. In the Fall of 1940, S&S tentatively offered *Western Adventures,* with John Burr in the editorial saddle. Its slant fell midway between *Western Story* and the juvenile *Wild West Weekly.*

Echoing editors who came before him, Burr complained to *Writer's Digest,* "The majority of stories submitted seem to fall into the 'sheriff and outlaw' class. It had always struck me as singular that more writers don't take advantage of the fact that there are a legion of other characters who belong in the Western picture and who might make appealing central figures for their yarns."

Even bottom-of-the-barrel *Double Action Western Stories* refused the discredited puncher. "Avoid the old 'two shots rang out' and 'the batwings flew back' mahoofsky," warned outgoing Columbia editor Abner J. Sundell.

Fiction House's *Frontier Stories* alone was ahead of the herd. Having long before reverted to chronicling covered wagon days, its editors boasted, "We use little or no straight cowboy stuff."

Now everyone was climbing aboard the Conestoga wagon. After the fall of France, pulp sales plummeted for anxious months as Americans were transfixed by war news emanating from Europe. Smaller houses folded borderline titles. Dell again suspended *All Western Magazine* for the whole of 1940, but revived it the following year. Owing to a lack of consistent editorial vision, the magazine never had much impact on the field once Carson Mowre moved on to greener pastures.

Over at Popular Publications, Rogers Terrill carefully began fine-tooling *Dime Western, Star Western* and the others under his charge. "We are making a sincere attempt to give the reader a wider cross-section of the West," he wrote. "A representative issue would include, perhaps, a railroad-building story, a cattle-trail story, a gambler story, a humorous story, a short animal story, a story of the early Missouri River boats, a mining story, and a lumbering story."

But Terrill also admitted that he couldn't walk away from basics, either. "We will still use straight cowboy, range-war fiction," he added, "and even stories of town tamers and gun marshals, providing they are well done. The last three types have, it is true, been terribly overdone during the last few years, but since we realize that taboos in general are dangerous and since there are many fine stories of this type still to be written, we'll not bar any single story type from our pages."

This marked the close of the original cowboy cycle, as Owen Wister begat it. The reason was simple, according to Norman A. Fox. "Peruse most Western pulps of fifteen years ago," he wrote, "and you have the impression that the population of the early West consisted entirely of cowboys, sheriffs and outlaws with a sprinkling of gamblers, prospectors, bartenders and starry-eyed gals who were always the motherless daughters of gray-haired ranch owners. Possibly the juvenile readers are still contented with the stock characters but the more astute readers have certainly grown heartily sick of them."

Switching over from cow-hero to folk hero was not easy for those who had fallen into the easy cowboy groove. To them, Fox offered some sage advice:

"To write about various occupations presents problems, of course," he wrote. "If you have learned the way of the genus cowboy, either through actual experience or by research, you can pour your lore into yarns and more yarns with nary a stop except to brew new plots or to clean your typewriter keys. But when you turn to stories involving lawyers, telegraphers, or postmasters, you have to find out how these gentlemen went about earning their daily bread. And you've got to have them show the tricks of their trade in your scripts.

"For instance," Fox pointed out, "you can't get a new kind of Western story by blandly calling your character a lawyer, dropping him in a ranch or a cowtown and proceeding to have him act just as an old stand-by character, the cowboy, for instance, would act. If he's a lawyer, let him get involved in a situation where his Blackstone proves mightier than bullets. You can still burn plenty of powder and bring in the scent of the sage and the rataplan of hoofs. And you'll have a rip-snortin' Western that hasn't been worn thin around the edges."

A strict new code dominated the Pulp West. By 1940, it was a severely altered landscape, as Walker Tompkins frankly admitted in "'Just Another Western—'" "For the past nine years I had been writing five book-length novels annually. It is doubtful if half of them would make the grade under the rigid 1940 market."

Before his abrupt departure from *Wild West Weekly,* Steb Stebbins asked the perennially popular purveyor of cowpokes Paul S. Powers to change mounts. "I want a real, honest-to-Gawd Texas Ranger of the frontier type. Hard-boiled, yet straight-shooting, and honest…The great 'I Ams' upstairs figure that Rangers are always popular and we ought to feature them as much as possible."

After trading one entrenched cliché for another failed to work, John Burr then asked Powers to clean out his stable of *all* clichés. "These days are vastly different from even a few years ago," he lectured. "The story that got by for younger readers just doesn't click today. I've had specific examples—from a nine and a twelve year old pair of buttons—and what they had to say about thin, no-plot stories written, as they expressed it, 'for just babies' certainly had point. They were country lads, too, but the stories in *WWW* just failed to interest them.

"Yes, Kid Wolf and Sonny Tabor are still popular," Burr continued, "but may I venture to say that they would be *even more so* if you could snap up your style and get rid of the old-fashioned clichés, phrases, etc., which were in vogue in the past. I think the writing which clicks today is the direct, crisp kind of writing. Writing with a 'bite' to it."

Never dreaming anti-cowboy fever was running rampant in editorial offices, greenhorn writers straightaway began getting tangled up in unexpected barbed wire.

Lee Floren discovered this the hard way. "When I was an undergraduate student I used to eye somewhat enviously the red and yellow covered Western magazines that cluttered up the corner newsstand. I even wrote a few Westerns. *I* liked them. So did my friends. But the editors decidedly did not."

Friendly rebuffs caused Floren to ask himself a simple question: What is a Western story?

"Of course, I had read many Western stories," he admitted. "Piles of magazines. But suddenly I realized I had *read* them, not *studied* them. Then and there I decided to read with a critical eye upon story-structure and forsake, temporarily, the study of methods of presentation of subject-matter. I even forgot I had first seen daylight on Montana's Milk River, that I knew a spade-bit from a snaffle bit, that I thought a double-rigged saddle better for roping than a center-fire kak. I concentrated on formula…."

The formula Floren laboriously extracted from piles of pulp like ore mined from hard rock was one that Walker Tompkins or any of dozens of more seasoned pulpsters could have told him in 25 concise words: "A *likable* Western hero attempts to attain a *worth-while objective,* or *goal,* in spite of apparently *insurmountable resistance.* But he overcomes this opposition by *plausible* and *convincing* means and finally attains his objective."

Unwittingly, Floren chose to test his new knowledge on a species of cliché that was already being cast aside as hopelessly overdone—the aging lawman yarn. "Using my newly-found formula," he recalled, "I wrote 5,000 words centered about an old sheriff who, for twenty years, had been the law in a tough trail town. Now, his opposition—the lawless element—

proclaimed him too old for his badge. The oldster would gladly have relinquished his badge to a worthy successor, but not to the candidate put forth by the lawless element: a candidate that would be pulled like a puppet, by strings of greed. And the oldster would not allow his town to dance such a death jig.

"But the town council, intimidated by the power of the lawless ilk, ousted the oldster and appointed the candidate in his stead.

"Did our hero get mad? Sure? Who wouldn't? Did he pull out? Not he! His town was in danger. He had an objective in life—that was to keep peace in his town, badge or no badge. And he did maintain peace, without a badge; though he had to squint through powdersmoke to do so."

This theme was so lame Leo Margulies had banned it years before. The odds were against Floren, but he didn't suspect it. After sending the story off, he wrote another using the same plot while he awaited the verdict on the first.

"That spring day in 1939 the mailman slipped *the* envelope into my mailbox. He was a talkative, good-natured man and he said pleasantly, 'Good morning.' But I did not answer. My tongue was lead. My fingers were thumbs. But I finally tore open the letter. It was from Harry Widmer, then managing editor of the Ace Magazines.

"'Born to the Badge' is a good yarn. We are scheduling it in *Red Seal Western*. Let us see more.'"

"Lawman Born" was the published title. Right off, Floren had to move away from the classic fare he confidently expected to write. What he had been studying was not what editors were now buying.

"I was doing graduate work at Occidental College and I was hungry, my wife was hungry and the cat starved. That was in the depression year of 1940. Sitting before a scarred table in our $17-a-month 'apartment' I had to scheme a way to get a buck out of an editor. So I deliberately 'created' two characters.

"At that time, magazine editors would only buy stories

without 'cowboy' characters. You could write a yarn centered around a lumberyard man, a tombstone engraver *et al,* and as long as it had a Western background it was okay. But no story could star a cowboy. I had been reading the history of the famous—or infamous—Judge Roy Bean of Pecos, Texas. I decided to fashion a character somewhat like Bean, only to make him more fitted through intelligence and training for the job of county judge. Judge Bates was born.

"An ardent reader of Dickens, knowing that Dickens strengthened his characters by giving them tags, I gave Judge Lemanuel Bates a tag—a whiskey jug which he always carries with him. Incidentally, he never gets drunk, regardless of how much he drinks. A tag is good thing for a character—it's a peculiarity, some physical gesture or mental habit that is owned by the character....

"A story with two leading characters is always stronger than a story with one main character because the writer can bring about conflict between the two protagonists, thereby adding to the uncertainty and building suspense. So I gave the judge a partner by the name of Tobacco Jones. Jones' tag is chewing tobacco and harping on the judge about the judge's bad habit of always drinking whiskey. Tobacco Jones was, to a degree, fashioned physically after our postman—a long, lean and hungry-looking individual who read postcards unashamedly and always took an hour out to sit under a tree in the California sun and read the latest magazine."

Taking inspiration to its furthest extreme, Floren made Tobacco Jones a Western postmaster.

"After I deliberately created two characters," he continued, "I put them to work. Characters are only interesting when they are neck-deep in trouble resulting from their efforts to reach a concrete objective. What would Tobacco Jones and Judge Bates try to do?

"I remembered that when I was a boy in Spokane, Washington, the kingpin of the local bootleggers died, and the other bootleggers met to give their departed friend a 'good' funeral. One got so drunk he fell into the grave. After the burial, they continued their drinking joust and complimented each other on the fine way they had kicked their brother through the Golden Gate. Why couldn't Tobacco Jones and Judge Bates give some departed friend a fine funeral?

"The plot germ glowed, spat sparks, and became a burning fire. I warmed my hungry hands over it and came out with a plot. The pair would travel to another town to officiate at the sudden demise of a young friend named Frosty White. While in this town, they would learn that Frosty had been murdered. Then they would unwind the plot, forcing the killers to face justice."

Floren sent "A Coffin for Frosty White" to Rogers Terrill's *Big Book Western.* Terrill snapped it up. Almost against Floren's will, the one-shot duo demanded a sequel. Dozens followed— every one a sure-fire sale. Such was the new market.

"Today the Western story reader is tired of conventional characters," Floren explained in 1941. "If you are a beginner, you have a much better chance of selling if your main character is an 'off-trail' character. The Western scene was not inhabited by only cowboys and sheriffs; there were other men—veterinaries, doctors, lawyers, lumber-yard operators, and many, many other characters, each of whom faced his individual problems as he adjusted himself to his environment."

And so the pulp Western was once more redeemed.

"The Western," Rogers Terrill summarized in his "Evolution of the Western," "has a rich variety of time and place. There's no denying that. But variety of time and place, we've learned, is not quite enough. This is merely a surface difference, and doesn't presuppose the more vital story differences of theme, character, complication and approach. Western stories, today, may be based on grand historical movements or on poignant little incidents in the lives of unimportant people."

Floren noted, "The leading characters in the last ten Western stories I have sold are as follows: Three marshals, a professional gunman (that was a hard one to peddle!) a rancher, a judge, a lawyer, a cowboy, and a gambler. So, don't think you have to make your hero a 'waddy.' Why step up to bat with two strikes already against you?"

Even after issuing clear orders, Terrill complained, "There have been very few gambling stories lately, very few railroad building stories, practically no stories concerning the stretching of the telegraph wires, not many good gold mining stories, and I haven't seen a good early lumbering story in five years."

Clever pulpsters devised new ways to sneak the new type of hero into the regulation formula. W. Ryerson Johnson reinvented the banned and banished town tamer, thereby having it both ways. He called his *Star Western* gunslinger Len Siringo.

"It followed the general pattern of the lone-riding ranny who came into a fear-ridden gun-bossed town or ranch or mine, used his wits and guns to get rid of the bad guys and put the good guys back in the saddle," Johnson explained. "Len Siringo was unique in that he always entered the story in the guise of someone apparently innocent and harmless—a wandering printer... tailor... grave digger... rain maker... preacher... doctor... lightning-rod salesman... whatnot. In the first part of the story he fought with the tools of his apparent trade, always successful against the bad guys, but apparently blundering into that success. Somewhere along in the course of the story his exploits became so remarkable that somebody recognized him as the famous Len Siringo.... And from there on he fought with guns, and rallied the heretofore beaten and bedraggled people to assist him in a grand battle of extermination of all those range rats. Then Len rode on to his next assignment...."

There were casualties, too. Established range knights-errant were summarily outlawed.

"Several years ago," recalled Norman A. Fox, "I wrote a short-story, labeled it 'Trigger McKeever's Gun-Gospel,' and sold it to Rogers Terrill for *10 Story Western,* which he was then editing. Trigger McKeever was a sawed-off little outlaw with a knack for poking his nose into other people's affairs, and though he was only one jump ahead of a posse, he tarried by the wayside to help an unfortunate in need. This he continued to do, for, after that first McKeever yarn, others followed, and every one I wrote—eight in all—sold to Rogers Terrill. Then I dropped McKeever. Popular Publications' demand of those days was for the emotional type character yarn for their Westerns, and McKeever apparently fitted to a T. But the change came, the trend demanded greater realism and more sweep, and McKeever, as delineated, became obsolete and lost favor in my eyes."

Fox instead created a fresh protagonist for John Burr's *Western Story Magazine.* Doc Comanche was a traveling pitchman in the vein of H. Bedford-Jones' long-retired Pawnee Joe. The more the mythic Pulp West changed, the more familiarly it shimmered.

Lest any writer think that editors no longer desired the comfortable recycling of familiar plots, Rogers Terrill set them straight. "We must, I think, comb the field of Western history to get fresh character types. We must try our best to make them real and human and colorful. But the stories must be different in more than even these elements! The same general plot outline and character types, for instance, may be developed by a skillful author into an heroic story, an ironic story, a quaintly humorous story (not slapstick) and yes—even an action story!"

At the end of "Just Another Western—" Walker Tompkins predicted the pulp Western had been turned around.

"To summarize, it appears that when the perennially popular Western pulp market was wobbling, editors, authors and agents got their heads together and evolved the idea of producing plots with authentic historic angles. Fortunately, the idea clicked with the buying public. The market revived in the face of adverse economic conditions. The swing toward historical fiction should last out the year, at least."

It lasted much longer. A decade later, Western wordsmiths were still talking it up as if brand new.

"But the really important thing which the newer trend in Westerns means," added Arch Joscelyn in his 1944 *Writer's Digest* essay, "Variations on a Theme," "is that now the whole deep, broad, wide sweep of the whole Western scene is opened up to writers. Only a few writers seem to have realized so far just what that means, and the vast possibilities inherent in it.

"For instance, Indians were once almost completely taboo in Western fiction. And the story had to be compassed within a comparatively short historical period. Likewise, most stories had to center around one character—the cowboy. Now most of these restrictions have been removed."

The period pulp editors preferred was 1860 to 1900—essentially from just before the Civil War to the advent of the automobile and the decline of the horse as the primary mode of American transportation, when impassible fords at last gave way to passing Model-T's.

But this had changed forever. "Every month on down from the trapper period in the early nineteenth century had some vital bit of Western history in it," stated Robert E. Mahaffay. "That's close to a hundred years of Western story material, varying widely. There's a market for all of it."

The cowboy had been ridden out of town on a rail. Soon, his familiar stamping grounds became off-limits.

"Just as certain stock characters have been overworked in the Western pulps," observed Norman A. Fox, "so have certain settings and themes. Undoubtedly we shall find lush range in the pages of the pulps until the end of time, and homesteaders will struggle for the same lush range.... There is just as much opportunity to develop some sizzling action and suspense against an historical background that hasn't been scratched right down to the bedrock."

Editors also drew their Western geography rather narrowly before 1939, as Walker Tompkins asserted in *Writer's Digest:*

"You can't miss if you lay your first Western story in Texas, New Mexico, Arizona, Nevada, Wyoming or the three northern provinces of Mexico—Coahuila, Chihuahua and Sonora. Less popular States include California, Montana, Colorado, Utah, and the Dakotas. 'Off-trail' regions which are replete with Western scenery and historical lore, but which readers do not seem to favor, include the State of Washington, Oregon, Idaho, Kansas, and Nebraska, together with all of Western Canada's cattle country."

But they didn't want the true West, as Lee E. Wells pointed out. "The setting is generally a definite geographic area, but the time is always vague," he wrote. "It might be any time in the old West. All the accepted trappings of background are used; the writers are careful to make sure that everything lends to the flavor of the old West as generally conceived."

The devil was in the details, according to August Lenniger. "If you live in the West you have a natural advantage over the Eastern writer because you'll have at your fingertips the little touches of physical atmosphere which go such a long way toward making a 'Western' ring true. You'll *casually* refer to a glade of quaking aspen with its silvery white bark; to the deep cool green of the tamaracks and conifers; to a grove of euca-lyptus or cottonwood, instead of vaguely to 'trees.' You'll portray your badlands with their multi-colored, crumbling spires and rimrock; you'll have your deserts studded with clumps of sage, prickly pear and mescal, with thickets of buckhorn, cholla and yucca, instead of merely 'cactus.' You'll know the difference between a butte, a mesa and a canyon. You'll refer to the Big Horns, the Tetons or the Sierras instead of to 'mountains.' You'll know how to handle all the little details incidental to describ-ing the routine action of a cattle or sheep ranch. And you *won't* put horns on a broomtail or have your hero throw his saddle on a whiteface!"

Lone Star scribe Eugene Cunningham asserted, "If you know your locale, know the topography of the country, the people who use it, the animals who frequent it, its oddities of all kinds, and then put a good, living, breathing character into it, the rest of the characters will just mechanically click into place, because if you do know your country you'll not get the styles of chaps, spurs, guns, saddles, bridles and bits mixed up, nor will you have a puncher native to a certain part of Texas talking a mixture of Montana, Wyoming, Utah, Rio Grande Border, North Texas and California dialects."

"Each state has its own traditions and its own way of doing things," advised fellow Texan Frank C. Robertson. "You can't write a story of the Southwest and ignore its large Mexican population. Even if you don't mention them their influence is there.... Utah has a large Scandinavian population, but you can't, as I once learned, use these people in a cowboy story although you may know dozens of Swedish or Danish cowboys. I named the hero of a Western yarn Olsen, which annoyed the editor who bought the yarn—after I had changed the hero's name to Parker. I was not, she reminded me acidly, writing a sea story in which the name Olsen would have been perfectly acceptable."

It was different in the slicks, according to one writer deserting the pulps for better magazines and more realistic pastures. "The pulp Western accepts without question a never-never land; the slicks won't," wrote Samuel W. Taylor. "Westmoreland Gray, MacKinlay Kantor, Ray Palmer Tracy, Ernest Haycox—good pulp writers all—have done swell Western stuff for the slicks, but without the stock characters and the casual acceptance of the never-never land."

Which was not exactly true, according to Luke Short. "… my favorite Haycox yarns don't lean on any known time or place," he observed. "In these stories, I suspect Haycox made his own geography, named his own towns and mountains and rivers; he peopled them with tough and abrasive characters whose only law was their self-will."

What had been the downfall of Max Brand, Haycox turned into a virtue.

"In writing a Western story," said Arch Joscelyn, "we must remember that it is largely idealized—not, in the better class of story, an expedition into a never-never land, for the old West that the reader prefers to read about certainly did exist. But, in general, it no longer exists. Therefore the story must be written in an idealistic vein."

"The locale is Western," Lee Floren explained, "but the characters and their actions are glamorized so that the shoe workers in Boston, the sailors in San Pedro, the iron-puddlers in Hammond, the railroad men in Denver, can pick up a Western pulp magazine and ride into the 'never-never' land of romance, of horses and guns and treachery and hatred, a land of fear and love and promise—but a land that never existed except in the movies… and a land that never will exist."

Because it never was, writers felt free to perpetuate its fading glory right up to their own unromantic time. "A great percentage of six-gun sagas are written around an undated period which roughly corresponds to the 1870s," acknowledged Norman A. Fox. "Yet you can write and sell modern Western stories where automobiles, radios, airplanes and Nazi spies play a part."

Stories of the so-called New West further distorted the distinction between the historical era and the pulp Western.

"A story of the Old West is by far the easier to write," said *Western Story*'s Bryan Irvine, "provided, of course, the author knows his stuff. In stories of the Old West we are permitted to use our two-gun hombre, the saloons, the dance-halls, the gambling tables, the stage coach, the mounted bandit gangs, the Indians and bad whiskey. There is always a ready market for semi-historical stories of 'The Covered Wagon' and 'North of 36' type, but they must be technically correct as to historical fact and they must be blended with enough entertainment and convincing fiction to satisfy and entertain the exacting or critical reader; he can't be fooled. Many good ideas or plots are spoiled by the authors' attempts to incorporate in stories of the New West characters of the Old West."

Editors demanded that the Western be accessible to modern readers, which meant the historical characters who peopled it possess modern attitudes and sensibilities. Curious developments resulted. Beginning in 1939, desperadoes bearing marked Germanic names started supplanting the border *banditos* in both types of tale. Nazi Brown Shirts were recast as owlhoot Black Hats. That was how editors kept the "Old West" up-to-date.

"We prefer the flavor of the Old West with the impression that the happenings are of today," Leo Margulies frankly told contributors. "If the setting is in the West of today, it must be idealized. The people must be modern in spirit, with boundless courage and endless endurance."

As one-time Fiction House editor Richard A. Martinsen rationalized it, "We editors know perfectly well that the 'Old West' doesn't exist any more. And so does the average reader of Western stories, I believe. We're not fooling anybody when we publish stories setting forth the West as it used to be, presumably, and trying to give the impression that this same old West actually exists today. They all know better." […] "But it is our job to keep alive the romance of it. That is what the readers want." […] "Whether such a West actually exists makes no difference to them. It exists for them in fiction, anyway."

Thus, *Writer's Digest* cautioned aspiring *Western Story Magazine* contributors, "Keep to the old-time era when a man might cry, 'My kingdom for a horse!' And never, never say the Old West is dead. Don't even let such an idea breathe through a sentence—not if you want a check instead of a rejection slip."

Old Frank Blackwell's dour shadow still lay hard across the length and breadth of the Territory of the Imagination.

"*Personally, I don't go for this stuff that we are writing about a never-never land. Nothing could possibly have been more real than the old West. Its mountains and plains, hills and valleys and deserts—they are still there. Who could call them unreal, or suggest that the men and women who peopled them were unreal?*"

—*L.P. Holmes*

IO

WEST OF NEVER-WAS

A T H E A R T a species of artificial folklore, the Pulp West was founded on a mixture of semi-factual tales and sheer imagination. Most editors of pulp Western magazines abhorred stories tied to a specific date or year. Tales hewing too close to actual history were dismissed as costume dramas, and summarily rejected. In spite of the undeniable fact that the Civil War occupied a central, if not pivotal, place in the unfolding of the great Western march, tales of the War Between the States were as welcome as cowpox. One reason was that Westerns were very popular in the South, and Northern editors understood that escapist reading should not inflame old Confederate wounds.

Observed Arizonan Oren Arnold in 1940, "America has known but two great epic periods—the *ante-bellum* South and the Wild West—and while one is now a tragic memory, the other is still at hand. We can, today, actually be very close to the old West, and awareness of this is an exhilaration. What if we do build it up a bit in our imaginations?"

"Seek always to resurrect the dead West which Buffalo Bill knew;" exhorted Walker Tompkins, "such is the desideratum and sacred trust of the pulp writer...."

The Timeless West, editors called this moonspun territory.

As *West's* Harry Maule explained, "The public doesn't want Indian stories or things *dated* back in old times. The idea is to give the story an atmosphere of timelessness, because adventure itself is timeless."

As Harriet Bradfield expressed it: "It is a state of mind almost more than an actual period in time."

Super Western agent August Lenniger outlined its metaphysical boundaries this way:

"The 'fictional West' is a curious paradox. It is the West in which the Indians are safely banished to their reservations and seldom indeed appear in the stories; it is the West of the stagecoach, the cattle-barons, the cayuse and the Colt, with occasionally a mention of the railroads. But the girls are fairly modern. They don't wander around in crinoline or gingham. Dressed in chaps, a gay-colored silk shirt and inevitable milk-white Stetson and or even in buckskin, they join their menfolk and can equal or outdo the lowly male in shooting, roping, or breaking broncos during the day—but at night they blossom forth in silk and satin and glide over the dance floor to the mellow music of strumming guitars."

It was, as Rogers Terrill dubbed it, "the White Man's West."

As for the cowboy himself, writer John H. Whitson put it best:

"The marvellous heroes who ride through the Westerns and the immaculate cowboys of the movies are like figments of the creative imagination. Cowgirls—they simply do not exist." [...] "The *real* cowboy is a hard-working and rather prosaic creature. If he carries a gun, it is to shoot rattlesnakes. The loneliness and hardships of the life account for his frequent wild outbursts on his visits to the towns." [...] "Accurately pictured he would not thrill the readers of Westerns."

No one understood this better than the cowboy himself. Western pulps were the preferred bunkhouse reading. Surveys showed that most of these magazines were sold either in the big cities of the East or in the rural West. *Writer's Digest* said flatly, "The majority of Street & Smith's *Western Story Magazine* readers are cowboys who like to see their own humdrum life glorified by the daring deeds of fiction."

This was no publishing myth. "The greatest readers of pulp

magazines are cowboys..." Jack Byrne asserted. "When a cowboy gets through his day's work digging post-holes and branding cattle, he sits down with a copy of *Action Stories* magazine or one like it. After reading a couple of Western stories, he'll exclaim, 'Gee! I wisht I wuz a real cowboy!'"

"What a job!" joshed W.C. Tuttle. "Forty-a-month plus frostbite! Out of the sack about five o'clock in the morning, the temperature about zero in the bunkhouse, outside ten or twelve below, and a wind blowing. You shiver into frozen overalls, fight your way down to the stable, where you harness a team of frosted horses, take 'em out and hitch them to a hayrick wagon... Man, it was romantic!"

The gulf between the way it really was and the manufactured daydream yawned as wide as the Grand Canyon. An anonymous writer once submitted a Western story to an agent, saying, "Here is a manuscript that depicts life in the West, on the ranch, as it actually exists. I have mailed it to eleven editors, and it has come home exactly eleven times. I know that it is truer-to-life than the stuff I read in the magazines. I positively refuse to write the slush they print, for it is not true."

Instead of embracing the offered masterpiece, August Lenniger threw cold water on its author:

"Never having roamed the wild and wooly places of God's great outdoors, it is not my business to argue with editors about the established atmosphere used in the stories they print. You may be right. Certainly no one for a minute believes that all cowboys talk in the way that Western yarns portray them as talking, or that they always keep their finger on the trigger of their .45. But if you want your stories to find space in the popular magazines, you must realize that a certain atmosphere has been established for the Western story, the cowboy story, the story of the North Woods, the Canadian Mounted story, for all the other types of story used by these publications—and whether it is a strict interpretation of the real life, *it is the established atmosphere for that type of story—the thing that readers want,* and that you, as a writer, can accept as *'the thing'* to use, or let it alone, in direct ratio to your desire for checks instead of rejection slips."

Few, it seemed, wanted the honest West and its authentic inhabitants. Or if they did, they were reluctant to buck the prevailing trend, set by Hollywood as much as New York.

"Lecturers often work up a fret about the premise that Ken Maynard, Tom Mix, Bill Hart, Will Rogers *et al* were just showmen and not real cowboys, and that many Western story heroes are patterned after them," noted Oren Arnold. "This fact (if it is a fact) is not insidious. Those men are not deceivers. They know we would never tolerate any presentation of a real cowboy, because he is invariably too shy, too inarticulate, too far removed in his thought processes and environment from the life and experience of the reader."

"Both movie makers and writers of Westerns have taken and still take some pretty fantastic liberties with the true tradition of the Hired Man on Horseback," allowed authentic Westerner S. Omar Barker. "There is no use pretending that the galloping go-getters showing off their shapely shirts on the screen can claim any close kinship with the cowboy of reality. Nor are the root-a-tootin' two gun toters of many Western stories much nearer the taw line of credible authenticity." […] "For the writer, however, there is no point in criticizing the fantastic foofuraw with which the vanishing *vaquero* has been adorned for fictional purposes. Writers write it, editors buy it, readers read it, and that's that."

"Because, gentle reader," cautioned Lee Floren, "you are not writing *Western stories*—you are writing *action* stories set in a Western atmosphere. The *Western pulp* editors today will not buy a true Western story. The true Western story would be slow and dragging in their estimation. For the West, despite popular opinion and the movies, was not built on gun-flame and powdersmoke—it was built by tears and hard labor and sweat. It was built by men and women who were real not glamorous. Glamour had no place there."

Not everyone saw it quite that way. "The old gun-totin', wild-ridin' West was just as real as anything that ever happened before or since," proclaimed Glenn R. Vernam of Kansas. "Life was every bit as tough as any man's fiction presents it. Nobody but the sturdiest of humans could have survived it. Law rode in individual guns and if you wanted to catch a scalawag, you took out after him on horseback."

"The best Westerns are those which are most true to life as it was lived in the pioneer West," added Arch Joscelyn. "True, there was no such amount of gun-action, of slam-bang stuff every minute, of murder and all the rest that you find pictured in many of the so-called action stories. If that had been true, the West would have depopulated itself in a week or so and have remained permanently a country for the Indian and the buffalo."

"Myownself, I have sold more Westerns without gunsmoke than with it," admitted S. Omar Barker, "but in that connection the point is not so much whether the oldtime cowpoke was a bangbang hero or not, as that he was of a breed unafraid to shoot whenever the exigencies of his hardy calling made it needful. The old West was no ordinary time, the cowhand no ordinary breed. If they had been, a lot of us typewriter cowboys would be herding sheep or escorting elevators for a living."

Barker called the cowboy right down to the ground.

Lee Floren's assessment of the pulp Western story as purely an exercise in action cut to the marrow of the formula's most unfortunate restriction. "The action story (such as a Western) is more concerned with material goals than is the slick-paper (or quality) story," he explained. "Thousands of Westerns have been written concerning the struggle for water, for grazing land, for mining claims. Undoubtedly, thousands more will someday be published, their characters fighting, dying, laughing, drunk and sober, and these thousands of unwritten stories will concern the goals mentioned."

One disaffected pulpeteer, writing anonymously in *The At-*

lantic Monthly took aim at the poor reader, blaming him for this sorry state of affairs:

"...the pulp reader had rigid likes and dislikes which must be catered to," he asserted in "A Penny a Word." "In the first place, he objects to any and all characterizations, on the ground that they slow the action. Character mutations are anathema to him: he wants types which are instantly recognizable. In Westerns, the hero is invariably tall and wiry, with eyes that can be blue as the desert sky or twin slits of steel. He is grim but he can laugh, usually just a quirk on one side of his tight lips. He pronounces doom in colorful terms and can deliver it with fist or six-gun. The villain must be large, florid, and powerful, or the small, crafty type; he is sneeringly boastful and possesses no trait to endear him to society. The sheriff is either a henchman of the villain, or the old-school, fast-shooting lawgiver. The reader must be able to identify each in his first appearance."

This was what writers and editors came to call "the pattern Western."

Frederick Faust saw it as literary tailoring. "If you go after the merchandising of Western stories as such," he advised, "you'll find that it's a simple group of rules by which one may cut the pattern of any number of yarns. And your bank account need never fail if you follow the rules, and clip carefully along the marked lines."

"Let's see what this pattern is," wrote one of the newer writers on the scene, Lee E. Wells. "The story is always strongly motivated, generally springing from depths of character conflict. These are often expressed through the old plot gimmicks of the land grab, the range war, the rustling combine.... The main character still retains much of the old romantic aspects, though 'dash' is generally sacrificed for other character traits. Nevertheless, he is generally strong with minor weaknesses that tend to make him more human and recognizable. We identify ourselves with him; we are eager to see him come through his trials and finally triumph, either over himself or others."

A chicken-or-egg argument could be made as to whether this is what the readership genuinely preferred, or whether it had become the preferred brand of beef stew because it was the only fare served up. Editorial timidity could easily account for the creative logjam.

Editor and publisher Harold Hersey, creator of the most successful Western pulp of all, *Ranch Romances*, delineated the essential dilemma of the Western pulp editor in his 1937 autobiography, *Pulpwood Editor:*

"To deviate from this formula is fatal. This is the way the average fiction fan visualizes the West, and, as he is the buyer, he gets what he wants—or else he reads the other fellow's magazine."

The crux of the problem was that the post-dime-novel Western derived principally from a single source, Owen Wister's *The Virginian*. The myth of the taciturn ruggedly individualist American cowboy knight is distilled from it. The novel was immensely successful, and was much-copied. Zane Grey, among others, hammered it into a cast-iron formula in the pages of *The Popular Magazine, Argosy* and a long line of best-selling hardcover novels.

"According to the author," Tom Curry explained, "it was a Western to end all Westerns. He stirred in every conceivable ingredient. And it is rare to find a Western that doesn't graze at least one facet of Wister's novel."

In the popular arena, writers and editors simply spliced the more adaptable ingredients of *The Virginian* onto the existing dime novel Western thriller, which resulted in the watering down of the genre at a pivotal period. If they had instead elevated the Western adventure story, the Wild West melodrama might have expired early in the 20th Century.

But the classic cowboy concoction couldn't continue forever. For one thing, it hogtied the writer to the point of near-paralysis of plot.

"The structure is rigid," noted Curry. "Deviations usually ended up in the writer's discard pile, though there are exceptions. The Western is an individual's struggle against overwhelming odds. It appeals to the basic human instinct of an eye for an eye, a slug for a slug. Shoot the villain is a must, but not until he has almost done in the hero."

"You didn't shoot a guy," W. Ryerson Johnson pointed out. "You gave him a chance to shoot you first. *Then* you shot him. The villain became more interesting than the hero because they had a little more scope. They could be more ingenious and mean. And you had to be careful not to make the reader more sympathetic to the villain so you made him bad. You made him *real* bad."

Johnson blamed the pulp editors. "It's hard writing these rigorous true-blue YMCA tough action stories, with deadwood characters and their patterns of behavior," he frankly admitted. "They wouldn't let you give anybody any human qualities. Either they were all bad, or all good. There were no graduations. I remember I got a letter from some editor, saying, 'Don't try to sell ideas to the pulps. Just keep it moving.' They wanted the action. Get rid of the characterization and get on with your story. You very quickly identified who was bad and who was good."

Deviations from the norm were what conservative editors called the "off-the-trail" story. Columbia Publications editor Robert A.W. Lowndes described the type thusly:

"'Off-trail' is generally differentiated from 'taboo' in that occasionally the former kind will be used, while the latter is unusable. A Western story from the heroine's viewpoint would be 'off-trail' for me, while a Western story revolving around warfare between the U.S. Army and the 'savage redskins' is taboo."

Although the term cut across genres, it was most avoided in the formula-bound Western magazines, where it was most needed and most appropriate. *Dime Western* was a notable exception. But even Rogers Terrill preferred its off-trail tales to be short filler material calculated to round out an issue, not interfere with familiar formula fare.

Early in his career, the self-described "old concoctor of cow country yarns," S. Omar Barker penned a supernatural story set in the wild and wooly West. "Back Before the Moon" raced around the mails for seven years. Seventy-five magazines rejected it before William Clayton took the yarn for *Strange Tales,* where its Wild West setting constituted mere background. Numerous Western anthologies reprinted it in later years, attesting to its enduring worth.

L. Ron Hubbard evidently had the same experience with his attempt at a fantasy Western. "Shadows from Boothill" was written during the period when he was writing for the top-paying *Western Story Magazine.* But John Burr ran it in the lower-paying *Wild West Weekly* where an editorial asking readers if they wanted to see more of that brand of beef was met by stony silence.

Even more prosaic variations presented a challenge. "I got tired of blasting six-gun bullets behind bat-wing doors of the Red Dog Saloon, roping steers, reining in runaway stagecoach horses, and in general forking broncs all over the Western plains," wrote W. Ryerson Johnson. "So I started looking for something a little out of the pattern, and decided to tell the story of barbed wire."

The upscale *Short Stories* took that tale. It was one of the few pulp markets where a pulp writer could sell an authentic story, not a fairy tale.

"The formula was so tight that writing them got a little boring at times," continued Johnson. "It was also phony. You were always having a situation, for instance, where a cowboy was getting shot-up or killed defending the cows of a ranch owner.

"'This is stupid,' I told myself one day. "No cowboy in his right senses is going to butt unquestionably into a bullet for 30 dollars a month."

Opening a yarn with what he thought was a more realistic situation—a remorseful ranch owner burying a hand who died defending his herd—Johnson had his super-cattleman deed over equal shares of his spread so that the whole outfit shared in the rewards, as well as the risks.

The editor who reluctantly took the tale growled, "What are you trying to do, spread socialism?"

Even humor—a real-life ranch staple—was largely frowned on in the more gunsmoky pulps after the Depression. Only a rare writer like S. Omar Barker or W.C. Tuttle could get away with it, and then only in the pages of the more lofty superpulps, like *Blue Book* or *Adventure*.

"To sell humor to a Western story magazine was even harder than to sell a story where a significant role was played by a woman," insisted Johnson. "In the man-action magazines, life in the West was grim and brutally earnest. Quick death stalked the cowboy's spurred heels dripping dust in the street in front of the Red Dog Saloon, or hard-riding the range in pursuit of outlaws, or just getting away from them. You brought in fun and levity at your peril—the peril of rejection by magazine editors dedicated to perpetuating a never-never land that existed only in the glowing imagination of the writer and in the transient 'suspension of disbelief' of the reader."

But it could be done. You just had to beat the sagebrush a little harder to find a receptive editor.

"I had fun with a few," Johnson admitted, "but only when I could get outside the rigid corny formula…There was a pattern of rugged, righteous, sober, seriousness to these Western characters that the editors were afraid to disturb. I got so tired of writing about these true-blue stalwarts that I tried a Western spoof.…I had cowboys getting knocked off their horses chasing the villain on horseback on top of a moving freight train. Tunnel knocked him off. I had cowboys roping caribou in northern Canada. 'The Mushroom Spread' was the first one. Featuring

Blazing Daylights Jones and Schemer McCann.... You wouldn't believe the editorial reaction I got. Undermining the character of the Old West, etc., etc. Orlin Tremaine, more imaginative than most writers or editors, finally bought one. And then ordered a series. But I don't think their hearts were in it."

Johnson sold his "Boxcar Buckaroos" series to Street & Smith's *Cowboy Stories,* which had become so desperate to break the mold that it experimented with up-to-date Westerns in which the cowboys piloted automobiles and airplanes. The magazine folded soon after, and Johnson's orphaned buckaroos landed in *Top-Notch.*

Pulpeteer Tom W. Blackburn made the mistake of exaggerating his Western resume to *Western Story's* John Burr during his formative writing days. Blackburn had spent five days on a Hawaiian cattle ranch, but boasted of deeper experience. He would soon regret the windy overstatement.

"Came back a letter from Burr greatly intrigued by my mention of cattledom in the Islands," Blackburn later recalled. "Would I forthwith do him a novelette along such-and-such lines (it was quite detailed) and rush it in for a lead in *Western Story*? Whew!

"Cattleraising in the Hawaiian Islands is one subject on which local libraries are singularly destitute of material." […] "Came another letter, wanting the novelette. I did the best I could by Burr. I wrote the best kind of a Texas locale ranch story I knew how—setting it down in the Islands. And I manfully threw in the only piece of Hawaiian cattle-raising color in my possession.

"It was a valiant effort. No one who has read it will deny that. But unless you have yourself received from Mr. Burr a rejection letter on a story which has offended his intelligence you cannot appreciate the nature of the epistle which accompanied that story homeward!"

No matter how much pulp editors tried to stretch the West over which they ruled, they found themselves stuck with its original boundaries.

Charles Haven Liebe of Tennessee started off writing Mountaineer tales, calling himself Hapsburg Liebe in print, but found "pseudo-Westerns" his most reliable product. After a move to Florida, he thought he'd stumbled across a rich new vein of story ore. "Down in the 'Glades and Keys there was raft of story material," he recounted. "It surprised me to hear that Florida had been a pioneer cattle state, and still boasted an immense bovine population running under registered brands as in the West. The average Florida cowboy proved to be as likable as his Western cousin. Ordinarily he used a long-lashed whip instead of a lasso on range so thick with trees and scrub that dogs figured in the cow hunts. With that whip he could snap off a rattler's head."

Liebe was mum on the particulars, saying of his failure to launch the Florida cowboy sub-genre only this: "Something new! And I muffed it."

Most likely Western editors simply lacked the nerve to expand the generic horizon. Under the title "Red Dice," Liebe's tale ran in *Black Mask*, where hardboiled editor Joseph T. Shaw was only too willing to buck Wild West expectations. The Sunshine State Western remained unexploited in the all-Western magazines.

Characterization proved the biggest bugaboo. How many ways were there to delineate the simple cowpoke? All attempts to stand the myth on its head and offer up variations on Jesse James and Billy the Kid met with ferocious reader resistance. Harold Hersey's *Outlaws of the West*, subtitled "A Magazine of Hair-Trigger Hombres", was bushwhacked under two title variations. The white-hatted gunfighter had to be kept pure and noble.

Only a "good" outlaw like Paul S. Powers' misunderstood fugitive, Sonny Tabor, could survive. He ran for over a dozen years in *Wild West Weekly*. After being pardoned by editorial fiat, both readers and his author fretted and chafed until he was forced back onto the owlhoot trail, thereby ensuring his continuing appeal.

"The Western Hero, in virtually every story ever written of the West, must be all white, or nearly so—never gray, or black," insisted Hamilton Craigie. "His type is the reckless, devil-may-care, gun-slinging hombre, with a heart of gold, a tenderness for women and children, and especially horses, but, often, with a bad habit or two, which is the prerogative of a he-man."

When greenhorn writer Steve Frazee attempted to fob off a slightly-tarnished cowboy on *Wild West Weekly,* the cold corpse was shipped back to him with a frosty note. But Frazee learned quick.

"I dumped my unreliable hero into the wastebasket," he admitted. "He made a thud like a sack of spuds falling off a pantry shelf. I adopted a well-tanned, steely-eyed Texan. Looking at his 'drygulched' pal he said, 'Brad, I'll get the skunk that did this if it's the last thing I ever do!' The Why of Tex was well-established. 'What' was the only problem left. He did 'What' against the usual obstacles, shot up four stinkers, collected a trifling shoulder wound, a girl, a little spread—and I took a check." His tongue firmly in cheek, Frazee remarked, "That Tex sure had character."

But that was *Wild West Weekly,* where "characterization" could be boiled down to terse utterances like Kid Wolf's laconic introduction, "Kid to mah friends. Wolf to mah enemies."

For after two years of foisting off more mature protagonists, *WWW* was forced to return to buckaroo basics, as exemplified by the cowpokes of Paul S. Powers, who had been furloughed by new editor Jack Burr. Readers demanded that they return. And they did.

Casting a cowboy out of unalloyed metal was also frowned upon. "When I was beginning to write," reminisced Jack Smalley, "an editor glared at me and said: 'At least give the guy a limp!' You see, I had failed to build up my character. He was tall and straight and good looking, with clear eyes and a sunburned face. He had no frailties whatever. So I gave him a limp and sold the story."

Such severe limitations virtually crowded the writer into the trap of creating an inadvertent gun-dummy.

"If you avoid stock characters you'll avoid stock plots," counseled Leo Margulies. "Your hero can be handsome, if you insist, but he will also be like most of the people you know, with all their variations in size, shape and coloring. The hero who is just a name attached to a pair of sixguns is a deadweight on a story."

Gradually, the difference between the pulp-paper and polished-paper schools of Western writing began eroding.

"Time was when the gulf between pulp and slick, especially in Western stories, was very wide," noted Walker A. Tompkins in "Improving Western Story Characterization" (*Writer's Digest*, April 1942). "But of recent years the line of demarcation is narrowing… F.E. Blackwell, former editor-in-chief of Street & Smith, saw the trend toward better quality in pulp Westerns back in 1934, when he remarked to me: 'When you pulp writers commence drawing flesh-and-blood characters, you leave me and show up in the slick magazines.'"

Current events were driving changing reader tastes, Tompkins believed. "Dig up a 1932 Western magazine and compare it with one of today's," he noted. "How awful some of those stories are! This demand for better writing gained new momentum with the start of World War II, which mushroomed the crop of escapist readers."

A prolific practitioner under his numerous names, Tompkins—nicknamed Two-Gun by his editors—started running dry in the characterization department circa 1939. He was brought up short when both Leo Margulies and *Western Story's* John Burr took him to task for his lame character delineation.

"You seem to think, Two-Gun," Tompkins quotes Burr as scolding him, "that just because you're writing Westerns for the pulps that you can devote all your energies to plot twists, and let your characters go hang. Readers aren't nitwits. Maybe you're laboring under the fallacious idea publishers used to have—that the industry is catering to a public with a fourteen-year mental level. Maybe so. But today's fourteen-year-old demands a lot better story than his predecessors. Ever listen to kids gripe about a corny matinee movie? You'll see what I mean. Even the kids want realism and convincingness."

Back in his 1938 *Writer's Digest* article, "Preparing for a Career in Western Pulps," Tompkins had been brazen enough to proclaim:

"Characterization—the lifeblood of quality fiction—is secondary to action and suspense, in writing Western pulps. Usually your hero is an epitome of all that is good and brave, while your villain is as uncouth and has fewer saving graces than a polecat. You and I know that a hero can have bad traits, and that there's a wee bit of good in the worst villains; but such third-dimensional characters are not strictly necessary in writing the average cowboy yarn."

Now he was forced to eat crow.

Buckling down, Tompkins moved up to the next level of pulp. As a result, 1941 became one of his best sales years. Even the second-generation pulp hacks were adapting. But the old ways were hard to mend.

In his 1942 article, Tompkins remarked on the new challenge of writing convincing Western heroines, citing an example that suggested while the gun-dummy might have been banished behind the barn, there remained a distaff edition composed of the same clichéd cardboard:

"Wayne D. Overholser, an up-and-coming young Western writer from Oregon, mastered the problem of heroines by compiling a scrapbook of clipped paragraphs from published Westerns, to serve as a manual to guide him in composing feminine characteristics.

"It is a virtual thesaurus of descriptions of cowgirl apparel, larkspur eyes, rose-petal lips, and so on. Overholser's got something there, too; a crutch to lean on until the knack of feminine characterization is acquired through imitation."

This was typical of the thinking of the early pulp writers. They were constructionists, writing to order in severely prescribed story lengths and supremely conscious of the fact that they were paid by the word. After the Depression, with their rates cut to the bone, pulp writers stopped boasting about how many pennies per word they earned and instead made fantastic claims about their sheer speed of production. This marked the decline of the million-word-a-year fictioneer—although most who made that claim might be rightly accused of counting their rejects, if not their carbons.

The post-1938 cuts produced new casualties not limited to cardboard cowboys. Authors fell by the wayside. Unable or unwilling to adapt, and discouraged by their word rates being knocked down to mere fractions of pennies, writers as established as Cliff Farrell and John A. Saxon fled the field. Luke Short moved up to the slicks.

"If pulp prices don't pick up," lamented one anonymous Western pulp writer in *Writer's Digest*, "I'm sunk. I sold my first novel nearly fifteen years ago for a cent and a half a word. Then, for years after, I got a straight two cents. Now I've been cut three times and my last check was a little less than one cent. The editor keeps telling me that he hopes that the rates will go up again soon."

Wrote Fletcher Pratt, "The million worder's fate was sealed when the half-cent pulps discovered that stories bought at this rate from cub reporters and boys just out of college were as true to the formula and rather fresher in approach than those of the old masters. Thus the million-word man committed hara-kiri by efficiency: ruined his own business by formalizing and formularizing it until anybody could do it."

This was not entirely true. Some prolific citizens continued to thrive—at a price.

"I was a working author as opposed to a 'talking author,'" declared Walker Tompkins. "I forced myself to keep a rigid working schedule: from 1 to 5 daily, five days a week, I chained myself to my desk. So-called 'inspiration', which lazy authors wait for in vain, never visited me. I used my formula to grind out plots and they worked for me every time. When mental blocks would finally lead to a full-scale drought, I wouldn't fight it; I would usually pack my bags and travel. Since you can write anywhere you can set down your typewriter, I could pick up my career no matter where I found myself." […] "Most of my output during the 1930s, my busiest period was, let's face it, pure crap. Rarely did I ever retype a page of manuscript—it went to the editor exactly as it came out of my head, so of course it lacked polish."

On the other extreme was Clee Woods, who took his work so seriously that he recreated a common Wild West experience in his own garage while his new bride stood nervously by.

"Hanging by strangulation was the fashionable way of lynching where big cotton-woods grow in Montana, back in the days that I re-create in my stories," Woods wrote, "and I had to know for one particular story about how long a man can hang by the neck before he goes unconscious. Also, how much it hurts. I could not go ask surviving victims of necktie parties, because I had never heard of one surviving. So I hanged myself. Betty insisted on standing by with the butcher knife to cut me down in case I went unconscious inadvertently before I got my feet back on the soap box."

This, just so Woods could accurately describe the sensations of a fictional character in distress.

Then there were the writers who ranged across genres, pecking out Westerns only when the market or the spirit moved them.

Minnesotan Frank Gruber was one such.

"I sold my first Western short story in December 1934," he reminisced. "This was during the time that I was sweating it out at the 44th Street Hotel, in New York, and it was a tight race as to whether or not I would be locked out of my room for non-payment of rent before 'the break' came. The hero of the piece was Leo Margulies, who was at that time editorial director of the large chain of pulps put out by Standard Magazines. I had made Leo's acquaintance and bombarded him with mystery stories, all of which were speedily rejected. Leo suggested that I try adventure stories. I did and they were rejected just as promptly. I tried love stories for *Thrilling Love*. They, too, were bounced. In desperation Leo asked me to try a Western story. He was that sort of a guy—he really wanted to buy a story from me. He gave me a couple of copies of *Thrilling Western* to read, when I admitted that I had never read a single Western story up to that moment.

"I wrote two 2000-word stories in one afternoon. I changed all the 'to's' to 'tuh's,' the 'you's' to 'yuh's' and the horses to 'hosses.' I submitted them both to Leo and he bought both. I have never had a single Western story rejected since."

Wayne D. Overholser of Washington State had a similar experience. Offspring of pioneers, he sold his first cowyarn to Margulies' *Popular Western* in 1936.

"I had no inkling I would turn out to be a Western pulpster," he later confessed. "At one time I was certain I'd write detective stories. I did, but the sales were definitely discouraging. Westerns went better for me from the first, and the reason may be found in my own background."

Frank C. Robertson likewise drew upon his outdoorsy upbringing. "My apprenticeship as a writer was, I think, somewhat unusual, yet quite beneficial," he joked. "I herded sheep on the Idaho range for five years, and if there is any occupation more lonely than writing, herding sheep is it. You get accustomed to people saying you are crazy—which also helps when you become a writer."

Simple pragmatism motivated S. Omar Barker, who admitted, "The practical reason for my writing Westerns is… the Western pulp magazine field was a wide open market."

Lester Dent, creator of the adventure hero Doc Savage, grew

up on a Wyoming ranch just after the turn of the century. He wrote only a handful of Western pulp tales during the pivotal 1932-33 period before giving up on the Pulp West:

"There are Wall Street secretaries writing stories about cattle rustlers who haven't seen a pickpocket," he joked, "whereas we really had cattle rustlers in Wyoming. And I can tell you about the time the range men and settlers of that whole section of Wyoming formed a posse and took out after a bunch of horse thieves. The horse thieves retreated to a place called Hole in the Wall—famous outlaw hideout—and fought off the posse for three days. When they got bored, the horse thieves chased the posse off. It really happened that way. Maybe that's why I can't write Western stories. I might tell the truth."

Considered one of the best Western tale-spinners, W.C. Tuttle damned the genre (and by implication his own contributions to it) when he confessed: "Give me a tale of the days of old, with plumed knights, stage-coaches drifting over muddy roads, tavern brawls, etc., and I'm useless until the end of the story. I can fairly smell the tap-room, hear the rattle of dice and the clash of swords. It is more like a moving picture than a tale of fiction. I often envy the writers of these tales. To me this is 'real' fiction."

Yet those interests may have helped make Tuttle the Western tall-tale teller that he was. Change "plumed knights" to "buckskin cowboys," and "clash of swords" to "blast of sixguns" and he might be describing the drover as Owen Wister first painted him in his seminal 1895 essay, "The Evolution of the Cow-Puncher."

"No doubt Sir Launcelot bore himself with a grace and breeding of which our unpolished fellow of the cattle trail has only the latent possibility," Wister wrote in *Harper's New Monthly Magazine*, "but in personal daring and in skill as to the horse, the knight and the cowboy are nothing but the same Saxon of different environments, the nobleman in London and the nobleman in Texas; and no hoof in Sir Thomas Mallory shakes the crumbling plains with quadruped sound more valiant than the galloping that has echoed from the Rio Grande to the Big Horn Mountains."

Despite all attempts at creating verisimilitude, the damning, inescapably discouraging truth about the Pulp West was that it was almost entirely spurious. Better writing, improved characters, and the freshest of new slants could not alter that fundamental fact.

Taking pen in hand, cowpuncher Hurst Julian took the entire genre to task in his 1940 *Saturday Review of Literature* article, "The Real Fiction in Western Stories."

"A recent survey of Western literature, covering almost every field and every available writer for the past several generations, close to three thousand stories and articles were examined before one was found which used all Western terms correctly and which had no impossible situations. It was written by a novice and published in the trashiest of Western pulps."

Julian blamed the reader, pure and simple. "The fellow who digs up the dimes at the news-stands will continue to dominate Western literature and determine its trends regardless of how little he knows about the matter. The West will be garnished according to his tastes regardless of how absurd they may be. The artistic and romantically-acceptable counterfeit has driven the genuine article from the market, and no one seems interested in trying to have it otherwise."

That was only one cowboy's opinion, however.

"I am well aware that anything like complete authenticity is neither an editorial requirement nor a reader demand in Westerns," conceded S. Omar Barker. "Being myself Western born an' brung up, I often wish it were. Nevertheless, I believe that both the editors and the ultimate reader do sense the flavor of reality when they came across it in a story, and that they like it."

Even Wister himself had encountered this paradox, back at the dawn of the new genre. "Once a cowpuncher listened patiently while I read him a manuscript," he recalled. "It concerned an event upon an Indian reservation. 'Was that the Crow reservation?' he inquired at the finish. I told him that it was no real reservation, and no real event; and his face expressed displeasure. 'Why,' he demanded, 'do you waste your time writing what never happened, when you know so many things that did happen?'"

Strangely enough, those pulpeteers reared in the honest West saw a strikingly different landscape.

"*There are two kinds of Western stories. The authentic kind,
written by men who have spent a great deal of time and energy
absorbing the background, language, customs, peculiarities,
appearance and traditions of a particular region. And the sort
of tripe turned out in great profusion, speed and regularity by
the New York school of blood and thunder pulpsters.*"

—*Nelson C. Nye*

I I

FEUDISTS

ROGERS TERRILL'S "The Evolution of the Western" brought forth a fusillade of letters from *Writer's Digest* readers—most of them Western writers who subscribed to radically different views of what constituted a respectable pulp oater. Not surprisingly, most of these missives came from out West.

The first shot was fired by range orphan Lud Landmichl of Riverton, Wyoming in the September 1941 issue:

"In the May *Digest,* Rogers Terrill... writes about the changes made in Western fiction along in the years '27 to '30, which brought about a consequent boom. Then the tragic collapse along in 1931.

"I know. I was in it, too.

"I wrote 'Westerns' day and night trying to keep up with the demand. I received letters and telegrams from Harold Hersey to rush more material to him, and I wrote for him steadily, because he took everything I produced. Often he'd run three stories of mine in one issue of a mag under different pen names. I was writing for *Quick Trigger,* and *Western Outlaws,* serials, novelets, and shorts.

"There was a little clique of us writing Westerns at that time, Glenn Connor, Coteau Gene [Stebbings], Capt. Walt Bethel, Wm. Colt MacDonald, and four or five others, myself included, who used to write letters to one another which were published in the back pages of the magazines. In those letters we razzed each other something terrible, but it was in good sport, and we all enjoyed it. It was great fun writing for the magazines in those days.

"Everything is so different now, so cold, so lifeless. It's simply deplorable that conditions should change so in a mere ten years. It is no less than tragic when one realizes what a tremendous reversal has come over humanity in such an incredible short time... Now we have wars, dissatisfaction and WPA.

"Stories of today, most of them, have gone the way of the human element, they are also insincere. For instance, check the Westerns of today against Western stories published twelve or fifteen years ago. There was more of the *real* West in those stories than there is in today's yarns.

"I don't mean that they are all insincere to the actual Western element, for there are still a lot of mighty good Western stories being written even in these hectic days.

"But they are thinning out. There aren't over a half dozen of them writing any more. The new writers going in for Westerns haven't got the sincerity, the knack of imbuing into their stories any of that *real* Old West atmosphere."

Landmichl goes on to cite his 37 years on the range, lamenting how automobiles and motorcycles were overrunning the great open spaces of yore:

"I have written about things I've seen and encountered in those early (for me) days of roaming around over sageland and desert. The stories were published in the old *West* magazine, in *Western Story Magazine,* and Sam Bierman put a lot of them in his *Two-Gun Western Stories Magazine.* A lot of the stuff, with photos, went into the slick pages of outdoors magazines, and sportman's books, and journals.

"Now I'm writing Westerns again. But these modern editors want a different sort of material than we used to publish. I'm afraid that some of them don't know what it's all about. A lot of the stuff they publish is faked up by *swivel-chair westerners* who live in N.Y.C.

"That's all right, and more power to 'em, if they can, over a cup of cawfee (?) induce the editors to buy their stuff. Personally, I just can't stummick [*sic*] it, and I know a few others who don't care a whoop for it."

Return fire came from Deport, Texas. The shooter was Ben Gardner. Under the contrived alias of "Gunnison Steele" he had helped make *Dime Western* the undisputed leader in the Western field:

"I've just read the letter by Lud Landmichl in the September *WD*, and it gave me a twinge. Quite obviously, Mr. Landmichl is living in the past. He had been unable—or has refused—to adjust himself to changing conditions and tempo in the writing game. I disagree with most of the things he said.

"I remember the days of the late '20s that he mentioned, when he and a few others were turning out reams of gosh-awful stuff for the Western books. I was just starting out then, selling my first yarn to Harold Hersey's *Quick Trigger Western*.

"Since then, I have sold over a thousand yarns, to practically every Western published, and a few other detectives, etc.

"Landmichl is right, times have changed since then. When he intimates that the Westerns written ten or twelve years ago were literary gems compared to those being written today—that's frankly ridiculous. I have at hand several copies of old Westerns. In a Max Brand story, the author takes two printed pages—approximately 1300 words—to describe the hero. In another, four printed pages are consumed in describing a gun-fight between two men, with a few pages in between shots to explain in detail matters that had absolutely no bearing on the story. Blood flows by the bucketsful, men die by the dozens; all stories follow the same general pattern, while the grammar in most of them would make a grade school pupil blush with shame.

"Is that what Landmichl means?

"Don't we all long for the golden days, when avid editors were pleading with pulpateers for just any kind of hooey, just so it blazed with fast action... or do we?

"The modern Western is not above reproach. I do mean—and as Mr. Landmichl has obviously discovered—that nine out of ten of the Westerns published ten or twelve years ago wouldn't have a chinaman's chance of being bought and printed today. As to the present-day Westerns being faked by swivel chair 'westerners' who live in New York City—exactly the opposite is true. Most of the top-notchers who turn out a top-heavy part of the copy, live in the West, and have for many years—Walt Coburn, Harry Olmsted, Ray Nafziger, Chuck Martin, Ed Earl Repp, to name just a few—and know the West inside-out. No better, maybe, than Mr. Landmichl—but they were wise enough to see the writing on the wall and change their writing style.

"They booted the old-style gun-dummy out the window, wrote a smoother, more compact story, got human emotion into it, quit 'writing down' and changed to a sensible, adult style. Has Mr. Landmichl done these things? I doubt it. I know two or three other die-hards who are still trying to sell the old slam-bang, gun-dummy, no-plot, no human-feel yarn—without success. They bemoan like Landmichl, that editors have changed; they expect Ye Ed to reach with eager arms—and checks—for their bewhiskered offerings. Why for gosh sakes, don't they wake up! As L.L. says, the modern Western editors want a different sort of material than we used to publish—and, make no mistake, they're going to get it! The old stuff is out, forever, and that's one reason a crop of newcomers have taken over.

"As he says, everything's different now. We have a war, half-cent word rates, a struggle for existence. A story has to be four times as good to bring one-fourth as much as it used to. But I still wouldn't swap jobs with anybody I know!"

Coming in on the side of Landmichl was another cowboy-turned-pulpster from the late '20s era, Joe E. Dash of Chicago:

"I went to work at twelve. At sixteen I rode a buckskin pony from the Pecos country of Texas to the Judith Basin country of Montana. I wrangled horses, punched cows and broke broncs to ride and drive. I drove stage, too, and freighted with a jerk-line. I spent all of fifteen years in the saddle and rode range from the Canadian border down to Old Mexico.

"During the last seventeen or eighteen years... my Western stories and Western articles graced the pages of the *Lariat, Big-Book Western, All-Western, Chicago Blade & Ledger, Two-Gun Western Stories, Black Mask,* etc.

"Mr. Gunnison Steele mentions that in the old Westerns, blood flowed by the bucketfulls and men died by the dozens, while the grammar in most the pulp stories would make a school grade school pupil blush with shame.

"Bucketfulls of blood are still dashed into the picture, only a bit more artistically—they sprinkle it on instead of pouring it over. As to poor grammar used then in the Western pulps, well, not a few of the editors preferred unpolished yarns, from cowpunchers. I sold chuck-wagon yarns then to Mr. Kelly on *The Lariat Story Magazine.* And Mr. Steele, you must consider that a cowpuncher had little time for schooling. I know—I had to get mine later. And the editors of the late '20s did not expect to find a purist amongst a group of flea-bitten waddies.

"Mr. Lud Landmichl said in his letter: 'A lot of stuff they publish today is faked-up by swivel-chair Westerners who live in N.Y.C.' There's lot of truth to that. Not so long ago I happened to be in an editorial office and had a good chance to look over several scripts written by two of our most prolific pulpateers. When I got through reading their yarns, I shivered in my boots. One of the writers had his setting in Montana. The rancher run out of hay, and—as the story went—the rancher fed his cattle sorghum stocks and mashes. The other yarn had the boys—as the story went—go up to the boss every Saturday to get their pay-check.... Well, in all my travels up and down the wide range, I have never seen a pay-day. You could draw your money anytime or just leave it ride until you went to town.

"Mr. Gunnison Steele, you mentioned something about top-notchers, who lived in the West and know the West inside-out—Walt Coburn, Harry Olmsted, Ray Nafziger, Chuck Martin, Ed Earl Repp.... Did you ever ask them, in what time they could bull-dog a steer? Sure, they are good writers.

"A writer can live in the West and know *nothing* about a cow camp, cowpunchers or range. Mr. Gunnison Steele, you say the 'old stuff is out, forever.' Well, that's taking in a danged lot of territory. Even a pulp editor would feel reluctant in leaping to that conclusion. It is not improbable for the Old Westerns to come back with a blast....

"I agree with Mr. Lud Landmichl that many Westerns written today lack the real Old West atmosphere. It just seems to me these Eastern Pilgrims have pulled the West right into their back-yard... Surely, I'm not going to bark at them for that. If they can convince editors that sorghum stocks are fed to Montana range cattle, and the boys play bridge in the bunk-house, and cow outfits pay off every Saturday night so the boys can go to the movies, you've got something! Pulp editors don't know the West, and they are taking a long chance, hoping nothing is wrong with the story's background. True, the Western can be faked, and that faking makes the readers rebel... What then is the outcome? The editors of the Western pulps know that answer only too well, and the old blind nag is gently led to the cannery to be shot at sunrise."

One of those accused of not being a true Westerner, Chuck Martin, came to the defense of himself and others:

"Dash wants to know how fast Walt Coburn, Chuck Martin, Harry Olmsted, and Ed Repp can bull-dog a steer. Walt Coburn was born on his old man's Circle C spread in Montana, up in the Bear Paw country. He's cowboy from boots to Stetsons, and nothing else.

"At past 50, he isn't bulldogging steers, but can he ride, rope and flank down what he catches? I have seen him do it.

"Olmsted never was a cowboy, but he sure knows the West,

and writes it *as it was*. Ed Repp's old man owned an outfit in the Mojave Desert called the Sunrise outfit.

"As for myself, 32 years ago I was riding the rough string for the T.O. outfit, known as the Santa Margarita Rancho, covering a quarter million acres. Then I made a hand for the California Land and Cattle company until I tried to make Mexico safe for Pancho Villa, and Madero. Then to England on a cattle boat, back to the States, and more work on cattle spreads. I raise my own stock horses on my ranch, and break my own colts. I work Calf round-up every Spring, and this year I taught my favorite colt to work a rope in three weeks. And I couldn't write a Western story worth a hoot in Chicago, or New York."

Martin then complained:

"I've had Editors tell me for years that I know too damn much about the West to write a good Western. They say I lost my perspective, being too close to the picture. Logically, this makes those New York cowboys prime beef, so when they finally whip us all out of the herd, we should make a splendid living writing about the night life and Cafe society in Chicago and New York. Our perspective won't be clouded. Sometimes I wonder how in hell I've sold 850 stories to national Magazines, and 29 published books."

But Martin was obliged to confess:

"There's a deal of truth in what those Editors say at that. A real Westerner unconsciously becomes too technical. The terms come so easy to us, but it does gripe us to see the squirts copy our stuff, and use the terms in the wrong places. There are just too damn many people back east, even Westerners who know better, but who write the way Hollywood and the East, thinks it should be. All except Walt Coburn. Walt would see 'em in hell first, in their bare feet."

In the same issue, William L. Hopson of Las Vegas, Nevada, makes the identical point:

"I wrote four years before I sold a Western yarn. That was because I was fool enough to try writing about the people I was born and raised among down in the Texas panhandle cow country and those I later met when I rode winters and poisoned coyotes for the state up around Dillon, Montana. It took me four years to get it pounded into my head that the average Western pulp editor—I said *average*—doesn't really care whether the stories are true to life or not. As long as he makes that profit for his publisher why should he worry himself about the stories not being true to life.

"Today the pulp game is in the doldrums. It would have been the same in spite of the war because even the kid readers are getting bored to death with the same old plot and the same old ingredients: sexless gun dummy hero with frosty blue eyes; virgin heroine as pure as the driven snow. Bold villain with an eye to fixing up the latter situation, unless he wants—as in most cases—only money. Bang, bang, bang, and the villain is dead, the heroine's virginity is saved, and the reader presumes that in time they'll get into bed together where nature will take its course and the two will get down to some natural business."

Little remembered today, "Wild Bill" Hopson was one of three employees of a Venice, California gas company who decided to break into the pulps in 1937. The other two were Richard Albert and Tom W. Blackburn, both of whom apprenticed as two of Ed Earl Repp's many ghost writers. Blackburn, whose Western background was impossibly sparse compared to Hopson's, eventually emerged as one of the top Western practitioners, while Hopson, who burned to transmute the West he knew into stories, ironically never rose above the stature of journeyman pulpster.

When first bit by the writing bug, it was only natural that William Hopson turned to the Western.

"I was born in the Texas cow country," he recalled elsewhere, "my father had been a hard bitten cowtown lawyer who about half the time got fined for throwing law books in the courtroom, and I knew every Hopalong Cassidy book by heart. So Westerns they would be, but not the kind published in all the magazines. No matter how much I loved Hopalong Cassidy, I knew such stories weren't too true to life. I would startle the editors and bring joy to their hearts by writing *real life* Westerns. After all, hadn't I seen a Texas sheriff shoot down a man at a dance one night, pulling the .45 Army-style pistol out of his hip pocket instead of a thonged-down holster? And the saloons. There would be no fights or shootings in saloons. Hard working cow punchers in real life worked from dawn to dusk and had little time to loaf in saloons like they did in Western stories.

"It wasn't until six years later, when I finally sold Leo Margulies my first acceptable short for $35, did I suddenly wake up to a ghastly realization," Hopson went on. "Editors were like grocery clerks. They were buying beans by the sack, putting them up in neat packages, and selling them at a profit. It made no difference if the clerks didn't like red beans. If the customer was satisfied, who gave a damn as long as the profits showed in the cash register?"

Hopson's letter continued:

"Frankly, I'd like to write about things I've seen and heard about from old-timers. About my cowtown lawyer father holding off the town toughs with two six shooters the night, as county attorney, he arrived and was to be chased right out again like his predecessor. About killer punchers turning preacher for awhile, running off with some guy's wife, then deserting her and going bad again. About cowtown divorces and remarriages, about love making at dances—these and a thousand other real life incidents. I'd like to write about my mother, heavy with child, sitting in our home with three of us huddled in terror around her while armed men strode into the house to kill my prosecuting attorney father to keep him from appearing in court next day.

"Of course, if I mix in *enough* gun dummy stuff and *enough* virginity for the heroine all this can be used—after which it becomes the old wornout formula stuff all over again. Take a guy like Walt Coburn. Although I can't personally stomach his stuff nor the mawkish sentiment he gets into some of his yarns, he knows the West backward and forward and crosswise.

Anytime he turns out a yarn you'll know it has an air of authenticity about it, from the caliber of a gun to the historical facts of the town. Yet to get the big rates he does Coburn, too, must write the 'smoke pole' stuff like the rest of us: strong, silent hero, virginal heroine, grumpy old-timer.

"If you really want to get an idea of just how god-awful outlandish and unreal our yarns are, just pick up a copy of grand old Charlie Siringo's autobiography, *Riata and Spurs*, which is within arm's length of my desk, along with a lot of others like it."

Finally, Hopson concluded with this lament:

"I live in hopes that one of these days some editor with courage will put out a new mag and let these guys who were born and raised in the West turn out any kind of a yarn they like about people they knew. If it's sex then put it in. If it's divorce, or even a prostitute central character—anybody; if they fit into a story *in an natural way*, put them in.

"When editors say they want emotion in a Western they get it about as follows: hero finds brother murdered. Hero's eyes harden; his lips thin, he grabs gun butts and squeezes them until the knuckles stand out white....

"In brief, if some editor would take one quarter confession story, one quarter love story, mix it up and stir well with one-half parts of gun dummy bang, bang, bang, I think he'd have something."

Writer's Digest dryly noted, "Q.E.D. to the subject, unless some executive editor of a pulp Western string, reads this on an ambitious Monday morning and wants to see what Reader Hopson suggests, or some version of it."

Evidently not, for the pages of *Writer's Digest* were quiet on the subject for a while. No one seemed to know or remember, but a decade before a similar controversy had raged in the *Digest's* pages over editorial worthiness and authorial credentials.

An outrageous claim by Allan W.C. MacDonald, who wrote as William Colt MacDonald, lit the fuse on that Depression-era feud.

"This stuff about 'Western story' writers who have never seen a roundup or a wild horse and who sit in stuffy city apartments pecking out slambang tales on a typewriter is so much noise," he wrote in 1932. "I'll admit that there may be some exceptions to the rule, but there isn't a 'Western' writer worth his spurs who hasn't spent a good deal of time out in these very much open spaces. To get the proper flavor in your stuff you either have to be a cowpuncher or live among them."

In short order, MacDonald was hooted down by Westerneers from both sides of the Rockies, half of whom claimed that no special background was needed, with the other side complaining that real Western knowledge only got in the way of commercial yarn-spinning. Unstated was the fact that MacDonald was born in Detroit, and had migrated to Hollywood to write Western movies. His chief claim to fame was creating The Three Mesquiteers for *Ace-High Magazine*, which he later brought to the silver screen. In fairness, it must be said that MacDonald spent considerable time living in various Western states.

If one believes the 1933 account of Utah writer Frank C. Robertson, the swivelchair Westerner stampeded the genuine article out of the Pulp West sometime in the early '30s:

"About ten years ago I sold my first story to *Adventure*. It was a novel. Immediately readers wrote in that a writer had arisen who knew his stuff. Well, I sailed right along for a while. And then this crop of east-of-the-Potomac-writers came along.

"Well, sir, first thing I knew, I began to get letters asking me why fer gosh sake I didn't go West and find out what the country was like. Didn't I know that all Westerners said 'yuhr' and 'thuh,' and didn't I know that cowboys always rode on a run and never stopped without letting out a yip? Didn't I know that they never walked; they always 'ankled?' And if they went places they always 'high-tailed' it. I didn't even know that cattle are always held in a herd, and that a steer can be the father of a band of calves.

"Until I was thirty years old I'd never done anything except punch cows, ride broncs, herd sheep, and work on ranches. I thought I knew it all.

"But I'm getting properly humble again and am prayerfully learning all over again from the boys east-of-the-Potomac. But, sir, it comes hard.

"I'm a stranger to the country which magazine readers now think was the West."

The Lud Landmichl of that fracas was an obscure Texas writer named P.S. McGeeney who lodged the following complaint in the January 1934 *Writer's Digest* letter column:

"I wonder why editors buy those so-called Western stories manufactured on Broadway by Britishers and Canucks (I presume), with 'Quirelys,' 'Hoosegows,' 'Saddle buckets,' 'Lass ropes,' 'Paddocks,' and meals composed of 'Beans and Frijoles;' 'Wough,' if they use Spanish phrases or words. It is to laugh, and I get a big kick whenever I read one of those Broadway Western yarns.

"Some years ago three of my books were published, and a number of short stories (Westerners as they should be 'writ').

"I've been out of the game though, directing pictures for a number of years.

"In the mean time a new crop of Editors have sprouted forth who do not know the WEST.

"Plenty of good, first-class, first-hand stories now lying dormant but our Eastern authors are not capable of finding them."

In ten years, nothing much seemed to have changed. Yet, inexorably, the Broadway shepherds kept crowding the cow-country boys off the range.

"I take strong exception to the idea put out here and there that the 'Romantic Frontier West' is a myth, despite the unrealistic quality of some Western fiction and films. Many Western stories in the pulps were authentic representations, and the cowboy as a folk hero is by no means a mere writer's myth."

—S. Omar Barker

12

—◦◦◦◦—

WILD WEST WARPATH

WORLD WAR II and the Draft began taking healthy males in 1942 and '43, creating a ferocious shortage of pulp paper and qualified authors to fill up the printed pages. *Writer's Digest* estimated in 1943 that only 50 writers produced half of all published pulp fiction, and between the service branches and the Office of War Information, half of those 50 were out of the fiction racket for the duration. Walker Tompkins, William Hopson, Nelson Nye, August Lenniger and others went into the Army. Allan R. Bosworth rejoined the Navy.

For those who were exempt, it was a new boom time.

As editor Harry E. Maule wrote in the *New York Times,* "This latest boom first got under way when the Armed Services Editions, a cooperative enterprise of American publishers under the sponsorship of the Council of Books in Wartime, learned that some millions of soldiers wanted more and more Westerns—all kinds of Westerns: 'straight action and the more analytical type....'"

The new boom inevitably extended to the pulps.

"...the war is the golden opportunity for the new writer," crowed Lee E. Wells. "The established boys are doing their bit with bayonet and tank, most of them. Those of us who are left behind can't possibly fill the demands made of us."

Old hands claimed it was like 1928 all over again. But for a new generation.

"Today, it seems that only the strongest and the youngest established writers can pull oars, or swim with the tide," reported Chuck Martin. "The Defense Billions have not filled the pockets of pulp Writers." [...] "The younger writers are pouring out mediocre copy. They are tireless, just as we were tireless back in the Golden Era. Their brains are fresh, and they are working for Editors who are in the same age bracket as themselves. These youngsters will never be top-notchers until they have learned to slow down. To THINK more, and work less."

Too old to reenlist, Chuck Martin found himself a California Civil Defense Chief Air Raid Warden in addition to his duties as deputy sheriff of San Diego County and cranking out five different Western series for Leo Margulies, two of which he was continuing for an absent Walker Tompkins.

In the game some twenty years, the Cincinati-born Charles Morris Martin might have been the quintessential old-school cowpoke-turned-pulpster. At 17, he went West to cowboy around California, working on two big cattle spreads. After a colorful career that included a Vaudeville cowboy singing act, Martin turned to fiction for his salvation following a 1922 car accident that left him with his back broken in three places. Editors cottoned to his salty style, and he took to punching keys instead of cattle on what he called his "tripe-writer."

"This was in the Golden Era when Bill Clayton was paying a minimum rate of two cents a word for all his mags, of which he had plenty," Martin fondly remembered. "These old-timers rode the crest of the wave where the current was going, and what an arrogant, free-spending crew they were. In those heady days, even pulp writers had a 'position in life to maintain', and Bohemia was in the United States; not only in Europe."

The flush times over too soon, the prolific Martin struggled through the Depression.

"We were told to do slow, careful writing, at about one-third the rate we had received for copy most of us will admit was

God-awful," he said. "Instead we ran, not walked, to the nearest typewriter and began hitting the little black keys harder, faster." [...] "Twice as much copy for half the rates, we all thought, would make us just as much as before."

Working for reduced pennies-a-word eventually took its toll.

"I broke down completely," Martin confessed, "and all the money in Hollywood could not induce me to work hard enough or long enough to go through a similar experience. I was working all day and half the night. Couldn't sleep or eat, and when the break did come I was so weak mentally and physically that I thought I was going to die, and was afraid I wouldn't.

"For more than four months I was in bed, and during that four months I lost my cover spots on magazines. I did a lot of heavy thinking and decided to keep on living, and it was necessary to make a comeback by writing short stories... very short ones. Healthy writers had all sold the long ones. It was then I decided that a sensible diet in writing was just as necessary as a ditto in food."

Martin bought himself a sixteen-acre ranch near Oceanside, California, where he erected his renowned Literary Boot Hill, in which he ceremoniously interred the Black Hats his heroes slew, with a proper pine headboard and fitting epitaph like "FLIP MADDEN DIDN'T FLIP FAST ENOUGH. KING COLT DID."

Fresh air and horseflesh soon restored his health. Over time, Martin worked his way back into the field, but his superprolific days were plumb over.

"That Million words a year racket was a tough grind," he admitted, "and as far as I know, there were only 11 of us in the Nation doing it."

Early in 1943, Martin wrote to *Writer's Digest:*

"The editors are crying for stories, but they won't let raw, unfinished stuff get by, nor will they lower their standards, which in all honesty were raised by the infusion of young, college-trained writers among the pulpeteers. The effect of

Superman is noticeable in a marked degree in modern pulp, which is not so far-fetched when one stops to consider the feats of young chaps in all the fighting forces.

"Personally, I sold 37 stories and books last year, working half a day at my desk. I work like hell for stronger sentences, tighter plots and real honest-to-Gawd Western color, which a hand never learns in college, and cannot crib from reference books."

Rancher-turned-writer Syl MacDowell seconded Martin's views when he told his fellow Westerneers, "If you're going to write the flowing history of the Frontier Period, you can't get it all by sniffing micro-organisms off of library shelves. The printed records are a fair source for whoever wants to catalogue them and give them meaning. But you must feel the West. Steep in it, physically."

Sound advice. But MacDowell betrayed his muleskinner past when he went on to exhort pulp writers to go the extra mile for their penny per word.

"What I'm trying to say is this: get out there and grovel in it. Bake your brains out under the desert sun. Freeze in a Montana norther. Learn the feel of thirst, of hunger, of desolating fatigue. Get into some unholy mess to work out of. Hunt or fish when your belly is hollering at you. Then you'll understand what it was to be a pioneer."

For those not so hell-bent for publication, Hamilton Craigie suggested the writer fall back on memories or his imagination. "It is important—as important as anything else—for you to *feel* that you are writing a Western story, to be aware that all the time there are clouds, mountains, arroyos, deserts, and Indians."

Chicago-born Nelson C. Nye took a more practical view as well.

"Intimate knowledge of the West isn't the first requisite of a Western story writer," he said, "but an overpowering interest in things Western certainly is. Ultimately, the man who has been born and bred in the range country has a fund of lore and background to bring to his writing that is mighty hard to obtain from reading. Still, a good percentage of Western writers have never been West of the Alleghenies."

Finding himself competing against the younger generation, Chuck Martin espoused the lone cowboy approach to fiction-eering.

"Ride a horse back in the hills, if you have a horse, and if there are any hills," he told his fellow old-timers. "Get away from your desk, and stay away from people. Jot down the ideas that will come to you BECAUSE you are an old-timer. Delineate your characters, work out a strong plot. You won't write as many stories, but you will sell twice as many. You will also buy textbooks from the magazine racks at ten cents a copy, and read the stories written by your competitors. Styles change every year, old-timer, and you better keep up with the changes."

Counseled August Lenniger, "Saturate yourself with the Western atmosphere—*as it appears in the magazines you wish to reach.* Visit your local library and get some real histories of the frontier West; read up on real outlaws; get some books on guns so you'll know the difference between a Colt and a Winchester; read up on horses and saddles and cows. Spend a month, or three of them if necessary, learning your trade—until you feel you're quite an authority on Westerns. When you can smell 'the clean tang of cattle' (as one Western writer I know often puts it), when you feel you're breathing the dust of a herd at the roundup, when you can taste the alkali water of the desert, then you're about ready to start writing your own first Western yarn."

Dwight Bennett Newton of Kansas City, Missouri learned that lesson the hard way. Since the age of 12, he dreamed of writing Westerns. Ten years later in 1938, his work was refused by all pulp editors. So Newton returned to college and earned a Masters in History. One day in May, his life changed.

"I remember I was sitting there and here comes a little envelope from Newsstand Publications," he recalled. "I set it aside and had my breakfast, because I wasn't going to eat any more if it was what I thought it was. But it was a check for $60, to D.B. Newton, for a 12,000-word novel. The letter said it was due out in *Western Novels and Short Stories,* and I went up to the drug store, and there it was, on the newsstand: My story. And that was the biggest day of my life."

The story was "Brand of the Hunted." Newton sold six Westerns that Summer. It took a college education, but he had broken into one of the lowest-paying pulp markets of all.

Naturally, there were those to whom book research was unnecessary, like Walt Coburn.

"I do little research," he claimed. "I knew the early cow country about which I wrote, cowmen, cow punchers, sheepmen, Indians, *et al,* before the barbed wire fenced the free range."

Most pulpeteers came into this world on the cusp of the Old West and the 20th Century, thereby missing the glory days of the cowboy. Born in 1901, Allan R. Bosworth grew up on a cattle ranch near Pecos, Texas. It left an indelible mark on him.

"I can remember many things about that nomadic life, and about the ranch country, and I have used them all. I can remember the rattle and jolt of wagon travel, and waking one night to feel flood water rising around me in the wagon bed, and the sights and sounds of two thousand head of cattle stampeding in an electrical storm. The smell of sheepdip brings nostalgia of which a Western writer—according to all popular tradition—should be ashamed. But I know there is just as much romance in the sheep industry as there is in cattle raising; I've sold stories about it, and hope to sell more. I know how a windmill sounds, and what hard work it is to put up barb-wire fence, and what it's like to sleep under a tarp in the rain."

For all that authentic background, Bosworth admitted that it wasn't enough. "That country was changing; I was fortunate in arriving on the scene just when the old, colorful days were shedding their last faint glimmer in the rimrocks, just when the Old West was dying hard, with its boots on. I heard the freight wagons jingling down from the railroad, ninety miles away; I was there when the first autos and trucks replaced them. I absorbed, without knowing it, some of the color. If I had known I was going to be a writer, I would have absorbed a lot more."

Some picked the brains of the previous generation of cowpokes, those who had rode the mythic trails.

"I had three old friends, who were all 84 the last time they were here at the ranch," revealed Chuck Martin. "I got most of my dope from them. Frank King, Tex Moore, and Jeff Milton. All dead now. Frank died last November at age 91. Grand old cowhand. I roamed all over Arizona, Texas, Mexico and California with those three. None of the three liked Wyatt Earp. Jeff was Chief of Police at El Paso just before John Wesley Hardin was killed there in the Acme saloon. Tex Moore hunted with Bill Cody. Frank was Customs collector at Nogales and El Paso, and a deputy sheriff for years. Back in the younger years I was to all three 'The KID cowboy'. At sixty I was still the Kid to those old mossy-horns. I loved all three of them."

No longer in the majority, typewriter wranglers such as Coburn and Bosworth and Martin nevertheless constituted the backbone of the field. Without their example, the swivelchair Westerners would have nothing to emulate.

"Of the fifty full-time Westerns authors now supplying 80% of the demand," Walker Tompkins estimated in 1943, "you can count the 'real cowboy' authors on the fingers of one hand: Walt Coburn, Chuck Martin and a few others being the notable exceptions. The rest of the Western authors come from ordinary backgrounds—New York lawyers, Jersey office workers, school teachers, farm workers, mechanics, grocers, doctors."

Typical of this emerging species was William Heuman of Brooklyn. Determined to make the Western pulps, he fretted over the fact that he'd never once laid eyes on cow nor cactus. Virtually unarmed, he began his first Western yarn.

"But I had seen the inside of a few Brooklyn saloons as a

boy and actually set this story in a saloon," explained Heuman, "thus keeping myself on safe literary ground."

Or safe enough for Rogers Terrill, who bought it.

Another one of Terrill's "boys" was William R. Cox, who confessed, "I got into Westerns in 1940, when the desk drawers of my editors became overloaded with sports and crime.… It was the strangest thing in the world, the first one for pulp. I just took a crime story and changed it into a Western. A guy owned the newspaper, he became the big rancher. His weak brother became the foreman, and so on. The private eye became the marshal. And I sold the same story I'd sold before."

On the other side of the corral were folks like Missourian Bill Gulick. Weaving a bit of overheard equine lore into a tale, he sent it to Terrill, who wrote back, "This story is so fresh and the horse color is so excellent, we are going to buy and publish it with great enthusiasm, in *New Western Magazine.*"

In the middle stood Washingtonian L. Ron Hubbard, who once complained that "My first Western stories were scornfully rejected by editors since they were 'not authentic,' having been written by someone who had been west of Hoboken."

But he lived West of "true West," after all.

The contrary view was taken by Massachusetts novelist John H. Whitson, who homesteaded on the Great Plains back in the authentic day. "A creative writer doesn't need to experience the things he describes," he wrote. "If he did there would be no novels in existence worth reading. I sold dozens of Westerns long before I had ever seen a wild horse or a Western ranch.

"Then in eight years on the plains I saw cowboys and wild horse hunters, helped break through blizzards that took human lives and winnowed the barbed wire boundaries of the Santa Fe with dead range cattle, saw cattlemen and settlers prosperous, and saw them broken and discouraged—saw good times and bad. Into my books, *The Rainbow Chasers* and *Barbara, a Woman of the West,* I put some of these things. It may have made them better, but they could have been written without it."

An emerging range-star of this phase was Frank Gruber of Minnesota, who after discovering in 1934 that Leo Margulies would buy any old Western he flung together, soon sickened of the work.

"I wrote perhaps a dozen more Western stories for Leo Margulies during the next year," Gruber admitted, "but during that time I was beginning to click as a mystery writer and became vaguely dissatisfied with the Western stories I was writing. I sold western stories to a few magazines, other than those edited by Leo Margulies. And I began to get some criticism that my Western stories didn't ring true."

A jaunt out to outlaw country combined with obsessive reading of Western history books suggested to him by Ernest Haycox transformed Gruber into a self-described "walking encyclopedia on peace marshals and outlaws," and one of the top writers in this ever-shifting field.

"With my newfound interest in the west," Gruber wrote, "I again began writing Western stories but the stories are vastly different from the ones I wrote four years ago. The stories are authentic. They ring true to me and I think they do to the editors and readers. I go to great lengths to make them authentic. At the moment I am writing a story in which a cavalryman is a major character. I've taken time out, merely because I want to make this cavalryman sound real, to read three books dealing with the cavalry in Kansas in the Eighteen-Seventies. I may not use more than six or eight lines from these books but I will know what sort of uniforms a cavalryman of that period wore, what his equipment was and something of how he regarded his life. In some form this will be transmitted to the story."

Authenticity had replaced sincerity as the essential ingredient. But it meant different things to different writers. Walker Tompkins saw authenticity as mere seasoning. "Local color is just another name for verisimilitude—that writing style which makes an editor (and future reader) think 'Gosh—this author knows what he's talking about. I'll bet he was a real cowpuncher before he started writing about his adventures!' Achieving verisimilitude, or the appearance of authenticity, is a simple matter of acquiring knowledge in various facets of Western lore which will embellish the action of a cowboy plot."

Color helped many a lame manuscript over the transom. It was the essential ingredient in a cowboy story. "I know Western writers who can make you smell the sweat of horses and hear the creak of saddle leather—and that is color," proclaimed Clark Venable.

Despite pressure to lower the fence rail, the Western appeared to be holding onto its maturity. But little by little, by the sheer formula nature of the genre, it once more started sinking back into what pulpster Thomas Thursday derisively called "Illiterature."

Responding to the question of the war's impact on Western pulp fiction, Rogers Terrill told *The Author & Journalist* early 1942, "If anything, I expect we shall be looking for a little more emphasis on early pioneer stuff and on the sort of high adventure and robust man-conflict which may make a little more glamorous to war-torn minds our kind of escape fiction. There will be a little less on psychological and social problems, and in general a slightly more adventurous and never-never story type."

There were good reasons for that. Chiefly, a certain percentage of the reading audience could be counted on to prefer the safe stereotype story. Especially, the young reader to whom the Wild Western was as fresh and new as Christmas snow. Thus, *The Virginian* continued to be recycled endlessly.

Its conventions were virtually unavoidable. Wister's unnamed protagonist had crystallized into the archetypal generic cowboy. Other classic elements were first introduced in *The Virginian*.

"Wister," D.B. Newton observed, "also gave us the first rustler, the first lynching, the first 'walkdown,' and even the Eastern schoolmarm heroine who remained a favored love interest for decades."

In short, *The Virginian* had everything.

"What is this *everything* that makes *The Virginian* live?" asked Harry F. Olmsted rhetorically. "'Complete characterization,' says Chuck [Martin]. Ask Rogers Terrill, Popular Publications Ed. He might say, 'Salt, brother. It's a salty yarn.' Mike Tilden, another solid editor with Popular, might fall back on his favorite fetish—'Epic types and authentic Western Period Color.' Plotting finesse, I hear somebody say. Intrigue. Gripping inner design. Honesty of conflict. Realism. On and on, far into the night. Anybody can point a finger at a convincing answer. It's easy. But not that easy."

Formularization was also a consequence of the size of the market. Editors had deadlines to meet, column inches to fill, and other editors to compete with. Top writers were in constant demand. The pages had to be filled somehow. Prolific authors could appear twice in the same issue. Usually the second story ran under a hokey pen name like "Alamo Boyd" or "Reeve Walker."

Writing ability more than historical accuracy mattered, as Walker A. Tompkins confessed in "Preparing for a Career in Western Pulps" (*Writer's Digest,* June 1936).

"Early in my apprenticeship I uncovered five fundamental truths of the cowboy story racket: first, that it's possible to be a successful Western author without moving West of Hoboken; second, that there are definite and readily-accessible sources of Western material; third, that certain locales are more likely to woo editorial checks than others; fourth, that certain clichés bring inevitable rejections; and last, that plotting can be learned.

"Locale was easy for me to get, since I lived in California within easy driving distance of local color. But the dope I began assembling first-hand could just as easily have been garnered by an office-bound Jerseyite who might have been nursing the fallacious belief that being an Easterner put three strikes against him."

W. Ryerson Johnson discovered the same thing when he switched from the dying Northwest Mounted genre to Westerns. He had broken in via a gun-trail tale, "The Yucca Kid," back in the Clayton era. Although born in the coal mining town of Divernon, Illinois, he soon rose to the status of cover-featured contributor to *Western Story, Star Western* and many others during the 1930s.

"The West of the pulp magazines was a very limited world," he wrote. "You could choose to write gun-town stories, gun-trail stories, ranch stories, an occasional wagon train, railroad or gold mining story—and that was about it. Cows and gold and guns.

"I thought all I'd have to do was read a batch of Western pulps… and I was right. I started in, reading first to get the story, reading a second time to get the feel of the presentation, the formula, the pacing, and to soak up some of the jargon and fictional conventions. For instance: they rarely called a revolver a revolver. It was a six-gun, six-shooter, .45 Colt, shooting iron, smoke pole. You could invent a likely name of your own if you wanted to."

Excessive artistic license led to writers like Chuck Martin foisting off paragraphs like the following as examples of authentic Western lingo:

"Elevate, you mangy old wart-hog! I shot that Bisley Colt from your filly's hand, and never broke the skin. With you it will be different, you long-jointed old pelican. Drop your Winchester and sky them dew-claws before I do you a meanness!"

This roll-your-own-hokum style of writing began falling out of favor after the synthetic slang got utterly out of hand. Thrilling Publications writer and editor Samuel Mines shot down this approach in his June 1943 *Writer's Digest* essay, "Western Corn (Pulp Grade)."

"For example," he lectured, "characters in Westerns rarely pulled the triggers of their guns. Usually, 'they triggered their Colts.' To some Western writers, 'leather yore irons' is a quaint manner of telling someone to put his guns back in their holsters. Cowboys are imaginative enough in creating slang, but real cowboy slang has a realistic base which is utterly lacking in this weak and unconvincing pseudo-slang. I'll eat both Colts and wash them down with the holsters if anyone can prove to me that a real cowboy ever said, 'leather yore irons.'"

Mines had the support of them who had been there, including Arch Joscelyn, who recollected: "I was born and raised in Montana, and have lived there the greater part of my life. I was raised on a cattle ranch. Our nearest town was three miles away. Through that town ran the old stagecoaches and the long freighter strings, before the railroad pushed across and put a stop to them. I saw them many times, saw cattle drives go by, and, on occasion, stop for a week on our own ranch. But I never heard, in those days, of a lot of the expressions and dialect used now in so many stories of the West. Some of them, I am sure, were never heard in any of the West."

Yet generations of use and abuse had ingrained this artificial lingo in the minds of all concerned, as Walker Tompkins pointed out:

"The vernacular used by fictional Westerners is a language all its own. Unknown in actuality, it gives a simulated atmosphere of how sheriffs and cowhands and rustlers are 'supposed to talk.' While real cattlemen may scoff at terms like 'hogleg' or 'smoke-pole' for a Colt revolver, your editor won't; because he is catering to the demands of thousands of pay customers, who want their characters to talk 'nacheral.'"

The origin of this invented lingo was part authorial laziness, part technical necessity. The gist of it was inspired by the Virginian's lazy Southern drawl, and transferred from his mouth to every paper cowpoke regardless of birthplace.

As Francis W. Hilton explained:

"These writers have taken the Virginian—who, it must be remembered, was a Virginian and not a Westerner—and put his slurred 'r's' and soft drawl into the mouths of their cowboys. The result is a jargon of deliberately misspelled words masking under the guise of dialect, and no more resembling the vernacular of the West than many of the gaudily-dressed and swaggering cowboys they would have folks believe infested the range."

As Arch Joscelyn pointed out, "The cowboy, that central and heroic figure of most Westerns, was usually a simple soul, in the better sense of the word. His talk was simple, but clear."

The reality was a species of linguistic bedlam, as Edmund Collier described it:

"In the early West there were more kinds of American spoken in one place than you could shake a stick at. Mexican, extreme Southern, extreme Yankee, highbrow Boston, Bowery, Cockney, Irish, high-class English, Scandinavian accents, might all be found in one trail-town." [...] "It is of course impossible to reproduce accurately all these different kinds of speech, and if he could they might be so unfamiliar to the ear of the reader that they would completely destroy for him the effect of the story. It is better, when in doubt, to have your character talk plain United States."

"Cowboy dialect or lingo, like all dialect, generally grows right out of the locale," Lee E. Wells explained. "Thus, a Montana cowboy is quite likely to use one term or phrase where an Arizona cowpoke would use another for the same thing. Maybe a Texas man would use a third slang phrase, quite different from the other two."

"If you want dialect," countered Arch Joscelyn, "don't worry too much about getting it from one section. You can't. No one could—though some writers who were old-timers in that section have it all over any one else."

"Would you write a Western yarn without using at least one sectional expression?" asked Walter Des Marais. "Therefore, it is well to use at least one sectional expression every paragraph. However, don't make all your characters use these expressions. Let but one character carry the dialect of the locale. This is much more effective than to allow every character to use the dialect.... Editors are about ready to scream whenever they see such charming display of colloquialisms such as 'yuh' and 'tuh'" for 'you' and 'to.' Even cowboys do not slay the regent's English."

"No matter how rootin'-tootin'-hell-for-shootin' your plot may be," cheered S. Omar Barker, "make your biff-bangin' buckeroos talk like cowboys. You can accomplish that end a lot more effectively by the judicious use of cow-country similes than by all the 'yuhs' and 'tuhs' born east of the Hudson. Of course yuh got tuh throw in a few 'yuhs' and 'tuhs' if the editor wants yuh tuh, for the editor is always right."

Editors were more picky about background details and local color. A writer had to know his firearms, his horses, and even possess a working knowledge of commonsense cow psychology. And woe betide the keyboard cowboy who didn't do his homework.

"No writer should attempt a Western without research," snorted the Lion of Standard Magazines, Leo Margulies. "It's too easy to slip. We catch some. Naturally, it makes us lose a little faith in the man. Take the pouch in which the Pony Express carried the mail. We constantly get stories in which the rider throws the pouch. Impossible. Pouch was built into the saddle."

Yet editors also shied away from too much detail on the theory that it "slowed down the action."

"The problems faced by the hero and heroine should be indigenous to their Western surroundings," counseled Margulies, "but we would prefer to limit lengthy discussions of cattle prices, beef shipments, rodeo stunts, rustler tricks, etc."

"We pulpeteers shouldn't kid ourselves that we're penning 'immortal literature,'" Walker Tompkins stated candidly in "You Don't Have to be a Cowboy," (*The Author & Journalist*, April 1942) "Our writings, sad to say, are as transient as the cheap stock they are published on. But that doesn't give the Western story writer any excuse to write phoney stuff. Accuracy in historical and technical detail is the yardstick by which is measured the successful author and the ha'penny-a-word potboiler."

But book learning, not hard Western living, seemed the preferred path.

"After I got well into the Western field," admitted Ryerson Johnson, "I did do some background reading, and settled upon two books. I found that I could get nearly all the information I needed to write acceptable Western stories from [Philip Ashton] Rollins' *The Cowboy*, and [Walter Prescott] Webb's *The Great Plains*. Webb supplied the historical perspective—the progression from open-range ranching to the barb-wire fencing era. Rollins, on the other hand, was meticulous in revealing the day-to-day details of cowboy life, everything from what he ate for breakfast to what he rode and wore—and his preferred branding and shooting irons."

This calculated commercial approach is what led the honest sons of the true West to write disparagingly of "Manhattan cowboys," creating the myth that most pulp stories were written by moonlighting clerks and bellhops.

"Most of the Western authors I know personally—good writers all, by sales standards—never bulldogged a steer in their lives, and don't hanker to, either," Tompkins said flatly. "Show me where the ability to work a lass-rope will improve my writing, and I'll start practicing on the neighbor's cat. The same goes for marksmanship with a pistol, or the knack of cutting a steer out of a boogery herd."

"I could travel all over the West," insisted Hascal Giles of Tennessee, "and that's not going to help me develop a character, or construct conflict and drama."

Tompkins continued, "Editors want entertainment for their readers, not capsules of historic wisdom. Erudition in pulp fiction, especially Westerns, bores the reader, who wants to escape from the hum-drum affairs of his banal existence. The author who can supply that vicarious excitement—be he an office-bound Manhattanite or a tumbling Texas tumbleweed—is the author who'll land the editorial checks consistently."

Nor were the pulp editors themselves above imposture. They

were Easterners, too.

"The editors of those Western magazines all assumed an air of infallibility and an encyclopedic knowledge of the West," observed Erle Stanley Gardner, later to gain great fame as the creator of Perry Mason, "probably gleaned from reading the manuscripts which came pouring in." […] "To be sure, the editors were demanding that their writers 'know the West,' but the big bulk of Western stories were being written by people who had never been out of New York, and who had secured their local color from reading Western stories written by other authors who, in turn, had never been out of New York."

And when one did venture westward, as W. Ryerson Johnson did, the plain truth could completely unhorse the man from the myth he was trying to perpetuate:

"Sitting in New York," he recalled, "I had sold around 100 Western stories before it occurred to me that maybe I should go west to find out how close it was to how I had been saying. Most of the Western writers I knew had never been across the Hudson River. I thought, 'Maybe we're missing something.'

"So I went west. Crossed the Hudson on the ferry and chugged into the sunset in the old Ford four-cylinder convertible. I covered Colorado, Texas, Arizona, New Mexico, and later the northern West.

"It was one of the biggest mistakes of my life!

"The West *was not* what I had been saying. It was not and never had been. I vaguely knew this at the time, but now I *really* knew. Disillusionment was complete. All that glamour and romance we put into it! Heroism. Intelligence. Elemental nobility. If it was there, I sure didn't sense it. The Western cowboy was no more than a dry-dirt farmer with the bib cut off the top of his overalls. He had his feet and brains both in the dust. Zane Grey's purple sage was an alkali-rooted weed, and the romantic rangeland stretched out and out in harsh, arid, dusty, rock-and-rattlesnake cluttered miles—a natural breeding ground, not for nobility, but for human insensitivity, ignorance and brutality."

A self-described "Hudson River cowboy," Johnson clearly saw the West through eastern eyes. Yet everywhere he traveled, he encountered an amazing circle of influence.

"I've sometimes speculated about the effect of the Western myth we bloomed to life in our stories—sitting in New York and creating those... adult fairy stories. I discovered when I went West that cowboys in their bunkhouses had stacks of Western story magazines leaning against the walls. Did our characterizations affect them? Did they try to live up to that grass-roots nobility and heroism we projected? Wouldn't it be interesting if, because of the image we projected, they moved over a little in that direction.

"When later I tried my luck in Hollywood, I discovered that there, too, Western pulps were stacked against the walls. But for a different reason. Hollywood writers drew from our stories in working up situations, characters, backgrounds and premises for their scripts.

"The same with us in New York. When we got stuck for a new story plot, we could go to a Western movie. Somewhere along in the storyline there was bound to be a decision scene. The hero could chose to take this course of action or that one. Whichever way he went, we could go home, start with a similar opening situation and angle our story the 'other way.' We came out with a fresh, new story. I guess we kind of swallowed up each other, New York and Hollywood."

In his book, *The Cattle-Trailing Industry, 1866-1890,* historian Jimmy M. Skaggs also skewered the notion of the heroic cowboy, writing, "If there is romance associated with the cattle-trailing era, it was created by reminiscing drovers, naive novelists, and stereotype-prone motion pictures."

After interviewing cowpokes throughout the West, Frank Gruber grumbled, "I must confess that quite a lot of these old-timers were great liars."

Yet London-born William MacLeod Raine, who worked

on Colorado ranches during that era's twilight before becoming a major *Western Story Magazine* writer, subscribed to the contrary view:

"Never in the history of the world has there been a phase of life comparable to that which existed in Cattleland within the memory of some of us not yet old... It has no parallel and can never have one. Because it *was,* the West *is...* It was a phase of American life the most free and joyous ever known, and it is written into the character of the cow country West forever. In it were courage, steadfastness and nobility to make the American heart glow with pride. It shall never be forgotten."

This romantic heroic notion actually predated Owen Wister, who is credited with coalescing it in cold print. In his 1897 paean, *The Story of the Cowboy,* Emerson Hough first painted the commonplace cowpoke in glorious hues:

"The story of the West is a story of the time of heroes. Of all those who appear large upon the fading page of that day, none may claim greater stature than the chief figure of the cattle range. Cowboy, cattle man, cowpuncher, it matters not what name others have given him, he has remained—himself. From the half-tropic to the half-arctic country he has ridden, his type, his costume, his characteristics practically unchanged, one of the most dominant and self-sufficient figures in the history of the land. He never dreamed he was a hero, therefore perhaps he was one. He would scoff at monument or record, therefore perhaps he deserves them."

Well into the pulp era, there were those who believed in it implicitly.

"Detractors of the Western story as a fiction medium claim that the cowboy has been shaped into myth-symbol," said Norman A. Fox, "and that the other frontier types have been glorified beyond reality as well. Yet for every dramatic scene the fictioneer has provided, history has provided an even more dramatic one, and the most colorful characters of Western fiction had their living counterparts."

New writer Victor H. White saw it that way, too. "With all their raw fist fights, gunplay, bravery and cowardice," he observed, "they rather accurately portrayed the kind of stuff of which Wyatt Earp, Doc Holiday, Buffalo Bill, and Wild Bill Hickok, to name a few, were made. They also pictured how Earp could playfully bounce a six-year-old-kid on his knee or how the love for a horse could influence an outlaw to make a better life. No Western pulp writer ever pictured Billy the Kid or Calamity Jane as being any tougher than they really were. And there was never a character in any Western who was a more engaging prospector or a more refined and convincing liar than Death Valley Scotty."

Frank Gruber wholeheartedly agreed. "This stuff is real to me. The adventures of some of these men absolutely authenticated, seem incredible even to a pulp fiction writer. Few fiction villains have ever been as formidable as was Ben Thompson who invited the highly touted Wild Bill Hickok to crawl into a hole and pull the hole in after him. Or John Wesley Hardin, the twenty-year old Texas kid who said to the same Hickok, 'What are you going to do about it?' Or Clay Allison, who journeyed up to Dodge to collect the thousand dollar bounty which had been put on Wyatt Earp's scalp by certain Dodge citizens."

"The old West did have many striking characters," countered Frank C. Robertson, "but few could ever be transferred bodily to a role in a Western story. Writers seeking to base stories upon 'facts' have blown up little Kit Carson to the size of Paul Bunyan, but he still doesn't fit well in fiction."

"No other facet of American history has been so abused," complained Oregon cowboy Glenn R. Vernam. "Nobody ever tried to make myths of the early banking tycoons, timber barons, railroad magnates, mining moguls and political carpetbaggers, all of whom created more hell and corruption than all the old-time Western cowboys."

Perhaps S. Omar Barker—himself no champion of the pulp interpretation of Western life—had it right when he split the difference between both camps and opined, "The romance of our folk-hero cowboy is a *legend* authentically born of fact, not a *myth*. There *is* a difference."

The last word on the notion of the cowboy came from an obscure Connecticut pulpster, James Howard Hull. In response to Walker Tompkins' "You Don't have to be a Cowboy," he penned "You Have to be a Tenderfoot" for the May 1942 *Author & Journalist*.

"What is a cowboy, anyway?" Hull asked. "Why, I have known hundreds of men whose work was the job of pushing cattle around in the great open spaces. Not one single one of them was a cowboy. No cowboy is ever a bullwhacker by trade. The real cowboys work at every trade in the world except bull-whacking. Being a cowboy is like being an American: it is a state of mind. If a writer is a cowboy, and can see himself objectively, and is impressed by what he sees, that impression, and that alone, is his material. All he needs beyond that is a small shelf of books, to give bodies to his heroes, the souls of whom are his own soul."

Hull cites his youthful exposure to Western yarns in *The Century* magazine as first imbuing him with the metaphysical cowboy imagination. An early pulp Western writer, he fell by the wayside as the field progressed.

"Twenty years ago I could write Western stories because I was still a cowboy then," mused Hull. "I thought at the time it was because I had traveled around the West quite a bit and camped with men who rode horses and packed guns. I sometimes tried to explain this to editors, but they were only amused. It was fiction they were paying me to produce, not information. The time came when I couldn't write Western stories any more. I thought at first it was because I couldn't write anyway, but no; I can still do that. It was because I was no longer a cowboy. I am sincerely sorry."

Continued Hull, "It was Bret Harte who first pointed out that it is always the tenderfoot, never the old sourdough, who achieves the spiritual experiences which serve his purpose as material for stories. To the old sourdough, everything is commonplace and without meaning. To the tenderfoot, everything sparkles."

It is exactly for these reasons that easterner Owen Wister's *The Virginian* remains a classic a century later, while Andy Adams' *The Log of a Cowboy* and other more authentic accounts of the working calf-roper, have faded from prominence.

The pioneer pulp editors were starting to fall away, too. After a stint at Munsey, Jack Byrne quit to freelance. But before long he was back ramrodding at Fiction House. Harry Widmer left A.A. Wyn's Ace ranch and *Western Trails* for Popular Publications. Ned Collier also left Wyn to write a book. Ruth Dreyer replaced him. She had been an associate editor on *Ranch Romances*. At Dell, Florence MacChesney rode herd on *All Western*, Art Lawson having settled in as a fulltime Western pulpeteer operating out of old Mexico.

It was a difficult grind. Kenneth A. Fowler toiled as a Street & Smith copyeditor under John Burr. "It is my conviction that there are too many incompetent writers plying the trade of fiction today," he asserted in his 1938 complaint, "Grinding to a Pulp." "It is an astonishing fact—for which I can provide astonishing proof!—that even the established, high-powered pulp-grinder is guilty at times of inexcusable lapses, is prone to the same faults and errors that are committed by his humbler compatriots in the writing game.

"For example, I choose this sentence from the work of a writer whose name appears frequently in the better Western pulp books—a sentence lifted from a 20,000-word story bought by the magazine of which I was associate editor: 'He acted decisively, exploding sideways, twisting his neck to look both ways at once.' *The New Yorker* would have liked that for its 'Neatest Trick of the Week Department'—if we hadn't been lucky enough to catch it.

"Another writer—without question one of the best-known

pulp authors in the country—was guilty of this weird grammatical miscarriage: 'They splashed through the mud to a shed beside the blacksmith shop, where the ponies had been sheltered from the storm, howling and singing and wild with drink.' The story didn't mention where the ponies got the hootch, but I have a feeling that it wasn't out of a grammar."

Damon Knight was just passing through the Western field on his way to becoming a significant science fiction writer, and came to consider editing Western pulps akin to recycling trash.

"When I was an assistant editor at Popular Publications," he recalled, "every species of pulp had its standardized stories that were rewritten over and over... In Westerns, there was the one about the drifter who takes a job at a ranch where the rascally foreman is cheating the woman owner. Popular... was the best of the pulp publishers then. The editors knew good writing when they saw it, and published it in the short form because they knew the readers thought of short stories as makeweights. What the readers bought the magazines for was the stereotyped repetitive plots that were recycled in every issue in the novelettes and 'complete novels.' These stories didn't have to be well written, and usually weren't. Well-paid professionals ground them out without paying much attention to what their fingers were doing, and assistant editors like me had to revise them line by line and word by word."

Like Hull, Knight discovered that he could no longer do it. The day came in 1944.

"In the Spring of that year I had grown increasingly restless at Popular," he wrote in *Hell's Cartographers*. "I sat with a thick manuscript on my lapboard, a Western novelette by Harry Olmsted, and found that I absolutely could not penetrate it. Olmsted always needed heavy editing, but in order to edit him you first had to find out what he meant, and I couldn't. When this had gone on for some weeks, I gave notice and quit."

Another Popular editor described making up a typical issue of a Western pulp magazine in a way that made untangling barbed wire by bare hand sound easy.

"There are really a limited number of variations on the Western formula," declared Bruce Cassiday. "The wire-war saga. The trail-herd saga. The cattle rustling story. The sodbuster-rancher war (a variation of the wire-war saga). The Oregon Trail (Covered Wagon) story. The Dodge City shoot-out. The father-son rivalry story. The duel in the sun. And, for esoterica, the riverboat saga. The plainstroopers vs. the Indians… And so on.

"So what happens when you as an editor of a Western magazine have three stories in the issue about hanging cattle rustlers? Of course, you try to keep them out of the same issue. But sometimes it isn't always that easy… by the time you scan all the titles and compare them, you've got the number of 'sod-busters' pared down, the number of 'hanging' themes down, the 'tinhorn gambler' with the cold deck reduced to one, and the 'trail boss' isolated. You've changed the titles so they don't all sound the same and you're pretty well satisfied with the contents as they are now.

"Then you've got to go through the stories to check the names," Cassiday concluded. "I've seen an issue of *Big-Book Western*—one of my magazines—that had four heroes named Clint! The following month there were two Bucks. No pun intended. And then two Montes. Never did run across a Cecil."

The plight of the pulp editor was illustrated by a comment author's agent Lurton Blassingame received from one of the breed. Blassingame wondered why there were so few old, seasoned editors in the business.

"The ghosts get them," he was told. "After ten or twenty years, they can stand it no longer. The ghosts of all the old stories they ever read jump out at them from the freshest looking paper, the clearest type. The editors begin to shadow box, to talk to themselves. And so they are quietly transferred to a job which has some freshness to it—the bookkeeping department, for instance—or they resign and write with gusto their memoirs of a few writers who had something fresh to say."

Ominously, Blassingame added, "There are more ghosts of trite Western stories haunting editors of cowboy magazines than there are ghost towns in the West."

"I once asked the great gunman Wyatt Earp if he had ever seen a man 'fan' a gun and hit anything. He said 'No' in such a way as to leave no doubt as to what he thought of the idea."

—John A. Saxon

13

BOOT HELL

THE YEAR 1943 began with a boom.

"Nearly fifty Western magazines are buying regularly now," reported Walker Tompkins, "a figure which eclipses detectives, women's slick magazines, and all other types of pulps including the ubiquitous 'comics' which are now enjoying such a phenomenal vogue...."

The Western was hot as a pistol. But it was all about to collapse. Again.

At the end of 1942, Popular Publications purchased the failing Munsey chain, with it the pioneer pulp magazine, *Argosy*. Rogers Terrill took over as editor, in the process surrendering all of his pulps, including *Dime Western*. It was an natural evolution, as writer Steve Fisher saw it:

"Rogers Terrill in those days was closer to the slicks than anybody, because his stories had to be all of a piece—all character and emotion, so to speak, and consistent throughout. The boys all hated him for it. It meant they always had to write a good story, and who could do that, at the rate of three a week?"

Terrill's longtime straw boss, Mike Tilden, swung into his saddle, insisting upon the traditional pulp story trail.

"Mike Tilden, God bless his heart, made you feel like a literary giant even when rejecting a story, and you went onward and upward," recalled Tommy Thompson. "Pulp people cared about you and Mike goosed me into *Argosy, Collier's, American* and *The Post* even though it meant losing a writer for *Dime* and *Star*

Western."

"Tilden, Heaven rest him, was into the sauce," added William R. Cox. "It was necessary to take him to the famed Tim Costello's Bar for steak and booze and tell him stories which one would go home and write. He accepted every one, just so you left him a list... His personal life was tragic beyond reason but he was a brilliant editor."

By this time, August Lenniger had risen to become the top literary agent for Western pulpsmiths. His job was to cull the weaker aspirants as much as encourage strong new writers to the proper pulp markets, as Giff Chesire discovered in 1944.

Chesire had sold a few Westerns on and off during the Depression, but soon deserted the field to toil as a construction company accountant. Illness forced him out of work. Boredom drew him back to the typewriter.

"Being a Westerner and having sold Westerns," he allowed, "I did a Western. It had anything any Western ever had. I mailed the finished product to Gus Lenniger, the agent, and set to work putting everything into other tasty little numbers.

"Item by item, [Gus] took out everything I had put into that story. I was amazed, infuriated, firmly convinced that the man had never seen a good Western yarn in all his life. I was prepared to write and tell him so. Would have, too, except for his final paragraph, in which he seemed to feel a little ashamed of himself, and which went something like this:

"'However, you can write. Since you have been connected with the engineering business, it seems reasonable to assume you know something about the construction game. They constructed somewhat, you know, in the early West....'"

Chesire swallowed his justifiable pride, executed a yarn along that theme, and his career was relaunched. The surest way to pulp success, he subsequently told *Author & Journalist,* was a fresh angle and "an agent who writes with a flame thrower."

Added Chesire, "I base my right to speak on my wealth of inexperience. I know nothing of the accepted technique of writing fiction. And, though this will likely cost me all my markets, I have rarely studied the magazines to see what they are using. Instead, I have a crisp, blistered memory of a winter day in '44 when I read a fourteen-page criticism of a story of mine. From that day I have jumped away from stock Western paraphernalia like a gun shy dog. My wife cows me into obedience even yet by murmuring things like, 'Waterhole... cowboy... rustler... range war... owl-hoot.'"

August Lenniger was the most powerful figure on the Pulp Range, the equal of any editor. He could make or break a Western writer. He made them by the score. He virtually saved the career of John A. Saxon during the Depression when Saxon couldn't rope and throw the new markets.

"Lenniger used to give me the very devil at times for sending him 'trial balloons' that were completely off-trail," Saxon admitted. "I was forever experimenting to see how far I could go and get away with it."

Some writers champed at the bit Lenniger insisted on putting in their mouths. One was Tommy Thompson, who walked away rather than knuckle down to his stern dictates.

"I was literally kicking ideas out of the way, there were so many of them," Thompson recalled of his early days. "And every idea was a fresh idea... I was with Gus Lenniger. I wrote stories like mad. He sold three or four... But Gus—for whom I have nothing but the highest regards—was not my agent. Every time I got a letter from him I felt like blowing my brains out. He was beating me into a pattern and I wasn't ready to be beaten into a pattern."

Those who stuck with them, however, swore by Lenniger—even as they swore *at* him:

"In the early days of our relationship," said Tom Blackburn, "he wrote some very tough letters about my work, letters he called 'sessions in the woodshed.' I was so furious with him at times that I seriously considered looking for another agent, but I never did. Looking back over my career, I'm glad I didn't. He wasn't always right, but he kept us eating, for that I am grateful."

He also knew how to peddle an author's wares, as L.P. Holmes fondly remembered:

"I'd write a yarn and Gus Lenniger would submit it to Editor A who would turn it down in scorn, adding that Holmes sure was slipping. So Gus would send it to Editor B, on the other side of the street and he (or she) would snap it up with the remark that this was one of Holmes' better jobs."

By all accounts, Gus Lenniger was a stern traditionalist, if not a true believer. "For nearly three quarters of a century," he once enthused, "the Western story has been one of America's leading favorites. Our grandfathers squinted under smoking oil-lamps at Ned Buntline's and Col. Prentiss Ingraham's melo-dramatic tales of how Buffalo Bill's timely arrival saved the beautiful braids from adorning the person of a savage Sioux. Today many millions of Americans, both young and old, still find their entertainment, 'escape', and perhaps as an outlet for their heritage of the pioneer spirit in avidly following the glam-orous deeds of heroism, self-sacrifice, romance and courage traditional to the conquest of the American West."

Fresh blood continued to pour into the field. Curtis Bishop had been part-timing it for years, but during the war went fulltime to feed the voracious pulp factories.

Bishop submitted a novelette to *Lariat* around this time which he described in *The Author & Journalist* as "…about a boom-town marshal who had exchanged the owl-hoot trail for the lawman's badge so as to be eligible to marry a Texas ranch-man's daughter. Into this trail town came a crusading preacher bringing a group of settlers from the Midwest. This minister wanted to clean up the red-light section of the boom town, which meant everything to the city because Texas trail riders wanted to bring their cattle to a town where they could kick up their heels. The girl fell in love with the preacher, one Julius Marlowe. Marlowe came leading his crusaders across the rail-road tracks, daring the gun-toting marshal to stop them. The lawman, Blue Strange, could do nothing else but walk out to meet the minister. But Strange was still in love with the girl and he couldn't shoot down Marlowe. He, a great gunman, took the preacher's bullet and fell forward on his face, dead."

"The Sixgun Saga of Blue Strange" provoked a bitter feud while still in manuscript, Bishop related.

"I'm told that up at Fiction House Jack O'Sullivan, Arch Robinson and Jack Byrne didn't speak for days over that yarn. O'Sullivan wanted Blue Strange to die, the other two thought he should live and go happily on his way.

"The result was a compromise. Into the story was written a prostitute who had loved Blue Strange for years and who knew that when he started out to meet the preacher he was signing the death warrant to his own happiness. She tried to stop him, even throwing a gun on him. In the struggle, Strange was wounded in his gun arm and, because of the pain, he missed his first shot at the preacher, and was killed by the crusader's fire."

Bishop contended that, "It isn't true that pulp editors want to publish the same plot issue after issue. I admit that there isn't enough variation, but I believe that is the fault of authors. Certainly the times I've come up with an idea that was a little different, without violating the fundamentals of a magazine's policy, I've received dividends—several times bonus checks over the usual per word rates."

Pushing the genre to its barbwire limits, Bishop took notice of another newcomer who had burst on the scene with a 1943 *Western Story Magazine* debut tale called "Bullets and Bull-whips."

"Occasionally I get very disgusted with myself for not realizing that even in Western stories, I should say *especially* in Western stories, this freshness is always available. I cussed for an hour after reading a story by Les Savage, Jr., in a recent issue of *Frontier.* He took a little-known fact of history and turned it into a swell story. Before the Civil War a boatload of camels was brought into the West by the war department at Jefferson Davis's insistence. I'll bet a drink I knew about that before Savage did—for I wrote a paper on it in college exactly eleven years before he wrote his story for *Frontier*. But while I was looking out the window, he was working at his typewriter.

"And the same guy popped up in a recent *Action* with a yarn based *not* upon the boom cattle days or the fight for more pasture, but upon the depression years of the early eighties when a steer's hide was worth more than a steer on the hoof. Yes, I had known about that, too. Does this guy Savage just worry, worry about his stories all the time! Doesn't he ever sleep or drink beer with his friends!"

Seeking the farthest reaches of the Pulp Frontier, writers and editors were reduced to substituting dromedaries for dray horses.

A letter from John A. Saxon kicked up the old controversy all over again. Written as a long, impassioned query to *Writer's Digest*, to which he hoped to sell an article, Saxon's letter ran as a mini-article entitled "Grown-up Westerns—Allegedly Wanted" in the March 1945 issue.

"Having had a hand in starting the present change in Westerns—and having fought bloodily for the change for ten years—I feel I know something about it," he asserted. "Having written and sold God knows how many hundreds of thousands of words of Western stuff, about ten or twelve years ago I began to get fed up with the juvenile approach and the 'bang-bang, hell for leather' stuff. It finally resulted in a down right rebellion on my part.

"My old friend and mentor Harry Bedford-Jones said, 'Well damn it, if you feel that way about it write 'em the way you want to and try and jam it down their throats.'

"So I finally wrote an 18,000 word lead novel which violated every set rule of Western 'literchoor.' Nobody got shot. The people in the story were all grown-ups. The sheriff wasn't crooked. The characters acted like all the people I had ever known from Montana to the Rio Grande and California to the Mississippi—that is people who had anything to do with ranches.

"But the pulps were not ready for that type of story. The front office said: 'No dice. What was good enough for the past generation is good enough for the present—and we are still holding circulation.'

"But one of the far sighted editors, Rog Terrill had an idea. He wouldn't go all the way but he started prodding his writers to do what he called The Emotional Western, the kind that leaves you with a choke in your throat at the end.

"Well, I did a raft of them. Cliff Farrell picked them up and did a lot of them. They ran about 50-50 with the blood and thunder buckety-buckety yarns for years.

"I still wasn't satisfied. August Lenniger, my agent, told me I was nuts.

"But, after thinking it over he came up with ANOTHER idea, another step along the road I had been plugging on for years. To The Emotional Western was added The Unusual Background, Unusual Characters Western.

"Then came Lee Bond,[2] Les Savage and another group of writers following the same trend but from different angles.

"That situation has prevailed for the last couple of years."

Saxon noted the demise of *Wild West Weekly* in 1943 and speculated it marked the beginning of a trend. "Are the Westerns growing up?" he asked. "Watch the kill-offs. Street and Smith's *Wild West Weekly,* the most juvenile of the lot (And I've written plenty of them too) was the first to go. More are following. More will go unless they 'GROW UP.'

"There will always be a market for COBURN, OLMSTED, and the rest of the old-timers, *BUT THE NEW WRITER CAN'T SELL BANG BANG EVEN TODAY.* The editors buy bang bang from the old-timers to get the name."

In truth, *Wild West Weekly* was a victim of the wartime paper

---

2   *Saxon means either Lee Floren or Lee Wells.*

shortage. Many magazines were folded in 1942 and 1943 that would otherwise have continued had paper supplies been more plentiful. Monthlies were reduced to bi-monthlies. Even the venerable *Western Story Magazine* was cut back to a mere monthly early in 1944. Its base rate of two cents per word was halved to a paltry penny. Martin Goodman summarily folded his pulp string in the Summer of '44. Most were Westerns, but he did keep one going—*Complete Western Book,* the title that launched his Red Circle outfit a decade before.

All across the landscape, the Pulp West was shrinking.

"Emphasis, everywhere, is on shorter lengths and more compact writing," reported *The Author & Journalist.* "The writer who can make six words do the work a dozen used to, is the writer who is going to sell nowadays."

Lee Floren had been happily changing horses to pursuit of new markets and better rates. "I left Ace, went over to Popular," he boasted not long after Pearl Harbor. "Rogers Terrill has praised me, berated me, and belted me. But it was all for my own good. John Burr shoved me into Street and Smith. Louis Silberkleit had sent me quite a few checks. I've sold to Fiction House and Erisman. Never Margulies, though. So 'round an' 'round it goes."

Floren was in a Mesa, California magazine shop where his wife counted 14 pulp covers carrying his byline.

"That was in 1942," he later recalled. "With a year of war behind the nation, I was an 'old man'—in my thirties—and Uncle Sam didn't want me. I was teaching school in a high school out in the mountains on the Mexican-California border; writing was a side-line for me, crammed in evenings after busy school days. For three years, I had pounded my typewriter, and been riding high and wide.

"The missus' next words brought me down. 'The paper cuts might knock the bottom out of your markets.'"

"They did.

"'I'll write booklength stuff,'" I said.

"That next spring, boiling in the California heat, I wrote my first 55,000 word novel, a Western. Bob Lowndes and Louis Silberkleit of Columbia liked it and sent me a three-figured check."

The Boothill Buckaroo landed in *Blue Ribbon Western*. Encouraged by fatter money, Floren wrote another.

"It slapped me back in the face so hard, it almost knocked me down," he lamented. "I looked at it. Bob Lowndes had a nice letter with it... but a letter doesn't pay the rent."

Floren discovered he had to adapt or perish. Short stories were a surer thing, yet had little resale value. But a rejected pulp novel was a dead loss.

Like so many others, he sought fresh cover. Following the tracks of Norman A. Fox, Nelson Nye and Chuck Martin, among others, Floren shifted over to the cheap lending library novel market to supplement their pulp work. Pay was poor, but old magazine novelettes and rejects could be rewritten or recycled to feed it.

Seeing sunset colors, other scribes drifted away from the field. Unwilling to stoop to a penny a word, Ryerson Johnson deserted the Pulp West for detective writing. Before he dismounted, desperate to discover a fresh twist, he concocted a Chinese cowboy armed with throwing knives instead of Peacemakers. Terrill declined Johnson's Shooting Gallery Kid, but John Burr embraced the novel series for *Western Story*.

More than mere magazines were casualties of the war. In 1944, Frederick Faust got it into his romantic head to become a war correspondent. May of that year found him with the U.S. Army in Italy, where in his halcyon prewar days Faust lived in a palatial villa pounding out formula Westerns. Refusing to carry a weapon, he accompanied a unit intent on liberating Florence armed with only a club cut from a tree.

At the start of the Battle of Santa Maria Enfante, Faust was wounded during one of the most ferocious artillery attacks of the war, dying quietly on the battlefield.

The King of the Pulps was dead. But no new prince had surfaced who could fill his boots. The last Western fabulist left behind many imitators, but no true heir.

His literary descendants soldiered on.

Stationed in the Pacific theatre of war, Sergeant Arthur W. Kercheval was flabbergasted to read in *Writer's Digest* that two aspiring pulpsters were stationed two miles from his 3rd Airdrome base. Jumping into a jeep, he raced over, discovering that Lenon H. Stringfield hailed from a town not far from his own Denver home.

"For two hours we talked a blue streak under the jungle moon," Kercheval told *Writer's Digest*, "covering every phase of the art of fictioneering from narrative hook to denouement. Naturally, we swapped questions as to what sales had been made, and they were filled with writer's awe when I admitted of marketing five Western shorts to the Wyn people, prior to my induction into the army. I had to enumerate them, for somehow titles always fascinated those of our breed—"Lazy .45s," "Tinhorn Saddlemate," "The Poker Pot Heroes," "Cold-Deck Canyon," "No Bids for a Bullet Boss," all appearing in either *Western Trails* or *Western Aces*. (At this writing I've learned of the acceptance of No. 6, "The Devil's Strongbox," scheduled to appear in a forthcoming issue.) My new friends decided without further ado that I had 'arrived,' which is far, far from the truth."

Kercheval survived the war to pulpsmith clear to the era's conclusion.

Staff Sergeant Walker Tompkins, stationed in Glasgow, Scotland for the duration, came to the defense of the juvenile oater in the July 1945 *Writer's Digest*:

"I've heard Senor Saxon expound his theories at bull sessions of the Fictioneers, a Southern California group of pulp writers, including such Western scribes as Harry Olmsted, Cliff Farrell, Tom Blackburn, George Shaftel, and others. Saxon, who is a court reporter in Pasadena when he isn't crusading for more mature Western stories, continued expounding in a long informative letter to me last winter, telling me that when I got back into civilian clothes I wouldn't find any more bang-bang juveniles being purchased by editors.

"I wrote back and stuck my neck out by saying that I disagreed with him. I told Saxon I believed juvenile Westerns would come back, and here's why I think so. Every year in America a generation of 10-year-old kids start devouring Western fiction. They'll want to supplement their reading of the comic magazines with cowboy stories. And they'll want blood to flow and six-guns to bark on every page."

Citing the popularity of Roy Rogers and Gene Autry movies, Tompkins went on to say, "Unless I'm badly mistaken, publishers and editors will revive magazines after the war to appeal to the millions of kids and teen-agers who flock to see bang-bang juvenile cowboy movies."

Tompkins also believed that *Wild West Weekly* was only suspended for the duration and remained confident that *WWW* and similar titles would return five years after the end of paper rationing.

"If not," he concluded, "I hereby guarantee to eat, without condiments, the original MSS of any of my friend Saxon's mature Westerns."

Tompkins was flat wrong. Whether or not he paid off is undiscoverable. After the war, he found Street & Smith to be "moribund," a virtual ghost town. "I had to fight my way back into the field," he later complained.

Tompkins concentrated instead on writing lead novels for what fellow contributor Tom Curry called "the super-hero Westerns" of Leo Margulies. In the forlorn post-war days, juvenile offerings like *The Masked Rider* and *The Rio Kid* were virtually the only novel-length Western magazine market remaining.

Spurred on by Chuck Martin, who called him "the daddy of the technique of full characterization in Westerns," Harry F.

Olmsted placed "After Selling Ten Million Words" in the September 1945 *Writer's Digest.* There, Olmsted conceded that the pulp Western was still undergoing growing pains:

"Let's take a gander at this business of 'Grown-up Westerns.' I was not aware that they had grown up. Growing, yes, but far, very far, from their ultimate stature yet."

Olmsted noted that among the bad old stuff then out of vogue, there still gleamed a few gems. But the pulp Western had clearly moved on from bang-bang.

"In my humble opinion, the stature of the Western was enhanced by a complexity embracing Chuck's 'characterization,' by subjective maturity of thought, authentic color dispersed in action, serious and convincing presentation, the language of action stripped of gross exaggeration, intriguing artifice and (more than any of the others) that the yarn be about something which the reader can accept as worth the reading effort. Couple all this with the writer's sharpest tool—enthusiasm."

John A. Saxon is not on anybody's list of major Western pulpeteers—*Twentieth-Century Western Writers* failed to favor him with an entry—but to hear him tell it in "Tabu Buster Or, Growing Up With the Western Story" (*Writer's Digest,* October 1945), he became a struggling pioneer in the direction of more mature frontier tales around the time H. Bedford-Jones gave up on the genre:

"I was getting pretty tired of 'bang-bang' and took Jones' words very much to heart," he recalled. "One of the first of my 'non-bang-bang' stories was an 18,000 worder I wrote for *Five-Novels,* entitled *Range Branded.*

"It got into print in this manner. I was having lunch with the late Florence McChesney, then editor of *Five-Novels,* and in the course of the conversation I said: 'I wish somebody would let me write a story in which about seventy-five less people die and where the protag doesn't even carry a gun.'

"Florence said: 'Well, don't you try that sort of a yarn on me. I won't buy it, and I'll probably get hell if I do, but let me see it.'

"Eventually she bought and published it. I made my first step in the direction of a goal which I was not to attain for many years—to write and sell a Western story in which the hero doesn't carry a gun, and there was *no shooting at all.*

"By now," Saxon went on to relate, "Cliff Farrell was really going to town in *Dime* and *Star* with his 'emotional' stuff. They were 'sob-story' yarns and Cliff handled them nicely—the sort of a story where the writer tries to leave you with a tear in your eye and feeling damned sorry for *somebody.*

"With the help of my New York agent, 'Auggie' Lenniger, to whom I'm afraid I have always been a pain in the neck, being strictly of the 'non-conformist' type myself, I hopped on the band-wagon and began to try to 'out-sob' Cliff.

"I started the 'Gunsmoke' series for Jack Burr of Street and Smith's *Western Story,* at the same time doing a lot of the old-time Westerns for other books that were inclined to let some other publisher do the experimental work.

"Hurrying through several of the Gunsmoke stories I can detect a distinct leaning toward the psychological development of character, a deliberate underplaying of violence, and an almost total absence of gunplay.

"During this same period I was writing a lot of stuff for Mike Tilden and Rogers Terrill of *Dime, Star, Ace-High,* etc.

"Popular Publications was beginning to like the 'emotional' type of story, so I stuck my neck out on it and wrote a thing called 'Greater Than Gunflame.' It came pretty close to being a sacrificial love story."

Saxon rode the emotional steed through the balance of the 1930s.

"In 1941," he admitted, "I got thoroughly fed up with Westerns and quit writing them. There was only one thing I hadn't accomplished and that was to write a Western story where the hero didn't carry a gun, and in which not a shot was fired. I had about given up hope of accomplishing it. Auggie Lenniger said I was nuts, and he was probably right."

Saxon switched mounts, riding the detective mare instead. That lasted three or four years.

"A year ago when I came back to the Western field it had changed once more," he wrote in "Tabu Buster." "For several years the editors had been calling for more characterization.

"Tommy Blackburn was going like a house afire with his 'Christopher Defevre' stories about the old Shakespearean actor who was roaming the country with a show-troupe and getting into about the same sort of adventures as old ["Pawnee Joe"] did years ago.

"Cliff Farrell, too, had become 'fed-up' and had gone back to one of the Hearst newspapers as night editor. He has done but little writing for several years, when all of a sudden he broke into the slicks with 'Fiddlefoot,' in [*The Saturday Evening Post*].

"But the old-timers can't stay away. Cliff is writing again now for *Dime* and *Star*.

"Once more I had to catch up with the parade. How far, I asked myself, had the Western progressed? How far was I behind the procession?"

Saxon turned out *Vanguard of the Steel Trail Legion* which landed in *Ace-High Western*, October 1944.

"I threw the book at them in the way of characterization, slow tempo, little or no gun-play and made my hero—of all things—a telegraph-operator who had been a spy in the Union Army during the Civil War," he noted.

"I caught onto the trend quickly. Minimize the gun-play, but keep the threat of the gun there at all times. The *threat* of impending action, and the *threat* of gun-play is much more effective than the actual happening thereof.

"I did a couple more and felt that I was back in the saddle."

Saxon experimented with a yarn told from the female point of view, called *Shifting Sands*, which ran in the *Toronto Star*, December 30, 1944. Then:

"Back to the man's viewpoint again I wrote 'The Outcast of Cliff City,' and I went whole-hog on it. The hero was a railroad man, an ex-convict, and the former member of a gang of bandits. He was married, had his wife with him, and shattering the greatest tabu of Western pulp fiction, *his wife was expecting.* It sold to *Ten Story Western*, and I suddenly realized that here, after long last, I had sold a story in which the hero didn't have a gun, no shots were fired (except off stage) and motherhood was no longer something to whisper about.

"Walker Tompkins, who used to turn out reams of stuff for *Wild West Weekly*... wrote me a letter from his army post in England saying: 'I don't believe it! Shades of Blackwell! A pregnant woman in a Western story!!! Buy yourself a drink with my compliments.'

"I did. I felt I had finally arrived."

Concluding, Saxon thought the pulp Western once more had a bright future:

"I have proved to myself that in the past few years editors have become pretty receptive to anything new *IF YOU DO IT IN AN INTERESTING MANNER.* The old hide-bound traditions as to what you can and cannot do in a Western story have been pretty well shattered. I like to kid myself that to some small extent I have had a hand in busting them."

A third writer also ventured to forecast the post-war Western. Stationed in Maryland's Aberdeen Proving Ground, Private William L. Hopson wrote:

"I try to think back into what now seems a long dead past, to a time when I worked three or four hours a day, arose at whatever hours I chose, went to bed at 2 P.M., looked as I liked, dressed as I liked, and took orders (for stories), only from pulp editors. But this army has changed all that was. It has changed our way of thinking too; mine and hundreds of other professionals, as well as thousands of amateurs who, though in uniform, still hope to find time to do some writing.

"It has changed our perspective, our thought processes, our evaluation of what might be called the things that once counted. I didn't realize this at first. I think few of the writers now in uniform did, either. But shrewd editors already were well aware of what the war has done to our national life, and a rejection from one of them on a story I had managed to turn out, after hours, on the typewriter in the 1st sergeant's office, brought home what I should have known.

"I had sold this editor numerous stories. I had filled orders for him, lunched with him, and quarreled with him in his office over revisions. He turned the yarn down cold. He would have snapped it up a couple of years ago. It was a good story as run of the mill stories go. It had plot, a couple of new twists, characterization, or so I thought; *but it was written in terms of two years ago, when Americans' personal God was still 'all for me and mine, and forget everything else.'*

"Most Americans have, up until the Japs struck Pearl Harbor, been firm in the belief that God created this universe for our benefit and that without us it would have been a foul place indeed. It was reflected in our speech, our ambitions, our manners while visiting foreign countries, and above all, in our fiction stories. These last named had but one plot: a handsome American hero fighting for a just cause, but always with the prospect of winning, in the end, the 'jewels,' a gold mine, or at least the goodly portion of an oil field or cattle empire."

Hopson was coming to sense in a sobering of American enthusiasm, the awakening of a world power. That he saw it as expressed in terms of the profession of writing Western stories does not diminish its validity. Because he perceived it in himself.

"I wrote the story, it was rejected, and the fault was not that of the editors," he confessed. "A rereading showed that somewhere in the gap between my last story as a civilian and this newest effort something had happened.

"To date I haven't sold a line of fiction since entering the service. But I've finally got a novelet under way. I do not say that I can finish it soon or that my agent can dispose of it after it's done; but I do know that in its scrawled lines is something new that never could have come out of the old plot machine in the other days.

"Fiction writers unable to get into the war, and the tyros who haven't yet cracked through, would do well to keep a close check on all mags, both pulp and slick, and watch for the work of the soldier writer. For they're going to see things start creeping into his work that weren't there before; things that are going to make themselves felt in the American short story.

"Thomas Wolfe was right when he wrote the title, 'You Can't Go Home Again.' Time changes and the things that were are gone. When Hitler is but a dark and bloody blot beginning to dry on history's pages, we in uniform won't be able to go back either. When that day comes, and we get back to full writing production again, there will be as high a standard of difference between the stories of then as between those of today and thirty years ago."

Hopson would live to see that glorious day, and exult in it. But not exactly in the way he envisioned it. For returning soldier-readers as much as soldier-writers were going to demand more than merely a higher standard of sincere pulp.

They would come to expect something entirely foreign to the Territory of the Imagination: true authenticity.

"I started writing Westerns with the attitude that this sixgun stuff is easy. You shoot three people in the first two pages, then have the hero wounded, a chase on horseback and then the villain gets it in the neck.

"I'll never forget how quick those manuscripts came back."
—Lee E. Wells

14

RETURN OF THE
REGULATION WRANGLER

JOHN A. SAXON'S essays ignited the old feud anew. Some complained that he was taking altogether too much credit for what was really a group effort, which Saxon readily conceded.

"It was not my intention to put a halo on my gray hairs by claiming that I was personally responsible for the origination of the 'non-bang-bang' Western," he wrote in the April 1945 *Writer's Digest.*

An avid reader of pulp Westerns from Tucson brought Saxon up short and hard.

"Ernest Haycox first introduced Western characters who talked, acted and thought like real people," journalist N.W. McKelvey pointed out. "Granted that Haycox has long since graduated to the slicks, he remains the founding sire of the school of mature Westerns. And as for present-day pulp writers, has Saxon ever written anything to equal William Benton Johnson's 'Homesteaders,' 'Night Marshal,' or 'Escape' which appeared in *Dime Western* as far back as 1940?—or comparable stories by such writers as L.L. Foreman, L.P. Holmes, L. Ernenwein and Peter Dawson?"

Then McKelvey gave it to Saxon with both barrels.

"Since I could find only one of Saxon's stories in a file of 70 Western magazines from 1940 to date, it would appear that *only* 'God knows how many hundreds of thousands of Western stuff' the old revolutionist has written."

Saxon's rebuttal—if there was one—was not printed.

S. Omar Barker of Tecolotenos, New Mexico offered his salty opinion in a letter published the following January:

"For the past 20 years I've written Westerns in which there was little or no bang-bang, sometimes no gun at all; Westerns with a Mexican hero, Westerns with non-cowboy protags as homesteaders, sheepmen, doctors, lawyers, trappers, game wardens, Forest Rangers, etc. A fair percentage of these were also told in the first person.

"Maybe I've been hogtied to my own self all these years and just didn't know it, but frankly I never found either taboos or patterns binding. Living way off here among the hoot owls, I've always had the country-boy idea that whenever I succeeded in putting some punch in my stories, some editor would buy it, regardless of taboos. And believe it or go suck eggs, so far it has always worked. Neither has my wife, Elsa Barker, ever encountered any serious barrier of taboo or pattern in writing Western love stories. Of course we don't try to sell Greek tragedies as Westerns."

One writer who did from time to time, and who gave the lie to Saxon's strict evaluation of the sexlessness of the pulp Westerns, was *Wild West Weekly* regular Allan R. Bosworth. As "Jackson W. Thorne," he occasionally contributed to the infamous *Spicy Western Stories,* where just about anything went:

"I wrote these with tongue in cheek," he explained in "Take to the Hills, Men!" (*Writer's Digest,* January 1947) "That was a good place to keep it, no doubt, considering that most of the stories had to begin with something like this: 'As her wiry little mustang galloped across the prairie, Sally's small but exquisitely moulded young breasts danced entrancingly under the silken shimmer of her blouse...' Paragraph. Something here having to do with the plot, perhaps, but not for long. In the next paragraph, you got back to Sally's bosom."

According to Bosworth, *Spicy Western* paid two and a half cents per word at a time when most of its competitors paid a cent, or less—which explained why he and so many others were drawn to its pages, which were littered with moonlighting Westerneers yarning under sagebrush pseudonyms.

"I doubt that the magazines contributed much to the uplift of anything," he conceded. "But one of the four stories I wrote for them proved my contention that a classic theme may be adapted to any field.

"I was showing one of the magazines to a newspaper friend, and I made him bet that I could take—and I pulled this out of thin air—the Cinderella motif and write it into a *Spicy*. I did, too. Instead of the prince going around looking for Cinderella with a glass slipper, my cowboy hero went around looking for the lass who could fill a size 40 bra, which had been sent to him by mistake from the mail-order house. The buxom babe, of course, had received the fancy headstall with eye-winker cups that the cowboy had ordered for his horse."

During the war, *Spicy Western* had been tamed down to an off-color nag renamed *Speed Western*. It was never part of the mainstream Pulp West anyway. Market notices often lumped it in with *Ranch Romances* with the dry comment: "This is not the regulation love pulp."

Another vocal exponent of bang-bang, Chuck Martin, jumped into the fray next. In "The Common Man, Western Story Division" (*Writer's Digest*, February 1946), he gave his own personal account of the ever-shifting mirage that was the Pulp West:

"We've been writing Westerns for twenty years during which two decades, three generations of writers have come and gone to do likewise, with each generation bringing some changes to the old basic Western theme.

"Was a time when the Gun Gods stampeded through the pages with their hog-legs blazing 'Bang-bang,' and raising plenty of hell. During that time the old-time editors told us: 'Don't tell us what your hero is thinking; let him TALK for himself!'

"So we mastered the art of dialogue. Came Twilight, and then the Dawn of the Next Era, which means that a new set of editorial ramrods took over the 'Pens which were mightier than the six-shooters.' They vouchered the checks, and the professionals were all writing for money. The first thing these new editors did was issue an edict about dialogue.

"'Too much talkie-talkie,' they admonished sternly. 'Get down inside your characters, use the single objective, and the PLOT must motivate all ACTION!'

"We wondered if they meant what they said, and some did. The old sloppy dialect had to be cleaned up, and descriptive narrative largely took the place of dialogue. The writers who could not make this change went to work in the studios in Hollywood, or back to driving a truck. Those who were elastic enough to conform, made the change.

"Then the editorial edict went out that there was too much emphasis on fast gun-slamming. They said the gun-dummies had to go; they've been saying it now for twenty years.

"Don't you believe a word of it, and don't take my word for it. Just go to any newsstand, pick up the current crop of Western mags, and glance at the titles of stories on the contents page. The six-shooter and the gunman still hold the fickle spotlight."

Pressed into wartime service keeping several series going, including those of Walker Tompkins, Martin struggled to keep up with the demand for his work.

"My best year, and I hide my head in shame," he admitted, "was 103 stories sold to the pulp Mags. Then John Scott Douglas spoiled it by telling me Frank Richardson Pierce sold 113 that same year. Several times I had as many as four stories in the same Magazine under different names for Leo the Magnificent Margulies. Clay Starr, Scott Carleton, Reeve Walker, Jeff Carson, Graham Cassidy, and the like."

When Tompkins was discharged, Martin gleefully unloaded the extra series. "The dirty dawg," Martin groused. "He wouldn't take 'em back. So final [*sic*] we both quit those series. So damn sick of those little buscaderos, 115 pounds soaking wet, always whupping three-four six-footers in every story."

Now past 50, Martin summarized his prolific career with a prescient epithet worthy of his own Literary Boot Hill: "The million-word-a-year man was sired by low rates, and killed off by his own exertion." He also once admitted his deficiencies as a writer by saying, "I have a couple of very frank editors who tell me that they only buy my copy for the color."

In "The Common Man," Martin spoke of the turning point that defined the Pulp West of the 1940s.

"Yores humbly began selling Westerns to Leo Margulies about fifteen years go. The 'Bucky Dorn' series, in which our hero was a bronc-stompin' deputy sheriff, which I have been, and still am.

"One day I received a long and earnest letter from Leo saying that a very fertile spot in the Western field had been overlooked. He claimed that the West had been built and populated by many different kinds of people, and that he wanted some stories about the 'common man of the West.'

"The telegraph lineman, the man who ran the general store, men of dozens of various occupations lived off the ranching community. Old time town directories, and handbills listed their vocations. How about these men for the heroes of Western stories as a change from the cowboy. August Lenniger, the agent, got hold of the same idea and was sending form letters to his Western story clients suggesting they try this new kind of hero."

Lee E. Wells was one of these writers. His rubber-stamp cowboy stories kept bouncing, and he couldn't fathom why.

"Lenniger… kept trying to get this idea across to me. August is a persistent sort of a guy and finally I did a short about a clerk in a Western general store. John Burr bought it. Followed shortly, two about cowboy life insurance salesmen in Arizona in 1880. Ruth Dreyer and John Burr bought both of them. Leo Margulies bought the next attempt, the story of an Irish railroad section hand in the West. By then I had seen the light. Few of my Western tales since have not had a basis in actual events in the old West."

Even Chuck Martin was dragged bodily into better markets, such as *Western Story*. "I learned a heck of a lot in the last couple of years under your not-too-gentle tutelage," he told Lenniger in 1943. "You and editor John Burr had to beat hell out of me, but I finally learned something of the newer technique in writing Westerns. Not only that, but I now like my copy better my own self."

Five years along, the historical trend was still going strong. Cowboys remained editorial poison.

"It was in June 1945 that I stumbled on a humorous and unique character for a Western pulp yarn," recalled Frank H. Bennett. "The story practically wrote itself. Rather, my character wrote it. I sent it to Standard, and, so it seemed, almost before I got home from the post office, Leo Margulies sent me a check and a note which said this was the kind of stuff they were looking for. Immediately I wrote another story around this character. They bought it, and so began my humorous series of 'Doc Swap' yarns."

Twenty-eight stories ran in *Texas Rangers* before traveling trader Doc Swap exhausted his bags of tricks and was retired by mutual agreement.

Norman A. Fox reported, "That prolific pulpster, Tom W. Blackburn, once showed me a lengthy roster of occupational characters which he had compiled. When Tom is ready to start pounding out another smoky saga he has only to go down the line to find his inspiration...."

Blackburn credited this anti-cowboy list with transforming his career. "My work gained in strength from the day I borrowed from Harry Olmsted a ragged little pamphlet that turned out to be a sort of business directory of an early Arizona town," he recounted in 1944. "Glancing through it set a train of thought in motion which is still paying me rich dividends.

"I sat down with that book and listed every trade in business in that town. There were nearly eighty of them. I saw suddenly that I didn't need events of great historical significance to build a sound, *historically-flavored* story within the confines of 5000 words. The sheriffs and marshals and badmen—the rustlers and bandits and gun-hands—had come in for too much share of Western glory in fiction. With that list of trades as a guide, and using problems which might face ordinary men in like trades in a rural town today, I set out deliberately to write fragmentary histories of these unimpressive heroes.

"It was a gamble. But it worked. I was careful to maintain an authentic flavor in background, dress, action, and dialogue. And I studiously avoided any opportunity to make my sawyer or peddler or cooper or gunsmith a superman. I made him, as closely as I could, the counterpart of the carpenter or blacksmith, whose shop you still find in country towns."

Blackburn swore that he had never failed to sell a story triggered by that list.

"Editors are more receptive to these little-used types of characters," explained Norman A. Fox. "Ask Street & Smith's John Burr how many stories he receives which deal with sheriffs and outlaws. Ask him—then duck!"

"But there were only cowboys, rustlers, sheriffs, and a few Indians scattered around, you will say," observed Lee E. Wells. "That seems true enough, but brother write a story with only that in mind and see how quickly the better editors such as John Burr, Rogers Terrill, and Leo Margulies bounce it right back in your lap!"

Old hands as well as new contended with this unreal new reality.

Chuck Martin wrote, "Leo Margulies told me that a Western story should be 'Folk-lore'; the simple story of the daily work of a cowboy, miner, or any of the common men of the West. He also wants the earthy salty humor of the real cowboy, as the late Will James so masterfully worked his craft."

"One of the best Western stories I ever wrote, according to the editors," said Zorro creator Johnston McCulley, "had the railroad station agent in a little cowtown as the hero. Another was built around a blacksmith and his troubles—not a cowpuncher in either of them."

"The possibilities here are as limited and as varied as were the actual types in the early West," continued Fox. "The old piano player from the saloon was one of my heroes and I've sold yarns built around a groceryman, a stage-actor, range-cooks, sky-pilots, a bookkeeper, a checker champion, a telegrapher and a host of other types including the cowtown medico and the cowtown newspaper owner."

But even this fresh new pasture came to be overgrazed.

"These last two have been worked a little thin in recent years," Fox admitted, "but there's no law against writing a good Western story about a barber, a photographer, a dentist, a blacksmith or any other type, occupational or otherwise, who might have been found west of the river where men were men and grew beards on their chests."

"Still to be written about, at any length," counseled Lee Floren, "are frontier merchants, lawyers, surveyors, railroaders and others who followed useful, if less celebrated, occupations."

"In this question of background the field is almost unlimited," claimed Lee E. Wells. "The old photographs and daguerreotypes prevalent in the West, many of which have been reproduced in books and magazines, mean that there had to be photographers. One of the trade often mentioned was Mr. Fly at Tombstone during the time of the Earp-Clanton feud. There were others at Dodge, Abilene, Carson City, Leadville, and countless other places. There were many more photographers who traveled from town to town taking pictures and constantly moving on. One of these nomadic photographers made the main character of a story, *Tintype Texan,* that John Burr bought for *Western Story.*"

Giff Chesire actually launched a series built around a piano tuner who was also a gunwizard. His Tunin' Tedro stories ran in *New Western*.

Some sagebrush scribes soon tired of the anti-cowboy.

"And so it went from year to year," bemoaned John A. Saxon. "Stories of gamblers, cattle-drives, cattle-trains, store-keepers, doctors, and what have you. Girl view-point stories, school-teachers, ranch-girls, girl-gamblers, milliners, waitresses, ad lib, and ad nauseam.

"I think Bob Bellem and I hit the top on lay-characters, when together we wrote a lead novel for Leo Margulies where the protagonist was a vetinary, and the villain was injecting fever into herds of cattle because he wanted to buy the cattle-land for a railroad. There was everything in it but the kitchen stove. The hero sent back east for serum. The villain side-tracked it. The hero went after it and the villain set a prairie-fire.

"Oh me, oh my—such fun."

The bottom of the barrel was suggested by Arch Joscelyn, when he wrote, apparently in all seriousness, "If you must have cowboy heroes, they still can have widely different backgrounds. How about a sailor with a wooden leg who has to pass himself off as a cowboy? Or a clown who wants to get material for a new clown act and thinks that a season as a cowboy will give him what he needs? In other words, freshness of characters and plot will go a long way toward overcoming the weakness which annoys editors more than all others put together—the same old plot with the same old hero."

The better Westerneers took a more serious approach to concocting what editors sometimes called "off-trailers."

"To be different, to shake myself out of the Western formula," recounted Tom Blackburn, "I tried writing a story without dialogue. One story I did was so empty of it that the hero—an Indian—had only one speech in the yarn, delivered twice: *'Me tired!'* The piece sold readily. Another was almost entirely en-closed in quotation marks. It also sold easily to the same market. These are examples of extremes, and were my effort to sound out a proper way to achieve writing individuality."

Blackburn once attempted a stream of consciousness action Western. "Over half of this story, when it appeared, was printed in italics," he recalled. Rogers Terrill's reaction suggested the revolutionary state of things:

"I'll have to agree with you that this is a pretty radical experiment for the pulps. Not only do you use considerably more stream of consciousness than we usually employ, but your idea of making a colorless little bank bookkeeper your hero was a little startling, to say the least—

"Keep on experimenting, fella, for I believe that some day you'll be selling these little off-trailers to the slicks!"

Quietly and persistently, writers like Blackburn and Lee Floren kept pushing the Pulp Frontier farther and farther into unexplored territory.

"…I read a well-known slick author," Floren said, "a specialist in the 'woman's' field, and, using information gained therein, I sat at my machine and knocked out a Western story. I wrote about *people*, not about *incidents*. I rewrote not a word of it and I do not believe I even reread the story. But soon a check came in for it from Harry Widmer of *10 Story Western*. He said he liked the 'slick' treatment that had been applied to the characterization."

Floren's "Gun Ghosts Can't Die!" appeared without fanfare in 1944. But it so shattered the action formula that former Clayton editor Allan K. Echols, struggling to write fresh Westerns himself, cited it as the wave of the future.

The simple story of a quiet saddlemaker with an outlaw past that comes back to haunt his new life, "Gun Ghosts Can't Die!" lays aside the classic situations and Western impedimenta and directly anticipates *High Noon* in the way the reformed protagonist is forced to face his troubled past alone, his own townspeople turned against him. Although Floren resolved his story situation through the traditional gunfight, he told a tale of purely human conflict. No cows, no gold, no guts—and no clichés.

Echols correctly recognized in Floren's approach the next step forward, but editors continued to cling to the old conventions.

"We have heretofore made the character the tool of the plot and we have reached a dead end," Echols asserted. "If we will start making the plot the tool of the man we can go on forever!"

Some veterans, such as Nelson Nye, had been doing that all along:

"I seldom start writing with a plot in mind; my yarn is devised as I go along, through the interplay of character. This system has disadvantages; it usually necessitates considerable re-writing; but it does avoid the 'cast-iron' plot."

A semi-retired Westerneer from Thermopolis, Wyoming named William F. Bragg made the identical point at the close of 1945 when he assessed the editorial experiment begun in 1940.

"In my writing days," he stated, "I noted that when editors grew weary, a sure sign of poor markets, they railed at the old familiar Western plot themes, locales and characters. But so far as I can see, nothing very radical ever happened to such things. After all the old West was the old West and the field can't be changed much. But human character is always interesting no matter in what field and I sometimes think if popular fiction went in more for characters and color and less over-strained plot incident, we'd regain a lot of our customers.

"I don't know why but probably because the erratic and fitful taste of the customers, the great American public, turned to other fields such as movies and radio," Bragg theorized. "However we were all probably guilty of one thing through the years. We got the swing of the so-called 'formula' and we stayed in the groove. Even today the deadly formula resurfaces here and there. It has burst out of the seams.

"Another thing that encourages this view is the way the movies and radio are falling into the same old formula pitfalls.

I think this is because the radio and movie writers are being edited too much. This happened to pulp writing along about 1940, and it never works out. The best material in the end is what the writer dreams of and not what some editor dreams of."

Most pulpsters, however, were still fixated on what *not* to write.

"If you start with a fresh and dramatic situation that could overtake almost anybody anywhere," suggested Giff Chesire, "and you are doing a Western, you will not set your story in the desert or in a saloon or on a trail drive or a beef gather, unless you absolutely have to. You will not make the character a cowboy or a deputy, or a trail wolf, or an old prospector, unless you must. You will try to find some other setting equally if not more typical of the old West—a fruit orchard, an apiary, an irrigation project, a diversified ranch, or a mail route. Your hero will be a tailor, a Watkins man, a taxidermist. He will not go through the conventional tricks, the things that come quickly and easily to your mind, such as whipping the villain in a bar brawl, shooting it out with a contingent ten times his number, doing deeds of wonder with lead enough in him to crush him to the ground. He will be governed solely by the logic of the situation, competing against a villain who, though formidable, is also governed by the logic of the situation."

Unfortunately, the irresistible logic of the Western was cowboys and cattle.

"It is difficult—and I doubt if beneficial—to avoid all the familiar stage settings," countered Johnston McCulley. "It is necessary to retain the cow town street, and saloon and school-house, the ranch buildings, the corral, the calf pasturage, the canyons and draws and background of hills and loftier mountains where called for—but they must be used in a natural manner without being stressed."

"I have tried to avoid the conventional cowboy story, but I think it was probably a mistake," asserted a new rider on the

Pulp Range named Frank Bonham. "That is like trying to avoid crime in writing a mystery book."

Eventually, the classic range rider was allowed back in. But he never dominated the field as he had prior to 1939. His day in the sun was done.

"A Western pulpster can always rely on those old stand-bys, the cowboy, the hired gunman, the prospector, or the sheriff," allowed Norman A. Fox. "A few thousand stories have been written about these salty sons, a few thousand more will undoubtedly be written, and I'll probably do my share of them. Yet there is no reason why I or any other writer should stick to a steady diet of bronzed sons of the saddle. The sunset side of the Mississippi drew all manner of men from the tamer shore. Many a gent who never felt the burn of a lariat can, nevertheless, be worked into Western stories."

"Certain books will use out and out cattle stories while others go in for the broader range of interests that were known to the American West of the Seventies, Eighties and Nineties," noted agent Ed Bodin in 1946. "In the strictly cowboy magazines, your hero would naturally be a boy who knew how to tie fast or dally, and which hip the brand belonged on. If your editor turns his writers loose in the tall timbers, the buffalo wallows and the gold mines, then brother, you can dig up almost any kind of buckskin man and decorate him with a John B and a Colts .44."

The Texas Trail story was back to stay, asserted Arch Joscelyn in 1944. "Innumerable stories of the longhorns, coming from Texas to Montana, have been written, and may others will be written," he confidently predicted. And he was right.

Attempts to take the all-conquering cowboy down a peg made some little progress, according to S. Omar Barker:

"…if memory serves," he wrote in "Courage on Horseback" (*The Author & Journalist*, December 1944) "that there was a time when many pulp editors would have turned thumbs down on any bang-bang buckaroo hero who betrayed the slightest natural human reluctance to slaughter his fellow man." [...] "I sold a Western not so long ago in which a sincerely religious young trail-hand not only had the courage to mount a water barrel and preach to a crowd of hooting hoodlums in Dodge City, but also the courage, born of his sincere belief in the commandment, 'Thou shalt not kill,' to face imminent death for himself rather than kill a fellow man. This, of course, was an off-the-trail story, but it sold."

Still, the Western super-hero died hard. A followup *Writer's Digest* letter by Saxon complained, "If you get a chance take a look at the cover of *Star Western* this month, which shows the thing I railed about in the article, a man driving a stage coach with the reins in his teeth and a blazing six-gun in each hand."

To which responded Montana writer Chis'm MacDel Rayburn, voicing what was doubtless a majority opinion among pulpsters who were growing uneasy with the increasingly-garish covers.

"In the matter of covers," he wrote, "I'll admit to a strong desire that the average Western cover be 'reformed' into a more accurate reflection of the material to go under said covers. I try my darndest on each yarn to do a job that the editor will be glad to get, one both of us can be proud of. I WISH the covers had progressed WITH the fiction content during the last few years—so that a fellow would *never* feel somewhat apologetic about said covers when showing mature friends a book contain-ing one of his yarns."

But the cover artists were just as hogtied to the Hollywood myth as were their writing saddle mates.

"In some instances, and certainly among the contributors to this colorful art form," Robert G. Harris recollected, "it was jokingly known as the 'Tit and Pistol' circuit. If in doubt about selling a weak cover idea, all you had to do was paint it red and you had a sale—or if you had a gun blazing away and lots of smoke, nine times out of ten you had it made. There wasn't such a thing as subtlety in these action paintings; you made a hit with art director and printer when you used the color right out of the tube."

Another practitioner agreed that the Western pulp cover formula was fixed in stone.

"It had to have action, color, six shooter spitting fire, hero in trouble but not defeated, no girl kissing," insisted Rafael DeSoto. A native of Puerto Rico, his first attempt to paint a Western pulp cover was derisively rejected because his "cowboys" were modeled after Argentine gauchos!

Even the King of the Pulp Covers, Walter M. Baumhofer, discovered to his chagrin that he dared not buck the all-mighty art directors. "Almost lost my pulp popularity, when, during my honeymoon spent in the West, I finally saw a genuine, dyed-in-the-sagebrush cowboy," he related. "After considerable argument with editors, finally put back the bright red shirt instead of the lovely sun faded colors I had just discovered."

Years after it was all behind him Robert G. Harris recalled, "I can still smell the gunsmoke and hear the creaking of the saddle—and the art director yelling, 'Paint it *red.*'"

With few exceptions, as the 1940s wore on and the stories matured, the more publishers felt the need to gun-dummyize the covers as a counterbalancing marketing device. Story titles became increasingly sensationalized. Fiction House and Popular Publications, in particular, seemed to be engaged in a duel of overblown titles like "Gunhawk of the Conestoga Caravan" and "They're Buying Beef in Hell!" It got so out-of-hand that one writer, sickened by purple retitlings of his realistic tales, and knowing some editor would slap on a fool white-heat title anyway, simply numbered his manuscripts in protest.

"I'm afraid people's impressions were based mostly on the lurid red-and-yellow covers," lamented D.B. Newton, "filled with sixguns and gritted teeth and leaking bullet wounds, and on the titles some editors persisted in hanging on our masterpieces: I always died a little when I saw my stories christened things like 'Wanted: Four Kill-Crazy Gunslammers' and 'Tin-

Badge-Backed Bushwhackers.'"

The writers had learned to avoid gun-dummy melodrama like poison. But their editors remained addicted to hokum—even if it was a more refined distillation of the pure pulp product.

Editor Robert O. Erisman captured the prevailing dilemma of the 1940s in a terse directive: "No plain gun-action any more. Emphasis is now on characterization, good writing and sound emotion—with gun-fight climax always, though."

As his star writer, Victor H. White, once explained, this was simply a necessary nod to historical reality. "We never left the punishment of the villain to chance. The pursuit of justice was the motivation of the Western pulp just as it was the motivation of the true Old West—a thing hard fought for, but finally achieved."

"*The Western, in most cases, is highly fictionalized, with stan-dard plots and characters greatly overdrawn and repeated ad infinitum. I have always been amazed at how these almost identical characters and situations are constantly published and republished.*"

—*Gordon D. Shirreffs*

I 5

DIFFERENTLY THE SAME

LATER IN that year of 1945, the specter of the gun-dummy was again casting its awful shade over at the Thrilling ranch.

"We've been yelling our heads off about bang-bang," Leo Margulies complained to fledgling writer J.R. Jackson. "It doesn't seem to do much good. I got a ten thousand worder from an old-timer who should have known better. He's been doing publicity for Columbia Pictures. I read a few pages. Nine killings. Ridiculous. I wrote him he'd sent me the scenario for a grade B Western picture by mistake. We don't want that."

Few publishers did. But there were some.

Over at Fiction House, they were inexorably slipping back into the Wild West wasteland of the pulpy '20s. *Lariat's* new editor, Jack O'Sullivan stated, "We want vibrant, melodramatic yarns of the open range, embracing strong characterization and a good meaty plot bolstered by lusty love interest. Give us as hero a cowboy or cowgirl; an outlaw, male or female; but don't give us a dummy hero or dummy characterization."

Writer Curt Brandon was a new face on the scene encouraged by the opening up to better writing that prevailed in most Western magazines.

"Of a sudden, a while back," he recounted, "I realized that several men were writing about the West as it was and employing, instead of the usual Brooklyn slang, the English language. Instead of the conventional pattern, they were telling the story straight, pulling no punches, straining for no embellishments."

Brandon started in the pulps, but was soon selling novels that he conceded had been previously unpublishable by New York standards.

"A generation ago a Western story was simple," he explained. "The hero returned to Texas from the Civil War, limping a little from a wound suffered at Gettysburg. He found his plantation fields overgrown in weeds and his fences collapsed. He sat unhappily staring at the ruins. Then he realized a tremendous thing. There were wild cattle feeding on his unkempt fields. He assembled them into a herd and drove them to Kansas. There he sold them for a prodigious sum and married his childhood sweetheart, who had been pursued for two years by a carpetbagger. The reader was left with the impression that every time he drove a herd to Kansas he married a new wife.

"That story was substantially true. It was a good story—once, and there was nothing wrong with it. Just as there was nothing wrong with the 'when you say that smile' and the tall, shy cowboy marrying the school teacher. People *do* marry school teachers…. *The Virginian* is not corny, not the first time. The fault I find with Western stories is that once one is written and approved by the public, both author and publisher are reluctant to let it go. They change a few minor details and out it comes again and again."

Lee Floren restated the evolving pulp cowboy recipe this way: "Your hero should have the genuine ring of the West. In the old tradition, he is usually a man of daring and personal integrity on the side of law and whatever organized social forces exist in rough, anarchic country. His gunplay, fist fights, hardship, championship of somebody who's being pushed around— all combine to show him as a symbol of decency and courage, as a focus of that struggle between good and evil which had peculiar and picturesque expression in the old West.

"But draw your hero in proper proportion to your story situation and to your 'supporting cast,'" he warned. "Sam Mines, veteran editor of *Giant Western*, once told me that he rejected many otherwise well-done stories because authors molded their heroes in such gargantuan proportions that they gave the impression of being blustering braggarts. Don't overplay your hero; don't oversell him."

That admonition was lost on Frank Gruber, who boasted, "My heroes are often patterned after Jesse James, Wyatt Earp, Bat Masterson or some of the other giants among the two-gun men. They are never weaklings. They may lose at times to inferior men, but that only bears out that even Achilles had a vulnerable spot. A defeat of a giant at times lends plausibility to a story...."

Defending his corner of the Pulp Range, Victor H. White contended, "There are those who say that a true picture of Western life was not given, that only the violent side was portrayed. I do go along with that fact that we writers emphasized violence and repeated it over, over and over again. I have violently killed many men on paper with typewriter! But I will not agree that the violence portrayed by Max Brand, Walt Coburn, Frank Richardson Pierce and the rest of us was more extreme, cruel or vicious than events that actually did take place in the West."

An up-and-comer named Thomas Thompson, struggling to carve out his own niche in the Pulp West, ultimately arrived at an observation that more than anything else codified the shrinking landscape:

"Why," said the author of *The Trojan Cow*, "just a few months back I thought a really epic Western was 50,000 cows going to Abilene. Now I know it is much more epic to have just one lone cow going to Abilene. Especially if it is a pregnant cow."

As Thompson explained to his agent, Joseph T. Shaw, it was a return to an inescapable fundamental. "I've thought a lot about *The Virginian*—. In that book there is no struggle of empire, no clash of hundreds of armed men against thousands of blood letting Apaches. And yet the book still stands as a Western 'epic,' and the only reason it does is because the epic proportions of the character itself."

Before he achieved epiphany, Thompson traveled down the traditional tumbleweed trail.

"I wanted to write Westerns for the pulps," he reminisced. "I couldn't sleep. It was all so simple. You introduced a hero who had a problem and you went ahead and solved that problem. Since this was a Western, best to solve the problem in gunsmoke."

"Gunsmoke is still popular," allowed S. Omar Barker, "but editors want its drama to depend more upon the interplay of conflicting human emotions that bring it about—or follow it— than merely upon a slam-bang description of fancy gun slinging."

Only the best of the best seemed to have absorbed that lesson.

"...drama and violence and tension are created not only by the rattle of hoofs on the Great North Road, or by 'Summoning up his last remnant of desperate strength, he made one final great lunge,' etc. etc.," cautioned Ernest Haycox. "Drama and violence and tension are created also by little things, by the two-inch shifting of a man's shoe as he changes the weight of his body on his legs, by the drop of an eyelid, by the voice of a man simply standing by, with a feeling in his bones that the sky will presently fall in."

"A good Western is only a good story if you can remove it entirely from its Western trappings, re-set it in another time and place and still have a good story," Luke Short insisted. "It's the characters—their human conflicts—that make for a good yarn. Never mind the trappings, that's just window-dressing."

But Short and Haycox had moved up to the slicks. What they called for constituted fine writing. The pulps were offering an altogether different product: tall tales coated with a thin veneer of nostalgic shellac.

What passed for evolution in the genre inevitably came down to pure technique.

"Twenty years ago," said Paul Ellsworth Triem, "the most salable Western story was one with a trick plot. A vocabulary of a hundred or so seasoning words—'hombre' and 'hog-leg' and 'bronc' were among the favorites—would give the yarn the Western flavor. The rest was trick. Well, just try to sell a story like that today."

Observed S. Omar Barker in *The Author & Journalist*, "You still come across Westerns in both the pulps and slicks in which the cowboy hero wears his horse's legs off up to the knees (and never knows it) by galloping the same pony hither and yon for a 40-hour week without even unsaddling, much less changing mounts. You still find fictional thousands of cattle grass-fat on an area that wouldn't support fifty head. You still find fictional ranches run by crews of buckaroos who spend six days a week bellying up to the bar. It is still a fact, lamentable or not, depending on your viewpoint, that numerous 'Westerneers' regularly sell stories which ranch folks cannot read without snorting."

"The trouble, as I see it," wrote Arch Joscelyn, "is that we've been educated to the wrong idea. A lean, cold-eyed waddie can go up against a big outfit which persists in rustling its neighbors' stock, and kill a dozen men, and that's all right. He can be sieved with shot from head to toe and hardly bat an eye, and that's all right, too. That's the tradition."

"The tradition—and it is a true one—of the cowboy as 'courage on horseback' was the legitimate father of the Western story in the first place," added Barker, "and whether as ranch hand, mounted lawman, or adventuresome drifter, the cowboy is still an acceptable hero; but today a much wider selection of occupational backgrounds is encouraged by most editors. In fact a drift away from the cowboy actually engaged in cow work seems to me to be definitely noticeable."

This drift went on both directions, Barker asserted.

"I have been interested to note a growing tendency among ranch folks to avoid calling their 'hired men on horseback' 'cowboys.' Why? Because the popularity of unauthentic Western stories and movies has robbed the name of its real significance, creating in its place the story-book cowboy of popular conception, stereotyped and considerably fabulous."

As wartime gave way to peacetime, arguments for and against authenticity continued to rage unresolved.

"Authentic local color," Arch Joscelyn espoused to *Writer's Digest* in "Variations on a Theme" (May 1944), "the real flavor of the West, is important in any good story, but you can't impart it to the story, the sort of story that editors favor these days, unless you know something of the West and its real, not fiction, history, but when it comes to getting that, your opportunity is as good as anyone's. Simply dig out the history in books, old letters and documents, maps, and so on, which are to be found in most state historical libraries and in many public libraries."

Two years later, Joscelyn began whistling a different tune.

"Editors write letters stressing the *real* West and their desire for it in fiction," Joscelyn described in his 1947 *Author & Journalist* essay, "History and the Western." "They break into print with more pleas of the same sort. Writers come forward and say that a new school of Westerns is emerging, that the old action Western is dying and the real West is coming into its own.

"Maybe the new era that some like to talk about is dawning. I'd like to think so. It would broaden the Western field 90 per cent. But so long as editors refuse to taste of the old days' meat and insist on just a skimming of the Western broth, avidly buying the old pseudo-Western whenever it's done according to pattern—just so long, I'm going to remain skeptical. So, until a change really comes, brother, you don't need to worry much about history or authenticity; it's more of a handicap than a help."

A year later, Wayne D. Overholser offered a starkly contrasting opinion in his *Author & Journalist* essay, "Beating the Sagebrush":

"I do not hold with the boys who declare that there is no place for authenticity or research in the modern Western," he asserted. "There are, of course, certain accepted formulas and basic plots; there are some taboos that change very little. It is true that many things have actually happened which are interesting, perhaps exciting, but which would not make good fiction. It is also true that some of the early Western story writers set the stage so that most readers today have formed a conception of the West that is hard to erase. Now no matter how false that conception is, they are definitely shocked if an author violates the tradition."

Editors could be shocked, too. They had cultivated the soil of their never-never land so well they began to believe in it.

Arch Joscelyn recalled, "If I write a Western with plenty of the old slam-bang action and the tried and proved plot, it sells readily—generally to those editors who are said to be most sympathetic to the yarn of the real West. But if I write the other type, I sell it—if at all—with much more difficulty, and much more reserve on the part of the editor."

Every Westerneer had an anecdote to back up Joscelyn's point.

"Once I wrote a story describing a range war in Colorado," recollected Curt Brandon. "I had the cattle kings employing twenty gunmen to ride up from Texas and throw their weights around. The editor returned it and deemed it implausible. I wrote him back the true version of the incident. There were not twenty of them, there were a hundred. They did not come a-horseback; the cattle kings chartered a special train for them. The editor changed his mind and bought the story."

As with many of his contemporaries, Lee E. Wells broke in via the formula route, and soon found himself in a box of his own devising.

"Like everyone else," he confessed, "the first stories were distinctly of the 'thataway' type, or vapid and pale copies of a lot of better writers. Then someone pointed out to me the high mortality rate of pulp Western writers... It seemed to be that the answer was to give the editors something different."

It was not as easy as it sounded.

"Something different" had been a pulpster curse phrase since the Great Depression. No editor could define its true meaning, but every Westerneer was expected to intuit it.

"I had read plenty in my time about getting 'something new, a different angle,'" admitted Wells. "The hardest thing about the Western story is obtaining that element the editors label as *different.*"

No one today remembers writer Charles Handley, but his experiences trying to decode pulp editorial needs are illuminating. For 15 years, he heeded the call for stories that were "different."

"I wrote one about a young cowboy whose wife was accidentally killed by bandits during a bank robbery," Handley wrote in 1946. "Having nothing to live for he went after the gang in the face of sure death, wiped them out and was killed. He got about forty-seven rejection slips for his efforts.... I wrote another about a simple kid who was kicked around by everybody. I poured poverty into that one in an attempt to gain reader sympathy. I guess the editors figured the hero would starve to death before they could get him to the news stands."

When every off-trail effort failed to land, Handley tried loading down his plots with true authenticity—with the same disappointing result.

"Leo Margulies was kind enough to say my writing was all right," he wrote, "but the story was too familiar. I should try again with something with a different twist to it.... I read that letter more than fifty times and still I couldn't for the life of me figure out what he meant by a different twist. My different yarns hadn't even brought a letter and my close-slanted one brought kind words that I should do something *different....*"

Eventually, Handley figured out the secret, and began selling.

"There are only a small number of acceptable situations in a given story field," he discovered, "that is, situations which the reader wants to read about, and he wants those presented again and again, only *differently the same.*"

Handley hit the nail on the head. Here was the central problem of the Western writer, whether he was a traditionalist penning historical Westerns, or a fabulist concocting the mythic brand. Don't stray far from familiar fields.

Norman A. Fox recognized the reality of this challenge.

"Maybe most of us who specialize in one type of fiction evolve a formula, consciously or subconsciously, and proceed to follow it with slavish monotony," he confessed. "Since there is nothing new under the sun, including story ideas, the trick of this writing trade is to give new twists to old themes. And the possibilities of diversifying the Western story by one device or another are as wide as the West itself."

Or as narrow as an editor's prejudices.

After peddling nearly 200 tall tales, Fox observed, "When I sit down to write another Western, I try to keep it from sounding like the carbon copy of the last one by shifting the occupation of the lead character, the location of the setting, or the period in which the story transpires."

Other prolific writers developed similar strategies.

"If we stole at all," said D.B. Newton, "it was usually from ourselves, by making a slight switch in the last story we wrote—perhaps trading places between the hero and the villain, and adjusting the motivations to fit—and sending the resulting story to a different editor."

The best prescription for this problem came from S. Omar Barker, who said, "Read Westerns. Read a whole damn lot of Westerns. Study how the writer does it, then do it yourself only different and better. If this shotgun advice doesn't seem to make sense, remember that most of the time neither do stories. They aren't supposed to. They're supposed to make *feeling.*"

This reality prevailed even in upriver magazines such as *Short Stories.*

"Let's take the basic yarn of a cowboy who is wrongly accused of rustling cattle, and appears certain to lose the girl and gold to a rival," cited editor Lamont Buchanan. "Hero set outs to prove his own honesty by finding the real rustlers, who, of course, turn out to be in the pay of his unscrupulous rival. Probably thousands of pieces have been written in some variation or another of that basic plot. And thousands more will be written, bought by editors, and enjoyed by readers.

"But each one will be different," emphasized Buchanan. "Each one will have some special originality brought to it by its author. New development of character, conflict, or climax twist. An old-time professional take the bit between his teeth and heads enthusiastically right into a rip- roaring new version of this ancient chestnut."

"In order to succeed, even in the lowest pulps, a writer must put some bit of his personality, his originality, in his stories," advised Lee Floren in 1946. "Without that, his story falls flat, he is done before he starts. The man who looks down his nose at the pulps does not succeed in that field. For the borderline between pulp and slick is so fine nowadays that even experienced 'hands' are sometimes at a loss to know, without an editor's opinion, whether they have authored a slick or pulp story."

Originality is a challenge for writers working in all genres. In the Western, this problem was especially acute. It was common knowledge that even a loyal pulp magazine reader lost interest after seven years of steady reading. When readers started deserting, the panic response was invariably the same.

"The editor decides that the stories were long winded, that they must be speeded up," explained Allan K. Echols. "The writer speeds up his stories. Physical action against its specialized background! We do the same old things better and faster. We cry for something new while crying that there *is* nothing new!"

Experiencing the Pulp Range from both sides of the editorial fence, Echols was forced to conclude that "the pure action story in any of its specialized fields must eventually destroy itself by repetition."

He came by this grim understanding through practical experience. "About twenty years ago, while editor of *Cowboy Stories Magazine*," Echols wrote, "I analyzed every short story that had been published in our magazine up to that time, and made up a 2-page list of story problems. I have rarely seen one since that was not on that list."

"No matter how you may labor with the old bean you can forget Polti's obsolete 36 dramatic situations," insisted Gladwell Richardson. "I did a long time ago because they just didn't work out in getting at the meat of plotting a Western story, whether it was short or long. After fifteen years and hundreds of Western tales of mighty heroes and women just like God made them, to me Western theme plots stack up like this:

1. Love.
2. Covetousness.
3. Achievement.
4. Animal.
5. Climactic.

"Just five? Yes, brother, and when you use one of these designations you will always wind up with another as a secondary plot to your tale."

Stephen Payne reduced it even further to one basic idea.

"It is: The forces of right and wrong clash, and right triumphs over wrong. Plain greed is the major motivation of all villainy. (Not the only motivation, but by a long shot the most common.)

"However, the manner in which the villain goes about it to acquire—always by unfair, underhanded and unlawful means— what he desires, and the manner in which the hero upsets and blocks his scheme, permit of *ten thousand and one variations on that same idea.*"

Either way one reckons it, allowed Gladwell Richardson, "These are strictly 'suit case' plots. Since we can't possibly get away from them and editors are always yelling for something 'new,' we are forced to do the next best thing, dress them up in new clothes. Put spring garb on them until they shine with the purity of apparent 'originality.' This is done with new locales, new twists to old situations, snow balls and having the main characters accomplish their objectives by a 'new' and unusual yet plausible and possible method. By this we mean what the general reader age believes to be plausible and possibly probable, not what we believe because we know the facts."

"But counteracting this basic truth is a happy parallel," added Walker Tompkins. "Namely, that new readers are coming along all the time, to whom these oft-told tales are thrillingly new. Our job as a writer, then, is to present our stuff in some guise which will sound original, despite the fact that under the clothing and muscles would be found the same old skeleton."

"And your yarns do not have to be too original," Thomas Thursday insisted. "Oh, I am aware that editors howl and moan for something 'different,' but God help the writer who fails to hurl his yarn into the same old groove!"

C. William Harrison pointedly concurred: "You don't avoid the trite. You use it and give it a new coat of paint."

"Plots?" scoffed S. Omar Barker. "You'll be hard put to find a basic plot that has not been used. Try anyhow. If you can't, a fresh twist or appealing character work can often put the old ones across again."

Norman A. Fox offered a perfect example. "The Western yarn about the hired gunman who finds himself pitted against the one person he likes is old stuff. You bet. But I worked a new twist into the denouement and Rogers Terrill used the yarn, 'Idaho—Merchant of Death!' in *Dime Western*."

It was a simple as that.

But there was such a thing as going too far down untraveled trails. Gladwell Richardson cautioned, "Building a plot around a spectacular and singular incident, even though you may have uncontestable proof that it actually happened in real life, may be entirely too unusual to be plausible and probable. As witness a friend of mine who wrote a Western tale about a fun-loving Arizona sheriff who issued the following invitation:

YOU ARE CORDIALLY INVITED
TO ATTEND THE HANGING OF ONE

His soul will be swung into eternity on December 8, 1899, at 2 o'clock sharp. The latest improved methods in the art of scientific strangulation will be employed and everything possible will be done to make the surroundings cheerful and the execution a success.

"Editors combed my friend's hair with their pens," Richardson averred. "They swore it couldn't actually have happened. Nothing so raw as that went on in the West of curly, yellow-haired heroes and bold peace officers. When he dragged out the original printed invitation they said it might have happened, but nobody would believe it."

"In other words," said writer Robert Turner, "Western readers didn't want to know that the Western gunslinging folk heroes were often cowards who shot first and asked questions afterward, some of them out-and-out psychopaths. They didn't want to know that many of the so-called dance hall girls were ugly, smelly creatures with bad teeth and, all too often, venereal diseases."

"I have had stories rejected—and so have other writers—simply because my stories were really the pure quill," agreed Arch Joscelyn. "The reason given as that they were not authentic! A lot did happen in the early West, and accordingly, a lot *could* happen in fiction. But most of the early history, as such, is considerably different from the average story. It is just as exciting, or more so. Just as bloody and tragic. Yet most of it seldom gets into print. Why? Because, I believe, of that old pseudo-Western tradition."

As D.B. Newton wrote, "For some curious reason the Western story had become saddled, early on, with the notion of a morality tale—right and wrong, good against evil—a concept that seems oddly at variance with the real West, where the ultimate issue was actually one of sheer survival, by almost any means."

Newton explained the rules of the range: "The pulps never wavered in their respect for the familiar moral stereotype. When we wrote for them, we tacitly accepted a strict, if unwritten, code whereby each character in a story, and his actions, had to be weighed and assigned an appropriate reward or punishment. The hero and all the other good people picked up the marbles; the truly evil had to be killed or, if a secondary villain, possibly sent to prison instead. As for a weak character who might at some point waver briefly and go over to the wrong side, he must at the very least repent his mistake and be shown at the end feeling very, *very* sorry!"

"The whole thing was stylized, of course," Ryerson Johnson allowed. "And that's one reason why the boys stayed in the pulps longer than most of them meant to. Because it got to be where you could do it most easily and with some certainty. You tell your story within that pattern of acceptance, and you could sell every one you wrote—if not the first time, then the second or the third time anyway."

The prolific Lester Dent outlined this rough-and-ready art better than anyone, creating a pulp masterplot that a generation of his typewriter-punching colleagues swore by.

"There may be an editor here or there who won't buy a formula, or contrived, story," Dent told them. "They don't stick around long.

"What they want is a story with the bones of the formula so cleverly covered that it isn't standing out like the bones in a starving cow. With a little practice it is not hard to cover the bones.

"They want a yarn that starts with a situation that precipitates the characters into conflict, jumps into the story quick, has as few characters as possible. They want the desires built strong; characters must be torn between them. The protagonist must be forced into a corner where he must make a final decision, and let there be no doubt anywhere in the yarn which character is the most important.

"If you can rig yourself up a story skeleton which ensures all this," Dent concluded, "and sell it over and over by putting a little different flesh and clothes on each time, it simplifies things."

Once again, ranch-raised S. Omar Barker put the issue into perspective:

"Editors are not supposed to be cowboys," he wrote. "They are supposed to know story values—how to select yarns that a majority of readers will enjoy. They do it, too, or they don't stay editors very long. They doubtless prefer stories of a reasonable authenticity, but the point is that they make story value, not guaranteed authenticity, their primary yardstick in buying Western stories."

Barker went on, "Some successful Western writers' yarns are authentic down to the last hair in a saddle cinch. There are other equally popular, top hand story craftsmen, who from personal experience might not even know which end of a horse to put the bridle on, yet write strong, entertaining stories with historically plausible plots and Old West backgrounds. I myself happen to have been born and raised on a ranch, but it is a demonstrated fact that *you do not have* to be a Westerner to write and sell Western stories."

Pointing to the top craftsmen in the field, Barker suggested even they couldn't cut the mustard in real life:

"...you should hear some of the real ranch folks' snorts that I've heard at Luke Short's tenderfootish methods of handling cattle (in his stories); not to mention some very significant snickers when reading Haycox and [Alan] LeMay. Yet these boys are tops... and among the 'authentickest' of our craft— swell yarn spinners, taking pains, at least, to be as authentic as they can, not like the Hudson Riverites...."

And something strange was happening to the Western writer. The further in time he became removed from the era he wrote about, the more he was inclined to consider his yarns semi-factual. With each passing decade, he increasingly saw himself as the honest custodian of legend, not a teller of tall tales.

Perhaps it was the psychology of the liar coming to believe his own fabrications, but the Western writer began to assume a growing importance in his own mind, somewhat akin to a historian.

"The Creator of that breed of man called the cowhand, cowboy and cattleman," wrote Walt Coburn in later years, "for some reason known only to Senor Dios, selected this cowhand writer among the chosen few to record the history of that hardy breed of pioneer, be it fiction or fact… I know that somewhere along the trail the Senor Dios laid a hand on my shoulder and shaped my destiny. Such is my belief and will continue to be until I follow the ghost rider on the pale horse on my last circle into the Shadow Hills."

Others seemed to slide into total fantasy. Walker A. Tompkins took to spinning wild windies:

"Once in 1934, as a young man of 24, I carried my Corona portable to the top of the Pyramid of Cheops and spent a day knocking out a novelette which I mailed to my editor in New York. It was published, as a recall, under the title, 'Tombstone Calaboose', no doubt the only literary masterpiece ever composed in such an exotic setting."

A check of the back files of *Writer's Digest* unearths his original report. Tompkins merely got the idea there. He didn't write that particular *Wild West Weekly* tale for years afterward.

Another one getting long-in-the-tooth was typewriter burner Tom Roan. His agent recounted observing the prolific pulpster in action:

"I watched him one day at his home in Atlantic Highlands, New Jersey," August Lenniger recalled. "Tom is a big man, and heavy, well over two hundred pounds. Suddenly, I saw Tom's hands drop from the typewriter, but I knew he was concentrating on something vital to his story. His right hand went to his side and he reached for an imaginary revolver. Then bringing it up in front of him as though aiming at some hated adversary, he pulled the trigger as he roared, 'Pow, pow, pow, pow, pow!'

"Then his hands went to the typewriter again. Curious as to what he had written, I tiptoed behind him and looked over his shoulder. I could have been a ghost so sure was I that he didn't sense my presence. I read the words he had just written: 'Five times his gun spoke hate—each pow of explosion a note in the dirge of death.'

"Tom had just killed a man on paper, but the illusion was strong. Tom was experiencing the emotions of the protagonist. No wonder his stories are realistic."

A former Alabama peace officer, Roan may have been suffering traumatic flashbacks rather than an attack of imagination-fever.

The pulp editors encouraged their writers to play up their Western backgrounds, whether real or imagined.

"Editors thought their readers liked to believe that their writers practically wrote the stories with their typewriters balanced across the saddles of their range ponies," commented Ryerson Johnson.

In the postwar era, the pulp Western struggled with its new-found maturity.

"Today, while gunfighting is still an acceptable ingredient in most markets for Westerns, there is also an editorial demand for cowboy heroes with some human qualities besides being split up the middle, with a gun in each hand," warned S. Omar Barker. "The editors of Western pulps are hollering for 'human interest,' and the writer who cannot supply a reasonable amount of it along with or in lieu of gunsmoke is shortly going to find himself, as the cowboys, say, 'between a rock and a hard place.'"

Returning veterans resaddled their typewriters. The brief wartime boom in readers and word rates was over.

"I broke in a couple of years ago," Ray Gaulden said in 1947.

"It was much easier then than now. Competition wasn't so keen during the war. I have sold fifteen shorts and two novelets so far this year. But, mister, they still send them back. The heavily fomularized Western is on its way out. If you don't believe me, just try one on Mike Tilden."

"We'll be perfectly willing to grant that there's no new general plot pattern as such," Popular Publications' Tilden readily conceded. "But the reader does want a certain amount of freshness and vitality. And one of the key ingredients may often be found in the characters. The reader is concerned about people, and people he can believe in, and moreover, people who are doing things."

Provided said people fall into the narrow editorial category of what constituted a pulp hero, that is. "It is good to have the hero a determined type of man who goes though hell and high water against tremendous odds to reach his goal," Tilden clarified. "Though many of the readers are boys of 8 to 14, the hero should usually be older. Authors tend to over-sentimentalize younger characters in this field."

"For a time you might get away with the purely action piece, but you'll do this only in the pulps," cautioned Lee E. Wells. "Even there you'll sooner or later come upon a time of reckoning. If you don't believe me, get a pulp Western of five or ten years back and one of today. Notice the change in the list of writers."

"For the Western story is gradually climbing up and up," said Lee Floren. "Two editors in my opinion, are responsible for this: they are Mike Tilden of Popular Publications, Inc., and Bob Lowndes of Columbia Publications, Inc. Both competent, they watch their 'copy' closely, and, when the writer lets his conversation 'fall out of character,' both are there to patch up the breech before the story hits print."

Columbia was one of the bottom-of-the-barrel pulp houses. In fact, editor Robert A.W. Lowndes himself admitted he had no particular fascination with the West, real or fictitious. He preferred editing his science fiction magazines. His hands-off policy was the opposite of Rogers Terrill's forceful approach.

"By the time I became a pulp editor," he allowed, "it was possible for a writer to write a Western the way he wanted to for a fair number of markets. Since I didn't know from nothing, I told all my writers to turn out stories they enjoyed writing and do them the way they felt the story required."

Even here, restrictions ruled. Colorado cowboy Lauran Bosworth Paine decided he could write better Westerns than anything he read in the pulp.

"Because I grew up in the Western ethos and environment," he allowed, "I am perfectly at home writing Westerns. I did it all at one time or another, and have the scars to prove it, from blacksmithing to trapping wild horses, to working in the saddle and harness shop, to working cattle, my own later, the cattle of others earlier, to riding in motion pictures, to horse and cattle trading."

Paine submitted six stories to Lowndes. All were rejected on the grounds that the writer was attempting to 'educate' his readers rather than entertain them. He changed his approach and got lucky with number seven.

"So I conformed until I was well-known enough to come back to telling about things as they were, which I do now exclusively," he boasted.

Obscure in America, Paine went on to write a staggering one thousand plus Western novels under 90 pen names—all for British publishers not stuck on the pulp myth.

Another downriver market was the Red Circle Group, owned by Martin Goodman and edited by Robert O. Erisman, now in his second decade there.

Paying low wages, Erisman had to be content with rejections and off-trails castoffs, but sometimes they were pure gold. In the early '40s, as Luke Short was shifting over to the slicks, his brother, Jonathan Glidden, broke into the pulp field writing as Peter Dawson. Erisman fell heir to many of Dawson's more experimental efforts.

"What amazed me was the excellence of these Dawson rejects; here was really fresh stuff for a change," Erisman recalled. *"The only thing that had killed these stories for the editors who first saw them was their split viewpoint.* Dawson had not stuck every word of the way with this hero. He'd follow the hero for a scene or two, then he'd switch over perhaps to the villain and follow him, then the heroine maybe, then back to the hero, etc.—always moving the story ahead, though, in his switching, and gradually pulling his threads together into a climax and point. He used, in short, novel technique in a short story."

Ironically, some of the freshest Western yarns were appearing in the crudest magazines—thanks to pulp editorial blindspots.

"Dawson, like most real artists, was simply ahead of his time," explained Erisman. "Because, as Dawson sensed, the patterns of fiction are constantly changing…. For today's Technique Taboo is tomorrow's Right Way."

But in the Pulp West, editors were still too busy ducking gun-dummy lead to focus on future fiction trends.

One of the few serious hardcover Western novelists still working, Arthur Henry Gooden (writing name: Brett Rider) complained, "A young man once conceded that he read all the Western pulp magazines and then, choosing episodes that appealed to him from the various tales, wove them into a synthetic 'Western.' He was averaging a hundred dollars a month, he boasted. He had never seen a cattle ranch and his cowboy language was acquired from a dictionary of Western slang."

Self-admitted Manhattan cowboy Robert Turner was one who fit that description perfectly. In his autobiography, *Some of My Best Friends are Writers, But I Wouldn't Want My Daughter Marrying One,* he explained how he pulled it off.

"…I wrote and sold tons of Western romance and straight Western stories… without ever having been west of the Hudson

dominant pulp genres. But just two years after World War II concluded, the Western again resurged.

Even action-crazy Fiction House moved in the direction of maturity. Editor Paul L. Payne describing *Frontier Stories* this way in 1946:

"We want to bring the Frontier alive again for modern Americans, so keep in mind that the Frontier was a place of brawling disorder. Primitive conditions, savagery, violence—and occasional flashes of great natural beauty. It also was a place of vast and unrelieved loneliness. Men were on their own there, pitted against pitiless nature, vengeful Indians, and treacherous whites. It was a situation to bring out not-too-well known sides of humanity—greatness and depravity."

Further evidence that the paper landscape had been irrevocably altered came from one of the field's oldest active practitioners, Johnston McCulley. For the April 1948 *Writer's Digest*, he penned an instructive piece for straying future Western writers, "The Western Story's 'New Look.'" Dividing the market into the Old Look and the New Look Western, McCulley explained it this way:

"The Old Look frequently comprised a situation where, to get action quickly, the story opened with a man holding a blazing gun and shooting down his foes. From a common sense standpoint, such a scene is properly a climax. Death is an ending, not a beginning.

"In the new Western story, physical action is subordinate to emotional action to a large extent. One man doesn't go gunning for another until he has had an emotional upset. He doesn't kill without a motive—revenge, prevention of injustice or self-preservation. Mental turmoil can be just as effective as physical turmoil if the writer knows his business."

Recalling that "Twenty years ago an editor wouldn't touch a yarn with Indians in it," McCulley observed that Indians are once again welcome in the pulps. Women enjoyed a larger role as well. "The swish of a skirt through a Western is desired by most editors now," he added, "but do not stoop to sentimental mush."

But McCulley's most important point lay in the sea-change among editors: "Editors are demanding better and better writing. The theory that readers of Westerns are mostly 'dumb clucks' has been proven wrong."

Finally, he suggested:

"Watch the Western motion pictures, the so-called Horse Operas. They have the New Look now, too. The hero doesn't indulge in intoxicants to any great extent; he isn't mushy in love. He doesn't whip out his gun every five minutes. Your Western hero should be a normal, mentally-balanced man ready for action but not begging for violence. Your hero must not incite combat, but he is ready to meet it if it comes."

McCulley called the state of the Western movie perfectly. The Technicolor horse opera was coming into ascendancy. The days of the rodeo-shirted range rider were drawing to a close. Audiences were bored with the singing guitar-strumming lariat-twirling trick-shooters of Hollywood.

Even a typewriter cowboy like Walker A. Tompkins found them unpalatable.

"I sold one story to Gene Autry," he admitted. "I don't re-member what my title was, but his title was *Colorado Moon*. I was quite shocked when I saw it. My story was very rough and tumble. Gene stopped his horse, unslung his guitar and sang a song between action scenes."

One anonymous cowpuncher spoke for jaded millions when he quipped, "These movie cowboys are jest too dang fictidious."

After a wartime drought during which few serious Westerns were filmed, the genre took a new direction in 1946 with John Ford's now-classic retelling of the Wyatt Earp legend, *My Darling Clementine*. This was followed by Ford's *Fort Apache*, and Howard Hawks' *Red River*, both starring John Wayne. *Red River* was based on a novel by a gangster-turned-pulpster named Frank Fowler, who once told a fellow writer: "Don't you get it? It's a rewrite of *Mutiny on the Bounty!*"

Shane (an *Argosy* serial-turned-book by a Terrill discovery named Jack Schaefer) and *High Noon* (adapted from John W. Cunningham's *Saturday Evening Post* tale, "The Tin Star") were right around the corner. One of the best mature Western sagas was *3:10 to Yuma,* based on an Elmore Leonard tale torn from the pages of *Dime Western.* Rogers Terrill's Emotional Western was riding hard for the Silver Screen.

But first it crossed the border into radioland, in the form of the first so-called "Adult Western" ever broadcast.

Gunsmoke grew out of CBS President William S. Paley's 1949 request for a hardboiled Western program he blue-skyed as "Philip Marlowe in the Old West." Production issues shelved the audition show until 1952, when producer Norman Macdonnell and scripter John Meston discovered "Mark Dillon Goes to Gouge Eye" while trying to develop a Western radio antidote to such juvenile fare as *The Cisco Kid* and *The Lone Ranger.*

Pure spleen drove them.

"It isn't often that a writer or any man is given an opportunity to destroy a figure he's always hated…." Meston told the *New York Herald Tribune.* "My hated figure is the Western hero who rides along looking like a transvestite, strumming his guitar, nasally singing a synthetic ballad, and looking for all the world like a fugitive from a cheap circus. I spit in his milk, and he'll have to go elsewhere to find somebody to pour the lead for his golden bullets.

"Now the best way to destroy something is to ride it down with something better. And I've got a guy I think outclasses any of these phony big-hats."

Set in Dodge City, Kansas, *Gunsmoke* revolved around Marshal Matt Dillon, his deputy Chester Proudfoot, medico Doc Adams, and the town prostitute, Kitty Russell. It was rough, raw and uncompromisingly realistic. During its first two seasons, no sponsor would touch it. That was just fine with

Norman Macdonnell.

"Sure," he told *Time*, "I'd feel great if someone did buy it, but there would be problems. We'd have to clean the show up. Kitty would have to be living with her parents on a sweet little ranch . . . And Matt, he'd have to wear buckskin and swagger around with his guns blazing. He'd even have to ride a pure white charger. Of course, if a sponsor did come along who would let us leave *Gunsmoke* as it is, then we'd really be pleased."

Dillon was a calculated blend of iconic Dodge lawmen Wyatt Earp, Bat Masterson and Wild Bill Hickok. Like them, he faced the West as it probably was.

"We got tired of the standard save-'em-just-in-time show," Macdonnell said of one early episode. "As the play progresses, Matt learns that the guy who was lynched was completely innocent. He knows who the lynch leaders were, but what can he do? Nothing, not in those days, against those odds. So he leaves, without doing anything tangible. And yet, after he is gone, he has left behind in the minds of the townspeople a sense of tremendous shame for what they have done."

"Dillon was almost as scarred as the homicidal psychopaths who drifted into Dodge from all directions," Meston once admitted. "Life and his enemies have left him looking a little beat-up. There'd have to be something wrong with him or he wouldn't have hired on as a United States marshal in the heyday of Dodge City, Kansas."

Three years later, *Gunsmoke* crossed over to TV, and James Arness replaced voice actor William Conrad. Macdonnell transferred the high production standards that had made the show a critical and commercial benchmark intact:

"We never do action for action's sake," he recounted. "For instance, we've never had a chase on *Gunsmoke*. We made a list of things that annoyed us in the regular Westerns. For instance, the devotion of the cowboy to his horse. That's a lot of nonsense. The two things a cowboy loves best are his saddle and his hat. And cowboy speech isn't full of things like 'shucks' and 'sidewinding varmint.' What's more, the frontier marshals made mistakes sometimes, and they weren't always pure. The other week's show is a typical example. Matt Dillon kills four guys and then is ashamed of himself."

Rogers Terrill or Leo Margulies could not have put it any plainer.

Sounding like the perfect pulpster of his era, Meston once reflected on his broken hero, "…the hardest thing for me, the writer, is to keep him—on paper—from goofing off into the never-never land of pure heroism; and the hardest thing for Norman Macdonnell, the producer-director, and Bill Conrad, the star, is to translate the script's attempt at authenticity into the living character of Matt Dillon. But we try, and try, and keep trying. Our attempt to create as realistic and entertaining a program as possible is not, of course, the only one of its kind. But we did precede and were on the air, trying, before the release of such pictures as *High Noon* and *Shane*. And we're still on the air, and still trying."

Gunsmoke elevated the genre and would outlast them all.

"*One cowboy I knew used to look at a pretty girl now and then without worrying one damn bit about whether her cattle were being rustled or not. But I guess he was an exception. A sort of a character.*"

—**Thomas Thompson**

16

COWGIRLS NEED KISSING

THERE WAS another corner of the Pulp West, an off-shoot that rivaled the main branch.

A sub-genre unto itself, the cowgirl romance magazine was the brainchild of a saddle bum of a pulp editor named Harold Brainerd Hersey. He never stayed in one place very long, and fathered more failures than successes, yet Hersey single-handedly turned the male-dominated Western field upside down in 1925 when he launched *Ranch Romances* for publisher William Clayton.

"I conceived the idea of combining the Western and the love themes in a single magazine under the title *Western Love Stories*," Hersey recounted in his autobiography, *Pulpwood Editor*. "Our distributors considered it too close an imitation of the Street & Smith titles. We were told to think up another. The result was *Ranch Romances* and it was an almost simultaneous hit with woman readers. Instead of the cowboy hero, we offered the cowgirl heroine. Bina Flynn, the editor we chose to handle the fresh idea, built the magazine into a huge success."

It was a success that outran Hersey, who did not long dally with Clayton. The publisher quickly released two companion titles, *Rangeland Love Story Magazine* (a retitling of *Rangeland Story Magazine*) and the hitherto-forbidden *Western Love Stories*. It took a few years, but eventually the industry caught on to the fact that *Ranch Romances* was outselling nearly every other Western pulp magazine by a country mile. When Bina

Flynn moved to Arizona, her assistant, a green-eyed redhead named Fanny Louise Ellsworth, took over. Under Ellsworth, *Ranch Romances* became a powerhouse twice-a-month title.

"I like stories with a good deal of action and a strong love interest..." Ellsworth told her writers. "The girl should be played up strongly. Every story should have a good climax, and a good way to play up the climax is to have an action fight, although gunplay is not essential; we can not use a slow story. The romance should be of the virile type that will appeal to the outdoor girl and young man. It must not get slushy, and never sexy."

Neither a love pulp nor exactly the regulation Western, *Ranch Romances* carved out a niche for itself by defying the narrow conventions of both.

Hersey delineated the *Ranch Romances* formula this way:

"There are two kinds of women in the Western pulpwoods: your sister and nobody's sister. Your sister rides like a man, the only difference being that she wears split skirts instead of chaps. She shoots like Annie Oakley but her skill at marksmanship usually disappears when the villain darkens her door. She develops the most amazingly feminine qualities, for all her outdoor mannerisms, when you least expect it—if the situation is tense she depends upon the hero's hairy-handed ability to save her from the conniving character who invariably passes over all the other girls, no matter how enchanting, to claim the unwilling affections of whatever maiden the hero adores in his strong, silent way.

"The language of your sister is as chaste as a Sunday school teacher's. She eats with a fork. She is often found riding the open range at all hours of the day and night on some excuse or other, unchaperoned and unguarded though she is aware that there is a large population lurking out in the sagebrush with only one idea in their collective mind. She knows, the sly minx, that a fast-ridin', hair-trigger cowboy will rush to her rescue if sex should rear its ugly head, but as sex just doesn't exist in the conservative pulpwoods her only danger is that the debonair gambler or badman will capture her for the foul purpose of insulting her by an offer of marriage. Sometimes the villain forces her to wear a spangled dress and dance with the boys in his honkatonk, but there isn't a reader alive who even questions her purity and ultimate release from a life 'worse than death.'"

The appeal of *Ranch Romances* can only be understood in the context of the times. The pulps tended to serve up predominantly male-oriented fiction. Some, like *Adventure,* published entire issues without a solitary female presence besmirching its invincibly masculine pages. When women did appear in the pulps, they were fey creatures apparently designed by nature for the sole purpose of being captured by evildoers and rescued by stalwart heroes, only then properly kissed. Rarely was one murdered for shock effect.

"The large mass of Western magazines featured 'man action,'" wrote Ryerson Johnson, "with women involved only slightly, or not at all.... When women were introduced into a story, it was—like the porcupine—carefully, so carefully. There was a cliché understanding that in the action pulps you 'cut a woman off at the neck, and didn't bring her back until you got to the knees.'"

While the basic ranch-and-range action formula was still present, in *Ranch Romances* the female reader could enjoy distaff heroines who did ride and shoot and fight like a man—at least until the genuine article showed up. This was as good as it got.

"The heroes in Western romances were always sickenly [*sic*] handsome and desirable to females," observed Robert Turner, who wrote bales of them. As proof, he plucked a specimen from his novelette, "Miss Fortune's Hard Luck Kisses":

He was very tall and spare and rangy, with great muscular shoulders under his royal blue shirt. He wore crisp clean levis, tucked into the tops of his back leather boots. He wore no hat and his hair was grain yellow, with deep, unruly waves and one undisciplined lock curling a little over his broad forehead, Swanee had never seen eyes so wideset, so gray-blue.

Early contributor J. Edward Leithead was present at the birth of the new venture.

"It was a new type of story for us, except the action part—we were well grounded in that," recalled Leithead, who also wrote as George R. MacFarland. "Men read it as well as women on account of the action in the formula."

Contributors included a mixture of the sexes. Westerneer Ray Nafziger wrote as "Robert Dale Denver." Frank C. Robertson, William Freeman Hough, L.P. Holmes, E.B. Mann, Austin Corcoran, Juliette Corey Foster and Marie De Nervaud were also prominent. Most continued with the magazine even after Clayton went bankrupt and Warner Publications took the title over in 1933, with Fanny Ellsworth's services part of the deal.

Pulp publishers possessed a herd mentality. When sales figures became known, knockoffs began jostling *Ranch Romances* for newsstand rack space. Their numbers grew legion. Most were pale imitations. Titles abounded. *Rangeland Sweethearts. Rangeland Love Stories. Westland Love Magazine. Thrilling Ranch Stories. Romantic Range. Romantic Western. Romance Round-up. Romance Western. Romance Range. Western Romances. Western Love. Western Love Romances. Western Love Story. Real Western Romances. Far West Romances. Golden West Romances. Rodeo Romances. Cowboy Romances.*

A *Gunsmoke Cowgirls* or *Quick-Trigger Romances* seemed beyond the imagination of the follow-the-leader publishers, although William Clayton was on the verge of releasing *Cowgirl Romances* when he folded his string back in '32. One daring outfit did issue *Fighting Romances from the West and East*. It perished after eight issues.

The fundamental difference between *Ranch Romances* and its herd of imitators was that *RR* showcased classic Western yarns with a strong love interest, while the others offered essentially love stories with a Western background. A small enough distinction, perhaps, but the difference meant acceptance or rejection by editors and readers alike.

Rangeland Romances regular Ennen Reeves Hall described the difference this way:

"In the action yarn we have our protagonist, a man, set out to solve the problem of who is rustling his cattle. But in a romance Western we change the viewpoint and the problem. Our heroine, who owns a ranch, is losing cattle. We have her try to clear her sweetheart of the charge of rustling or try to satisfy herself of his innocence. In other words, for a romance Western, a girl's problem is tackled from an emotional angle and the story is laid in a Western, or period, setting."

Explained August Lenniger, "The blood-and-thunder Western action story in which the girl furnishes a prize for the hero's success, won't do. Nor will a sweet-and-simple love story. You have to concoct something better than a stew of which the ingredients are a quick-trigger cowboy, a tomboy heroine and a black-mustachioed villain, boiled over a sagebrush campfire."

The love Western pulps leaned more to the so-called "modern" Western than the masculine-oriented magazines. This was a kind of story set in contemporary times, but with all the expected Wild West trappings. Usually set in a dude ranch populated by sprightly gals tricked out with names like Dallas or Starla or Texanna, sometimes at a rodeo show, they were an attempt to bend the mold rather than break it. Hollywood popularized this mixed-breed concoction.

Action was not the main ingredient, as *Western Romances* editor Carson Mowre once explained:

"While the stories fall under the 'action' head, they are not the blood and thunder type. Rather, they are 'conflict' tales with the girls experiencing the adventures side by side with the hero."

It was widely recognized that the female protagonist took the place of the old Western "sidekick" role.

Mowre's successor, West F. Peterson, set out specific guidelines:

"The heroines must not be of questionable character; rather, they should be wholesome, pure, and in themselves symbols of the best in rangeland life. A little passion now and then is not to be scorned, but something should be left between the lines— it needn't be laid on with a calcimine brush...."

Peterson's successor, Clifford Dowdey, elaborated:

"Our stories must be emotional. The heroine is either the central character or one of two central characters. She should *not* be a prize standing on the sidelines and handed over to the hero at the end. All the action and plot must revolve around the hero and heroine jointly, and she must take active part in the action. Our plots must be built on Western situations and advanced by strictly Western action; love, hate, greed, which furnish the motivation must be of primitive intensity, in keeping with the frontier background."

Thrilling Ranch Stories' Leo Margulies added, "It is important that the heroine fight alongside the hero and help in the motivation, especially in the lead novels. Western dialect is okay for the hero—but never for the girl."

One pulp wag dubbed the genre, "love on a compost heap."

As with the straight cowboy titles, all distinctions between the Old West and its modern counterpart were uncertain and deliberately obscured by editors.

One such, *Western Romances'* Art Lawson, stated frankly, "While we all know that the fictionalized West is the Old West, the illusion should be maintained for the uninitiated that it is truly the West of today."

Writers toiling for this vast market could encounter rocky going. Refused manuscripts didn't necessarily fit downriver magazines. Lawson complained of receiving too many rejects "...from Western writers who add a girl and four kisses to a Western plot; and from love story writers who put pants on the heroine and throw in a horse."

As the field proliferated, and other love Western pulps came on the scene, the formula was remixed. Depending on arcane variables of slant, sometimes an editor insisted that submissions be told from the cowboy point of view. Abruptly, he reversed policy and demanded cowgirl viewpoint yarns. Certain editors preferred action stories laced with romance. Others sought romantic tales with just a hint of gunplay.

Of *Real Western Romances,* Robert Lowndes admitted, "I started the magazine, but we eventually decided that it should be a love pulp with Old West settings, rather than a Western magazine with strong romantic elements added."

Announcing *Rodeo Romances* in 1942, Leo Margulies straight-facedly noted: "All types of stories with any connection with rodeos are wanted. These need not be about rodeo contests, as this would make a monotonous book."

Women could write under male bylines, and vice versa. Of course, women also wrote for the regular action Western magazines, but usually with their sex disguised. B.M. Bower was really Bertha M. Bower. When she married cowboy Bertrand W. Sinclair, she became Bertha M. Sinclair. May Eliza Frost was obliged to call herself Eli Colter. Chloe Kathleen Shaw wrote as C.K. Shaw in the Western action pulps and Kathleen Shaw in the Western love magazines. Longtime *Western Story Magazine* contributor Cherry Wilson got by with her own name, perhaps because readers didn't quite cotton on to the feminine connotation of her personal name, cowboy nomenclature being what it was. Inexplicably, the superprolific Anita Allen committed her subliterary sins as Marian O'Hearn.

Male Westerneers were also subject to editorial concerns that their names didn't sound "Western" enough. Thus was George Rosenberg obliged to become George Armin Shaftel. Oscar Schisgall used Jackson Cole at Thrilling and Stewart Hardy for *Western Story Magazine.* For some reason, Chester W. Harrison preferred the more Eastern-sounding byline of C. William Harrison. Herman Hascal Giles dropped his first name "because I think cowboys shoot people named Herman."

When Frederick Dilley Glidden was deemed too Eastern a handle, he became Luke Short. Only later did he claim to have discovered that a gunman friend of Wyatt Earp had gone by that name. Wife Florence used Vic Elder in her Western romance fiction.

Before editors would print his stuff, Short's brother Jonathan was labeled "Peter Dawson" after a popular brand of Scotch. Forgotten was the fact that Peter Dawson was one of Frederick Faust's many pen names. Leslie Ernenwein substituted his first initial so editors wouldn't dismiss him as a romance writer. And poor Gladwell C. Richardson received so many rejection letters addressed to "Miss Richardson" that he was forced to adopt the hairy-chested pen name, John R. Winslowe. After that, he had no trouble selling his wares.

Harold Hersey's original *Ranch Romances* formula was refined, but rarely improved on. As the Golden '20s gave way to the grim '30s, the emphasis subtly shifted toward the female audience and male readers largely abandoned the sub-genre. Many he-man Western writers shied away from the Ranch Romance sub-genre, but others considered it fair game.

"The Western love field is often shunned as being specialized," wrote agent Adolph L. Fierst in "Love in the Saddle" (*Writer's Digest*, April 1937) "It is really nothing of the sort. It offers a rather unique market—it is open to all writers who can do the ordinary love pulp stories, and it offers a welcome variation to people tired of knocking out the machine-gun-action Westerns.

"The Western romance is essentially a love pulp story, with all the love pulp requirements—the girl yearning for the hero, the difficulties she faces, and her eventual triumph over his sales resistance. The difference between a Western romance yarn and the ordinary love pulp is the Western atmosphere, the Western background, and the fact that the difficulties are usually physical, rather than psychological. If you write the ordinary Cinderella story for, let us say, Miss Fairgrieve's *All Story*, you give us a situation which the gal, in love with the boss' son, finds him entirely indifferent to her charms, or engaged to a society girl, who is so mean that she might easily be mistaken for Lucretia Borgia. Your heroine, as sweet and simple a wench is ever went into a clinch, does all her man chasing on the highest possible plane. She's given to periods of anguish in which she bravely keeps back the tears when the prospect of landing her victim looks hopeless indeed. Of course, the fact that she eventually does land him should come as a complete surprise, not only to the reader, but to the heroine.

"What happens when your cowgirl falls in love?" Fierst asked. "Fundamentally, the same thing; but the solution of the problem is entirely different. The gal must be able to sling lead with the best of them; she will fight shoulder to shoulder with her Tarzan on horseback, very much in the manner of our pioneer women; she will, because of her more direct nature, be in a position to help the man by direct physical action, by interfering in his affairs, and by displaying the other cute feminine tricks the big bashful heroes are supposed to fall for. If I'm not mistaken, the late Texas Guinan was the original cowgirl of the films.

"Your straight love pulp heroine must win the man by her sweetness; your Western heroine must do the same thing, but she must also rise to the occasion with a gun whenever such action is indicated. As a concession to her frail femininity, she might use a small pearl handled revolver, instead of the portable cannons the heroes drag around and laughingly referred to as six-guns."

Some writers who balked at the bullet-torn, powder-burnt version of the Pulp West found the grass was infinitely greener on this side of the fence. For its editorial gold was infinitely more golden.

"When I got going well on detectives," said Frank Gruber, "I quit writing Western stories altogether. I just didn't like them. I was writing an artificial type of Western, which didn't ring true to me. I read the stories of others who were appearing in the same magazine and they were as unreal as my own. There was much about rustlers and cowboys and outlaws. And cowgirls. I think, though, that it was the dialect that really got me down. I'd cringe every time I'd come across a phrase like, 'dern yore ornery hide, yuh dod-blasted side-winder!' or 'Waddy, I'm goin' tuh drill yuh.'

"For a year I didn't write a single Western story but in the back of my mind was the urge to write a—to me—intelligent Western, in which the hero didn't say 'yuh' or 'tuh.' After mulling it over for quite some time I finally wrote a 25,000-word story in which there wasn't a single rustler or even a cow. I found that I really enjoyed writing this story and after getting the check for it from *Ranch Romances* I decided there might be something to Western stories, after all."

Most of these titles were interchangeable. One exception was *Rangeland Romances,* which Rogers Terrill launched in 1935. Taking a leaf from the emotional formula that had cata-pulted *Dime Western* into one of Popular Publications' top-selling titles, Terrill described the magazine's special slant in its June 1936 issue:

"Over a year ago we started a new magazine with a new idea. We started a romance magazine in which the hero and heroine fight side by side, live an adventurous life together, experience hope and despair, defeat and success, and finally love together. We brought out a magazine that was true to life; that was about characters who really could have lived and done those things that the author writes about. Very carefully, from the start, we avoided the 'story book' kind of thing. Because we know, and you who read *Rangeland Romances* know with us, that the most gripping, most glamorous, most beautiful stories are those that come the closest to us—the stories that you and I could have lived, ourselves, had we happened to have the right opportu-nity."

This took the *Ranch Romances* formula to its ultimate expres-sion: the super-cowgirl, equal in all ways to the super-cowboy of yore.

"Our Western heroine isn't the shy, sobby clinging vine," explained August Lenniger. "She has pioneer blood in her veins and she fights for her rights and her man. If he's too dumb to propose when he should, she'll not wait til leapyear to give him a hint! But while she can cuss with the best of 'em when necessary, the Western heroine doesn't drink, smoke, or have time for such frivolous vanities as cosmetics."

"If you wish to write for these Women Westerns," warned Walter Des Marais, "then remember that your heroine is no modest little violet. She can do everything a man can do, except cuss, smoke or chew. She must not weep or blush, and she can take all reverses on the chin. If she doesn't, well, the reader turns away in disgust."

"The heroines must be daughters of today," instructed Leo Margulies, "not Victorian milksops."

But the shivaree stopped far short of hot-blooded biological reality. "Often enough," Margulies explained, "she is the daughter of a rancher worth half a million dollars or more, which is big business, and as a rich man's daughter, she has had an expensive education and all the luxuries her position would naturally command. Her love life is clean, with kiss the ultimate in passion." He dubbed this papery confection the "cattle princess."

As Laurence D'Orsay elaborated in *Writer's Digest,* the true pulp cowgirl was more tomboy than woman:

"You can let your hero have a girl pal, unless you are trying to hit one of those magazines which believe that *Homo sapiens* consists of one sex… but don't let him know that she is a girl, and don't let her know it. Let her behave like a nice, plucky boy, and let him behave like a kind elder brother. If there is any real love interest at all, let it be perfectly clean, chemically pure, romantically elevated. By the necessities of your plot, the hero and heroine may be forced into situations ordinarily considered compromising to a girl…" […] "But, if it be a genuine red-blooded yarn, you must never suggest that the situation is compromising or embarrassing. Because, of course, it isn't. Your hero is a superman who wouldn't dream of doing anything wrong, and your heroine is a superwoman who wouldn't dream of letting him."

As for sex, it simply did not exist this here neck of the woods. Fanny Ellsworth put it this way: "All of our babies come out of the cabbage patch."

The writing required was a thing unto itself:

"You lie, Mace Stevens!" said Trixie without changing voice. "You lie like the very devil! For the truth is in your eyes. Look at me!"
Her fingers caught his chin, twisted his face toward her own. With a hoarse oath Mace scooped her into his arms. "By God," he gritted, "you're *mine!* You'll do to ride the mountain with, from hell to breakfast, Trix!"
Locked in his arms, her own tight about his shoulders, Trixie Clifton found herself alternately laughing and crying.
"You're damned right I'll do!" she whispered against his lips.

More male writers wrote for *Rangeland Romances*—at one point retitled *Rangeland Love Stories* after *Ranch Romances* threatened suit—than any other title in the sub-genre. Some simply specialized in it. Former editor Art Lawson fell into the field after a period of alternating between detective and confession stories.

"Changing overnight from a wronged young maiden to a hardboiled dick was quite a strain," he recounted. "I… was going crazy when Harry Widmer rescued me on his big white horse. Harry had come to the conclusion that the only thing I could write was romantic Westerns. So I started turning them out for Harry and others under not only two names but three. One of these was William Fargo, whose stories usually had an historical background. John Logan wrote bang-bang stories. He died. An editor shot him. Art Lawson is still around writing Western romances."

Lawson admitted that it was a grind.

"They were easy for me to write, and I had a couple of editors who liked them. But I was fed up with the lonely little girl on the out-of-the-way ranch and the good looking outlaw who happened by singing and strumming his guitar. So I have varied this Western background. Since I once lived near the Mississippi, I use that river a lot, and the Missouri, too. I like the old historical background of the trappers and mountain men. Once I camped close to the Brazos de Dios—so I use that Texas country that turned from cows to cotton, then to airplanes and oil. For four years I lived in San Francisco and have found it a starter for gold rush stories. But somehow, though I spent a couple of years in Mexico and later took my bride down for a winter's visit, I have seldom used that background in fiction. It was mighty hard to sell the few stories I tried. They were from the Mexican viewpoint, I suppose, and that was the wrong slant for readers in the *Estados Unidos del Norte.*"

Authenticity in this sub-genre was handled gingerly, or avoided altogether.

"I learned early in these pulps never to describe the make of a gun or its calibre—the hero just picked up a gun and shot it," recalled writer Bill Severn. "The magazines would get a fantastic kickback of mail from readers if they found a mistake."

Emotion was the only authentic coin in this realm.

"As in every kind of writing, you had to put yourself in the reader's place as you wrote, give her what she wanted," explained contributor Robert Turner. "And, of course, when a *Rangeland Romances* heroine first got kissed by the handsome hero, all hell broke loose.

"As Harry Widmer, the editor, once explained to me: 'You have to give the reader the impression that the doll is very close to orgasm or even right *there*, without writing dirty and even making it all sound maybe a little spiritual, if that's possible.'

"Well, we always tried," said Turner. "As follows:"

A little moan formed in her throat and she flung her arms around his neck and clung to him while all the blood in her veins seemed to turn into flowing flame. And the gentle night wind caressed both their faces, crooned in their ears.

Behind Swanee's closed eyes the night seemed to burst into

a shower of stars. Her heart seemed to be filling her whole body. She couldn't manage to breathe and she felt dizzy and as though she were whirling forever through lovely rainbows and fleecy white clouds and pink mists. It was wonderful.

The kiss could also be used to express the darker passions, as Ennen Reeves Hall illustrated by quoting from her *Rangeland Love Stories* tale, "Darling of Double-Cross Range":

> There was nothing of tenderness in his kiss, no wild stirring of ecstasy. It was rough as Tru himself and it swept Lyndal off her feet. All her hunger for love rose like a consuming force in her as she found herself responding in a way she had never meant to do.
>
> Tru's arms tightened and his lips pressed closer. And suddenly revulsion was a black flood sweeping over Lyndal, smothering her. This wasn't love, she knew in a blazing flash of under-standing. She struggled for freedom but her struggles only delighted Hays. Lyndal thought she must know how the black mules felt when his strong hands were on the reins—as though they must fight free of some strange power that would enslave them. But fighting Tru was as futile as pitting her puny strength against a stone wall.

Harry Widmer explained, "A kiss is the ultimate of sex our censors will permit. So we like to give our readers as much of a thrill as we can within the limits of plausibility and the Post Office Department."

During World War II, editors drafted more and more women writers into the Pulp West, both in the romance end and what some called the man-action Western. They were, to use a phrase of the day, "broken into the field."

After the war, there came another market shift. Women characters became more acceptable in the action Western magazines. Simultaneously, pulps like *Thrilling Ranch Stories* and *Rodeo Romances* dropped their *Ranch Romances*-style slant in favor of the straight male viewpoint laced with glamorous cowgirls. Readers accepted this drift away from the romantic side of the range because the line between the two types of magazines had grown blurred.

"Girl interest needs to be handled smoothly and, for today's blasé reader, in terms of modern norms prevailing between men and women," explained Harold Preece in "If Your Hero's a Heel." (*Writer's Digest*, July 1954.) "In the various Western love pulps, the female protagonists are fairly sophisticated and have robust personalities matching those of the men who catch their fancies. Bad girls—lady bandits, card shufflers, dance-hall demi-mondaines and the like—require exceptionally strong characterizations and, for current reader tastes, that unfortunate pseudo-glamour which converts an old harridan like Belle Starr into a seductive bronc-riding Brunnehilde."

Taking his cue from the prevailing anti-cowboy fever, Robert Turner applied the Tom Blackburn lesson in his own cow-confections. "In a whole bundle of stories sold to *Rangeland Romances* and *Rangeland Love*," he admitted, "the heroines were, variously, Post Office mistresses, wagon train mistresses, scouts, barbers, and whatnot."

In the post-war period, the straight Western pulps also got a little sexier. But not much. Titles ran to concoctions like "Gun-Mistress of the Smoke-Pole Pack", "Lure of the Boothill Siren", "Bride of the Hang-Tree Hellion" and "Saucy Witch of the Wagon Trails" but suggested far more than the stories actually delivered. Covers flirted with cheesecake appeal. Inside, the same sexual restrictions applied. Readers looking for steamy sex got gunsmoke instead.

"I believe that in many ways the Western story has grown up in recent years," offered Wayne D. Overholser in 1948. "At least we can consider man and woman relationships with more reality than Zane Grey did, and magazine stories are miles ahead of many Western movies in which the hero can kiss his horse, but must never, never touch the lips of the woman he loves. A writer can't shoot too far ahead of the reading public or the editors who make the vital decisions with a pen in one hand and a checkbook in the other, but at the same time he had better see to it that he is not left behind."

While it doesn't sound like much, this was leagues ahead of the pace-setting attitudes of Frank E. Blackwell circa 1931:

"You know, we never have any bad girls in *Western Story Magazine*. Our girls are the kind of girls that all girls should be. They stand for something to be won; a kind of loving cup or medal. So you see, I am for romance, the rolling plain, a good horse under you, a moonlight night and a fair one who has put a light in the window for you."

The leading Western love pulp was still going strong. *Ranch Ro*—as it was known in the trade—was also changing with the times, and its superior word rates and growing flexibility continued luring mainstream Western writers into its tender pages.

Texan Elmer Kelton, then coming into the field, noted the subtle shift:

"Sex rarely crept into a Western pulp. I remember a mild form of shock when in a Wayne D. Overholser story a young lady—not the heroine—showed up with an illegitimate child, and another, also by Wayne, in which the hero and the heroine spent the night together in a barn because of a storm. Nothing untoward happened, of course. *Ranch Romances* was a family magazine. Just being together overnight was far out for the time."

This was a response to the emerging paperback book market, which unlike a subscription magazine, was not subject to postal inspection of its contents, and could more boldly explore forbidden frontiers.

Overholser's son, second-generation Westerneer Stephen, explains:

"In the late 1940s Fanny Ellsworth saw a decline in sales. Reading some of the new, more realistic Western novels made her take another look at the cabbage patch. As a result, some well established writers at *Ranch Romances* disappeared from the table of contents. New names were seen there. Among them was Wayne D. Overholser."

"Wayne's stories have just the right amount of sex," Ellsworth claimed. Which was, nearly none.

Throughout all these permutations, the Western romance pulp kept to a single track.

"The difference between the straight, or action, Western and the romance Western is the basic problem," explained Ennen Reeves Hall. "The basic problem is a love problem... Let your gal tackle her problem fearlessly. Western love pulp heroines are young and have plenty of guts and gumption. When they see a man they want they go after him, but they stay ladies of virtue, even if tempted almost beyond endurance. No married heroines are allowed, no divorce, no illicit love affairs, nothing risqué.

"In spite of these taboos you have to inject a large dose of sex into a Western love story," Hall added. "As a general rule, every Western love story should contain several more-than-warm love scenes. The gal should get kissed several times—really kissed, not just pecked at. Never write these love scenes objectively. The reader doesn't want to see Nellie getting kissed. He wants to *feel* it. That's why he's reading the story... Kisses must say a lot without saying too much."

Jack Byrne, still holding down the fort at Fiction House, commissioned from Les Savage, Jr. a series for *Action Stories* that broke entirely new ground. Senorita Scorpion was a glamorous gunslinger who enjoyed great popularity, although she spawned few memorable imitators. Outside of *Ranch Romances* and its copies, the Wild West Wonderland of Woodpulpia remained a man's country.

As Harold Hersey wryly observed, "The Western writer in both pulpwood and smooth-paper fiction is an expert at dodging sex. He does it so well that one doesn't miss it. If the time ever comes that a cowboy heroine is caught reading Havelock Ellis, or a cowboy discussing his libido, you will know that a new era has dawned in the popular saga of the West."

That new era lay just over the imaginary horizon.

"*Back in 1949 the pulp magazines, in which a generation of Western story writers had managed to sustain life on word rates ranging from one half cents to two cents a word or slightly higher, suddenly began to wither and vanish one by one. It was panic time, made worse because all around us we could see the rest of the country enjoying unprecedented affluence while we went quietly and desperately broke.*"

—*D. B. Newton*

17

END OF AN EPOCH

THE SUN began setting on the Pulp West in 1948.

A recession settled over the real landscape of post-war America that year. Inflation created a new paper crisis, and the economic contraction dealt a body blow to the pulp magazine industry. The expected Summer sales slump hit the pulps in the Spring that year, lingering to year's end. Formerly healthy monthly magazines overnight shifted to bi-monthly or quarterly frequency.

The first to feel the pinch were the writers, many of whom had climbed back to three cents a word during the busy wartime years.

Predictably, Leo Margulies put the onus on the range-savvy and the greenhorns alike.

"During the lush days of the war and the three years of boom that followed," he accused, "selling stories was so easy that many freelance writers believed anything would go. To an extent they were correct for we had so many pages to fill that we couldn't be as critical as we normally were. The result was that many writers became careless in writing and lackadaisical in assembling good plot material; and developing it along proper technical lines. That particular honeymoon is over, to the consternation of some authors who were getting away with murder. They think we have stopped buying altogether. We haven't."

Ironically, the American Folklore Society decided during their annual meeting held in December 1949 to elevate the

U.S. cowboy to the status of true American folk hero. Citing outdated statistics showing that Western magazine circulation had soared 28 million copies between 1945 and '48, Mody C. Boatright of the University of Texas proclaimed, "The cowboy meets the test of any folk hero. He must have prowess—brave, strong, unconquerable. And he must have cleverness, defense of the weak against the strong. The cowboy has both prowess and cleverness."

It was an honor bestowed too late for the pulp bulldogger. From late 1948 and all through 1949 the industry struggled against utter collapse. Inventories were full. Publishers began salting their magazines with decade-old reprints to save money. No one knew how to reverse declining fortunes.

Allan K. Echols once again took the field to task:

"A million sheriffs have broken up a million range wars with only slight variations in their looks and tactics," he wrote. "We have blurbed a yarn like that something like this, 'Armed only with courage Sheriff Black breaks up a blazing range war...'; when in truth we should have said, 'Armed only with two .45's and a repeating Winchester, the usual tools of his trade, and backed only by the government of the County and State, Sheriff Black goes out and earns a day's pay doing the job he hired out to do.'

"It's the same with a million detectives, professional adventurers, or what have you, all going out to do a day's work. All of them 200% brave, all dead shots, all with eyes that narrow to mere slits. Not a personal problem in a carload. No fear, no character trend that would cause him to hesitate to counter the villain's move... not people, just names identifiable by slight individualizing tags, such as the color of their eyes."

The Territory of the Imagination was dying. The surest sign of its impending fate was the abrupt cancellation of *Western Story Magazine* after 30 years and nearly 1300 issues. September 1949 was the cover-date of the final number.

But the death was bigger than that. Street & Smith had in

fact cancelled all of their remaining pulps, blaming paperback books and television.

"The recent sharp drop in their newsstand sales was, of course, not due to television alone," Harriet Bradfield reported. "Other pulp companies have been making changes in view of this drop, which has affected sales of Western story magazines most keenly."

Readers and editors alike were shocked.

"I, who at the age of 12 had dreamed of appearing in Street & Smith's *Western Story Magazine,* suddenly found myself with the last story in the concluding number," remarked D.B. Newton. He'd been in the game only 11 years.

"My God, what a world that was," wrote a surviving Street & Smith editor. "How could it not have lasted forever, as it seemed destined to. Times changed with pix mags and the war, but those people could not. They rode the range and barbwire fencing, so to speak, did them in forever...."

It was said that Street & Smith's distributor forced the decision.

Simultaneously, Aaron A. Wyn folded his veteran Western titles, *Western Trails* and *Western Aces.* A follower to the bitter end—even if it meant going over a cliff.

In a strange way, Walker A. Tompkins' wartime prediction began to come true, but not in the pulps. In the post-war comic book field, readers had grown bored with Superman and Batman and their imitators. Publishers beat the bushes for a new kind of hero—and found one in the commonplace cowboy. Former pulp house Fawcett built a new line around Hopalong Cassidy, Roy Rogers and other Saturday afternoon matinee White Hats. Other publishers brought out *The Lone Ranger, The Ghost Rider* and *Kid Colt, Outlaw.* It all started in 1947-48, when driven by TV exposure, *Hopalong Cassidy* circulation doubled to eight million copies per year. No pulp editor ever dreamed of such astronomic numbers. No pulp magazine character was featured on television. Within a few years the cowboy ruled roughshod over a new kingdom.

One comic book publisher demonstrated the same acumen that kept his pulp magazine chain at the bottom of the pile over the course of a long career.

"I went to Martin Goodman one time," said Marvel Comics editor Don Rico, "and I said, 'Look, we're doing a whole lot of Westerns; how about instead of imagining things, let's use the real West.' He was excited as hell. He said, 'What do you have in mind? What kind of a hero?' I said, 'How about a guy like Wyatt Earp?' He said, 'Who? Who'd ever go for a guy with a name like Wyatt Earp?' Six years later he apologized to me."

A dramatic shift was also taking place in the emerging paperback field. For ten years, the paperback had co-existed with the pulp magazine as a vehicle for reprinting hardcover books. But in 1949, Pocket Books released the first paperback original, sending shock waves through the hardcover book field. The novel was *Range Boss,* a Western.

In the months that followed, *Range Boss* would quietly sell nearly a half-million copies, paying its author, pulpster Dwight Bennett Newton—the same scribe who had closed out the epoch of *Western Story Magazine*—not a penny or two per word, but ongoing royalties after a handsome advance.

The Paperback Revolution was on. And the pulp magazine was taking a beating from all sides. Escalating production costs and competition from emerging media rivals like TV further hammered circulations. Top writers saw their rates slashed. New writers had their wares summarily rejected, often unread.

"Woodpulp is gravely ill," conceded Allan K. Echols in his 1951 *Writer's Year Book* essay, "The Waning Woodpile." "Many of us love the old girl, and depend on her completely or partially for our living. So it is up to us to try to keep her alive and find out what is wrong with our meal ticket."

Without mentioning him by name, Echols indicted Owen Wister. "In a typical Western short story," Echols noted, "an antagonist lays such a trap for a hero that the hero is forced to ride all over the county in a whirl of dust and gunsmoke for a certain number of pages while the villain pushes him around unmercifully. Then the hero gets a bellyful of all this riding and shooting and goes out and kills the son-of-a-bitch.

"But defensively, of course! Meaning that he wouldn't have had a problem in the world if the villain hadn't decided to push him around a bit.

"That has been going on unvaryingly for fifty years. It is action for its own sake. It is admittedly interesting to the immature mind... But until pocketbooks hit the stands, the mature pulp reader had to take this material, suitable for immaturity, or nothing. Now he has something better. And so does the kid who has fallen in love with Dell comics. Today, these two readers, not the editor, makes the decision, and their decision is against pulps.

"If the publisher's balance sheet shows him that the present reader doesn't like the fifty-year-old story, then why doesn't the publisher give him a better one? The cold fact is that for the last twenty years pulp has not had to bother about the type or quality of story it offered for sale, because it had no competition on the news stands."

In most surviving Western pulps, the dreaded gun-dummy remained unhanged and kicking.

Likewise Walt Coburn. With the collapse of *Western Story,* he had seen his oldest and most dependable market go up in smoke and cinders. Coburn had dominated it since 1938. Now Popular Publications alone had to carry him. Or perhaps it was the other way around.

In September 1949, *Writer's Digest* ran a profile on the now-venerable 59-year-old by Fred Gipson, himself a seasoned Western pulpeteer, who would go on to pen the classic, *Old Yeller.* "Rangeland Word Wrangler" retold the tale of how after busting a kneecap working his brothers' ranch in Bloody Basin Arizona, Walt Coburn turned to writing Western pulp, tutored by *Western Story Magazine* trailblazer Robert J. Horton.

Published to coincide with Popular's launch of *Walt Coburn's Western Magazine,* the piece indicated that the field was still struggling with its juvenile past, suggesting Coburn was a major factor in turning that around:

"You can point out to Walt that his leadership in writing authentic flesh-and-bone range stories has done more than anything else to raise standards of Western pulp fiction. Mike Tilden, a Popular Publications editor who buys the bulk of Walt's yarns, will verify this.

"The Dead-Eye Dick type of fiction, written by authors who'd never been west of the Mississippi, brought down so much bitter scorn upon the pulp Westerns that they've never yet wholly recovered.

"But Tilden says that Walt's ability, which is nothing short of genius, for recapturing the old West and bringing it colorfully alive again, year after year, is gradually lifting the Western pulps to their rightful place among current fiction magazines."

But the years had not been kind to the Cowboy Writer. Gipson acknowledged that Coburn had a problem.

"But quart-a-day drinking will finally catch up with any man," he wrote, "and it caught up with Walt. He never missed a deadline with a story, but there were too many times, he says, when he had to goad a story out of his whiskey-fogged brain."

Unstated was the fact that after 1946, Coburn tended to write drunk. His meandering yarns had to be salvaged by copyeditors who swore that only shreds of his original compositions survived the blue pencil.

Coburn claimed to write in the saddle, neither plotting nor pre-planning his work.

"My plots came from the stars," he asserted. "I might awaken in the middle of the night with some idea which would keep me awake. Perhaps it was nothing more than a single character, or a catch phrase I had heard, or a horse which reminded me of one I once knew, and the man who rode that forgotten horse. Dreams took shape, the plots just came from nowhere."

Coburn was entirely self-taught.

"I went after the job of pulp writing as if it were a game from which I got a big kick. I had no set plan of work, no idea in my head, just a kind of cockeyed, haphazard way of putting down words on paper. I liked to have a strong dramatic situation pictured in my mind, such as a stage setting with the characters on it. These characters might be based on some cowhand or outlaw, gambler or bartender or lawman whom I had known on the range or around some cowtown. I turned them loose on paper, let them act out their parts and speak their dialogue. I made no notes of any kind but carried the story in my head. I had no plot to start with so let the characters do the work, act out the whole yarn, the plot developing as the story unfolded."

Sometimes, Coburn got his plot-threads tangled up in mid-yarn, but invariably the solution would come to him in the middle of the night. He cautioned greenhorn pulpeteers from following his loose pattern.

"In the past few years," Coburn noted, "the whole set-up has changed. The editors will toss that kind of a yarn back in your lap. They want a story mapped out beforehand, re-written and re-written until it's cut to the bone. They want a tight-twist story, and to hell with what you actually know about the cow country. They don't care what is inside the heart of a cowhand or an outlaw or a sheriff. They don't give a damn about how cold or hungry or played out a man on horseback gets, because the cow country is gone and the present generation of readers, so they claim, wouldn't be interested.

"A gent that's never been west of the middle west, can write and market a so-called Western story. A man that doesn't know which is the Injun side of a horse can sell a Western, if he's any kind of a writer. There's plenty of good reference books in the public libraries and you can pick up the vernacular from the rodeo boys around Madison Square Garden. It won't be the kind of lingo I listened to when I was a kid punching cows but there aren't enough of the old-timers left to pick out the flaws."

Called by Gipson, "The King of the Pulps"—an honorific formerly bestowed upon Max Brand—Coburn presided over a fading empire. Longtime editors would say the handwriting had been on the wall since that desperate spring in 1932. Others pointed out that the field never bounced back after World War II and the post-war cultural shifts.

In the same issue, William Hopson, now residing in Douglas, Arizona, resurfaced to lament the sorry state of things:

"Reading my *Writer's Digest,* I note the usual number of old names slipping into obscurity and the usual number of new names coming to the fore.

"As an old-line pulpster I'm not setting the world afire at all, and am not in the least ashamed to admit it. Markets are not what they used to be in earlier days.

"I really would have liked to live and work back in the days when mags like *Argosy* were coming out every week and when the late Max Brand had a couple of serials running in *Western Story Magazine* every week. Those were the days when Bedford-Jones made a reported $65,000 a year, W.C. Tuttle got up to 10 cents a word for pulp, and Max Brand had his luxurious villa in Italy and dictated to two secretaries. Or so I've heard. I broke into the game during the early years of the depression, and didn't make a decent living at it until the late '30s. Today, I'm about in the same boat as the rest of the Western story writers: slow markets and low pay.

"Like a lot of other Western pulpsters, I don't know what has happened, or is going to happen, to Western sales. I can't believe that television and comics are solely responsible for the drop in markets. Today in Hollywood when producers of alleged entertainment are causing theatres to be empty—except for those who come to buy popcorn—there isn't a Western picture, no matter how corny, that doesn't make money.

"Last night I saw John Wayne in a picture that made him a big star—*Stagecoach*, from a *Collier's* short by Ernie Haycox. The theatre was packed.

"So people still must like Westerns. If they aren't plunking down their dough at the news stands every month, then the fault must lie with either the writers or the editors, or both. Once a writer develops certain steady markets, where the editor will almost buy 'em without bothering to read, it's so easy to fall off into sloppy writing—a sort of the-hell-with-it-they'll-buy-it-anyhow frame of mind. On the other hand, the editors won't let you write anything a bit different from the plot formula of thirty years ago.

"The one editor who has always turned me loose and let me write 'em *my* way is Ray Palmer. How I love that boy! I think that's one reason why, during this slump, *Mammoth Western* has been adding pages to its contents.

"In the old days we had the weekly pulps running yarns up to 90,000 words as weekly serials. Came the slump and we cut to one shots in a monthly at 40,000 words. They've gone over big for years and are still going over, but not like they used to. Readers are buying the same old length every month, and they're reading the same story by the same writers over and over and *over* again. Stock plots, stock situations, stock characters!

"I'm at a loss to understand why more realistic stuff can't be written. The only answer I can figure out is that publishers are afraid to risk money on anything but strong silent heroes and snow-white heroines. (Not long ago I wrote a story about a young girl who had been forced to get a divorce. Yep, you guessed it, it bounced. She was a real nice youngster, too. In fact, being a bachelor, I'd like to have met her.)

"One of these days an editor will come along with a new wrinkle on Westerns and give them a shot in the arm. I earnestly hope to a benevolent God so, as do the other pulp writers. Because any four of us in the game today, specializing in book lengths, could probably supply the whole 40,000-word market. I've turned out up to 13,000 words of finished copy in one day, and there isn't a guy in the business like Lee Floren, Arch Joscelyn, or Two-Gun Tompkins who can't do 10,000 words under pressure.

"The average professional pulpster can still make a living, more than he can by punching a time clock, and the average editor is still playing ball with us. But with markets like Dell's *Five-Novels Monthly, Western Story,* and Wyn's two Western pulps gone under, it puts the editor in the most enviable position today he's been in in years. He can pick up his telephone and call a dozen literary agencies and get bales of salable stuff in an hour. But everyone seems to be hopeful of an upsurge, and the editors seem to be trying to spread their checks around as evenly as possible among their writers.

"But all this is half a cake. What the pulp field needs is an editor who will offer the same revolution in this field that *The New Yorker* gave the humor field, that *Time* gave to *Literary Digest,* that *Life* gave to the newspaper picture supplements, that *Seventeen* gave to *Calling All Girls,* that *Farm Quarterly* gave to the farm field, and that *Popular Photography* gave to *Camera.*

"It's that new editorial vision we are waiting for; a vision that will break with all the clichés of yesterday and today; a restatement of reading values based on integrity."

There were indications that it was happening, but not from the editorial side of things. A new powerful generation of writers was emerging. Men like Louis L'Amour, William Heuman, Frank Bonham, Giles A. Lutz, Gordon D. Shirreffs, Lewis B. Patten, Steve Frazee, Barry Scobee, Elmer Kelton and Elmore Leonard were starting to crack the pulps. But they would enjoy their greatest successes in paperback and hardcover after the pulp field finally collapsed.

One of this new wave, Thomas Thompson, transitioning from the pulps to the slicks, discovered that a slicker species of gundummy was making *Saturday Evening Post* editor Erdmann Brandt gag.

"A Western novel needs a strong lead character, and usually has one," Thompson wrote. "But, unfortunately, characterization usually stops right there. He is strong. Strong as hell—and silent. And a little stupid when you look him over carefully. He is the big boy who stalks around through 60,000 words and comes in finally to wipe out the baddies in the nick of time and is about as believable as the fair maiden he saves—and she a cold dish who simpers so sweetly no self-respecting cowpoke would give her bed space. Lurking around these two as secondary characters are very often a set of completely believable human beings.

"Quoting Erd Brandt: 'The trouble with the average Western serial we see is that it has no sunshine. It is written in a monotone.' And there again is that strong silent boy lousing up the story. He squints, looks wise, knows all (but derned if I'm a-tellin' it, because I ain't a-hankerin' to hurt your feelin's, Ma'am.); in rare instances he is allowed a fleeting smile (generally a sad one), and he goes about a-sufferin; and a-sufferin'! Said Mr. Brandt, in discussing this man, 'Throw that bum out, he's breaking my heart.'"

The humorless Ernest Haycox approach had finally gone flat.

Harkening back to the unusual character formula, Thompson continued: "Remember the era in the pulps where we all wrote stories about the crippled old man or the sad little boy or the poor little barber down the street?" [...] "Too often, obsessed with the idea of character, we have cut off a man's leg, given him a special stirrup, crossed one of his eyes and said, 'There, now, is a character.' But we didn't delve into his insides, his mind and his heart, and there is where character lies.

"We've got the surface of our boy pretty well whipped. There isn't one of us who can't describe incredibly narrow hips and feet too small for the width of the shoulders and hair the color of a new lariat. We've even dug inside a bit. He's strong. Doesn't talk too much. He's trustworthy, loyal, brave, reverent, clean and kind. Now, maybe, it's time to ask ourselves *why* he is all these things.

"Let do something radical—put a heart and soul in the guy," Thompson concluded. "And I know this is asking a lot but, once in a while, when something funny comes up naturally, let the poor bum laugh. It will relax the deep lines of fatigue in his blocky face and soften those eyes that have seen too much in too few years."

The days when a Hamilton Craigie could straight-facedly suggest ransacking old dime novels for material were long past. The new generation possessed a far more sober attitude, and it showed in how they spoke of their craft.

"You don't have to slant the cowboy story," admonished Curt Brandon. "Write him as he was. He was good enough without your embellishment or your imagination to grip the fancies of the world. His was a story more fabulous than you can create; just take it, work with it, and try to make it make sense. You can't clothe him, in the span of one novel, or one story, with all the glamour and the grandeur that was his. Afoot, wobbling along on his high heels as he tried to walk, he was somewhat of an awkward character, a man easy for a writer to make human. In the saddle, with a rope in his hand, he was on the prodigious side."

Offered writer Harold Preece, "What counts in all Western writing is the mood you set for your final showdown—the manner in which you build toward your last meeting between two men whose interlocking destinies bring them face to face ultimately with guns or fists." Probably no one compressed the formula into a single sentence with more honest economy.

This new attitude blurred what was formerly a barb-wire demarcation between the two main schools of magazine Western writing.

"There is, these days, a tendency toward better writing in the pulps," observed writer Ray Gaulden in 1949. "The old slam-bang style, the bucking and jumping, the snarling and rasping, isn't found so much now. The line between pulp and slick Westerns has narrowed a great deal. Steve Payne, trying to nail that difference down, was of the opinion that the difference is made of intangibles which can only be discovered through trial and error writing. Happily, there is a middle ground. Many stories, written for the pulps today, are selling to the slicks and many a writer is salvaging his hybrids with the in-between markets such a *Blue Book* and *Toronto Star.*"

Thrilling's Samuel Mines described the shift as one away from formula action and toward plot tension: "There was a time when every Western writer began his story with a fight—whether it was important to the plot or not—and then made sure he had another fight about every thousand words along the way. Today we're publishing many Westerns without a shot fired in them, without a punch thrown—but they do have a strong feeling of suspense."

Sounding exactly like his predecessor, Rogers Terrill, Popular's Mike Tilden insisted, "The Western has come of age. It is no longer a ride-'em-cowboy treatise with a shoot-out per page and a carcass per paragraph. It is a realistic, living story of the true drama of frontier America. It is a credible, vital, true-to-life re-creation of the past, told in terms of the fight for human decency against insurmountable odds in a savage environment."

As the postwar period lengthened, authenticity was spoken of less and less. The new mantra, a reflection of changes taking place in related genres and other media, could be encapsulated a single term: suspense.

Amid collapsing Western magazine circulations, the romance Western titles showed less of a decline. The sharp distinctions between the two began to blur.

"Today we see more of the 'romantic' Western story than formerly," observed Columbia's Robert A.W. Lowndes. "But there is little essential difference between the romantic and the straight Western—except that the women are made more of. That is, you can have a good straight Western story without a mention of the female; in a romantic Western, the girl is crucial; her feelings, character, actions, and motivations dominate—

even if she is not the main character. It helps to make the girl the protagonist, but it isn't necessary. One test, though is simply this: could the girl be taken out? If she could, and after taking her out you'd still have a story there, then the story isn't a romantic Western; only if the story becomes meaningless without the woman can it be considered 'Western Romance.'"

But the real action was shifting inexorably over to the so-called pocket book. "It is thither that the highly skilled professional pulp writers are being irresistibly drawn—leaving the pulps to the beginners," observed Red Circle's Robert O. Erisman. "The pulps still use plenty of material from the seasoned professionals. But I think all pulp editors will agree that it is becoming harder and harder to keep the topflight boys on the string, even with rate increases, and that new writers can be the only practical answer to the problem."

In this dramatically shrunken market, old hands and tenderfeet alike fought for their place in the sinking sun.

"Today, landing in the writing game by way of the Western is no easy thing," asserted veteran pulpster Johnston McCulley. "You have to be fresh in treatment and newer in viewpoint than the veterans. It is not enough for the hero to shoot the meanie and strut away triumphant."

Some fresh pilgrims fell victim to the same old editorial quicksand. Californian Ray Hayton was a prime example. A 25 year old Army Air Corps veteran who relocated to Manhattan in April of 1947 on a strength of a few pulps sales, Hayton thought by moving close to his markets, he could carve out a career. He was wrong. Two bleak months of peddling pulp brought him to the brink.

On June 10, Hayton was found dead of a self-inflicted gunshot wound. He left no suicide note. Unless the title of the otherwise-blank Western manuscript found in his typewriter was a mordant attempt at one. It read: "Trail to Hell."

Respect for the veteran pulpsters was one of the first courtesies dispensed with. Newcomer Worley G. Hawthorne took a swipe at the venerable Walt Coburn in a rebuttal letter triggered by Fred Gipson's revealing portrait:

"I've been a peaceful cuss all my days, but I've got an exception to take up with that wrangler Walt Coburn. He's been in the saddle more years than I have, but when a cowhand says, as Walt did in Fred Gipson's article in the September *W.D.*, that editors 'don't care what's inside the heart of a cowhand or an outlaw or a sheriff,' I've got to stand up in the stirrups.

"Walt is saying, as I understand him, that editors are not interested in character. His phrase, 'inside the heart,' makes me draw that conclusion. He tries to rope me into believing that editors are only interested in a 'tight-twist' story.

"Sure, they like tight-twist stories, but they also like stories with living characters in them. I say this because my first saleable Western, *Bridle the Wild Heart,* was primarily a character story. Even the title indicates that. One of the main complications of this story—which sold to Fiction House in July—is based on the 'cold or hungry or played out' condition of the cowhands on a long trail drive.

"That's why I believe editors do care what's 'inside the heart of a cowhand.' I hope I'm never proved to be wrong, because it is that 'inside the heart' quality that I strive to get into each story I write. Because I have sold my first story, strong with the 'heart' quality, and because my agent has accepted for sale other stories with much the same qualities, I'm sure that editors want more than the 'tight-twist' story.

"Yep. I know. I'm talking up pretty pert for a tenderfoot Western writer. I've never been west of the Pecos, don't know 'the Injun side of a horse,' have never see a rodeo in Madison Square Garden, but I do know that editors are interested in the inside of a cowhand's heart."

Hawthorne was never heard from again. His mount was about to be shot out from under him.

"*Some sort of hoof-and-mouth disease struck the straight West-erns, and their carcasses littered the prairie like those of long-horn steers in the famous 'die-ups' of the eighties. I was present for the obsequies. A score of shoot-'em-up pulp titles were in-terred in a narrow grave just six by three. There was a glow of sunset on the rimrocks, and an intermittent, fitful, spo-radic split-second stab of six-shooter flame from a crowd of pulp heroes and villains turned out to pasture. Not one of them dreamed of a television resurrection. They just went that-a-way.*"

—*Allan R. Bosworth*

18

THE LAST ROUNDUP

BUZZARDS WERE flying lazy circles over the Pulp West.

Faced with stiff competition, desperate experiments were undertaken. Popular's *The Pecos Kid* failed to unseat Thrilling's *Rio Kid*. Avon put out a single issue of *Pioneer Stories*. Fiction House's *Indian Stories* lay scalped after three issues. The industry verdict: too off-trail. Leo Margulies tried to hop on the emerging TV Western bandwagon when he hired Louis L'Amour to pen as "Tex Burns" new adventures of Clarence Mulford's *Hopalong Cassidy*, then taking television audiences by storm. Another TV tie-in, Avon's *Wild Bill Hickok Western* was killed before the first issue could go to press.

In 1950, Fiction House finally retired *Lariat Story*, and with it, companion title *Action Stories. Frontier Storie*s limped on, obviously lame. Only three issues would be published for each remaining year.

The primary proponent of the action Western left, the Thrilling Group, announced late that year, "The big news on Westerns at Standard Magazines is that... a whole set of longstanding taboos has been knocked in the head and the horizon of the Western story pushed right up to the sky.

"The finis of the horse opera which covered its lack of ideas by physical action and shooting, has been a long time coming," continued supervising editor Charles S. Strong. "Today's Western is a *story* with a locale but no violence. The days of gunplay, cowboys and Indians are over."

A prolific Westerneer back in his prime, Strong blamed comic books for absconding with the juvenile fans. The focus shifted to the adult reader. But true change was measured in inches. As an example of Thrilling's bold new direction, Strong offered this:

"…scheduled for a future issue of *Giant Western*, is Giff Chesire's 'Torment Haven,' in which a man and girl, snowbound in an abandoned mine, act just the way you'd expect a man and a girl to act in such circumstances. There is no flagrant sex in the story, but there is at least, praise be, a diplomatic recognition that it exists."

This was Wayne Overholser's recent *Ranch Romances* wrinkle taken to the next step—or perhaps merely a tamer version of *Spicy Western Stories*. Progress it was not.

Just when the situation seemed impossible, the cavalry came to the rescue.

"Twice in the last 10 years," wrote *Writer's Digest's* Aron Mathieu, "just as the pulps were ready to perish, they were rescued from what seemed like oblivion by the same turn of events that put the used-car market back on its feet when new car manufacturers made tanks…. Today, December 1951, the pulps once again are in the black. Two years ago, 80% of them were in the red. How did the change come about?"

The answer was paper. In 1950, the Korean conflict broke out. Anticipating a long war, the government rationed paper. Allotments were soon reduced.

"Suddenly," explained Mathieu, "the retreating pulp publishers found themselves issuing fewer titles (because they had killed off the losers) and printing fewer copies of and fewer pages in the pulp titles they retained. And the scarcity of newsprint kept away any competitor from vying with them. With some surprise and considerable aplomb, Messers Pines, Steeger, Byrne and Goodman, *et al*, backed into a profit."

Noting that "the magazines that are selling now are not one

whit better than their sisters which were failing two years ago," Mathieu predicted this unexpected reprieve from the gallows would last only if the basic product was reformed.

A certain sign that the end was near was the abrupt resignation of Leo Margulies upon his return from a nine-month European sabbatical in the Spring of 1951. "I needed the rest," he was quoted as saying. Dark rumors swirled of a breakdown. After 20 years of editing a 40-pulp chain, perhaps a nervous collapse was inevitable.

Before he quit, Margulies uttered a pronouncement that seemed guaranteed to tear the heart out of the struggling writers he left behind, if not undermine all efforts to move the Western action story into fresh vistas.

"The curse of the Western story," he thundered, "is the laziness of its writers—they fail to find fresh slants in an unbelievably unlimited field."

Charles Strong replaced him, with *Ranch Romances'* Fanny Ellsworth as Managing Editor. *Ranch Ro* had ended up in the Thrilling corral.

During this transitional period, veteran *West* editor Edmund Collier helped ride herd over the chain's Westerns. He gave it up after less than a year. Summing up the dismal state of the field in his August 1951 *Writer's Digest* piece, "What About Westerns?", Collier wrote:

"Today many professional writers of Western stories are discouraged, and new men are shying off from the field. The market has been passing through one of its unavoidable periods of adjustment. When these occur the writer searches his soul for means of improving his work, while the editor goes on a furious hunt for new people who can supply him with better fiction. This is constructive, but the improvement cannot at any given moment be colossal."

Collier, who broke into *Ranch Romances* back in 1926 and over the years edited Western pulp for Doubleday and Ace, spoke of a general exodus from the Pulp Prairie.

"The causes of the present disruptions are both economic and artistic. Manufacturing costs are up. Display preferences have gone to pocket books. The amount of original fiction published in the pulp paper magazine has been radically retarded. There are fewer titles and once again reprints are rife. Comics and television have solved the writer's first problem—where to go for the money he received from the Western pulps—by writing for the comic books, television and radio."

Observing that "the popularity of Western stories is as great as ever," Collier made no bones about what he thought Western writers should do. He urged them to switch from pulp shorts to novels because of the wider primary and reprint markets available. He also took a final swipe at the still-extent supercowboy pulper, which he called the formula Western.

"Writers frequently say that editors hound them to get away from such formula Westerns, to produce fresh, original work—but that as soon as they follow the suggestion, they receive nothing but rejections until they return to the old stereotypes."

It was an old complaint. And a valid one. Bruce Cassiday, one of Popular Publications' last Western editors, spoke for two generations of his breed when he remarked, "It's the clichés—that is, the repetition of clichés—that is the problem. They are the backbone of the Western genre. The entire Western canon is a Rocky Mountain of clichés. It's for the clichés that people read Westerns!"

Cassiday allowed that even a novel new approach didn't necessarily work twice:

"There's nothing new under the sun. Especially in a Western. Western writers were always on the lookout for material in other genres they could refurbish into sagebrush scenarios. For example, one enterprising pulpster did a pretty good rewrite of an old classic he titled 'Gunslinger from Abilene.' Scene for scene, act for act, 'Gunslinger from Abilene' was our old friend *Hamlet Prince of Denmark,* complete with murdered cattle-king father, usurping ranchero uncle, maddened fiance, her bushwhacked father, her vengeance-hungry brother, and the big shootout at the Elsinor Corral. We bought that one. The same writer submitted 'The Merry Wives of Albuquerque' later, but we turned it down. Too much blood and gore."

The reformation Aron Mathieu called for seemed well underway.

"There has been a sharp rise in the last ten years in the interest of the public in Western Americana," wrote Lee E. Wells. "We are becoming more and more conscious of our heritage and I believe the public will demand that the writer interpret this Western phase."

Change struck right to the genre's roots. No longer was any portion of the Pulp West sacred—not even the fundamental milieu.

Thus it was in 1952 that Columbia's Robert "Doc" Lowndes made the astonishing announcement, "On the way out are stories of the timeless West, a never-never land cut off from the rest of the world. On the way out, too, if not already out, is the gunman who can fight although bleeding from every pore, the perfect marksman, the hero who isn't afraid of any danger."

"We've just cut out a lot of the senseless bang-bang," admitted Samuel Mines, still editing for Thrilling.

Warned Harold Preece, "If you want to make the grade in Western pulps you'll have to set your sights higher than did anybody who entered the field 20 or even 10 years ago. You can't ride in on a medley of shooting running through a scrap of plot. That combination clicked during a long period when readers had less schooling and all of American life held a certain quality of naive innocence. Then we Western writers could get by with a hero who was a knight in buckskin, a villain who was an unadulterated prototype of Old Scratch, a heroine who was brave but passionless and Indians who were either Noble Red Men or scalp-hungry fiends. The whole thing was a simple dish cooked up for simple people and pulp editors shied away from anything else."

Whether he realized it or not, Preece was spouting the same editorial line his predecessors had back in 1927, 1932 and 1939. Everything had changed, yet nothing had changed.

"The basic plot-theme of salable Western stories back in the heyday of Western pulp magazines was *male courage and fair play* pitted, but physically and emotionally, against *danger and villainy*," reminded S. Omar Barker. "It still is. But whereas the fictional hero of those days was most often a cowboy, lawman, gunman, or all three in one, today's editors welcome yarns with the lead male character engaged in any conceivable Old West occupation, from piano-tuning to printing, soldering, surveying, homesteading, horseshoeing, Buffalo peeling, or button peddling."

At Popular Publications, Harry Widmer finally cashed in his editorial chips after 20 years in the game. He went to work for August Lenniger. Mike Tilden added Widmer's Westerns to his own responsibilities, and cast aside the once-true-but-now-trite Rogers Terrill formulas.

With all the old clichés in coffins, Tilden advised, "Since there is no new plot in the Western, the writer must find new angles and emphasis, usually through emphasizing characterization." He failed to say how.

Popular Publications president Henry Steeger cited the new post-war reader as the true driving force behind it all.

"During the war," he said, "15,000,000 American men put on uniforms and fought a war all over the face of the globe. They came back more confident of themselves, but they also brought back a demand for more realism and less hokum."

But the pulp magazine industry was built on a rock-solid foundation of hokum. Sales continued to lag. Publishers raised cover prices, slashed editorial salaries, yet demanded ever higher quality from beleaguered writers, whose rates were subject to unannounced cuts.

"The pulp magazine is essentially a fiction magazine," observed Fanny Ellsworth, "and like everything else in this post-war world, it has grown up. At one time a story could be sold on the basis of action alone; today the story must be about something or someone, real problems and real people. Why? Because anyone who has made an effort to sit down and read a story doesn't want to feel as if he'd have done better to sit back and watch television.... If fiction is going to compete successfully against other forms of entertainment, it must offer something the reader can't so satisfactorily find elsewhere—vicarious experience."

"Despite allegations to the contrary," Lee Floren wrote in 1952, "one has to be a good writer to sell a story even in a Western pulp these days. A few years ago an author could load down a Western yarn with roaring guns and flying fists and he could shove action into the script whether logical or not. Today, to sell a Western pulp magazine, an author has to write a *slick* story. He has to write for *Satevepost* and mail it to a pulp editor. Editorial policy has drastically changed and action for action's sake is out—definitely out!"

Floren was singing the same old song. He was probably one of the last to do so. For the end was near. Floren cited three countervailing trends—TV, the paperback and a new crop of green but promising writers.

"The new Western story writers are almost all college graduates with a sound basis in the fundamentals of fiction writing," he said. "Some of them have completely run old hands out of the game."

One was William R. Cox. In June of 1951, he complained to his agent, Joseph T. Shaw:

"'Lawman,' the first of my experimental Westerns dealing in character seems not to be what they want, doesn't it? The fact that none of them sold really sunk me. I used to do Westerns galore and sell them; was suddenly socked with a rejection saying 'this is the old fashioned type story,' and took a deep holt and tried to learn what they wanted. Reading the magazine taught me nothing. So I tried character stuff. Now it seems I have failed at it. What is left to me in the business?"

Cox quit wordslinging six months later.

One stubborn cowboy clung to his saddle. "For the old-timers who were caught unawares at the present cycle of the pulp markets," Chuck Martin told *Writer's Digest*, "I have scant sympathy. The handwriting was on the wall, for all who write to read. The danger lies in too close specialization. If one field shows a slump, there are a hundred other fields. But you must learn to look ahead. I was caught in 1930, but this time I was looking."

Others followed the familiar slick trail of those who had gone before them a generation ago.

Popular Publications editor Alden H. Norton reported, "Luke Short doesn't write for our magazines any more. He is selling serials to *The Saturday Evening Post*, for which we can't blame him. But let us not lose heart. A new, young, vigorous crop of writers are finding their way into our pages. The pattern always repeats itself."

Famous last words. Even the new blood was getting spooked. Thomas Thompson addressed the death rumors troubling the greenhorns in "Why Write Pulp?" for *Writer's Digest*.

"One faction tells them in effect, 'You are wasting your time writing for the pulps. They are dead and you'll be dead, too, if you get mixed up with them.' Another faction says, 'Go ahead and write for the pulps but prepare to be robbed, beaten and quartered.' And a third faction says, 'Successful writers come up through the pulps; you can't be a slick writer without being a pulp writer first.'"

Yet the old definition of what constituted pulp had been strung up and stretched out.

Said Fanny Ellsworth, "Beginning writers will find the pulp fiction market—and remember that 'pulp' refers to paper, not what's printed on it—an excellent testing ground for their new and undeveloped talent."

Ominously, the very term had become the newest taboo. As

Paul Chadwick remarked, "The word 'pulp' is really nothing but a trade name. It has more to do with the publishing business than it has with actual writing craftsmanship."

There was even talk that the new brand of Western story needn't be terribly Western.

"Except for the necessity of remembering correct items of background and atmosphere," Johnston McCulley observed, "forget you are writing a so-called Western. You are *writing a story*. Have the characters as natural as you would if they were a part of the modern scene with which you are familiar."

As Robert O. Erisman put it in 1952, "The modern Western gets more modern and less Western daily: all the characters tend more and more to talk like present-day people, with Western 'color' throughout correspondingly toned down."

That same year, Lee Floren attempted to lecture his *compadres* on the fine art of writing slick Westerns for common pulp magazines:

"How do you make a character realistic and lifelike?" he asked. "You do that by making his actions, his thoughts, logical to his characterization. Your main character is a redheaded, headstrong young fellow. He is strong on brawn and shy on brains. He had homesteaded a piece of land (an old formula in Westerns) and the villain, the local rancher, tries to run him off his land upon which he has legal claim.

"You have shown your reader that the hero has a rough temper and likes to fight. How, then, will he solve his problems? Through brawn and gunsmoke, of course. What if, suddenly, he backs down, caves in, and suddenly uses his brain power, of which the reader knows he has very little?

"Your hero is out of 'character.' He has suddenly lost his reality to the reader. When that happens the reader loses interest. When the reader loses interest you, as an author, have made an enemy. Because he does not like you he will not buy another magazine with your name in it. Because he will not buy the magazine the publisher does not like you and he will not buy another story from you. It's that simple and because of its simplicity some authors almost starve to death."

Everything Floren wrote was truth—yet clichéd beyond redemption.

Clearly, the Pulp West had entered a last, vicious cycle.

Seeing their markets failing, nervous pulp writers organized the Western Writers of America at this time. The principal instigators were Tommy Thompson, Dwight Bennett Newton, Norman A. Fox, Wayne Overholser, Harry Sinclair Drago, and first president Nelson C. Nye. William MacLeod Raine, who had been writing since the genre's start, was named Honorary President.

In the first issue of WWA's *Roundup,* Raine made an amazing statement that flew in the face of the genre's checkered history. "The founding of WWA may mark a milestone in the history of our regional writers. Our fiction is far less stylized and pattern-built than that of other types which receive more consideration from the pundits who review books."

Apparently, Raine never read Western pulps.

From the WWA's inception, a fresh schism developed between the pulp practitioners and those exploring virgin territory in paperback books. Despite the undeniable fact that the organization was founded by pulpsters, a writer couldn't be a voting member unless he had published three novels—pulp magazine lead novels were exempt.

As WWA's second president, Noel M. Loomis, outlined:

"One side calls the other 'pulp writers,' implying they use action for action's sake, while those of us who cut our eyeteeth in the pulps are likely to exhibit a great deal of disgust over the obvious attempts at self-professed 'modern' writers to use the Western as background for a shocker. It is hardly necessary to point out that adultery, incest, homos, queers and masochists can become as monotonous in fiction as a six-shooter that shoots 44 times."

But all this hoorah was too late for the Golden West of the

pulp magazine. It really started imploding in the Summer of 1953 when the Thrilling Group put out to pasture *Thrilling Western, Thrilling Ranch Stories, Popular Western, Exciting Western, Texas Western, West, Rangeland Love Romances, Giant Western, Masked Rider Western, Range Riders* and *The Rio Kid.*

For the Korean War had finally ended. Paper controls were lifted. Production costs continued to spiral upward. Belts were pulled tighter. The pulpeteer legion pushed on, praying for a miracle. All they got was more ruction.

That same summer, the St. John Publishing Company, issuer of the celebrated suspense digest, *Manhunt,* decided that there might be a market for a similarly realistic and suspenseful companion in the frontier fiction field. *Gunsmoke* was a ray of hope to writers sick of Hollywood-style pulp cowboys, and attracted top names.

"As far as I can recall," contributor Robert Turner wrote, "only two issues of *Gunsmoke* were published, even though the writing in a great many of the stories was superb. It just didn't go, partly, I believe, because of what Don Wollheim of Ace Books once told me. He said the general reading public that was hung up on Westerns wanted the standard stories, the bigger-than-life Western heroes. They didn't want stories about heels, stories from the viewpoint of a killer. They didn't want the West the way it really was, but as the fantasy world that Western fiction had made it to be down through the years.... So *Gunsmoke* magazine died."

The surviving all-fiction titles, paper dinosaurs from the beginning of the pulp magazine era, began winking out of existence. *Adventure. Blue Book. Short Stories.* All gone.

In July 1954 *The Author & Journalist* carried a survey article by S. Omar Barker called "Fiction Should be Plausible." He could not help but acknowledge the drought plaguing the field.

"I can remember when prospering Western pulp magazines were so numerous that a competent fictioneer could find ready acceptance for a dozen short stories and novelettes a month—

if he could write that many. How come it ain't thataway no more? You've noticed those colorful and ubiquitous 'pocket books,' haven't you? Wal, ol' podner, the Westerns went that-away!

"We have been hearing a great deal recently about the new approach in Westerns," Barker noted. "Next to the striking changes in markets, I believe the most important changes implicit in 'the new approach' can be fairly summarized this way:

"Not less plot, but more careful motivation; not less action, but better writing to give it dramatic effect; not necessarily less gunsmoke, but more convincing occasion for it; not less Wild West atmosphere, but less dependence on exaggerated lingo to attain it; not necessarily new plot situations, but more emphasis on the human nature involved in them; not less Old West, but more accurate regional-historical background for it; not less rip-snort, but more human heart-sweat to go with it; not less thrill of adventure, but a closer tie-in with everyday frontier living; not necessarily an absolute authenticity, but at least an awareness of the Old West as a place and period inhabited by people, not puppets—all of which adds up to a somewhat more adult story, which still should not be adult enough to wean youthful readers away from an established Western story tradition."

Western pulp fiction was at long last growing up. But it was too little, too late.

The timing of Barker's article was unfortunate. For, with the August and September 1954 cover dates, Popular killed off *Dime Western, Star Western, .44 Western, New Western, Big-Book Western, Max Brand's Western Magazine, Fifteen Range Romances, Western Rangers Stories, Western Ace-High Stories, Rangeland Love Stories, 10 Story Western* and *Western Story Magazine,* which had been purchased from Street & Smith and briefly revived. It was an unprecedented Western magazine massacre.

Over at Fiction House, they finally gave up the ghost town, too. *Frontier Stories* had been put down the year before. All that was left were a matched pair of semi-reprint titles *Two Western Books* and *Two Western Action Books* designed to compete with the paperbacks. They were interred early in the Spring.

The pulp publisher which had prematurely pronounced the Western dead in 1927 and again in 1932, finally cashed in its chips forever.

By the end of 1954, writers like William F. Bragg and others were wondering in print where all the pulps had ridden off to. Many predicted they would return. *Writer's Digest* was more sanguine, blaming the first editor to ramrod the pioneer Western fiction magazine:

"An editor's job is to select and emphasize. Many all-fiction editors select their fiction from a formula composed of old hats and older saws. Their emphasis, since the days of Frank Blackwell, re-affirms old credos and rejects the realities of devious human behavior. This, plus poor printing and dated illustrations, can't compete."

In response, Bill Bragg wrote, "As one who for many years was a full-time writer of popular fiction particularly in the Western field, I would say first that the 'pulps' are not dead. 'They but sleep.' Perhaps some of the fiction magazines were edited by 'unimaginative editors,' but the men who handled my first faltering copy for such excellent magazines as *West, Western Story, Star Western, Dime Western, Thrilling Western,* etc., were far from unimaginative. I refer to such editors as Blackwell, Jack Byrne, Ronald Oliphant, Anthony Rud, Harry Maule, Mike Tilden, Leo Margulies, Jack Burr, Art Lawson, Arthur Sullivant Hoffman, Fanny Ellsworth, Fred Clayton, Roy DeHorn, Rogers Terrill, Harold Hersey, and a score of other fine people who set my feet on the successful 'freelancers' pathway until World War II, when a flood of reprint magazines, and TV temporarily—and note that I remark 'temporarily'—played havoc with the popular fiction market."

Regrettably, Bragg was wallowing in nostalgia, not reality. The Pulp Range he had grazed upon was then in the throes of a permanent drought. No miracle rider, no rainmaker like Rogers Terrill, loomed over the darkening horizon.

The emerging paperback book market was largely credited by *Writer's Digest* with making the pulp paper story obsolete:

"When the war ended and the news stands loaded up, because paper was free again, the pulps received only a token display of their 'straps' (the flat binding edge) which listed their name, volume number and price. This was a poor substitute for full front cover display. Meanwhile, the paperbacks had their own wire racks which amply displayed the bosoms and violence and seduction on their front covers. Pulp sales died, and the pulp publishers lapsed into defeatism. Their competitive answer was lower pay for editors, writers and illustrators. Naturally, the pulps promptly went to hell." [...] "The pulps will stay dead until someone new comes into the business who, instead of imitating Silberkleit's Columbia Publications decides to fade him dead away."

It was a dream never realized.

Popular kept *Fifteen Western Tales* going until 1955, changing to the slick *Argosy* format, but in vain.

Events had elevated what had formerly been a "dump" market—Martin Goodman's Red Circle Publications, publisher of ephemeral titles like *Gunsmoke Western*. Suddenly, it was a major chain. Editor Robert O. Erisman capitalized on his shifting fortunes by drastically de-pulping his magazines, consigning the old formulas to oblivion, and buying slick-magazine rejects whenever he could.

In 1956, Erisman told *The Author & Journalist*, "Where we once used only very solid, standard stuff in our lead spots, letting the off-trail stories come later in the books for variety and where they would be sure not to disturb the 'regular' Western reader who was looking for standard Western reading—where we once used only these standard leads, we now tend more and more to hit the reader right off with what we hope will be a pretty unexpected story."

Erisman admitted the regulation Western yarn was now what he employed for filler. Unmentioned was the fact that under numerous pen names, editor Erisman himself wrote those lead novels almost exclusively. Like the Pulp West itself, the Red Circle market was more illusion than substance. A year later, that chain had evaporated, too.

Two seemingly impregnable titles lingered. *Texas Rangers* miraculously survived until February 1958, the same month *Ranch Romances*—the last surviving twice-a-month pulp—went quarterly. A last-gasp attempt to launch a traditional pulp magazine based on the *Wagon Train* TV show came and went in 1960.

Astonishingly, *Ranch Romances* struggled on to 1971, although in its sunset years as a reprint vehicle. The last true Western pulp line to succumb was Columbia's *Double-Action Western, Real Western, Famous Western* and *Western Romances* in 1960. In this case, the distributor jerked the hangrope.

The irony of Columbia's dogged persistence in the face of the ever-declining fortunes of the Pulp Western magazine was that, contrary to Ned Collier's 1936 prediction that any 1956 pulp survivors would unquestionably hew toward the authentic West, Columbia dished up an unabashedly juvenile product.

The bang-bang formula had outlasted all others, altered in only the most minor of ways.

"I am old enough to remember when *Bang!* was a generally accepted onomatopoeic symbol for the sound of a shot," joked S. Omar Barker. "Then along came *Pow!*, followed variously by *Ping!*, *Whomp!*, *Zing!* et cetera *ad infinitum.*"

When the powdersmoke finally cleared, the despised and many-times-lynched gun-dummy had been the last hombre left standing. Yet even in death, he was triumphant, his epithet a stark yet simple truism: He Was What The Public Expected.

After three decades of editing Western pulps, "Doc" Lowndes said frankly, "I would be perfectly happy if I never had to read another Western."

One of Lowndes' most indefatigable contributors had been Eric Rober, professionally known as T.W. Ford—the self-same once-young Fiction House editor whom Rogers Terrill recalled bemoaning the death of the pulp Western thirty years before. Still grinding out Westerns, Rober died in the early '50s. The genre had outlived him.

The venerable pulp magazine had gone the way of the Conestoga wagon. It was obsolete.

"There seems to be no single, basic cause of the downfall of the pulps," wrote author James L. Harte. "I'm not convinced, as some of my contemporaries are, that loss of readership, chiefly to the pocket books, is a large factor. I am more convinced that snobbish publishers and, in some measure, incompetent editors are a fairly large part of the picture. When Street & Smith drops such names as *The Shadow, Doc Savage,* and *Wild West Weekly,* which it seems to me, based on lengthy research into readers' preferences, any publisher could make money on, my conviction of publishers' snobbery grows. Many of them, despite that they've built fortunes and publishing empires on them, do not genuinely like pulp fiction. Naturally, such a condition makes pulp fiction more stereotyped, less likable. It's a descending spiral."

Tom Curry named two villains. "Two factors dealt the *coupe de grace,* not only to the pulps but to many slick-paper general magazines that used polished, high-toned Westerns by master craftsmen," he noted. "The paperback and TV slaughtered the fiction magazine as surely as any gunfighter ever plugged another through the heart. But the Western survived."

Noel Loomis pointed an accusing finger at the beleaguered writers, opining that "...the old million-words-a-year-men laid the foundation for killing off the pulps." He went on to assert that "...it seems to me that back in the '20s a lot of writers who discovered how to sell to the pulps in quantity, operated almost solely on that basis and refrained from spending any more time writing or studying than was absolutely necessary. Unfortunately, editors aided and abetted them. The pulps did not grow with the readers. If there is any question in your mind about the trend, go to some news stands that ten or fifteen years ago stocked big piles of pulps. In my town, in every case the pulps have shrunk to a fraction of the volume they totaled in 1935 or 1940. Ask the old-time newshawks."

Writing in *The Roundup,* novelist Clifton Adams blamed Norman A. Fox's old "double-barreled" approach to pulping.

"The pulps still had their loyal but limited market when they went under for the third time," he asserted. "As I see it, they tried to hold their loyal market (a juvenile market) and be 'adult' at the same time—from the outset an impossible combination. They resorted to lurid covers and sexed-up stories in an attempt to reach their juvenile-adult market, but they forgot that sex can be mighty dreary unless it is brought off with some skill. The pulps tried just about everything in the book to stay afloat but ignored the one thing that could have saved them. Quality."

"Low budgets never allowed top editors like Mike Tilden to get the strongly characterized, skillfully written stories all of them would have liked," added William Hopson. "They had to select the best they could get, no doubt wincing painfully every time they initialed an O.K., and the majority of it was pretty gun dummy. The hero was a face supporting not one but two guns, and the readers finally wore out before the pistols did."

"One reason definitely is *not* any lessening in the popularity of Westerns as such," insisted S. Omar Barker in 1958. "Stories of the Old West, authentic or unauthentic, have never been more popular than today. But a vast number of Western fans who once *read* short stories now watch them on TV. In my opinion TV has been the biggest single factor in pushing pulps out of the picture. Probably the popularity of so-called 'comic books' has also played its part.... Other probable reasons for the demise of pulp Westerns may have been increased production costs, distribution difficulties, poor newsstand display, and perhaps the inexorable element of change in a changing world."

"When the thing finally collapsed," reflected Tom Curry,

"the publishers blamed the editors, who in turn blamed the writers, and the only thing they could do was go home and kick their wives."

The better writers fled to better markets. An upbeat communication from William Hopson in the December 1954 *Writer's Digest* told of the new Western boomtown the hardiest survivors fell heir to:

"I'm just as anxious as all of us to see the pulps come back. A good many years ago I wrote a piece for the *Digest* about Western novels; and I said I didn't know what the future would be but that some publisher would come up with a new wrinkle. Well, through paperbacks like Bantam and Gold Medal originals I'm making more money than I ever made in my life, and it's piling still higher. I'm slogging away like an old steady workhorse and selling everything I can turn out." [...] "That's what comes from working instead of crying."

Dwight Bennett Newton, the writer whose unassuming novel kicked off the boom in the first place, saw this transitional period as a reaffirmation of his craft:

"We starving ex-pulpwriters were back at work again, writing and selling four or five books a year, and at far better pay than we'd ever known in the magazines. Moreover, we all at once discovered we were what many of us had secretly always wanted to be—novelists, instead of mere pulp paper hacks. It was a good feeling."

Others called it a day. William F. Bragg, for example, moved on to the Wyoming State Legislature. Harry Olmsted retired to operate a Navajo trading post rather than retool. Decades of fictioneering had earned him no equity in his own output. Routinely, he had sold all rights.

"In those days," Olmsted explained, "a story in the mail was dismissed, forgotten. Once I dropped it in the slot, my thoughts would be centered on the one that'd go out next week. The new day's work, and tomorrow's completion left me with no interest in subsidiary rights."

"We were so bubbling over with the next yarn!" said E. Hoffmann Price. "We knew there was no end to the supply, we knew we'd never tire, never go stale, we knew that a thing done was an end. When a yarn bogged down, or got kicked around, we'd not revise it unless an editor asked us to. Better scrap it and start something that did move."

Many operated that way. Surviving practitioners were forced to break new trails. Walker Tompkins transferred his facility with the Western fairy tale to television, as did D.B. Newton, Frank Gruber and sundry others. Luke Short turned his hand to Western screenplays. Tom Blackburn was central to the Davy Crockett revival of the 1950s, scripting the famous Walt Disney TV series and its hit theme song lyrics. Johnston McCulley sold Disney all rights to his Zorro, ultimately working on the popular TV series.

To a man, they credited their pulpwood training with enabling them to make a successful transition. Tommy Thompson put it like this:

"What I had learned from the pulps was, you tell the best action story you can and you put some real, honest-to-God people into it and you add a few spoonfuls of honest emotion. I never quit doing that kind of pulp story. The only difference was, they paid me better and called it television."

S. Omar Barker concentrated on the slicks, until they too folded up, victims of television. Accustomed to writing short stories and novelettes, he couldn't convert to the new markets for Western novels.

"I've tried," he confided to Wayne Overholser, "but my stuff always turns out to be short stories."

Many, like John A. Saxon—who kicked the bucket in 1947—and H. Bedford-Jones, another casualty of 1949, simply disappeared from print. In 1950, pioneer Ernest Haycox rode off into his last sunset while at the peak of his magnificent career. Chuck Martin went to his reward in 1954. Ironically, he died with a six-gun in his hand. Under doctor's orders to slow down,

Martin battled deadlines, collapsing markets and failing health until the day he shot himself in the living room of his Boot Hill Rancho.

Yet Frederick Faust's untimely battlefield death seemed only to increase the public appetite for his work. And Ernest Haycox's work also lived on, despite his 1950 death. Remarkably, Hamilton Craigie, who once claimed to have been one of the original Confederate soldiers mistaken for postmen on the streets of Philadelphia in 1869, continued selling Western fact articles right up to the bitter end. If his 1837 birth year is to be believed, Craigie was still turning them out at the improbable age of 110 plus.

Perhaps the period's spiritual close was marked by the death of William MacLeod Raine in 1954. In the game since 1898, his serial *Wyoming* had kicked off the first issue of *Western Story* back in 1919. Wayne D. Overholser eulogized him with these words: "His passing marked the end of an era, for he was the one working writer of Western fiction whose career reached back to the days when the events about which we write actually took place."

As the pulps were collapsing, Leo Margulies launched a modest line of digest magazines. Fifteen years passed before he dared issue another Western title. The first issue of his *Zane Grey Western* was assembled from castoff 1950s pulp manuscripts. It did not long endure.

Frank Blackwell had passed away in 1951, at the age of 73. It is doubtful if in retirement he read so much as a single Western story.

Rogers Terrill, the editor who did the most to salvage the pulp Western from a premature Boot Hill burial, left Popular to start the Rogers Terrill Literary Agency. Author's agent August Lenniger, an equal force in the reformation of the Pulp West, tied up with the Western Writers of America and edited their annual anthology for years. He continued wrangling authors until 1978, when, after fifty years in the business, he sold his agency.

Jack Byrne ended up at G.P. Putnam's Sons. Calling himself the "surviving dean of pulp magazine editors," he contacted Leo Margulies in 1965, reporting that people kept asking whatever became of William Clayton, Harold Hersey and others of that vanished breed, and inviting the old lion "to cast your mind back to those fine days when you and I were kings and every night was pay night at Nick's and Jack Delaney's."

Unable to crash upscale U.S. markets, Walt Coburn wrote for British hardcover publishers until the sad day in 1971 when he hanged himself.

Others simply drifted away. "Two-Gun" Tompkins turned to non-fiction, admitting, "Westerns sort of bore me."

Prevailing wisdom said TV finally killed off the pulp Western, that people could enjoy their horse operas with less effort by watching it on the tube than by reading it.

"Within three or four years after TV established itself comfortably in American homes," recalled Ryerson Johnson, "Western magazines bit the dust. It was easier to drink your beer and watch *Bonanza* or *Have Gun, Will Travel.* You didn't even have to turn pages."

Old-timer J. Edward Leithead recollected, "I had seen it happen before—the movies knocking out dime and nickel novels—but, like many another writer and illustrator, I didn't want to believe that the present slump was the 'handwriting on the wall' for Western fiction. For forty years people couldn't get enough of it—and then *bam!* it was over."

Agent Lurton Blassingame saw the sea change this way:

"I had friends who would always ask me to bring them some Western pulps cause they knew I could get them for free through my business. By the early '50s none of those friends were asking for Western pulps any more. They were watching the 'Lone Ranger' on television."

Television certainly was a culprit. But the true killer was not to be found outside the page of pulps, but inside. The evidence?

It comes from an unimpeachable source. Circa 1927, John A. Saxon had occasion to take the testimony of Wyatt Earp in the Lotta Crabtree trial. But let him tell it:

"At the time I met Wyatt Earp he was over seventy, but had the appearance of a much younger man. As a writer of Westerns I tried to sound him out concerning the 'early days' but he was never a loquacious man and it was hard to get him to talk.

"However, one time I did get him to open up a little on the subject of Western stories, many of which concerned his own experiences. I had asked him if he had ever read any of them. He looked at me for a long time and finally said: 'Yes.'

"'What do you think of them?' I asked.

"'If any man had ever acted as most of these so-called gunmen are portrayed in the Westerns I have read,' said the great marshal, 'they would have been killed off in twenty-four hours. People would have considered them too crazy to be allowed to run loose.'"

What killed off the pulp Western magazines? The same thing that elevated them to fortune and fame. The deadly and ultimately unkillable combination of the gun-dummy and the Broadway Westerner. Or as John A. Saxon once quipped, "Buckety-buckety, bang-bang, and another villain bit the dust...."

"The Western is not going to die. Even television couldn't kill it. They just put on new wheels, that's all."

—Thomas Thompson

EPILOGUE

THE GUN-DUMMY did not perish with the pulp
magazine. He simply moved on.

"In the first flush of the pocket books," wrote Frank Gruber,
"the Western story was overlooked but when the publishers
scraped the bottom of the barrel of mysteries and straight
novels, they tried Westerns. To their astonishment they found
that they sold as well as mysteries. Soon they were outselling
mysteries."

This unexpected boom led Gruber to proclaim a new Golden
Age. "The Western story has reached its greatest height of
popularity," he stated in 1955. "The pulps died, the small
Western motion picture series died, but TV discovered the
Western story, the pocket book publisher found the Western
story and at long last, the motion picture found the Western
story."

That same year, Jack Schaefer proclaimed in his anthology,
Out West, "Despite the long past of the Western story and the
millions and millions of words that have been written in the
field, the dramatic and significant possibilities of the material
have as yet scarcely been touched."

Interviewed at this time, President Dwight D. Eisenhower
revealed that his favorite authors were Harry Sinclair Drago
and Bliss Lomax—blissfully unaware they were one and the
same.

As always, the gun-dummy wore out his welcome pretty

quick.

By 1955, the juvenile TV Western fare symbolized by *Hopalong Cassidy* and *The Cisco Kid* began to fade in popularity. That was the first season of the so-called "adult Western" hero. The cycle commenced with *Gunsmoke, Bat Masterson* and *The Life and Legend of Wyatt Earp.*

A new gold rush, same as the old gold rush, ensued.

Working on NBC's *Tales of Wells Fargo,* Frank Gruber told *TV Guide,* "When I first began writing Westerns in 1934 I learned a discouraging fact. There were only seven basic Western plots. I tried for months to invent an eighth and met with failure. Now, 24 years later, I am still writing those seven basic Western plots."

Yet a boom in one medium seemed to slide seamlessly into a new bust in another.

"The old Western novel is a dead duck," declared William L. Hopson. "The better publishers are no longer content to buy a cold-eyed *pistolero* slamming into a strange town (or valley, basin, ranch, homestead, *et al*) to clean it out and then gallop out the other end with something beside him in skirts that might well have been taken from the window of a millinery shop."

Hopson could have been repeating the tired old pulp editor's refrain, but he was not. He was referring to the paperback Western novel, already outmoded and drifting aimlessly into its first prolonged rut.

Bereft of his pulp markets, Hopson had flung himself on this vibrant new market like a wrangler out to throw and hogtie a calf. Under his own name and that of John Sims, he ground them out as fast as he could, while he could.

"This is not Hal Everts or John Prescott or Tommy Thompson writing," he admitted. "It's pick-and-shovel stuff from a run of the mill Western writer, nearly all of it first draft from the carbon, with hardly a revised word. It's also why I never had a serial in the *Saturday Evening Post.* It's the only way I can write. But most of it has an authentic background through long and painstaking research. Most editors of both hardcover and paperback are demanding it these days...."

Hopson now had the freedom he always yearned for. As he told fledgling Westerneers:

"You don't have to write literature to get into this market for a better and more authentic novel of the West. L.P. Holmes, one of the top producers in the field, hit the nail on the head. Lew said:

"'Readers still like the man on horseback with a gun on his hip. They're not too well educated, they don't like too complicated plots or many involved characters.'"

Writing in *The Roundup*, pulpster-turned-paperbacker Joseph L. Chadwick added:

"Our rider with a gun need not be of a never-never West. Indeed, I like to think that he typifies the Old West—that he is the prototype of Goodnight, Chisum, Slaughter, Story, Milton, of a hundred other men of horses and guns who actually lived far more adventurous lives than any of our fictional heroes... I dispute the contention people who buy Westerns want to read about grocery clerks, bookkeepers, or what-have-you."

Chadwick was not alone in that thinking. Another reformed pulpster, Dan Cushman, took Tom W. Blackburn to task in *The Roundup:*

"When I was working on my first million (words, that is), I recall reading an article in *The Writer's Digest* by some fellow who had come across the directory of a Western town and was plodding through it doing a story from the viewpoint of each merchant, tradesman and laborer one by one. It was stupid, of course. From the viewpoint of the Western writer it was worse—it was self immolation. When he should have been out where the wolf howled free, this dull Haycox had his boy chained to a stool in a bank office. Of course, he outwitted the bank robbers and won the boss' grudging admiration, but it wasn't quite the same."

The clock had been turned back to the regulation cow-hero vintage 1927, but true freedom lay in the domain of sex.

Hopson again:

"When Ernest Haycox invented an addition to the Wister plot—a good woman and a good-looking bad woman, the latter almost getting into bed with the hero in a storm-bound cabin—everybody hopped onto it. After all these years we're still on it. Seems like even now every time I write a new frontier novel I swear I won't, but somehow or other the darned thing keeps creeping back in again. One good, one good-looking bad...."

At long last free to write of the true West he knew, Hopson found his novels praised with that golden word formerly denied him, and generations of pulpsters: "authentic." Ultimately, he produced one epic that remains a minor classic, *Cry Viva!*

But those flush days proved predictably short-lived.

"When the paperback boom hit like a new Texas oil field about five years ago," Hopson recounted in 1955, "fly-by-night publishers cropped up by the score, crying for copy. To a reader with two-bits, a book was a book."

Quantities of Western novels soon choked the wire racks. Quality varied widely. The painfully predictable bust came in 1955, the year network television went nationwide.

"Luckily for me," confessed Hopson, "my agent foresaw the inevitable result of overcrowded newsracks and lost no time dumping 20-odd of my old gun-slamming 'Westerns' while there was yet time. The sprinkling of three or four he couldn't hurriedly get rid of before the bottom fell out and the publishers went the way of the old cornies, couldn't be sold anywhere today."

Fortunately for the gun-dummy and his typing puppeteers, fresh grazing ground lay close at hand. The TV Western trend of the 1950s was starting to stampede. After riding the Davy Crockett phenomenon to its end, Tom Blackburn went over to Warner Bros. to script *Cheyenne* and *Rawhide*. Tommy Thompson signed up with *Bonanza*. And Dwight B. Newton rode *Wagon Train* through several seasons.

"Trend?" said one network programming executive in 1957. "It's an avalanche."

That autumn, *TV Western Roundup* reported, "This year there'll be the adult Western, the dude Western, the eastern Western, the northern Western, the southern Western, the flying Western, the girlie Western, the Indian Western, the animal Western, the old film Western, the rootin' tootin' Western...."

Not everyone saw it as another golden age. "The Wyatt Earps and the Bat Mastersons of television are nothing but exploded myths!" scoffed 78-year-old Harry Sinclair Drago. "I think it is a crying shame that kids have to watch this stuff."

"These men were really 'townies'—gamblers or town marshals who knew how to use a gun and hung around saloons and houses of prostitution," explained Gordon D. Shirreffs. "Some called them fighting pimps."

But it was the adults who were driving the herd mentality. In 1959, an unprecedented 32 Westerns saturated the air. Of the top ten shows that year, eight were Horse Operas. Out of the 60 shows cancelled in the previous TV season, not one was a Western. One-third of all 1959 Hollywood productions were of the Western genre.

The old Pulp Range had given way to the new Electronic West. "In spite of some opinion to the contrary," observed Victor H. White, "I contend that Western pulps exerted a greater influence than any other medium in cementing a picture of 'How the West was Conquered' in the minds of our people. And it is fact that their stories became the nucleus of the majority of Western television presentations."

The last effort of any significance mined the motherlode. One of the first to go to color, *The Virginian* was broadcast in 90-minute episodes from its 1962 debut. It lasted nine seasons.

"You'd think people would get tired of looking at the southern end of a horse every week," bemoaned one anonymous TV producer.

Eventually, they did. By the early 1970s, TV viewers had succumbed to trail fever. *Gunsmoke* endured to 1975, setting a 20 year record that remains unbroken to this day. Before the genre had once again been exhausted, perennial cow-hero actor Chuck Connors had starred in the remote and improbable *Cowboy in Africa*.

"There were too many *bad* Westerns," explained *Bonanza* producer David Dortort. "The public saw through it, and they began switching off the Westerns, the bad ones—and, unfortunately, the good ones with them."

Although TV programming has gone through many cycles in the decades since, the Western show never returned to the small screen in remarkable numbers.

In the Summer of 1959, with TV Westerns at their all-time peak, Norman A. Fox got one of his Western manuscripts back from a hardcover publisher. With it was a note: "After careful consideration, we have decided to discontinue the publication of Westerns."

Figuring that was that, Fox went on vacation. Upon his return, he found a followup letter, saying, "We have decided to continue the publication of Westerns, as we are convinced they are what our readers want. Please return manuscript at once."

And so it went. Sunrise and sunset in predictable five year cycles.

"The Cowboy has become a great America folk-hero...the Centaur of the West, the Lancelot and Galahad of the mesa and sierra," observed Robert West Howard that same halcyon summer. "Now, the meat-packers didn't create The Cowboy as a symbol of human-freedom and democratic goodness. Nor... did the Chamber of Commerce do much about The Cowboy until a few years ago. The cattleman certainly didn't do it; the cowboy is still a shovel-boy on the manure pile in his vocabulary.

"The Western Writer created The Cowboy, just as the Western Writer created The Golden West as that lovely land where human-freedom achieves full stature."

After twenty years, the prevailing wind once again shifted away from the cowboy story. "I never wrote one for the simple reason that they never existed historically," swore Gordon D. Shirreffs. "Cowboys were too busy herding cattle and repairing fences to be walking around town blowing hell out of anybody who crossed their path. They never had enough money to buy cartridges to become expert shots."

In books, the Historical West was revived. Again. "The men who were writing polished-up pulp material for softcovers couldn't make the second transition into historically accurate material and failed," recalled Shirreffs, one of the few pulp survivors who did.

"And that was the worst thing about writing for the pulps—" lamented fellow survivor Clifton Adams. "I learned about every bad habit there is to be learned in this business and I have been trying to unlearn them ever since."

The so-called slicks eventually succumbed to the same forces that crushed the pulps. *Collier's* went out in 1957, in the middle of serializing Luke Short's *Doom Canyon*. Responding to fevered Western fans, *The Saturday Evening Post* published the conclusion. When the *Post* expired a decade later, it was after running Charles Portis' *True Grit*.

In the decades that followed, the Western genre has waxed and waned. *The Searchers.* Anti-Westerns. *The Man Who Shot Liberty Valance.* *Hombre.* Spaghetti Westerns. *The Wild Bunch.* *Butch Cassidy and the Sundance Kid.* Adult Westerns. *Slocum.* *Edge.* Piccadilly Cowboys. *Lonesome Dove.* *Dances with Wolves.* *Unforgiven.* *Tombstone.* Elmer Kelton. *Open Range.* *Brokeback Mountain.* *Serenity.* *3:10 to Yuma.* *Australia.* *Cowboys and Aliens.* *True Grit.* *The Lone Ranger.*

During this time, a new giant rose to prominence. Before the war, he had been an obscure pulp adventure writer. After being mustered out of the Army in 1945, Leo Margulies asked him what he intended to do with his writing career. He confessed not to know. Margulies then growled the golden word he had uttered to Frank Gruber and so many others: "Westerns."

When Bantam Books decided that marketing one prolific Western writer was smarter than three slower ones, their first choice Luke Short declined the ordeal of writing three novels a year. Their second choice said yes.

Louis L'Amour went on to become the most popular Frontier novelist since Zane Grey and Max Brand, not to mention the best-selling writer of his time. Only his 1988 death called a halt to the golden gravy train.

"Whole generations of writers have come and gone," Dwight B. Newton wrote in 1979. "Most of us must get used to the fact that all but our very latest works are normally out of print, and that in our turn we can expect to join the ranks of George Washington Ogden, Dane Coolidge, F.R. Buckley, William Patterson White, George Gilbert, Robert J. Horton, Cherry Wilson, Kenneth Perkins, Robert Ormond Case... all top names, remembered with fondness by older readers, but now apparently on their way to oblivion. What of that? It's not bad company to be in."

Critics and editors alike have periodically declared the Western story dead and buried. Stubbornly, it refuses to remain interred. The U.S. cowboy rides eternal.

Squire Omar Barker one last time:

"The oldtime cowboy spent far more of his time in the saddle and hard at work than he ever did shooting off sixguns, either in play or in earnest. How, from the horseback hardihood, dash, and courage of this character there has developed the worldwide tradition, more than a little fabulous, of the cowboy as any Old West hero with a gun, would make an interesting study. But... the important fact is that the story of Western adventure as an expression of that tradition, continues to be perennially popular, and will probably continue to be written and published in one form or another even long after our advance agents arrive on Mars."

Way back in 1941, Rogers Terrill explained why—and his words still ring true today:

"…The Western story, with its flavor of high adventure, its glamorous and colorful setting, its patriotic appeal, its opportunity for the dramatic presentation of heroic accomplishment, and, lastly, its variety—is, in my humble opinion, the most worth while contribution to American recreational life so far made by pulp magazines."

EPITAPH

"Well, they have gone into the night, a vast and silent caravan, with their buckskins and their boots, their spurs and their long rifles, their wagons and their mustangs, their wars and their loves, their brutalities and their chivalries; they have gone to join their old rivals, the wolf, the panther and the Indian, and only a crumbling 'dobe wall, a fading trail, the breath of an old song, remain to mark the roads they traveled. But sometimes when the night wind whispers forgotten tales through the mesquite and the chaparral, it is easy to imagine that once again the tall grass bends to the tread of a ghostly caravan, that the breeze bears the jingle of stirrup and bridle-chain, and that spectral camp-fires are winking far out on the plains. And a lobo calls where no wolf can be, and the night is dreamy and hushed and still with the pregnancy of old times. But gone are the days when the prairie schooners carried their cargo of empire into the sunset lands and gone the reckless, roaring days when the trail herds went up along the old Chisholm. The old time cowboy with the Spanish mustang and the longhorn steer has followed the raiding Comanche, the buffalo hunter, the whole-sale cattle rustler and the old scouts into silence and oblivion."

—*Robert E. Howard, Texan*

GALLERY

CLIFTON ADAMS   S. OMAR BARKER   H. BEDFORD-JONES

TOM W. BLACKBURN   ALLAN BOSWORTH   WILLIAM F. BRAGG

NOEL M. LOOMIS, NELSON NYE, S. OMAR BARKER, JOHN SHELLEY, LESLIE ERNENWEIN, ELMER KELTON AND FRANK C. ROBERTSON.

MAX BRAND   JOHN F. BYRNE   ARTHUR H. CARHART

WALT COBURN   EUGENE CUNNINGHAM   TOM CURRY

STANDING: CHARLIE HECKELMANN, WAYNE OVERHOLSER, BILL GULICK, S. OMAR BARKER AND NOEL M. LOOMIS. SEATED: NORMAN A. FOX AND TOMMY THOMPSON.

Dan Cushman   Lester Dent   Allan K. Echols

Allan V. Elston   Robert O. Erisman   Leslie Ernenwein

Cliff Farrell   Lee Floren   Norman A. Fox

STEVE FRAZEE

FRANK GRUBER

BILL GULICK

CHARLES W. HANDLEY

C. WILLIAM HARRISON

GEORGE C. HENDERSON

HAROLD W. HERSEY

L.P. HOLMES

WILLIAM L. HOPSON

ARCH JOSCELYN

RYERSON JOHNSON

ELMER KELTON

J. EDWARD LEITHEAD

AUGUST LENNIGER

HAPSBURG LIEBE

NOEL M. LOOMIS

ROBERT MAHAFFAY

LEO MARGULIES

CHUCK MARTIN RICHARD A. MARTINSEN HARRY MAULE

DWIGHT NEWTON NELSON NYE HARRY F. OLMSTED

WAYNE D. OVERHOLSER STEPHEN PAYNE PAUL S. POWERS

GLADWELL RICHARDSON   FRANK C. ROBERTSON   LUKE SHORT

ROGERS TERRILL   THOMAS THOMPSON   MICHAEL TILDEN

WALKER A. TOMPKINS   GLENN R. VERNAM   LEE E. WELLS

INDEX

A

E

G

H

K

L

M

N

O

P

Y

Z

ABOUT THE AUTHOR

W ILL MURRAY was born in Boston in 1953, so his acquaintance with the Old West was naturally confined to the TV shows proliferating during the Golden Age of Television. He watched them all, from *Cheyenne* to *The Virginian*. His favorite remains *The Rifleman*. TV Western theme music is wired into his brain.

Murray freely admits that while he loves the Western genre, he was never a big reader of Western stories, preferring to enjoy them in their cinematic expression. Writing a book on the subject—never mind one that took a dozen years to research and assemble—was the furthest expression of his literary aspirations. But his love of pulp fiction, specifically the pulp-fiction magazines of the first half of the 20th Century, led him to write hundreds of articles and a few books on the subject. It was during these explorations that Murray stumbled upon some fascinating then-contemporary articles written by some of the field's most prolific writers, which opened his eyes to the incredible story of the Pulp West.

Attempting to pen an article on the subject, Murray discovered that he had taken a bucking bronco by the tail. He also became fascinated by the authentic voices of the word wranglers of the past, and decided to tell their story. The result is *Wordslingers*, possibly the last word on this rarely explored subject. Although *Wordslingers* is subtitled, "An Epitaph for the Western," Murray firmly believes that the genre will never become extinct. But he keeps his fingers crossed.

A prolific author of action-adventure novels, Murray is the co-author, with the legendary Lester Dent, of Altus Press' Wild Adventures of Doc Savage series under the name Kenneth Robeson (www.adventuresinbronze.com), the most recent of which, *Skull Island*, pits the Man of Bronze against the immortal King Kong. He has forty other novels to his credit, including entries in the Destroyer, Executioner, Mars Attacks and Nick Fury, Agent of S.H.I.E.L.D. series. Murray has produced only three Western stories, one starring Lee Falk's Phantom, another a Lovecraftian horror tale, while the third appeared in *Spicy Zeppelin Stories*.